SEA LION

Also by Franklin Allen Leib

THE FIRE DREAM

FIRE ARROW

SEA LION

FRANKLIN ALLEN LEIB

NAL BOOKS

NAL BOOKS
Published by the Penguin Group
Penguin Books USA Inc., 375 Hudson Street, New York, New York 10014,
U.S.A.
Penguin Books Ltd, 27 Wrights Lane, London W8 5TZ, England
Penguin Books Australia Ltd, Ringwood, Victoria, Australia
Penguin Books Canada Ltd, 2801 John Street, Markham, Ontario, Canada
L3R 1B4
Penguin Books (N.Z.) Ltd 182–190 Wairau Road, Auckland 10, New Zealand

Penguin Books Ltd, Registered Offices:
Harmondsworth, Middlesex, England

First published by NAL Books, an imprint of Penguin Books USA Inc.
Published simultaneously in Canada.

First Printing, June, 1990
10 9 8 7 6 5 4 3 2 1

Library of Congress Cataloging-in-Publication Data

Leib, Franklin Allen, 1944–
    Sea Lion / by Franklin Allen Leib.
        p.   cm.
    ISBN 0-453-00729-5
    I. Title.
PS3562.E447S4   1990
813'.54—dc20   89-77095
                                                                CIP

 REGISTERED TRADEMARK—MARCA REGISTRADA

PRINTED IN THE UNITED STATES OF AMERICA
Set in Times Roman
Designed by Leonard Telesca

**For Victoria,
a lovely girl I was privileged to hold
for a moment in time**

Acknowledgments

The author wishes to thank two very wise men of the market, John Harris and Louis Schirano, who advised me patiently about the Euromarkets; and Ma'soud Ibrahim and Eddie Teo, who guided me through Singapore.

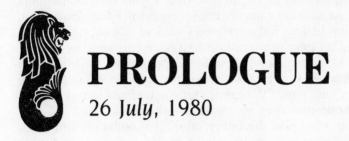

PROLOGUE
26 July, 1980

THE KAWASAKI MOTORCYCLE HURTLED south across the Johor
Causeway between Malaysia and Singapore. The night was black
and starless, blanketed by a thick cloud cover that promised rain.
The bike bounced and skidded on the mist-slicked concrete as
the driver continued at speed. From his seat on the pillion behind the driver, Holden Chambers saw the flashing amber lights
of the Singapore immigration checkpoint approach. The driver
wore riding leathers and a black plastic helmet, and he was
hunched over his handlebars. Chambers clung to him grimly,
nauseated and afraid. He felt woozy and disoriented, certain he
had been drugged earlier in the evening. His thin safari suit
flapped open at his chest in the rushing air, and he was chilled
despite the liquid heat of the night.

The motorcycle accelerated through the narrow covered channel of the border post and slewed through a gap between the
parked police cars beyond.

"Why don't you stop?" he screamed at the back of the driver's
head. Their papers were in order, and they had left their pursuers
in Malaysia far behind. Chambers felt his words torn away as the
wind caused his cheeks to balloon and his mouth to flap and drool.
He was sure the driver had not heard. He turned in the seat and
saw the Singapore police cars start in pursuit, lights flashing and
sirens wailing. The motorcycle accelerated through the sparsely
populated districts of north Singapore, and the police cars soon
faded behind the racing bike.

Holden Chambers had been taken north into Malaysia to rendezvous with a mysterious informant called Sea Lion, who had
been sending reports of an impending coup d'etat against the
Singapore government. Chambers's employer had directed him
to either verify or discredit Sea Lion's rumors. In the early evening
he had been met by a contact introduced to him by his bank's
branch in Singapore, a man who called himself only Elias. Elias

had driven him north on the motorcycle, saying little. Chambers was taken to a military camp in the forest north of the causeway. Sea Lion himself had not appeared—or had not identified himself—but the military preparations had been very real, as had the zeal of the Malay soldiers. A sudden appearance by Malaysian police vehicles had sent Elias scurrying for the Kawasaki, dragging Chambers behind him. "We cannot let you be found here, Tuan!" Elias had shouted as they motored into the blackness.

The bike hurtled past the intersection of Woodlands and Mandai roads, with its village, its quaint Malay inn, and its double flashing stoplight. Holden guessed the speed of the motorcycle to be close to a hundred miles per hour, as his fear and his chill fought to overcome the drug he had been given. Why had they drugged him? What had he not been supposed to see, or see less than clearly? He remembered the table of council in the center of the camp and the stocky gray-haired man in uniform speaking, exhorting his officers in Malay, gesturing with a swagger stick. He thought he should have recognized the man, but his fogged brain would not help him. Nearly to Choa Chu Kang Road, he thought, as the motorcycle banked through inky-dark curves, pursuing the racing, shuddering beam of its brilliant headlight. Looking past the driver's helmet, he saw faint flashes of light, which might have been heat lightning. As the bike rounded a curve, Chambers saw they were rapidly approaching a road block, and the lights were the blue-and-white roof lights of police cars.

Elias braked sharply as the men in the police cars heard the bike's motor and began turning on their headlights. Elias swerved and gunned the bike toward a dark gap on the right side of the road. Chambers's guts contracted in terror and he tried to scream, but once again the wind whipped his words and his breath away. He gripped Elias around his narrow waist, wanting to crush the breath from him, to make him stop. Chambers could see dancing shadows in the roof lights and headlights: running men, many carrying weapons.

The dark gap at the side of the road erupted with powerful white lights, apparently mounted on an armored car. The vehicle's cannon or machine gun was a dark tube below the primary searchlight. With no place to go through and no room to stop or reverse, Elias braked the bike sharply into a skid, first right, then left and down. Chambers resisted the impulse to let go and try to roll free, and instead he pressed his face into the driver's leather-clad back and tucked his legs up under the driver's legs. The bike skidded on its left side along the rough pavement, sending a shower of sparks past Chambers's face, then struck with a jarring thump against the side of a police car, which bounced backward from the impact. The motorcycle's engine screamed and then abruptly died. Chambers rolled off the road and down a steep bank into a deep ditch. He felt his legs immersed in warm water up to his knees and he smelled the fetid odor of sewage. He was suddenly warm. He opened his eyes and peered upward; he didn't think he was hurt, but he didn't feel able to move. The drug retook control of him, and he tried to breathe deeply. The black-and-white car above him on the road had "POLIS REPUBLIK SINGAPURA" in block letters on the door, alternately lighted and dim in the rotating roof lights.

Two men in the khaki uniforms of Special Branch police descended to him and lifted him gently back up to the road surface. A third policeman stood over him, holding an M-16. Chambers heard the angry buzzing of a light helicopter, and then saw its lights and felt the strong, gritty downdraft as the craft landed.

"Sir? Can you hear me, sir?" asked one of the Special Branch officers.

"Yes," said Chambers.

"Are you bad hurt, sir? The ambulance comes, quickly."

"I don't think I'm hurt." Chambers's head was spinning, and his hearing was suddenly restored in the absence of the roaring Kawasaki motor and the rush of air past his ears. His body felt numb and cold. "Let the doctor have a look, though, please."

Three men got out of the helicopter and walked toward him. They stopped a few meters away, silhouetted in the powerful floodlamps mounted on the helicopter and on the armored car. "Is he alive?" muttered the thickset man in the middle, in a gravelly voice Holden thought sounded vaguely familiar.

The policeman with the M-16 slung his weapon and saluted. "Yes, Colonel. He seems to be all right."

"What of the other?" The man addressed as Colonel advanced into the lights of the police car and squatted a meter from Chambers.

"Badly hurt, Colonel. Taken away in a police car."

As the man peered at him, Holden saw the swagger stick under his arm and recognized him as the one who had been addressing the officers of the rebel group in the forest in Malaysia: the man clearly in charge of the gathering. Chambers had met the man many times at official receptions in Singapore. He was a police colonel; Chambers couldn't recall the man's name, but he knew him as the Minister of Home Affairs of the Republic of Singapore.

The minister stood, nodded to the policeman. "See that he is taken to hospital at once, and kept guarded after he has been taken care of. I will want to question him in the morning."

"Yes, Colonel," said the policeman, saluting again. The big

man acknowledged the salute and strode back to the helicopter, which lifted off immediately.

Chambers closed his eyes against the blown grit. What am I doing, lying drugged, battered, and apparently under arrest on a road in Singapore? His hazy mind drifted, taking him back to the event which had started the chain which had brought him to this place, the night four months before when he had first met Barbara Ramsay.

SEA LION

I
NORTHEAST MONSOON
The Mists of Spring

1

Hong Kong, 24 March, 1980

HOLDEN CHAMBERS RUBBED HIS eyes and glanced at his watch. Six o'clock and the end of another busy but uneventful day. The sun slanted in through the windows of his corner office in Gloucester Tower and warmed the room despite the air conditioning. Gloucester Tower was one of the newest and smartest office blocks in Hong Kong, situated in the middle of Central District at the corner of Des Voeux Road and Pedder Street.

He straightened up his desk and pressed the intercom buzzer for his secretary. He was the managing director of Traders Asia Limited, the merchant-banking subsidiary of Traders Bank and Trust Company of New York, the eighth-largest bank in the United States. Since Hong Kong and New York had no common business hours, it had become his custom to end each day by dictating a summary of the day's events, plus any observations he might have on the market and its trends, which would be sent to New York and London in the form of a telex. David Weiss, Chambers's boss in New York and the head of the bank's International Capital Markets Group, liked to feel involved with his subsidiaries and offices around the world, and Chambers figured his newsy little summaries forestalled many a middle-of-the-night telephone call.

Margaret Lam perched on the edge of the chair in front of Chambers's desk, writing down his terse comments about the Hong Kong, Tokyo, and Singapore stock markets, movements of the various Asian currencies against the U.S. dollar, and movements of the U.S. unit against major European currencies. He discoursed about upcoming major borrowings to be organized in the Eurodollar market, opining as to which mandates ought to be pursued by Traders and at what price and structure. Finally he thought he had enough to allow Weiss to feel "hands on," so he just stopped and studied Margaret's crown of coarse but very shiny black hair as she read his words back to him.

He had long since decided that she was one of the reasons that managing Traders Asia was an easy and even a happy task. Margaret ran the office, and to a large extent she ran Chambers's life as well. She kept his business and his personal calendars, paid his bills, rendered his accounts, and sent them off to New York for reimbursement. She advised him of problems with the Chinese staff, from whom he was cut off by language, culture, and ancient prejudice, and gave him thoughtful counsel as to how to solve them. As a result, the entire staff, from the volatile foreign-exchange traders to the shy junior secretaries, thought him wise and strangely prescient.

He nodded slowly as she read aloud. She had a way of drawing herself up when she read back his dictation that made his thoughts sound important. Margaret believed in him, and she attributed the success and rapid growth of Traders Asia to his efforts alone. She was proud of him, and somehow that made it important that he continue to excel. Indeed, her approval meant far more to him than the opinion of anyone at Traders Bank and Trust Company, and certainly more than the opinion of the man to whom the telex was addressed, whom Chambers considered a pedestrian thinker, a plodder, and a meddler. If the nightly telexes kept Weiss happy and out of Hong Kong, Chambers would gladly continue to send them.

Margaret looked up at him when she had finished. "Is it all right?"

He nodded and smiled at her. "Letter perfect, Margaret. Send it out and then good night."

"You remember you have the reception tonight for the new head of Pacific Capital Corporation?"

"Yes. At the Mandarin?"

"Yes. The Connaught Rooms."

Figures, he thought. Trust PCC and its parent, First New York Bank, to treat the arrival of a new managing director as a royal event. The Connaught Rooms, which could be divided into as many as five separate reception rooms but would be one vast hall this evening, could accommodate over eight hundred people for stand-up cocktails.

Margaret plucked the invitation from the pages of his appointment calendar and handed it to him. With a shy smile she pointed to a newspaper clipping, then placed it next to the invitation card. "Don't forget your horoscope."

Holden grinned. She cut his Chinese horoscope out of the *Hong Kong Standard* every morning and brought it to him with his morning tea. He picked it up and read it again.

Someone you will meet today may bring you great joy, and later, ruin.

Holden folded it carefully and put it in his shirt pocket. Chinese horoscopes were not ordinarily so gloomy, and they usually gave you a way out, like "today would be a bad day to start a new business." It was nonsense anyway, he thought, but, seeing that she was plainly worried, he promised, "I will be very careful, Margaret. One has to tread with care any time one deals with PCC."

"Good. Shall I have Ah Wong wait for you at the Mandarin at seven-thirty?"

"Okay. If I get bored earlier, I will call him at the car park at my flat."

She stood up, smoothing her dress across her thighs with one hand still clutching the steno pad across her rather full breasts. It was a strange gesture, prim and sexy at the same time, and entirely Margaret. "Good night then, Mr. Chambers."

"Good night, Margaret. See you in the morning." He gathered his jacket and shut off his office lights. The lift carried him to the silent lobby without stopping. Gloucester Tower was connected to Alexandra House by a passageway above street level, and Alexandra House was connected to Prince's Building, which was in turn connected to the Mandarin. The walkways were lined with expensive shops where they passed through the office towers, and where the footbridges passed over Des Voeux Central and Chater Road, Chambers could watch the gridlocked traffic of red and silver taxis and busses compressed by road construction that never seemed to end. A sudden shower accompanied by gusting winds had the pedestrians scurrying toward the harbor, with its ferries and bus terminals. He could faintly hear the futile bleating of auto horns beneath him.

When he reached the Pacific Capital–First New York reception at exactly six-twenty in the evening, the line at the door had dwindled: Hong Kong's freeloading drunks tended to arrive at the five-thirty sharp set forth on the invitations to receptions of this sort, at least when one of the great houses such as First New York was the host. The minor houses—the Europeans, the Japanese, and nearly all the Americans after First New York, Chase, and Traders—had no face to lose. Holden knew his late arrival would be noticed, with approval by some and malice by others. He was pleased to find the man in front of him was John Malcolm, the managing director of Llewellyns Bank (HK) Limited. John was very British, very witty, and a good friend.

Chambers dropped his business card into the silver tray at the end of a long, covered table, behind which were seated three pretty Chinese girls dressed in blue silk *cheong sams*, the skin-tight, high-collared, and slit-to-the-thigh national dress for women in Hong Kong. The card was passed along and Chambers received his plastic name tag, which he thrust into his pocket. John Malcolm had allowed the girl to pin his on, then took it off as Chambers joined him in the receiving line.

"Good evening, John," said Chambers, shaking the bigger man's hand. Malcolm was a bear of a man, with blond hair thinning away from his forehead and pale blue eyes twinkling under shaggy eyebrows.

He drew Chambers to him with his powerful grip. "Good evening yourself, squire! First NY and Pacific Capital have themselves a right slap-up do here, eh?"

"Well, they do, John. You know them better than do I—you cut your teeth with them."

Malcolm waved his hand in a broad gesture of refusal. "You always hold me to that, you right bastard. But that was years ago, and in Canada. They don't recognize the rumpled beast I have become."

Holden laughed. Malcolm had been brought out from his last posting with Bank of America in Dubai to Hong Kong by Traders two years before, to be Chambers's deputy and probable successor. They had liked each other from the beginning, but it had been plain to both that each thought himself better qualified to run the shop, so Malcolm had moved to Llewellyns when the top spot there became open. Chambers had received a thorough dressing-down from David Weiss for letting Malcolm escape and had wept publicly at Traders's loss, but in truth the two men held each other in such high regard that they felt more comfortable as competitors than they had working together.

"Nice to be singled out for such individual treatment, eh, John?" said Chambers, looking over the pressing crowd that stretched farther than the eye could see in the tobacco smoke.

"Only a few thousand of the movers and shakers, as well as the rooted to the ground. Hope the buggers have enough beer for this mob," said Malcolm gloomily, as if he really thought they might not.

Chambers smiled and nodded with mock concern. As the two inched toward the First New York and Pacific Capital executives in the receiving line, he asked, "Do you know anything about this Richard van Courtland they have let loose on us?"

Malcolm shrugged as they shuffled along behind the three representatives of the Bank of China, who were entitled to elaborate courtesies. "I knew him in London, a bit. Knew him as a junior at Nibble." Nibble was the inevitable nickname of New York International Bank Limited, the London merchant-banking subsidiary of First New York.

"First-class Berk," he went on matter-of-factly, even though only inches away from shaking the hand of the Hong Kong branch manager of First New York, Geoffrey Crawley. "Right cunt, if you ask me. 'Course, that was years ago, but I would doubt a profound change."

"What's he done since? Any guess?" said Chambers.

"Not really. Corporate planning, I have heard. Strategic. Some in Nibble think him an odd choice for Hong Kong, but I haven't yet found out why."

Chambers nodded as Malcolm shook the hand of Crawley and mouthed pleasantries. The line moved more slowly than usual: The mainland Chinese from the Bank of China ahead of them were new to this game and tried to respond to the banalities mouthed by their hosts rather than just pressing through to the food and ample booze beyond.

Chambers shook hands quickly with Crawley and was passed on to Richard van Courtland. The new managing director of Pacific Capital Corporation was a tall man with a ruddy complexion, little eyes, and plastered-down black hair tufting gray over his ears. Chambers thought a complexion like that came from exercise and energy. Or booze. Booze, he decided after smelling the faint sour scent of vodka on van Courtland's breath. His expensive tie was tightly knotted despite the heat in the room as the air conditioning in the vast hall struggled to catch up with the sudden influx of people. Van Courtland was sweating, showing stains through the chest of his wilted blue Oxford-cloth shirt.

"Holden Chambers," Chambers said simply. "Traders Asia. Welcome to Hong Kong."

"Thank you, thank you. Enjoy the party," van Courtland said, dismissing him quickly. Holden hurried through the last few First New York officials, then chased John Malcolm toward the nearest of the many service bars.

The Connaught Rooms were so vast in the haze of hundreds of cigarettes as to seem dimensionless. Elaborate crystal chandeliers hung from the high ceiling, softly lighting the dark paneling and the blue carpets bordered with gold. The long chamber always reminded Holden of sepia prints of the grand saloons of one of the enormous nineteenth-century ocean liners—the *Great Eastern*, perhaps—except that everything was so obviously brand new.

John Malcolm turned away from the bar with a large glass of beer for himself and a tall scotch and soda for Chambers. They drifted away from the busy bar into the mass of noisy bankers, many already drunk, and many others browsing through the various food bars of roast beef, hams, morsels of Peking duck, steamed dumplings, and sushi. Malcolm looked around and spoke softly. "Well, squire, a right bloody potlatch the First New York has thrown at provincial Hong Kong, eh?" His eyes twinkled.

"Disgusting, John. Let's get into the sushi—"

"Holden Chambers? You are Holden Chambers?"

Chambers turned toward a melodic female voice and saw an attractive dark-haired woman, American by her accent, whom he was quite sure he had not met before. Her name tag read "Barbara van Courtland, Roland, Archer and Co." above the Pacific Capital logo. Malcolm also turned toward her.

"Yes, I am. And this is John Malcolm, of Llewellyns."

Barbara shook hands firmly with both of them. "I recognized you from your photo in the *Morning Post*, from the Korea Shipyards signing last week. A very impressive deal." Her smile was brilliant if a bit self-conscious.

"Thank you," said Chambers. He noticed that her eyes remained fixed on him even while she touched the Englishman's hand. Malcolm arched his bushy brows, harrumphed, and drifted toward the busy sushi bar.

"You must be Richard van Courtland's wife," he said.

She carefully unpinned the name tag from the collar of her sleek pearl-gray woolen dress and stuffed it into her purse with evident annoyance. "Yes, I am. First New York wrote the tag up that way; I am Barbara Ramsay. I have never used my married name."

"And you are with Roland, Archer?" asked Holden. Roland, Archer was the largest securities firm in America, but it had little presence in Asia.

"Yes. I hope to be doing business with many of the merchant banks here. You mustn't think of me as some mere appendage of Richard and Pacific Capital. Please?"

Holden raised his glass to her. "Done. You don't have a drink; let me get you one."

As she smiled, he felt a strange, compelling attraction to her, despite the thick gold wedding ring on her left hand. "Champagne, please, Holden, if they have it."

He favored her with a winning smile of his own. "If they don't, Barbara, they will get it. A moment." He darted to the bar, pushing aside several people with a discourtesy unusual with him.

"Why am I so afraid she'll wander off?" he found himself mumbling aloud.

He secured a glass of champagne quickly enough and found her standing alone and looking uncomfortable, her feet slightly pointed toes in, her hands rubbing each other in front of her crotch. She was smiling bravely but uncertainly; the nearly all-male throng swept around her but did not approach. She is going to find Hong Kong and Asia difficult, he thought. Women in Asia had not escaped traditional roles. Somehow, however, Barbara Ramsay seemed game for the challenge, he thought, handing her the champagne and gazing into her luxurious dark-brown eyes.

"Thank you," she said, taking the glass, seeming about to reach for him to keep him from going away.

"What are you going to do for Roland, Archer in Hong Kong, Barbara?"

She tossed her fine head of dark-brown hair in an impatient gesture. She seemed about to reply, perhaps an answer already prepared for a question many times asked, but then she stopped and looked at him frankly, the gaze of an equal. He was impressed and amused at the same time.

"Christ, Holden, I don't know yet, really. The fact is, I am here because Richard is. I am flattered to believe Roland thinks enough of me to make a job for me here until he and I return to New York in two years, but I can tell you that I do not intend to twiddle my thumbs or have babies or boss around house servants during that time. I am going to be successful here, Holden, and I am going to need to figure out how. I meant it about wanting to work with the merchant banks; Roland here is just retail, as you well know, and I am a capital-markets person. But I have to make my own way, and I think that is going to be more difficult here than even in the male-sexist environments of Wall Street and London." She turned away suddenly, a look of discomfort on her face. "I am sorry. I don't know you well enough to burden you with this. Please excuse me."

She turned back toward him, her eyes pleading, and then again away, apparently seeking some escape, but the guests continued to jostle them on all sides. He reached forward quickly and plucked her half-empty glass from her hand. "Let me get us another drink," he said softly. His own glass was empty, and had been through most of her short speech. Her expression softened, and Holden read it as relief that she would not yet be abandoned in this school of indifferent predatory fish—indifferent, not hostile, because they had not even noticed her presence.

Holding both full glasses in his left hand, Chambers placed his right hand gently on Barbara's elbow, and guided her toward the busy sushi bar. John Malcolm and Chris Marston-Evans stood to the side of the sushi serving bar, watching Holden and Barbara approach. Marston-Evans was capital-markets director of Warrens Limited, the merchant bank of the Imperial Bank of Hong Kong—the Bank, simply, to the financial people in the colony. Malcolm looked amused, pushing *maguro* and *hirame* pieces of fish, wrapped around balls of steamed, cold rice into his large mouth. Marston-Evans looked somewhat bemused; he usually did. Holden felt the crowd part before him as he approached the crowded bar, with its Japanese chefs dispensing sushi as fast as they could. Barbara looked up at Holden, and he fancied she appreciated his guidance, and the way the lesser predators moved away to let him get to the trough. He set both glasses on the edge of the table, and directed the chefs to fill two small plates. *"Simima-sen, dozo. Sushi-desu,"* he said. *"Nitsu, desu, domo."* He received the two plates, and the wooden chopsticks handed him by a girl in a blue *cheong sam*, and presented a plate, chopsticks, and her glass of champagne to Barbara. Malcolm and Marston-Evans approached, and at last Barbara had something of a friendly audience around her. She smiled her thanks. Holden noticed she found the chopsticks awkward, but she managed them carefully as she ate the succulent fish. "Lesson one, Ms. Ramsay," he said with humor, but very softly. "Eat well off the largesse of the great Pacific Capital."

"At each and every opportunity," joined Malcolm.

"Thank you," said Barbara. Her dark brown eyes make her face almost beautiful, thought Holden.

The four of them ate, the men returning several times to revisit the sushi bar, and then drifting through other tables, sampling each of the different foods being served. Bachelors tended to make their evening meal at functions of this sort.

Chris Marston-Evans, who hadn't spoken a word since being introduced, drifted off to join some young, rather flashily dressed Englishmen who probably worked at the Bank or one of its endless subsidiaries. Malcolm and Chambers moved with Barbara happily tucked between them, greeting acquaintances. Both men pointed out significant persons in the crowd, giving Barbara thumbnail sketches of the important and the merely self-important, and introducing her to each with whom they spoke. Malcolm's descriptions were particularly wry and witty as he got along with the beer. Chambers had switched to champagne.

"Are these parties always so crowded?" asked Barbara, despairing of remembering even a few of the names she had been told.

"It's a free feed," said Malcolm, accepting a shrimp-filled steamed dumpling from a pretty waitress with one hand, and exchanging a full glass of beer for his empty one with a passing waiter.

"Hong Kong has a pecking order, rather a rigid one," said Chambers. "You would have to be pretty obscure or very disreputable to be left off the list for a party of this size, but we all show up anyway, because First New York is far and away the most important American financial institution in the colony."

Barbara nodded, looked from Chambers to Malcolm. "It's a free feed," he repeated, in exactly the same tone as before.

Barbara laughed. "Does Traders give receptions like this? Does Llewellyns?" she asked.

"We are having one in a month," said Malcolm. "Half the bloody management committee of Llewellyn's Bank from London is tramping through Asia, doing their annual shopping, I suppose. Now Holden, here, he hasn't given a really major homage to the community for years."

"Why not?" asked Barbara.

Holden shrugged. "I don't find them particularly effective, Barbara. The usual excuse for giving a party like this is to introduce a new senior officer to the financial and business community, as we are tonight, or to expose a senior officer from our own headquarters—which really means to show off our own power, more often than not. I expect the vice-chairman of Traders here in about two months, and I will give a couple of small lunches, and maybe something like this for about eighty people, people who will be able to genuinely impress the vice-chairman of the importance and depth of the Hong Kong market."

"Not to mention the importance and depth of Holden Chambers," mocked John Malcolm gently. "Although, Barbara, our Holden here really shows his great face by having in only the movers and shakers; much greater risk. You showcase the chairman of the Bank, the financial secretary, the shipping magnates, the chief manager of the Bank of China, and you run a risk of looking small if some or all don't turn up."

Barbara frowned. "I can see that. I have the managing director to whom I report in London due out here in a month. Do you think I ought to do something like this, perhaps on a smaller scale?"

John beamed, bowing to a waiter and making another full glass for empty exchange. "It'd be a free feed."

Holden laughed. "Frankly, Barbara, I don't think I would. Take him around, visit people in their offices, people you think will say useful and supportive things about whatever you decide to try to accomplish. Hand-pick some of the lads for a lunch or a cocktail. If you invite the mob, your MD is likely to find out not many really know you, and that is the worst impression you can make in cliquey, gossipy Hong Kong."

"Thank you," Barbara smiled. The advice was clearly good. "Can I ask you now to put up with office visits from me and the great man, to confirm tomorrow?"

"Of course. Delighted," said Chambers.

John Malcolm screwed his big face into a look of mock displeasure. "Well! I dunno how much of my valuable office time I might spare, though I would surely show up for the lunch and cocktails." Barbara didn't know him well enough to be sure of his humor, even though Holden was grinning broadly at the two of them. "But John, you have been so kind—"

"Oh, Christ, then, woman. Don't whine! Bring him 'round without fail."

The receiving line had at last broken up. Richard van Courtland was making his way across the room, his face red and sweaty, and his mouth pressed to a glass of very dark whiskey. John Malcolm looked toward him and away. "I say, Holden, could you give me a ride up the hill when you are ready? My bus is on the blink again, and besides, I need to discuss a bit of business with you."

Holden glanced at his watch: seven-thirty. Ah Wong, his driver, would be lurking in front of the Mandarin. He set down his champagne glass and bowed to Barbara, and then shook her hand. He noted her handshake was firm and cool, and that her eyes said she was sorry he was leaving her. He took a calling card from a small leather wallet in his pocket and handed it to her. "I am delighted to meet you, Ms. Ramsay, and I do hope you will teach us some new capital-markets tricks. Give a call to my office to set up an appointment; my secretary's name is Margaret."

"I will. You too, John. Thank you very much for taking such good care of me this evening." She waved.

"Good night to you, Barbara," said John. Glancing at van Courtland heading their way through the crowd, he said softly to Holden, "Let's hop it, squire, the beast approaches."

"Right. He doesn't look like fun at all."

"Which is why we must talk. I picked up a rumor that he may try to get the Indonesian mandate as a sole lead—freeze us out of the best position and fees."

"Let's go find my car."

Holden and John made their way slowly toward the door. Barbara caught up with them and placed her hand lightly on Holden's arm. "Holden, wait," she said. She held a scrap of newspaper in her hand, and her expression was between worry and hurt. "This piece of paper was wrapped around your card; I thought you might want it."

He smiled and plucked it from her fingertips. He knew what it was but he read it again.

Someone you meet today may bring you great joy, and later, ruin.

"It's my Chinese horoscope, Barbara. My secretary cuts it out for me every morning."

"It's a little bleak," she said, her eyes unhappy and her smile forced. "I hope you don't take it seriously."

He looked at the pretty woman, and at her husband beyond, who had halted some five yards away and seemed to be watching them through the moving crowd. "Of course not, Barbara. I hope to see you again soon."

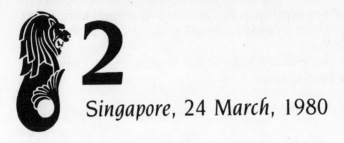

2

Singapore, 24 March, 1980

ABDUL RAZA SAT SLUMPED in the back seat of the blue Datsun saloon and watched the lights of Singapore City thin out as the car rolled north into the sparsely populated northern part of the island. Past Bukit Timah and into Woodlands Road the traffic thinned as well, and Raza's driver picked up speed, flicking his headlights up and down as he passed large goods lorries lumbering toward the Johor Causeway and Malaysia beyond.

Raza was a stocky man, very fit for his forty-six years. He had large, intelligent black eyes in a smooth brown face divided by a hawk's-bill of a nose. His hair and mustache were thick and black, both clipped short and shot with gray. He wore a tailored safari suit as black as his mood. His large fists were balled on his muscular thighs and his teeth were clenched. He was angry and embarrassed, for himself, for the office he held, and for his miserable son, Joseph, who awaited him in a cell in the police station in Johor, just over the border in Malaysia. Joseph, the pampered favorite of his late wife; Joseph, the gifted child who would not be taught; Joseph, the rebel; and now Joseph, the self-styled revolutionary and petty smuggler. Raza seethed. All his life he had worked for the betterment of the people of Singapore, and especially the advancement and integration of the Malay citizens into the Chinese-run economy, and now his son wanted to overturn all that because of the rantings of a demented old mullah thousands of miles away in Iran.

Raza stared at the back of his driver as the car slowed at the checkpoint on the Singapore side of the border. The driver was wearing normal chauffer garb of dark slacks, a short-sleeved white shirt, and a necktie. Lee continually tugged at his tight collar. He's unused to the hard collar and tie, thought Raza. The uniform he normally wore was open at the neck.

The Datsun was passed through quickly on both sides of the frontier. Phone calls had preceded them, and they were expected. Lee drove west along the coast road, past the elegant mosque

built in the Moorish style by an architect sent to the sultan by
Queen Victoria, and the ugly modern Islamic Centre. The police
station was at the base of the hill surmounted by the fortresslike
government offices, likewise built by the British. Lee parked the
Datsun in back of the modern concrete building, just behind the
double lines of black-and-white police vehicles. Raza got out before his driver reached the door. "Get your dinner, Lee," Raza
said, straightening his tight jacket. "Be ready to depart in forty
minutes."

"Yes, sir," said Lee, returning to the car and driving off toward
Johor City. Raza took several deep breaths in an effort to calm
himself, then straightened his back and marched into the police
station.

He was recognized by the desk sergeant as soon as he entered
the squad room. The sergeant broke off his conversation with an
old Indian man standing before the sergeant's high desk, and
came down to greet Raza. "Good evening, sir," said the Malay
sergeant, saluting smartly. "I am sorry to have you up on such a
sad errand."

"Not as sorry as I am to be here," Raza said curtly. "But I
should apologize to you for your inconvenience."

"Professional courtesy," said the sergeant. "I only regret we
did not know the boy's true identity sooner." The sergeant winced
as Raza stared at him. The boy had identified himself as Yusef
bin Sirdar, and the investigating constable had knocked the lad
around a bit while getting his story. Raza was sure to notice the
bruises. "We didn't know he was your son until we ran his prints
and the university files came up."

Raza nodded. "I am sure you acted correctly, Sergeant. May
I see the boy now?"

"Of course. He is in one of the interrogation rooms downstairs.
Let me show you."

Raza followed the sergeant down into the basement, past holding cells containing a few dull-eyed men. The basement was air-
conditioned and quite cool, but the stink of unwashed bodies,
urine, and vomit fought the smell of strong disinfectant. The
interrogation rooms were at the end of the corridor, and the
sergeant let Raza into the first. The room was divided in two by
a window of one-way glass. A long table and chairs were pushed
up to the window. On the other side of the glass Raza saw his
son seated on a metal chair facing the glass, staring straight ahead
at his reflection without apparent interest. Raza saw a purple
bruise under Joseph's left eye, pushing up so the eye was swollen
nearly shut.

"Do you wish to go right in?" asked the sergeant.

"Give me a minute to collect my thoughts, Sergeant," Raza said slowly. "May I see the charge sheet?"

"It's right here, sir," said the sergeant, handing over a thin blue folder embossed "POLIS REPUBLIK MALAYSIA." "Also the results of the interrogation."

Raza took the folder and placed it on the table. "Thank you, Sergeant. Please return to your duties."

The man saluted and left the room. Raza pulled one of the chairs forward and sat down, then opened the folder and read the charge sheet and the single sheet of notes from his son's questioning. His son's stare seemed hostile, boring into Raza's eyes, blaming him, although in fact the boy couldn't see him and could not be aware of his presence.

Raza studied his son. The boy was the image of his mother, slight and pretty. Even the bruise staining his cheek and eye seemed to add to the picture of feminine vulnerability, and on that smooth, beardless face the angry scowl looked merely petulant. Raza knew he had neglected the boy when he was a child, perhaps because his mother had shielded him from the father she considered coarse. Raza had loved Fatimah, even worshiped her for her beauty and refinement. Perhaps he had always agreed with her that she had married beneath herself, although her aristocratic but impoverished parents had thought the young inspector in the Federated Malay States police a good enough catch. The boy had always been Fatimah's; in fact, she rarely let Abdul come to her after he was born. She taught Joseph—her name for her son; his legal name was Yusef—to paint and to draw and to play the piano, and she agreed with him that it was unimportant that he excel in arithmetic or play rough sports, even though his father clearly thought a boy should know such things. Only when Fatimah fell ill with cancer and quickly wasted and died did the boy really begin to respond to his father, and then it was with fear and contempt. Raza knew the boy blamed him in some way for his mother's death; she had always said the torpid air of Singapore made her weak. Perhaps, thought Raza, I was selfish to keep them in Singapore, where I prosper. Perhaps they both had reason to hate me. It had been a relief to both father and son when the boy went away to Kuala Lumpur to university. The boy rarely came home to Singapore, even at holidays, but at least his marks had improved.

Raza looked away from his son's face and reread the charge sheet and the notes from the interrogation of Joseph and another boy arrested with him, one Jarid Khan. He closed the folder and got up, feeling stiff and weary from the long ride through the night and the hard wooden chair. He opened the door to the inner room and went in, closing the door behind him. The lights on the ceiling seemed much brighter than from the other side of the one-way window, which appeared as a mirror from inside the small cubicle, and his son now seemed small and frightened in his metal chair. "Hello, Joseph," said Raza, taking another metal chair from a rack on the wall and placing it before his son.

"Father," said the boy, in barely a whisper, "why are you here?"

"Surely you knew I would be called," Raza said, twisting the chair around backward and straddling it.

"I didn't give the police my right name," the boy said.

"But they took your fingerprints. You know about fingerprints, don't you, Joseph?"

"Yusef," the boy said. "I prefer to be called Yusef."

"Your mother always called you Joseph."

The boy turned to look at his father with what Raza thought was a surprisingly steady gaze. "My mother liked the English and their ways. My mother is dead, and so is Joseph." It sounded to Raza like a prepared statement. "I am a Malay, and my name is Yusef."

Raza folded his arms over the back of the chair and rested his chin on his wrist. "We are all Malays, Yusef."

"Even those who serve the Chinese pig-eaters?" the youth shot back.

Raza smiled mildly. He had heard all this many times before. "I am a public servant, Yusef. I serve all the citizens of Singapore."

"Perhaps you have forgotten the Koran, Father. A proper Muslim is servant only to God."

Raza shifted his weight in the cold metal seat. "Perhaps so, Yusef. But I did not come across the causeway for a civics lesson in eighth-century Islam. You are in a great deal of trouble."

"So the lackey police have already told me," said Yusef, touching the bruise under his eye and turning his face away. "All I did was agree to take some Malay Students' League posters down to Singapore."

"Over two thousand posters, Yusef, according to the charge sheet," Raza said. "That is a violation of the Malaysia Riot and Sedition Act, and it could get you two years in prison and then put out of the country."

"What do you care?" flared the youth. "You are fat and happy, licking the hand of the Chinese tyrant, Lee But Yang."

Raza smiled again. Lee But Yang, the Prime Minister of Singapore, was indeed his boss. Why did these ranting youths always sound the same, in any country or any language? "Then there is the small matter of a Webley .455 revolver found in the rucksack of your companion."

Yusef turned back to look at his father. "I know nothing of that. Either the police planted it on Jarid, or it was in the sack when he picked it up at the Student Center."

Raza ignored this evasion. He had wearily listened to hundreds of its kind for years. "Possession of the revolver could add another two years to your sentence, Yusef, but if the gun is traced as a police weapon, which seems very likely, and if the officer who signed it out last was assaulted and the gun stolen . . ." Raza paused. What did he expect his son to do? Beg for his help, his forgiveness? He longed to take the youth, weeping contritely, into his arms, yet at the same time he did not want Yusef—not the delicate mama's boy Joseph but the man-cub Yusef—to beg.

"I told the policeman I knew nothing of the gun and that I did not believe Jarid did, either," said Yusef with a steady gaze, which greatly pleased his father. "The pig cuffed me around, but it is the truth. Are you going to hit me as well?"

"No," said Raza, shaking his head slowly. "I am going to do something I shouldn't: I am going to have you released and the charges dropped. But I would at least like your word that you will leave aside this Islamic fundamentalist foolishness and concentrate on your studies."

"And if I refuse?" the youth sneered. "You will let them put me in jail?"

I should, thought Raza. A few months' hard time in the old Pudu prison in Kuala Lumpur would drive this folly from Yusef's mind forever. Raza looked at the boy, trying so hard to look fierce. But the criminals in that place would be riding his smooth brown arse through the blocks before he had spent his first night, important father or no. "You will not refuse, my son," said Raza with an edge of fury in his voice that made the boy wince. "You will finish your studies with honor marks, and you will report in the fall to the Royal Military Academy at Sandhurst. You will be delighted to know I have obtained your appointment only last week."

"Sandhurst!" the boy sputtered. "I'll not go there! I have no interest in the army."

"Content just to be a terrorist?" said Raza, sensing victory. "You can go to Oxford or Cambridge if you can get admitted, but you will finish your education in Britain—as your mother wished."

The boy seemed to shrink. "I won't go," he said without conviction.

"You will," said Raza, leaning forward. He tried to make his voice gentle, but the edge remained. "If you are arrested again, I won't be able to keep you from joining Jarid in the old rock Pudu prison."

Yusef looked up. "Jarid will go to prison?" The idea was strange to him; somehow he'd thought his powerful father would protect them both.

"Most assuredly," Raza said. "He might have been forgiven the leaflets, since none were actually distributed or taken abroad, but the revolver tears it."

"Can't you . . . get him off?" Yusef's voice was suddenly whiny, and Raza was repelled.

"Why should I?" he asked.

"Jarid is—is a very close friend, Father."

"Not too bloody close, I trust," said Raza sharply.

The boy slumped. "You always think I'm bloody queer. I'm not. I have never touched another boy."

"Nor a bloody woman either, I'll warrant." Raza fought to control his anger. His arms on the back of the chair bulged with tension.

"I've no time for women." Yusef looked at his father, anger to anger. "And you should know that homosexuality is cursed in the Koran. It is abomination."

Thank heaven for small favors, thought Raza, rising from the chair. "This Jarid will do his time, and you will stand surety for him on the outside. As long as you behave yourself, I will ask that Jarid be treated as a youthful offender and kept apart from the general prison population."

Yusef looked up at his father, his face contorted with pure hatred. "You rotten, blackmailing bastard!" he said.

Raza's backhanded blow caught the youth under his eye, exactly on the purple bruise. Yusef let out a single sharp cry as he and the chair fell backward onto the concrete floor. Raza stood over him, pointing a finger at a spot between Yusef's eyes. "Think anything of me you like. Hate me as you like, but on your mother's grave, I swear to you that you will not be a criminal. You will be a man and a decent one, and you will have the education I promised her before she died. Now I give you one last choice: return with me tonight and resume your studies at Singapore University where I can have you watched, or give me your word to stay here and finish your degree, with no more politics."

Yusef got up and faced his father. His lip was quivering. "I'll finish in Kuala Lumpur, Father. See that you keep your word about Jarid." His voice was cold as ice, and it tore at Raza's guts.

He looked at his son and nodded slowly. The boy's chin trembled and his eyes were moist. "I accept your word and your condition. Now, for God's sake, don't start blubbering." Raza realized that he himself was near to tears.

"I'll not cry for you, Father. Mother did that enough."

Raza turned away quickly and fumbled for the doorknob. Once outside the cubicle, he clutched his stomach, feeling the boy's words like steel knives. He forced himself erect, then picked up the blue police folder and found his way back to the sergeant's desk in the deserted squad room. He placed the folder in front of the sergeant and took a deep breath.

"Will you want to take the boy home tonight, sir?" asked the sergeant.

"No. Can you get him back to his school in the morning?"

"As you wish. I hope you put the fear of God into him, sir, if I may say so. I would hate to see a son of yours ruin his life with youthful indiscretions."

"I hope I did too, Sergeant. If these impatient children can just get old enough without stumbling, they'd learn how hard one has to work to succeed."

"Quite so, sir. Good night and safe home."

"Thank you, Sergeant. I will speak to the general tomorrow and tell him you were most helpful." Raza walked outside into the cool evening. Lee jumped out of the front door of the Datsun and let Raza into the rear, then guided the big car out of the police compound and back toward the Johor Causeway.

3

28 March, 1980

HOLDEN CHAMBERS WAS IN good spirits as he left his office, even though he had been working nonstop since lunch and it was now past eight o'clock. He had been on the phone most of the afternoon in a three-way call with a Traders attorney, Ray Adams—the Hong Kong resident partner of the New York firm of Danger, Close—and representatives of BenMinco, the Philippine mining conglomerate. They had ironed out the last details of a debt restructuring to be led by Traders Asia that would bring in a handsome fee. The deal had taken months to nail down, largely because of the volatile personalities of the Philippine joint-venture partners, but it was done, and Chambers looked forward to an evening with no business problems whispering inside his mind.

Ah Wong was waiting at the curb on Pedder Street behind the wheel of Traders Asia's white Mercedes. Holden pulled open the left rear door and climbed in. May-Ling Wong was seated behind the driver. Chambers leaned across and kissed her on the cheek as Ah Wong pulled into traffic. He reached Connaught Road and turned east. Apparently May-Ling had given him directions.

"Well, May-Ling, my dove, where are you taking me for dinner?" said Chambers, taking her tiny hand in his. She was luminously beautiful, tall and slender with glowing tanned skin and almond-shaped eyes, very large for a Chinese girl. Her glossy black hair just touched her shoulders and was turned under at the bottom. She wore a simple yet elegant black silk dress, a fitted red-leather jacket, and matching red shoes. She squeezed his hand but looked nervously at Ah Wong, as though embarrassed to be touched by Holden in his presence. He was touched by her shyness and moved to the other side of the seat. They had been lovers for two months, and Holden felt himself becoming more and more attached to this girl of twenty years who could be a submissive lotus flower when she wished, then turn around and flash the precise and aggressive temperament of the honors law student she was.

"The Shark's Fin Restaurant, in Causeway Bay," she said in a deferential whisper, as though she thought he might disapprove. She knew it was one of his favorites, as long as he had an experienced Chinese gourmet along to choose the dishes.

"Wonderful, May-Ling," he said, looking at her erect figure in the seat beside him. Once again she looked at Ah Wong and seemed pained. Was something wrong between them? He resolved to ask in the restaurant.

Ray Adams, Chambers's lawyer and friend, had introduced him to May-Ling. A secretary in Adams's office, hired part-time while she was still an undergraduate, she wanted desperately to be a solicitor and even a barrister. Adams liked her so well he had convinced his firm to pay her school fees in exchange for her agreement to work in his office at least two years after she was admitted to the bar. Holden had at first been irritated and later amused by the whispers in the European community that he had "taken up with a Chinese woman." He found gentle May-Ling so much more interesting than the brassy English girls who came out East with the annual "fishing fleet" in search of husbands and screwed whomever they liked until they found them. "European" in Hong Kong meant everyone not Asian, and the European and Chinese communities mixed little outside of business. Most of the solicitors and nearly all of the barristers in the colony were European men, so May-Ling faced a formidable challenge. All the same, she was as determined as she was smart, and Holden was confident she would succeed, especially with her first placing with Danger, Close assured.

A fine rain was falling as Ah Wong pulled to the curb at the Shark's Fin Restaurant. Ah Wong got out and opened the door for May-Ling, exchanging a few words in Cantonese. Chambers let himself out before the driver could race around to his side of the car. "Two hours at least, Ah Wong," said Chambers. "Go home and have dinner with your wife and sons."

"Miss Wong say 'leven o'clock, Masta," said Ah Wong. "Okay?"

"Fine. Eleven o'clock, then." Chambers gave May-Ling his arm, and they went into the ornate red and gold decorated restaurant. The maître d'hôtel approached and bowed. May-Ling spoke to him in rapid Cantonese, and he bowed again, then led them to a small private dining room with a table for eight. A waitress in a gold *cheong sam* entered with tea and hot towels, took their drink orders, and bowed from the room, sliding the brocade screen shut.

Chambers decided he wanted an explanation of May-Ling's strange uneasiness in the car. "Darling, you seemed put out on the way over here. Is there a problem with Ah Wong?"

She smiled, then looked down at her hands, wrapped around the porcelain tea cup. "Not," she whispered, "not with Ah Wong."

"What, then?" he asked, reaching across and touching her forearms. "Something I did?"

"You should not call me May-Ling in front of Ah Wong," she said, looking him directly in the eyes. "It is an intimate name, only for my family. When you call me that, Ah Wong will know that we are lovers."

Holden swallowed. He was glad for the interruption of the waitress, who brought a long whiskey and soda for him and an orange juice for May-Ling. The waitress closed the screen. "I am sorry, May-Ling. But we *are* lovers, and Ah Wong surely knows that." Ah Wong had often driven May-Ling from his apartment to her home very early in the morning.

"Of course he knows," she said. "That isn't the point. If you call me by my Chinese name in front of him, it is as though you are *telling* him. It makes me a mere concubine in his eyes."

Chambers shook his head. "Face?"

"That is what you Europeans call it." May-Ling smiled, still looking sad. "In China the form is often more important than the facts."

"I'm sorry. I meant you no disrespect. Have I never done that before?"

"No. Just tonight."

"But my *amah* calls you by that name."

"Ah King is a sixty-year-old Chinese woman and the mistress of my barbarian's house," she said with a little giggle. "It would be rude of me not to tell her my baby-name."

Chambers smiled ruefully and sipped his whiskey. "I guess I still have a lot to learn."

"Ten thousand years' worth, my love."

"So what do I call you among Chinese? Miss Wong?"

"Of course not, silly. Marylin, just as you used to."

"And that is okay?"

"European names are not important to us."

When he had first come to Hong Kong, Holden had had the good luck to sit next to Michael Sandhurst, the former chairman of the Bank, on the aircraft from San Francisco. The man had been in a talkative mood and had told Chambers many things he later found useful and indeed sage. One that flashed into his mind was the simple statement that any Westerner who ever told you he understood the Oriental mind was a damn fool. "Thank you for telling me, May-Ling. You are a gentle teacher."

She pushed her chair closer and kissed him. "Enough of this. You are sweet, and even wise, for a long-nosed *gwai lo*."

He put his arm around her waist and kissed her back. "At least you got us a private room so that we can behave in an appropriately barbarian manner. But I am famished. Should we ring for menus?"

She gave him a look of mock horror. "Once again you insult me. I have ordered everything, like a proper Chinese woman would for her man. Some of the dishes have been being prepared for hours."

"What are we having?"

"Everything you like. Shark's fin soup, of course, scallops two ways, steamed fish, hot and spicy prawns, and Peking duck. Sweet steamed dumplings for dessert."

The screen slid aside and a waiter stepped in, bowed, and placed a steaming tureen of shark's fin soup in the center of the octagonal table. The waitress followed with bowls and spoons, and stirred the soup with a ladle. May-Ling dismissed her with a word and served the soup herself, adding a spoonful of vinegar to each bowl. Shark's fin soup was Holden's absolute favorite Chinese dish, fragrant and chewy, and sharpened by the vinegar. They ate in silence for a moment. Holden was ravenous, and May-Ling refilled his bowl twice.

"I could live on this stuff," he said appreciatively.

"Save room. The steamed fish, especially, will be delicious."

"Did you order wine?"

The screen slid back, and the waitress entered with a bottle of white wine in an ice bucket. "Of course," said May-Ling with an amused wink. "Hock until the duck, then a claret."

Holden laughed as the waitress pulled the cork and served them. "Good," he said. May-Ling nodded, and the girl withdrew. "I get the feeling I had better watch *anything* I might say tonight."

"No, love." May-Ling laughed, the sound as musical as a wind chime. "I am finished punishing you. I want to talk to you about my career, after I am admitted to the bar."

"How much longer?"

"A year next June. Mr. Adams wants me to do corporate work. He wants to expand Danger, Close's practice to serve British and indigenous Hong Kong companies."

"What do you think?" The waitress entered to clear away the tureen and the bowls. The waiter followed with a platter of scallops done with scallions in a delicate orange sauce.

"At some point I want to become a barrister," she said, tasting the dish before serving him. "I'd never really get very far with an American firm unless I qualified in New York."

"Would you want to go to New York?"

Her eyes widened as if she thought the question were too frank. Perhaps it was, he reflected. "Do you plan to return to New York?" she asked.

"Not for many years," he said. "I guess eventually." Please don't ask me if I would take you with me, he thought, realizing that he had no idea of the answer. She wouldn't, though. He knew she would never be that direct.

She seemed to study him. "It's an odd question. You Americans so love your country that you seem to assume that anyone, from any part of the world, would go to live in America if only they could."

"We are joyful in our provincial arrogance," he said, struggling to control a slippery scallop with the long plastic chopsticks.

"Americans are joyful in everything," she said, picking up a scallop and wrapping it with scallions with swift, deft movements, then popping it into his mouth. "I have never been there, but I imagine it as a vast country, with all kinds of people, alike only in their lack of traditions. People of a nation so new that it considers the lessons of the ancestors to be no more than fetters to be cast off. China is so different; in China tradition guides us and molds our every thought and act. A Chinese without China is beyond our conception."

"And yet you have accepted much of the West," he said, a bit stung. Including me, or so I had thought.

"Of course, love," she said, reaching over and touching his hand. "I don't mean to criticize; I am only trying to explain. I am Chinese but Hong Kong Chinese, with an education in the British schools. I am already a strange hybrid in the eyes of more traditional Chinese. Hong Kong to most Chinese is as much a part of China as Shanghai or Canton, and you Europeans are merely visitors, traders. The strange ones are people like me who learn your ways as if you were of any importance."

Holden sipped his wine. May-Ling took the bottle from the ice bucket and refilled his glass. "Does this hybrid status bother you?"

"Only a little," she said, frowning. "Some call us banana Chinese: yellow on the outside but white on the inside. But I think the hybrid can only exist here in hybrid Hong Kong. If I went to China, I would have to be Chinese, which would mean losing a lot that I find important and useful about the West. If I went to America, I would lose my Chinese side." She paused and traced her right eye with a fingertip. "Even though I would still have my Chinese face and my Chinese soul."

"So you want to stay here," he said, not at all sure that was the logical conclusion to her statement.

"Until I want to leave," she said, giving her bell-like laugh. "Do not press your European logic on me, love." She bent over and nipped his ear. "Just remember, a Chinese is molded by his past; the future is the concern of the gods."

The waiter and waitress returned and replaced the scallop dish with an elegantly arranged platter of prawns in a pungent sour sauce. "This is a marvelous dinner, May-Ling," said Holden, as the waitress closed the sliding screen.

"That's better," said May-Ling, smiling. "Think like a Chinese: The future is the next dish."

Holden dozed, his head on May-Ling's shoulder, as Ah Wong drove through the light traffic from Causeway Bay to Central and then up to Mid-levels. She had been right: Each dish had surpassed the one before, and he had drunk virtually all of the wine, since she had rarely taken more than a sip. He wondered where their relationship would lead, and he wondered as well why he had never thought about it before. Did he want to spend his life with this lovely woman, or was she appealing to him simply because she was exotic, part of the mystery of Hong Kong he wished to master? Would she change, and perhaps wither, if removed from Hong Kong, the city that could nurture her bicultural identity? How far into the future did *he* see? And how would her Western side, the incisive-minded lawyer, develop in tandem with her passive, nurturing Chinese side, especially if he took her to America? Would she even go if he asked her? Maybe the gossips were right: Maybe the gulf between East and West not only ought not to be bridged but could not.

Ah Wong dropped them at Holden's flat and departed, leaving the car parked beneath the building. Holden and May-Ling took the slow lift to the ninth floor, and he unlocked the door. Ah King, his *amah*, or house servant, had long since retired. May-Ling said she wanted a shower. Holden made himself a whiskey and put a record on the stereo, a concerto by Ponce performed by Andrés Segovia. He switched the stereo to the bedroom speakers and lowered the volume, then went to join May-Ling in the shower.

Their lovemaking was long and languorous. She shivered at the gentle, grazing touch of his hands as they stroked her skin, and his mouth as he kissed her everywhere from her eyes to her mouth, down her belly and down her legs, arousing her and causing her to squirm and moan. The wait for him to find her golden door was agonizing, even though she knew he would, and when his tongue entered her, she cried out sharply. She had never slept with any man but Holden (although she had sworn to him she was not a virgin), but she could not imagine a Chinese man taking such care with her, giving her so much pleasure before wanting his own. She grasped his hair and pulled him up from her groin, and she came the moment he entered her, thrashing beneath him and clawing his back, moaning in low barks. She felt his weight on her as he thrusted toward his own climax and enjoyed the slick feeling of their mingled sweat and the tickling sensation of his chest hair. Finally he raised himself above her and gave a moan of his own, and then settled beside her, his lips touching her throat as his breathing slowed. He said nothing; he never did. Why do I love this man? she thought, stroking his back and his neck as one might a child. We will never be the same. Why did I seduce him that first time and give him my virginity—a bride-price in China—and then deny it? It is because he encourages me to use my mind in new ways, in ways a Chinese man would find threatening and unseemly. Yet I try to make him more Chinese, more sensitive to the ancient dictates of my people. Do I want to be his woman, or just his pupil and grateful lover?

I never want to lose him, she decided, realizing at once that she was taking a very un-Chinese view of the future. But I might. She stroked his hair, and he raised his head and kissed her deeply on the lips. She stirred with pleasure and reached for him, bringing him back to erection. She knew he was tired, but she wanted him again.

He ran his hands down her back and under her slim buttocks as he picked up his rhythm. I could so easily love this woman, he thought. If she demanded it, I would marry her. The realization chilled him even as the warmth of his excitement blossomed through his body. She could command me for the asking, yet she would never ask. He stifled her sharp cries with a kiss as he came deep inside her.

4

8 April, 1980

HOLDEN CHAMBERS TURNED HIS two-ton-class racing yacht, *Golondrina*, toward the long starting line in Junk Bay, just outside the eastern approaches to Hong Kong Harbor. The winches screamed briefly as the yacht came hard on the wind and bore down to the line. The line was relatively square, and he had decided to start at the windward end. John Malcolm stood behind him, calling the seconds down to the start. The one-minute gun sounded just after they turned.

The sky was filled with thick, low clouds spitting rain, and fog blew along the clefts on the shore. The unseasonal southeasterly wind was expected to hold and even freshen during the night, and the sailors knew to expect many shifts in direction and changes in velocity of the wind as it swirled around the high, mountainous islands of Hong Kong. The overnight race would start at five o'clock, an eighty-mile course first to windward around Wang Lan Island to the southeast, then a reach or run around the southern side of Hong Kong Island to Southeast Soko well to the west, then a tricky reach among the unlighted small islands between Hong Kong and Lantao around Cheung Chau rock. The tidal currents were strong and unpredictable in the western approaches, and success depended upon knowledge of those currents, especially if the wind went light. After rounding Cheung Chau, the course took them on a beat against wind and current through the narrow channel between Lamma Island and Aberdeen Harbour, on around the southern coast of Hong Kong around Po Toi Island, and a probable reach back to the finish at Shek-O rock, only a couple of miles southeast of the start line.

Two other yachts, two-tonners of similar design to *Golondrina*, were heeled over hard, heading for the same starboard end of the line, where the race officer on the committee boat waited to fire the start gun. The remaining thirteen boats of the fleet, mostly smaller, were planning more conservative starts lower along the line. The top of the competition was the three two-tonners, powerful boats with hulls nearly forty-five-feet long and enormous masts and sails.

"*Sea Bird* looks early, Holden," said Malcolm softly. "*Welsh Dragon* certainly is. Thirty seconds."

Chambers nodded. "Think we should luff them up?"

"At least get close to *Sea Bird*'s quarter. Reg is going to have to tack any second, and then we can go after Hamish." Reg Lloyd raced *Welsh Dragon*, currently ahead in the overnight race series. Hamish MacDougal's *Sea Bird* was a very close second and *Golondrina* third.

"*Dragon* is tacking!" shouted Chris Marston-Evans, who was standing in the bow pulpit.

Malcolm waved his acknowledgment. "All right, Holden, let's get under Hamish's stern. He should have tacked immediately with Reg, and now he will have to fall off or luff to avoid crossing early. We could push him right into the mark if he does that."

"Are we feeling aggressive tonight, John?"

Malcolm smiled. "This is the last overnight, and they are both ahead of you in the series. Look! *Sea Bird* is easing her sheets and falling off. Let's go!"

Holden eased the helm slightly to pick up speed, and the trimmers in the cockpit, all Australians—the "three Bruces and Kevin"—adjusted the jib and main slightly. *Golondrina* closed rapidly on *Sea Bird*'s quarter as the pale-blue boat slowed.

"Steady, Holden. Twelve seconds. Maxwell, ready trim!" Bruce Maxwell, a superintendent of the Royal Hong Kong Police, was leaning over the lee rail, his face inches from the rushing water, watching the trim of the genoa jib. He raised a gloved hand to acknowledge he had heard Malcolm's command. Hand signals were preferred on *Golondrina* over shouted commands, which often could not be heard. John Malcolm was the tactician-navigator, and most commands would come from him, while Chambers concentrated on his steering, watching for tiny wind shifts and odd waves that could slow the boat at a critical moment.

"*Dragon* has tacked again! She is coming up on our quarter!" shouted Marston-Evans.

"I have him. Chris, call *Sea Bird* up!"

"*Sea Bird*, get up! Up, up, up!" called Chris shrilly across less than six feet of gray water racing between the two boats. Holden almost laughed. Chris looked like a skinny terrier in the bow, barking at *Sea Bird*'s burly, red-bearded skipper, who was leaning way out and trying to guess his chances of holding the big boat back long enough to avoid the early start.

Hamish MacDougal turned and grinned at Chambers, giving him the back of his hand, the first two fingers extended in a *V*. "Oh Christ, laddie, all right!" he shouted to Holden. Then, to his crew, "Ready about! Lee-ho!"

Sea Bird's blue transom slewed around, clearing *Golondrina*'s quarter by inches. *Golondrina* now had clear air, and she picked up speed. She was practically at the start buoy. "John, am I early?"

"No. Great. Five seconds, four, three—"

"*Golondrina!* Get up! Get up!" called a voice from close astern. Holden turned and saw *Welsh Dragon*'s dark-red bow swaying above his head, ten feet away but looking closer. Her bow man loomed above him and again called him up.

John Malcolm slapped his shoulder. "Fuck him, Holden. Drive the boat. One second, start!"

The committee-boat gun fired a single cannon as *Golondrina*'s bow drew even with the orange buoy. Holden winced and waited for a second gun, which would mean he had crossed early. It did not come.

"Bloody good start, Holden," said Malcolm.

Holden nodded, beaming. "Bloody good start, lads!" he called to his crew, who acknowledged with waves. Chris Marston-Evans came back to the cockpit and relieved Bruce Maxwell, who ran the deck on the lee-side primary winch, and the bigger man leaned back and stretched.

"What's my course around Wang Lan, John?" asked Holden.

"Crack off two degrees, sail her for speed. Let's win tonight, Holden."

"Yeah, let's do that. Great fucking start, John, and thanks."

Malcolm grinned. "Does that kind word mean a round of beers for the lads?"

"Absolutely. Let's get everyone a drink before we have to get busy with the spinnaker."

Golondrina led the fleet out through the eastern approaches toward Wang Lan, going fast in the gusty breeze, *Welsh Dragon* forty yards behind and *Sea Bird* just behind her. The rest of the fleet was strung out behind the two-tonners in a single file. A damn fine evening, thought Chambers, as Kevin emerged from below with the cans of beer.

Golondrina rounded Southeast Soko just after ten o'clock, still leading the fleet. There was a light on South Soko, a fairly large island, but it was on the far side and largely obscured as they made their approach from the east. The passage between South

Soko and the barren rock that was Southeast Soko, the mark that had to be rounded, was no more than fifty yards wide and often turbulent as the tidal current surged through. Holden had rounded the rock perhaps twenty times, and always at night, but the narrow slot always made him nervous, and he was glad to leave it behind and turn the helm over to John Malcolm.

Chambers dropped down into *Golondrina*'s cabin, rubbing the strain from his eyes. The wind had been flukey all evening, and the spinnaker run had been slow. He could feel *Golondrina* heel as Malcolm brought her clear of the Sokos and onto her reach for Cheung Chau. Ginny Campbell, the eighth member of the crew and the usual cook, was refilling thermos bottles with hot coffee from the galley stove and passing up sandwiches and oranges for the crew on watch.

"Would you like some coffee, Captain?" she asked, favoring him with a smile and a grope at his crotch. Ginny was small and pretty, with that wonderful creamy skin some redheads get, and stunning blue eyes. She loved to sail, she would tell you, almost as much as she liked to screw.

"No thanks, Ginny," he said, dancing away from the grope. "I am going to put my head down for an hour." He crawled into the navigator's berth, aft of the chart table and near the companionway. If Malcolm needed him, he could get back on deck quickly. Bruce Maxwell, Bruce Moore, and Chris Marston-Evans were bedded down on pipe-cots on the weather side of the boat. There were no frills in *Golondrina*'s cabin—just the galley, the pipe-cots, and the head and sail stowage forward. Frills were extra weight.

Holden closed his eyes and enjoyed the sound of the water rushing by the hull. Wind is picking up again, he thought, smiling. He loved the night races with a fast boat and a good crew. He felt he had come a long way to this place, and he felt powerful, immortal. He was thirty-one years old and life was good. The rushing water and the soft murmur of voices from the cockpit soothed him, and he dozed.

Holden Chambers thought himself typical of the merchant bankers of Hong Kong, including the few privileged to style themselves as Lions. The coiner of the nickname, which the Hong Kong men preferred to "gunslinger"—the name the market movers of London had accorded themselves—was Robert Burleigh of Chase Asia, who had conferred the first Lion mantle upon Jack Carroll, the former managing director of Pacific Capital Corporation. Jack Carroll had been in Hong Kong since 1974, trying to put syndicates of lenders together to raise money for Asian-government borrowers, a game the London merchants reserved to themselves. Jack's greatest success had been an export credit for Garuda, the Indonesian state airline, for $50 million in 1975, but when the two jumbo rescue credits for the Government of Indonesia itself—which together totaled $450 million—had been organized later the same year, Carroll and Hong Kong had been frozen out and the deals done entirely in London.

Syndicated lending—the arranging of major loans using other banks' money along with your own, while gaining a fee for putting the deal together—was easy enough, Carroll knew, if you had *other players* in the market, but in 1974 Hong Kong had none, at least in the Eurodollar market. When Burleigh and Chambers had arrived in Hong Kong in 1976, eager to make names for themselves and their banks, Jack Carroll saw a chance to make his, and Hong Kong's, own market.

Robert Burleigh conferred the title of Lion upon Carroll during a drunken revel at the American Club in Ice House Street after Carroll had brazenly outbid his own parent, New York International Bank Limited, for the 1977 mandate for the Development Bank of the Philippines deal. Nibble had cut Carroll off with only $25 million underwriting room for the deal, while secretly bidding themselves with fifty, hiding behind the Morgan Bank with a like amount. Carroll had gotten Chase and Traders to come up with fifty each, and then he had simply declared that PCC had fifty also, and the Filipinos had agreed to do $150 million—fifty more than Nibble and Morgan had offered from London. Carroll had put the offer on the table Saturday morning in Manila, saying apologetically that because of his fine price and terms, he could only hold his three-bank group together through Monday midday. Saturday morning in Asia is Friday night in New York and the wee hours of Saturday in Europe, and Monday midday in Asia is still Sunday in New York and long before opening in Europe on Monday. When the Development Bank took the deal, Jack had taken a tongue-lashing from his bosses in London and then in New York, but the deal held up, and a month later, Burleigh, Chambers, and Carroll had celebrated long into the evening and the Lions of Hong Kong were born.

Holden remembered that deal and that celebration with pleasure. Chase, First NY, and Traders were fierce competitors in London and New York (at least as competitive as one could be in the clubby, buttoned-up world of those two mature markets), but in Asia they cooperated, albeit never officially or publicly, because they all needed the market to grow so that each could prosper. Holden gave Carroll a lot of credit for being sharp enough to know that Nibble would never let PCC out from under its imperious London thumb until there was truly an Asia market, operating without respect for the clocks of London and New York. Chase and Traders needed to get into the game in Hong Kong, and both Burleigh and Chambers had the balls sufficient to do it Carroll's way. Carroll's deal for the Development Bank of the Philippines had declared the new rules in one weekend, and the Lions had never looked back. None of their London or New York offices had tried to move into the Asian loan-syndication market on its own since.

Holden had joined Traders Bank and Trust in New York fresh out of Yale in 1972. Traders was a respectable bank, not patrician and prestigious like Morgan and not aggressive and modern like First New York, but decent, and it paid the going rate. He had decided early in his training period that he wanted to be in the bank's International Department. The International and United States departments were very competitive for the brightest trainees. At the time, the United States Department was more prestigious. The International bankers, the USD men said, were a bunch of playboys who couldn't tell one side of a corporate financial statement from the other, and worse yet, drank wine at lunch and wore colored shirts and Gucci shoes, rather than martinis, white button-down shirts from Brooks Brothers, and wingtips like real bankers. Chambers, who had almost majored in drama at Yale, decided he infinitely preferred signing up with the playboys.

He was assigned first to the Argentina desk, and when, in 1974, Traders entered the newly emerging loan-syndication market, he was selected as one of four assistant vice-presidents to launch the group, under one of the bank's brightest stars, David Weiss. And two years later, when the Asia Division, which had no one from Syndication assigned to them, asked Weiss to send one of his protegés to South Korea to talk about a syndicated credit for the Korea Development Bank, Holden quickly volunteered. He was in Seoul, Tokyo, Hong Kong, and Singapore for four weeks, and when he returned, he brought with him a proposal for a merchant bank to be set up in Hong Kong to develop syndication opportunities in Asia. He modestly offered to go to Hong Kong himself to set up the bank and run it.

In August 1976, Weiss secured for him a promotion to vice-president, sent him off to Hong Kong, and commanded him to report on his activities to all interested bank divisions. Holden tried to comply, but he soon found out that reporting to everybody meant reporting to nobody, and furthermore, that reporting to nobody meant that he could only survive if he made nothing but money for the bank. Thus he was prepared to play the game with the similar loose cannons of Pacific Capital and Chase Asia, and in time, he thought, to play it better than either of his major rivals.

He felt warm breath blown into his ear and opened his eyes to find Ginny Campbell crawling into the narrow cot on top of him. He yawned and pawed her playfully. "What's up, Ginny?" he asked.

"You, ducks, if I get lucky." She nipped his earlobe. "But Big John says Cheung Chau rock and asks if you want to come up on deck."

As Holden slid out from under her and sat up, she stretched out and yawned like a contented cat. "You always leave a bunk so *warm*, Captain!"

Holden kissed her cheek, cool from the night air. "Sweet dreams," he said. He pulled on his boots and his heavy sweater and climbed into the cockpit.

5

9 April, 1980

RICHARD VAN COURTLAND DROVE the big Mercedes fast and aggressively through the Sunday traffic in Wong Nai Chong Gap and down into Repulse Bay. Barbara Ramsay sat in the left seat, memorizing the route as they went, thinking that if her husband ran true to form she would probably have to drive back.

They passed the elegant old Repulse Bay Hotel, with its famous restaurant on the long veranda. The hotel was due for demolition so that another high-rise apartment building could go up. How sad, thought Barbara. Hong Kong had so little of architectural or historical interest and so many artless vertical glass and concrete boxes.

They started around the south side of the island, which was sparsely populated because the red-earth slopes of the mountains were too steep to support buildings. The slopes were covered with wild tropical shrubs and stubby flowering trees and rang with the calls of brightly colored birds. The sudden transition from the high-rises and urban bustle of Repulse Bay stirred Barbara; it made Hong Kong seem raw and tropical, a jungle just over any hill from the civilization perched precariously on the coastal plains. The traffic thinned as they rose into the hills, but Richard was unable to speed up because he was trapped behind a red-and-yellow double-decker bus, one of the older ones that was able to navigate the sharp switchbacks of the narrow back roads. The dirty, dented relic ground up the rising slope in low gear, belching black smoke. On a particularly sharp turn, Richard executed a daring and dangerous pass, using all the car's power and nearly all the brakes to get around the bus and back into line before colliding head-on with a goods vehicle hurtling at them downhill. Barbara was badly frightened but said nothing. Richard didn't take any criticism of his driving, and didn't even want conversation.

He had found that a friend of his from his London days, Colin

Leach, was living in Hong Kong, representing the Australia and New Zealand Banking Corporation. Leach had married the eldest daughter of Hamish MacDougal, head of one of the old Scottish trading families, and seemed, therefore, set for life and very happy about it. Colin had invited Richard and his wife to the weekly Sunday lunch at the MacDougal home on Big Wave Bay Road in Shek-O, the wealthy enclave on the remote east coast of Hong Kong Island.

The traffic had dwindled to nothing as they drove down into the valley that contained Tai Tam Reservoir. It was a driver's road, and Richard attacked it with grim concentration. Barbara admired both his skill and daring, even when it frightened her. Once away from the traffic she relaxed and watched the thick green forest rush past.

They had been living in Hong Kong for just over a month, and though the place still felt strange, the fast, insistent pace at which business skimmed across the surface of the mysterious city made feeling brand-new and rootless seem ordinary. They had settled in quickly, since a flat owned by First New York had been available. It was a large airy apartment on Baker Road in the upper Mid-levels, with a spectacular view of Victoria Harbour and the city and mountains of Kowloon beyond. Their furniture arrived from New York and was installed; an *amah* was located and hired; and cars and drivers were provided by their respective employers.

Barbara found herself a cramped office in the Roland, Archer suite on the mezzanine level of Connaught Centre, the enormous skyscraper at the harbor's edge which dominated the Central District skyline. She mapped out and began a calling program, the intent of which was to find out what the banks pouring into Hong Kong from all over the world wanted to do with their money. She called on European bankers, mostly newly arrived, and paid special attention to those from Japan. Many of her afternoons were taken up by the wives of Richard's colleagues, and she ate lightly and played tennis and learned all about *amahs* and schools and shopping and yearnings for home. Her business contacts with the "stuffees," as the minor banks were called because they swallowed the loans and issues brought by the Lions but initiated little business of their own, proved little more satisfying. Few of the minor houses had any firm idea of their mission and most seemed content to remain stuffees. She wanted to have as clear an idea of the market as possible before calling on the Lions, because she thought it unlikely that they would welcome an upstart Yankee investment bank, no matter how big it was in its home market, into their profitable inner circle. She knew she would have to call on them soon, however, as the managing director from Roland, Archer Limited to whom she reported, Nigel Cross, would be coming to Hong Kong in less than three weeks, and he would surely want to call on the banks who moved the market. The minor bankers were courteous and solicitous, but they didn't know the answers to Barbara's questions, and she had no better idea as to what to do with her career than on the day she arrived. The only thing of which she was sure was that the Lions of Hong Kong defined themselves, and that she would have to do likewise.

Barbara Ramsay was a headstrong, independent woman, and comfortable being so. She enjoyed competition, and when growing up she had resisted being forced to compete only with women. While in high school, she had argued successfully that while there might be a need to separate boys' and girls' basketball teams, there was no reason for separate debating societies. She had no qualms about playing the role of the submissive female when it suited her, especially when the reward for patronizing stupid men was the advancement of her own career. Barbara thought of maneuvering men through her charm and her looks as a kind of mental bullfighting, getting a man moving in one direction because he found her attractive, and then stepping aside and using his own momentum to carry him out of her way or into the barrier.

Barbara had grown up in the Cleveland suburb of Chagrin Falls in a family which she considered as white, Anglo-Saxon, middle-class protestant, and dull. In high school she was an exceptional student, but she hadn't yet learned to suffer the arrogance of the boys who pursued her, so she ended up studying a lot and dating little. In college at Vassar she became a more thoughtful person, and she discovered women could, especially in the absence of men, become just as arrogant and foolish. By the time she reached the Graduate School of Business at Harvard, her leggy good looks had ripened toward beauty, and her feminism had been refined by tolerance, but she still sought competition at the highest level. She decided on investment banking by the middle of her second year, set about making friends who might one day be colleagues or important clients, and was graduated in the top ten percent of her class.

Barbara joined Roland, Archer and married Richard van Courtland in the same year she had received her MBA. Richard had been a class ahead of her at Harvard, and had all the right pedigrees. He was seven years her senior, and had been working at First New York Bank for five years before taking a leave with the company's blessing to go to Harvard for his master's. After returning to First New York, Richard had risen quickly in the merchant banking division. A year after they were married, Richard was offered a posting to London, to the syndicated-loan unit at New York International Bank Limited. Barbara had said she wouldn't go with him unless her own career at Roland, Archer could be preserved, and her employer had come through with a posting to Roland, Archer Limited, its small but growing merchant banking subsidiary in London.

Barbara complained to her colleagues at Roland, Archer about having to move with Richard like a camp follower, but she admitted to herself that being sent to London had helped her own advancement. Roland had her working on stock underwritings for large national accounts during her first years in New York. It was dull work, consisting mostly of editing prospectuses and even proofreading. The move to London forced Roland to move Barbara into Capital Markets, because that was all Roland, Archer Limited did, and Capital Markets was where the big money and the fast-track careers were made. Roland needed bright, successful women to show it was trying to bring women along and up the ladder, just as they had to hang on to any other "minorities" that could make the grade, so Barbara got her capital markets assignment ahead of many men who sought it. It hadn't hurt, of course, that her husband was sent to New York International Bank Limited.

Barbara worked very hard in London, learning the intricacies of deal structures, pricing formulae, and trading and clearing mechanisms of different instruments. She used her time in London to prove herself a diligent and loyal worker, and to get herself noticed as a quick study. She found the work of mastering the Eurobond business more time consuming than difficult, but she had lots of time, because while her male colleagues were for the most part happy to help her master the game, they did not include her in the totally male-dominated social life of clubs and wine bars in which each working day in the City was concluded.

Three years later, Richard was transferred back to New York to do a stint in Corporate Planning—dull, but considered crucial for early advancement to senior management, as long as one didn't stay too long and become labeled as a staff man. Barbara had asked to remain in capital markets, and with the support of her colleagues in London was given a position in a newly formed unit in New York which was marketing interest rate and currency swaps. The unit was successful, and its members became well known on the executive floors of Roland, Archer's huge black headquarters on Liberty Street. By the time Richard was given the assignment to run Pacific Capital Corporation, Barbara was once again ready to move.

Roland, Archer had no capital markets office in Hong Kong, although one had been under consideration for some years. Barbara made it quite clear that she had no interest in moving into the existing retail office, which sold U.S. securities to wealthy Chinese clients, and argued that she could at least begin the groundwork for some Asian issues, preparing the way for a more senior person when one became available. Barbara knew that none of the gunslingers in capital markets in New York or London wanted any part of getting too far from the action, away from the big bonuses the steady flow of deals provided. She thought it unlikely that anyone would be sent to watch over her until she had proved the market real by doing the first deals, and by then, it might well be too late to take it away from her. Her colleagues endorsed her plan; after all, it couldn't hurt to have her look the market over; she might be awfully junior, they all said, but she was damned good. Moreover, since Roland wouldn't have to provide any housing or living allowances (it being assumed that First New York would provide all that), they would be getting her on the cheap. Barbara had smiled sweetly at this suggestion, and demanded at least her own company-supplied automobile.

Barbara broke out of her reverie as Richard turned the Mercedes sharply onto the very narrow road which ran along the top of Tai Tam Dam. The reservoir was low, and the drop looked steep on either side. Richard accelerated off the dam and around two very tight hairpin turns, and then the road rose again, on one side the mountain and on the other a wall which concealed the dropoff. Richard drove as though he knew the road, although Barbara knew he didn't, and she had to remind herself that he was a skillful driver even as she wished he would slow down. The two-lane road was much narrower than a similar road in the States would have been.

At the top of the rise they found the road that led to Shek-O. They rocketed through a patch of woods, and then they began seeing the sea on both sides as they descended through a series of switchbacks called the Dragon's Back, which finally forced Richard to slow. At the bottom of the hill, they turned into Big Wave Bay Road, passed the golf course, and into Shek-O. There were a few more cars now, as people headed for the beach at the end of the road.

Barbara and Richard were looking for number 6, which took some concentration, since the numbers on the house signs ran in no obvious order. They passed number 3, then number 33, then 27 and 8 before finding 6, a paved driveway to the left, rising steeply between high masonry walls. Richard parked the Mercedes in the ample carpark that adjoined the driveway on both sides.

"Helluva road," he said, stretching his fingers and cracking his knuckles. "Helluva road." These were the only words he had spoken since leaving their flat forty-five minutes before.

Barbara got out of the car and stretched. The house was new; indeed, it didn't appear quite finished. It seemed built of enormous blocks of white stucco and had a faint Mediterranean style. It was grand in scale, even viewed from what must be the narrow end. She walked across flagstones to the huge double front doors, which were elaborately carved in a tropical hardwood. Richard followed, and together they looked for a doorbell. "Here it is," he said, finding an old-fashioned French wrought-iron twist bell set into the stucco, under a small brass plaque that said "Seaview—MacDougal."

He twisted the bell handle and heard a faint ring from within, immediately followed by the thunderous, rolling bark of a huge dog. Barbara stepped away from the door, startled, as she heard the scrabble of the beast's claws on a hard floor within and again the monstrous bark. "Seems we have been announced," remarked Richard dryly.

The door was opened by a pretty teenage girl with pale skin, sea-blue eyes, and reddish-blond hair. Her hand rested lightly on the shoulders of a Rhodesian Ridgeback whose head came up to her elbow. "Guests, Mummy!" she called back into the house, opening the door wide. The dog stood his ground, blocking the door, until the girl pushed him lightly to one side. "Let them in, Kima."

"Richard van Courtland," said Richard importantly.

"And Barbara Ramsay," said Barbara. "Hello."

"Hello, I'm Constance MacDougal; call me Contzi. You must be Colin's friends from America," said the girl, extending her small hand to Barbara. "Please come in. Don't bother about Kima—he hasn't eaten anyone in days. Mummy!"

Richard followed Barbara into a large hallway, floored with marble of a pleasing greenish-gray shade. The Ridgeback retreated, head down. He is shy, thought Barbara. There was a dining room to the left of the hall, and to the right down two steps was a vast living room with a fireplace stretching nearly across one wall. The wall toward the front of the house was all glass and overlooked a terrace and the sea beyond. There was comfortable upholstered furniture near the fireplace and a grand piano in one corner. The rest of the room was filled with packing crates, rolled-up rugs, and paintings leaned along the baseboards. Barbara noticed the faint smell of fresh cement.

"We are just moving in," said Contzi unnecessarily.

A tall, slim woman in dark slacks and a man's white shirt, her hair tied in a bandanna, came down the stairs at the far end of the hall, a vase with roses in her hand. Her features matched the girl's, refined to mature beauty. Barbara placed her age at perhaps forty-five, though she looked younger. She had an air of energy and warmth. She set the vase on an antique table and came to greet them, a smile of welcome bringing fine lines to the edges of her eyes. "Please come in. I'm Alice MacDougal."

"Richard and Barbara Ramsay," said Contzi. Barbara suppressed a smile while Richard set the record straight. Alice took them into the living room and pointed absently at the couches and chairs near the fire, which burned very low. "I hope Colin told you we are just now moving in. I hope he told you these lunches are very informal."

Colin hadn't said anything one way or another, and Barbara wore a blue-gray linen dress and Richard a somber gray suit. "We are glad to be here," said Barbara, smiling at the woman, liking her. "But it seems we are early."

"Colin said to be prompt at twelve o'clock," said Richard. "Sorry."

Alice MacDougal waved her left hand as she turned toward the fire. The only jewelry she wore was an enormous diamond ring on the third finger. "Not to worry. As I said, these lunches are informal to the point of being chaotic, but we have fun." She clapped her hands once, quite loudly. A Filipino manservant appeared from the hallway. "Delfin, please serve drinks to our guests. The Bloody Marys are ready, I hope?"

"Yes, missy," said the Filipino, smiling and showing a gold tooth. He turned to Barbara and Richard, "Missy? Master?"

"Yes, thank you," said Barbara. "A Bloody Mary would be perfect."

"Same," said Richard, and he turned back to his hostess, who was now staring out the window-wall. "What a magnificent house you have, Mrs. MacDougal," he said, at his most charming. "And the view!"

"Alice," she said, with a slightly flirtatious smile. "Thank you. We have just built the house, and it is still a mess, but the view is certainly intact. Very good *fung shui*, at that. Look!"

Barbara drew beside Alice as she pointed out toward the sea.

They could see the rock of Shek-O, with its wrought-iron light tower surrounded by surf in the middle distance. The water was slate-gray under the turbulent cloudy sky, and beyond the rock a containership sped northwestward toward the eastern entrance to Hong Kong Harbour, a bone of white water under her bow. Across the channel a jungle-covered mountain jutted from the sea, and a narrow passage between it and a peninsula of the mainland glittered where the sun was breaking through a rent in the cloud cover. It was truly beautiful. "I have heard of *fung shui*, Alice," said Barbara as Delfin returned with the Bloody Marys in very large glasses, "but I don't know what it means."

Alice took her glass, and raised it to her guests. Barbara returned the salute; Richard was already taking a large gulp. Barbara was ashamed of his lack of courtesy, but Alice seemed not to notice. "Cheers," said Alice. "Now, *fung shui* literally means 'wind and water.' We look out at the Eastern Approaches between the two hills on the other side of the road. Water between dragons—hills—is good *joss*, good 'luck.' If you look across, you can see Fat Tau Mun—that's the pass between the mainland and Ting Ling Island—and you have water between dragons a second time." Alice's tone was both whimsical and charming.

Barbara smiled and nodded. Out of the corner of her eye she saw Richard wave his empty glass at the steward, Delfin, who took it and retreated to the pantry. "Your home, and this setting, are truly special, Alice."

Alice smiled. "But you must let me show you the rest, rubbish tip though it appears." She took Barbara's elbow. "Richard? Care to have a look around?"

"Ah, thanks, Alice. I will just enjoy the view for a moment, if I may. It's restful after the drive out." Delfin returned with Richard's drink, rebuilt.

"Of course," said Alice sweetly. "Sit and relax. Barbara and I will just be a minute."

Alice led Barbara through the dining room, with its *koi* ponds beyond the sliding doors, through the pantry, the huge kitchen with its bustling, giggling Chinese cook and helpers, and the climate-controlled wine room. The rest of the downstairs was servants' quarters, she said, and she led Barbara upstairs. Barbara followed, silent and seething. Richard had never been polished, not in New York and not in London, but his colleagues had seemed prepared to accept his roughness because of his financial brilliance. Somehow politesse, just basic *manners*, seemed much more important in Hong Kong. Despite its rough-and-tumble business practices, Hong Kong retained a veneer of gentility.

Barbara admired the regal way in which Alice, obviously surprised in her work clothes by their early arrival, had serenely taken them in and made them at home. She wondered how many bloodies Richard would inhale before they rejoined him and how soon he would become embarrassingly drunk.

"The second floor is mostly for the children," Alice said, leading Barbara into a large room, messy with furniture and toys. "This is the playroom, and the younger children's bedrooms and baths surround." Alice waved at the rooms in a circular gesture, her diamond flashing in the pale light coming through skylights thirty feet above. "The upper gallery, which looks over the playroom, has rooms for my older girls."

Barbara looked up, at the balcony that circled above them. Each room would have a view of some sort, either of the sea or of the mountain behind the house, she thought. "It's lovely, Alice," she said.

"We have six children," said Alice, smiling. "Contzi is my third. Carol and Mary—your friend Colin's wife—are older, and Philip, Catherine, and Anne are younger."

"How very nice," said Barbara. "You must be very happy." Please don't ask me when I plan to have children, she thought.

"Oh, yes," said Alice, leading off up a flight of stairs that reached a level about halfway between the two floors of the children's wing. "I would have more, but I got so cranky when I was carrying Anne, my older sprogs told me I should stop." She laughed, touching a large family photograph hung alongside the stairway. "There is little Anne. She is just eight now."

Barbara studied the photograph. The MacDougals were a very handsome family, from the grinning red-bearded giant of the father and the slim, youthful, dark-haired mother. Three of the children had their father's coloring and three their mother's, and all looked guileless and radiantly happy. Barbara couldn't wait to meet them.

Alice continued the house tour, showing Barbara the vast master bedroom with its large bathrooms at either end, the private veranda, which ran around the house at this level and from which they could see the swimming pool and the terrace, and the formal garden, a riot of color from blooming roses and tropical flowers and bordered by bougainvillea, giant ferns, and tall palms. From above the pool, they once again faced the sea, which had now taken on a greenish-blue color as the cloud cover thinned and broke up. A sailboat with a blue-and-white spinnaker came into view, running toward the harbor to the northwest.

"Oh, look!" exclaimed Alice. "Here they come at last."

Barbara smiled and looked a question. Alice pointed to the sailboat. Another appeared behind it, also under a blue-and-white spinnaker. "You see? Hamish is racing. They started yesterday afternoon, and it was a short course. They should have finished around dawn, but the wind must have gone light during the night. That is why no one is here yet, Barbara. Most of the guests, or at least the men, are on the boats."

Barbara felt better about their early arrival having obviously been a gaffe. "Which boat is yours?"

Alice squinted. "I can't see without my glasses. We have blue-and-white spinnakers, but so does *Golondrina*. Can you see if one of the boats has a blue hull?"

Barbara shaded her eyes. The sun was suddenly quite bright. "The first boat is white, I think, and the second boat is definitely blue. I can see a third now, and it has a red hull."

"Oh, dear." Alice sighed. "The second is ours, and the one in front must be Holden Chambers. The red boat will be Reg Lloyd's *Welsh Dragon*."

Holden Chambers! thought Barbara. She hadn't heard his name since meeting him two weeks before at the First New York party. She had thought about him, with his handsome face and humorous grin, and his easy, confident charm. "Then the white boat belongs to Holden Chambers? Will he win?"

"Well, it seems he has," replied Alice, turning toward the door back into the house. "Or at least he has beaten my Hamish. There is a handicapping system, which I don't really understand, but Hamish gives Holden a time handicap."

"Will your husband be upset?"

"No," said Alice, a hint of annoyance in her voice. "Sometimes I think I care more about the races than Hamish, though I rarely set foot on the bloody yacht. Hamish likes Holden; like as not he will bring him on to lunch." Alice held the door for Barbara. The two women stepped inside, and Alice closed the door. The wind off the sea was damp and still slightly chilly.

I hope he does, thought Barbara. "We will wait for, ah, Hamish, then, before lunch?" She was quite happy to wait, but she couldn't help worrying about Richard, applying booze with no food to absorb it. He hadn't eaten breakfast; he never did.

"Oh, yes, I am afraid so," said Alice, looking at Barbara thoughtfully. "Wee Hamish will be an hour at least reaching his mooring at the yacht club in Causeway Bay, then he *must* stand the lads to a drink at the bar or even two. He will bring Colin with him to lunch—Colin is in Hamish's crew—and doubtless several others from the yachts." Alice paused and once again glanced across at Barbara. "Nice chaps, all. Some will bring their wives. I told you these lunches are informal, even unruly."

"I am sure it will be great fun," said Barbara, following Alice down the stairs. In the living room they found Richard, a full glass before him on a glass table, making conversation with Kima, the giant Ridgeback, who sat well away from him, his expression suspicious. Barbara noted that Richard's eyes were hard and bright. Damn, she thought.

"Perhaps I will ask Ah Fong to make us some little snacks," said Alice. "We may not see the actual lunch before three; I wouldn't want you two to go hungry."

"Oh, thank you, Alice," said Barbara, feeling relieved and showing it. "But we shouldn't want to change your plans."

"Rubbish," said Alice, beaming. "It is no trouble, and I can see that that wretch Colin led you to expect we would eat lunch at lunchtime. I will just have a word with Ah Fong to give us a snack, and then I think I will open a bottle of wine. Will you join me? Richard?"

"Thank you," said Barbara, gratefully. Richard would be much restored by a snack, and she herself would be famished well before three o'clock.

"Yes, that sounds very nice," said Richard, springing to his feet. "I am sorry to be such a bother, but we really didn't ask Colin the right questions. May I help in any way?"

Barbara felt her tension slipping away. Richard could be charming when he relaxed, and it looked as though his Bloody Marys and his talk with Kima had helped him unwind.

"You can help me choose a wine," said Alice, leading Richard into the wine room.

The "snack" prepared by Ah Fong turned out to be delicious omelettes, followed by cheeses and various fruits in a salad. They chatted through the meal, with Contzi and her younger sister Anne joining them and asking many questions about America. After the meal, Contzi persuaded Barbara and Richard to take a short walk down the road to look at the beach. Richard went happily, abandoning his full glass of wine, and chatted pleasantly with Contzi. Barbara tagged along, enjoying the wildness of the lush tropical vegetation and the nearly deserted beach, so different from the high-rise crowding on the other side of the island.

Maybe I am not being fair to Richard, she thought, but he seemed to function so well in London and New York, where cliques of bankers got things done and individuals weren't expected to and, indeed, didn't stand out. Out here the solitary Lion was king, and for that reason Richard's lack of individual presence seemed much more worrisome. But he was under pressure, and he didn't really drink all that much more than the others. But he just didn't seem to feel the place, in the way he thought a Lion should; and in a way she thought she was beginning to understand.

Despite the sun's gradual overpowering of the clouds, the air was still damp and cool in the breeze, so the walk was kept short, and when they returned to the big house, they found that the other guests had begun to arrive.

Mary Leach greeted them warmly. "Colin phoned from the yacht club. He said they were having a beer with the crews and that Hamish was bringing Holden Chambers and two of his crew with him. They should be here in under an hour."

"How was the race?" asked Richard.

"Colin said it was fine until about two A.M., when all three of the big boats sailed into a hole south of Tai Tam and they just sat for two hours with no wind. *Sea Bird*—that's Daddy's boat; Colin crews with him—sailed through Holden's *Golondrina* at one point, but when the wind came back, Holden got it first and regained his lead. Holden won the race, but Daddy came second, and since he was ahead of Holden by a wide margin in the previous races, Daddy won the series."

"They race all night?" asked Barbara.

"Oh, yes," said Alice. She had changed her slacks and shirt for a simple knitted dress and combed out her hair while they had been walking. "They take it awfully seriously. There are day races as well, but the overnight series is considered the real test for the big yachts. The China Sea Race begins next week, and they will be off to Manila."

"To Manila!" said Barbara. "How long does that take?"

"It is over six hundred miles across the South China Sea," said Mary. "About four days for the faster boats, followed by four days of intense partying, and then they sail back."

"Do you go down with them?" Richard asked Alice.

"I don't sail down. I may fly down," she replied. "Every year I swear I won't; I don't know whether Hamish behaves worse if I am there or if I stay home. It is an enormous party."

"I'm going," said Mary, mischievously. "I will get enough dirt on Colin to keep him docile for another year."

In the hours that followed, the house began filling with boisterous, happy guests. Delfin moved in and out of the pantry to satisfy drink orders. Carol MacDougal appeared, apparently just risen from bed. She was deeply tanned and the loveliest of the

MacDougal girls. She explained the tan and the late rising by telling Richard and Barbara that she was on spring break from the University of California at Santa Barbara and had flown in to Hong Kong only the day before.

Just before three, the roar of a powerful sports-car engine overwhelmed the conversation, joined by its loud klaxon. Kima gave a joyful yelp and bolted down the stairs and to the front door, which Alice moved swiftly to open for him. The guests surged out into the driveway, shouting and laughing. Barbara could see Holden Chambers backing a white Triumph TR-6 into a narrow slot, its engine rumbling with joyful menace. Hamish MacDougal sat in the passenger seat, his red hair and beard tangled from the wind. His head protruded at least six inches above the top of the sports-car's windscreen, and his left shoulder extended well outside the door, which popped open with a snap as Holden shut the engine down. In his massive right fist, Hamish held a pewter tankard aloft, and he roared a greeting at the mob. "God save all here!"

After much milling around, everyone reentered the crowded living room, Hamish's tankard was refilled by Delfin, and drinks were served all around. Colin Leach arrived a minute later and, after him, John Malcolm and Chris Marston-Evans. The race was relived minute by minute, with Chambers, supported strongly by Malcolm and Marston-Evans, maintaining that they had led from start to finish and that, further, their victory had been ordained by God himself. Hamish and Colin complained good-naturedly about Yankee luck on a wind-shift snatching away *Sea Bird*'s victory, deserved by superior seamanship and crew effort, not to mention British virtue.

Barbara noticed that Carol had at last become fully awake when Chambers entered the room. He had given her a chaste kiss on the cheek, and now they sat next to each other on the raised ledge in front of the fireplace, Carol holding Holden's arm and chattering excitedly in his ear. Barbara felt a twinge of something like jealousy, and then she surprised herself by crossing the room and thrusting her hand at Holden, putting on her best smile. "Congratulations, Holden. I heard that you won."

As he took the hand, he looked confused, and for a horrible second Barbara thought he might not remember who she was. "Why, thank you, Barbara. We were lucky this morning." He squeezed her hand and noted she seemed reluctant to take it back. "Have you met Carol MacDougal?"

"Yes, hello. Carol was telling me earlier about her school." Carol's smile stiffened and Barbara immediately regretted the remark. The way she had said "school" seemed to dismiss Carol as impossibly young, compared to Holden Chambers—and to herself, which, of course, had been exactly her subconscious intent. She felt color rising in her cheeks and decided it was best just to plunge on. "The race must have been exciting," she said, realizing how lame that sounded.

Chambers smiled at Barbara with a look of quizzical amusement in his eyes. She had never in her life felt like such an obvious flirt. Her cheeks burned as she waited for him to speak, and she thought frantically about escape.

Carol gripped his arm a little tighter and smiled sweetly at Barbara. Her voice had only the slightest hint of malice and of triumph. "Oh, look, Holden, here's Mummy at last. Lunch is finally ready. I do hope you like curry, Barbara."

Holden and Carol rose, and Barbara took a step backward to let them pass. Carol started toward the dining room, still with a firm grip on Holden's arm. As she pulled him away, he stopped and looked back. Barbara in turn looked at him, knowing she was not hiding her chagrin. She thought his eyes looked soft, even understanding. "The curry is excellent," he said softly, then followed Carol into the dining room.

Barbara stared at the fire for a moment to calm herself, then went to find her husband, who was sharing a joke with John Malcolm and Colin Leach. She stood on the periphery of the all-male circle like a dutiful wife. The delay allowed her color to return to normal and to ensure that their position in the buffet line was well away from Holden and Carol.

Barbara drove the big Mercedes carefully up the narrow road from Shek-O, going very slowly around the switchbacks, which the headlights couldn't illuminate until the car was fully around. Richard sat in the passenger seat, his head occasionally lolling with the car's motion, nursing a pint of beer in a plastic glass that Hamish MacDougal had pressed on him as they left.

The party had gone on and on, as the guests, many sitting on the packing crates in the living room, had eaten curry and salad and eventually dessert off their knees. Most of the men and not a few of the women had gotten pretty drunk, as Hamish MacDougal made it a point to refill glasses with beer or wine or whatever anyone was drinking. Barbara admitted to herself that while Richard was perhaps a bit far gone to manage the long drive back into town, he was by no means out of line with the boisterous behavior of the group.

Barbara slowed to a crawl as she crossed the Tai Tam Dam,

which seemed even narrower in the pitch dark. She saw the lights of another vehicle at the far end, and it stopped and waited for her to complete her crossing. Thank you, she whispered to herself, and realized she was driving in the middle of the road.

"Saw you talking to that bastard Chambers," said Richard matter-of-factly. He had been so quiet that she jumped.

"I congratulated him on his race win," she said. She had not in fact spoken to him after that, although several times during the meal and afterwards she thought she had seen him looking at her. She still smarted with shame at her display in front of him and Carol. "Did you speak with him?"

"Saw no reason. Don't like the bastard," he said, sipping his beer.

"Why not?" she asked.

He shrugged and looked across at his wife, watching her bite her lower lip as she concentrated on her driving. "For one thing, he sits at my rightful place at Hong Kong's table. First NY invented the Asia syndication market, and if that jerk Jack Carroll hadn't let Chase and Traders and even Bank of America get into the game, we would still control it. Even now we have more of the market than any other bank, but fucking Chambers still carries on like the stud rooster of the barnyard."

Barbara smiled in the darkness. Richard had gone to the University of Texas, and his drawl and his rural figures of speech both became more pronounced when he drank. "I thought you had a mandate from New York to get some of your lost market share back," she said.

"Mandate's one thing. Problem is, people in the various countries' finance ministries and central banks listen to Chambers; God knows why. Two weeks ago he persuaded the Indonesians to give a mandate to a management group of Traders, Llewellyns, and B. of A., even though I offered them a lower fee for an exclusive."

She shrugged but didn't answer. They were encountering more traffic now, and she felt the beginnings of eyestrain. He fell silent beside her.

Bus traffic slowed them through Repulse Bay, although she was able to pass two double-deckers as they moved to the left in the special climbing lanes on the long hill on Repulse Bay Road. Richard seemed to doze, and Barbara was glad to be not more than ten minutes from their flat. Just beyond the end of the climbing lane, a car pulled in behind the Mercedes, flashed its high-beam lights, and accelerated past in a blur of white and a burst of engine noise. Richard squinted through the windshield.

"Fucking cowboy! Why, that's Chambers in his fucking Triumph!"

Barbara nodded slowly, watching the receding taillights. Holden Fucking Chambers, she smiled to herself, aware how glad she was that he was alone in his little car.

6

11 April

CHAMBERS WALKED INTO TRADERS Asia's offices at his usual
arrival time of nine-thirty. Margaret stood behind her desk, wring-
ing her hands in front of her and looking extremely agitated.
"Good morning, Margaret," he said pleasantly. "Something up?"

"Mr. Weiss is here," she whispered. "He arrived half an hour
ago, and is sitting at your desk, reading your telexes."

How rude, he thought, instantly angry. And how perfectly typical. He nodded to Margaret, then pushed open the door to his
office. David Weiss sat in his chair, his feet up on the polished
surface of the desk. "Good morning, David," said Chambers,
forcing down his anger. "This is an unexpected pleasure."

"Ah, Chambers. Good of you to slide into work so nearly on
time. I have been reading this intra-Asia traffic without interest
for the last half-hour." He looked at Chambers briefly over his
half-lens reading glasses, then returned his gaze to a long telex.

Chambers hung his jacket on a hanger on the back of his door,
hoping no one in the Asia network had picked that morning to
send a telex either expressing anger at Traders Asia or a snide
comment about their masters in New York.

Prior to the formation of the Syndications Unit, David Weiss
had occupied a corner office in Traders Bank's London branch.
He was a feisty man, undeniably brilliant, and a virtuoso in the
fast-dealing London Eurodollar market. He seemed to report to
no one, never wrote anything down, and calmly did the complex
calculations needed to price an issue for syndication in his head.
Confronted with a group of earnest young officers who needed
to be managed and used to increase the business, he at first seemed
to resent their presence, and the concomitant need to get money
and office space and to deal with such other nuisances that subordinates brought with them, but he knew he needed bodies to
project his power, so he tolerated them and even indulged them
with trips to London to bask in his glory. He never gave up the

idea, however, that he could handle the business worldwide better without them, and he never missed an opportunity to tell them how useless they really were. He had a tongue that could abrade flesh and draw blood.

Weiss put the telexes down, took off his glasses, and stood up. He was a compact man, only five-eight, but he always seemed charged with energy, which made him seem larger. He wore a shaped Italian suit, five years out of fashion, which fitted well over his muscular, athletic body. He had a round face topped with a shiny mop of black curls, worn a bit long. He had bushy black brows and a thick mustache under a prominent nose. The effect of the brows, nose, and mustache, plus a receding chin, made him look at once aggressive and slightly simian. What always caught people and held them, thought Holden, were Weiss's eyes. Shiny and black against pale skin, those eyes penetrated and were impenetrable; they gave him an air of knowing every secret, of being in total control. Weiss extended his hand, but the gesture did nothing to counter the effect of his eyes: ruthless intimidation.

"We didn't expect you," said Chambers. "We would have liked to make some appointments for you." Might as well have done some work, long as you're here, he thought.

"I am quite able to make my own appointments, Holdy," said Weiss, sitting again. "I am here just today, to work off a bit of jetlag. I am off tomorrow afternoon to Tokyo to attend the Asia Group conference."

That's bullshit, thought Chambers. He could have taken the Pan Am nonstop from New York to Tokyo and rested there. He was up to something. "I didn't know you were to attend the group meeting, David."

"Thought I should, since you apparently can't be bothered."

"I am sending Walter Faring. It will be good experience for him, and as you know, I have the China Sea Race beginning Sunday."

David Weiss sneered. "Your sailing outing is more important than liasing with your colleagues?"

"David, I see these guys more often than they see each other. I do business with these people. I don't need to go to these empty meetings. Besides, Walter will benefit from watching three days of the station heads preen and posture and lie about their market shares and their individual importance."

Weiss laughed, a short, mean bark. "I didn't know you held your colleagues in such low regard, Chambers."

"Individually they are fine men, David, and most of them work at their jobs. You yourself have often said, and not just to me"— Weiss looked up sharply, responding to the criticism—"that the

Asia Group is totally lacking in leadership, and therefore the individual station heads do as they like."

"And you want young Walter to see that first-hand?"

"Indeed. He doesn't yet know these people. He needs to see them as they are. To that extent alone this meeting may have value for us."

Weiss stood up and turned toward the window. "A cautious man might not want his number-two to learn the business too quickly." He turned back, a quick movement like a karate turn, and pointed at Chambers with a long finger. "If Faring comes along rapidly, you might seem less than indispensable here."

"I am sure, David, that Walter is already fully capable of supporting a new head of TAL, should you wish to appoint one."

Weiss grinned, cocking his thumb over his pointing finger and firing the imaginary pistol. "Why, Holdy, how can you imagine I could do without my Prince of Asia?"

Holden allowed himself a small smile. "One senses at times that one is not loved."

"Nonsense, my boy, nonsense!" Weiss crossed the room and grasped both of Chambers's shoulders in a loose embrace. "Of course you are loved; cherished, even. And to show it yet again, let me invite you to dinner this evening."

"Delighted, of course," said Chambers. To be harangued and abused through six courses, he thought with an inner twinge. "What will you do all day? Do you want to see anyone?"

"I have a full slate." Weiss's smile and raised eyebrows suggested mischief. "Just meet me at Gaddi's at eight."

"Do you want the car?"

Weiss grinned more broadly. "Shouldn't want to inconvenience you, Prince. I have one of the Rolls-Royces from the Peninsula. Until eight o'clock, then?"

He could just be doing his holiday shopping a bit early, thought Chambers, but I am guessing he is up to something, and he doesn't want my driver to tell me later where he has gone. "Good, David. I look forward to dinner."

"Charmed." Weiss made a deep bow in the Japanese fashion and strode from the room.

Weiss had lunch with Richard van Courtland at the Overseas Bankers Club, where he was sure to be recognized and reported upon. The thought of him being seen conferring in low tones with Chambers's arch-rival as well as the energy Chambers would have to expend guessing what was said amused him greatly. His conversation with van Courtland was in fact about old friends and haunts in London, and in the end Weiss begged off early in the afternoon, leaving van Courtland to drink his cognac alone. He had been a bore in London and hadn't improved in Hong Kong.

Weiss rode back to the Peninsula Hotel in the brown Rolls-Royce he had hired for the day. He changed his woolen suit for a light-weight cotton safari suit, then left the hotel for his afternoon appointment. He waved away his driver on the hotel steps and rounded the corner into the broad Nathan Road, walking north past the smart shops and the big hotels. He carried a tourist map of the city and consulted it at each corner, until he reached Carnarvon Road and through it the short, narrow street that was Hanoi Road. It was very crowded with stalls selling all manner of cooked food, and Weiss had to push through the mob of shouting, sweaty patrons. He began to feel somewhat uneasy; the place had a feel of brutality, even possible violence, and Weiss wished for the serene courtyard of the Peninsula or even the broad openness of Nathan Road only a few hundred feet behind him. At last he found the restaurant in which he was to meet Mr. Dennis, a man recommended to him by friends in London as one who could be trusted to conduct a discreet enquiry.

The Nine Dragons Inn was warm and crowded with diners, even at three in the afternoon. The air was hot and damp, though cooler than in the road, and redolent with pungent smells of cooking fish, oils, and spices. Weiss gulped and tried to breathe shallowly. The maître d'hôtel, a small, wrinkled old Chinese in a stained dinner jacket, met Weiss just inside the door. "I am looking for Mr. Dennis," said Weiss. The man nodded without apparent interest and pointed Weiss toward a table in the corner by the window. Weiss slid sideways between the many small tables and reached the corner one. Sunlight coming through the dirty glass brightly lit the empty chair nearest Weiss while leaving the occupant of the chair opposite in deep shadow. Weiss squinted in the glare, but could see little beyond that the man was tall and thin and European. "Mr. Dennis?" he asked.

"You will be Mr. Weiss. Please sit." The man's voice had a whispered quality, as though purposely disguised. The man neither stood up nor offered his hand.

When Weiss sat down, he found he still couldn't see his companion's face. The sun on his own face was uncomfortably warm. "I say, d'you suppose we could find another table? I am roasting here, and I can't even see you."

"In my business, Mr. Weiss, one seeks out places just like this." Weiss thought he could see the ghost of a smile from the shadowed man. "Besides, I am sure we can conclude our business quickly, and then you can return to the Peninsula and its admirable air conditioning."

A waitress appeared, a pretty Chinese girl with a sullen expression and a tight T-shirt revealing pert breasts. Dennis spoke to her rapidly in Cantonese, and she nodded and went to the tiny service bar. Weiss leaned forward in an attempt to see into the gloom, but without success. I wonder if this character has tables staked out in different parts of the city for every hour of the day, he thought as the girl returned with two T'sing Tao beers in long-necked green bottles. The man picked up one bottle and drank from the neck, ignoring the glass the girl had left. Weiss decided that was probably wise, so he sipped from the bottle also. The beer was smooth and icy cold, and it tasted like a German pilsener.

"A mutual friend in London sent you to me, Mr. Weiss," said Dennis. "May I ask why?"

"I was told you do private investigations."

" 'Confidential enquiries,' we say. But yes, I do."

"I want the activities of a man here investigated, very quietly. His name is Holden Chambers."

"He works for you," said Mr. Dennis.

"Yes." This guy has already started, thought Weiss. Once again, as in the street, he felt threatened in this exotic place.

"What sort of investigation are we talking about? Personal conduct, sexual aberrations?"

"If you can find any of that, well and good, but what I really need to know is how he is conducting his business. As you said, he works for me, but he doesn't tell me what I need to know. I want, in a phrase, to know the secret of his success." Weiss paused and once again tried to peer into the shadow. "I understand you have experience in banking."

"I have been in banking," said the man, without offering further elaboration.

"Have you ever met Holden Chambers?" asked Weiss. "Would he recognize you?"

"No, and no, Mr. Weiss. I live in Hong Kong, but I almost never work here. The police are quite efficient, and it would be too easy to become known."

"I see. Well, if you take this on, you will have to watch him in Central as well as in other countries in the region when he travels. Can you do that?"

"For a price," the man said. "What do you suspect?"

"This Chambers lives off his reputation as having an uncanny ability to call market movements, price deals just right, and the like. I don't believe he is all that smart, and he gets it right far too often to be just lucky. I think he must have an edge: Either he is colluding with other market players to fix the game, or he has inside information as to what borrowers will do before their intentions are made public. I want that edge, Mr. Dennis."

"And what will you do if you get it?"

"That's my business." Weiss leaned back and smiled at the shadow.

"If I am to work for you, I will have to know." The whispered voice carried a hint of menace. "And besides, it would seem to me that you could send out your bank's internal auditors to look at his files for a lot less than I will cost you."

Weiss was not accustomed to being intimidated; that was *his* game. Once again he leaned forward toward the shadow. "I have done that, Mr. Dennis. He gives them complete and unsupervised access to his files, other than a single locked cabinet labeled personal, which does indeed include his household accounts, though I know not what else."

"So what will you do with this 'edge' if I find it for you?"

"Perhaps I intend to replace him, but I want his connections, whatever they are, intact after he is gone. Is that sufficient?"

"For now." The man chuckled. Weiss wasn't accustomed to being chuckled at, either, and he began to get angry. "How do you wish me to report?"

Weiss took a card from his pocket. "By mail when possible, marked private and confidential, of course. By guarded telex or telephone when absolutely necessary, and always to me personally. Progress payments will be to the bank of your choice."

"I am sure you have brought a down payment for expenses?" Again the man chuckled.

"I did." Weiss took a brown envelope from his shirt pocket and placed it in front of him, firmly held down by his left hand. "Ten thousand pounds, Mr. Dennis. I assure you, I have had you thoroughly checked out, and I will expect results." The man nodded, but his chuckle grew louder and higher pitched. "I suppose you will want to use a code name for yourself in communications."

The man shrugged. "Dennis is good, I think. Could be a first name or a last; not unusual enough to be noticed if someone should see it on your desk."

Weiss frowned. "A bit risky to use your own name, isn't it?"

"Well, Mr. Weiss, since you have had me 'thoroughly checked out,' you will know that Dennis is neither my first name nor my last, and indeed it is a name I have never before used." The man's laughter was barely audible, an irritating clicking sound.

Weiss fought an impulse to stuff the money back into his pocket and bolt from the crowded restaurant. "Very well, then," he said, taking a gold pen from his pocket. "Dennis it is, but if this operation uncovers anything unusual or leads to anything beyond a simple investigation, I want you to use another code name."

"As you wish. What is it?"

Weiss wrote the name on the inside flap of the envelope, then pushed the money into the shadow. The man picked up the envelope without opening it and slipped it into the inside pocket of his jacket. "Use the second name only as a danger signal," said Weiss, putting a note of authority into his voice.

The man nodded. "You will hear from me when I have something, Mr. Weiss, and I will send you instructions for future deposits of funds to my bank." The man leaned forward but didn't rise. "And now if you would precede me out of this humble restaurant." The man patted his jacket over the pocket containing the money. "I'll take care of the drinks."

Weiss got up quickly and left, pushing rudely out of the crowded street and striding rapidly in the damp heat, driven by his anger. When I get back to London, he thought, I had better find out a bit more about Mr. Bloody Dennis. The money he had given the agent was of course untraceable, and the man had come on good recommendations from people who certainly would know, but Weiss couldn't help feeling he had just had his pocket picked by a man he would never even be able to describe.

Ah Wong dropped Holden Chambers at the Nathan Road entrance to Gaddi's, the Peninsula Hotel's—and some Europeans said Hong Kong's—principal restaurant. Holden told the driver to get his own dinner and not to worry about coming back until nine-thirty. Chambers was fairly sure Weiss would chew on him until at least ten.

He found Weiss already at a corner table, sipping Perrier and talking to the captain. Weiss almost never drank alcohol in any form and was known to regard those who did with suspicion and often contempt. Chambers considered playing the role and having a booze-free evening but then thought better of the idea, and, as he was seated, ordered a bottle of Veuve Cliquot and two glasses. Weiss nodded, letting it pass with a small smile.

Weiss waxed avuncular during the long dinner, treating Chambers to all manner of amusing stories of New York and London and uttering not a single critical word. He seemed as happy as Chambers had ever seen him. After the oysters and the soup and the roast duck and the salad and the dessert, Weiss actually accepted a cognac from the after-dinner drinks trolley and sipped it along with his espresso. "Well, bubby," he said, around the large Davidoff cigar he had selected from the tray brought by the cigarette girl, "any message you wish me to impart to your Asia Group colleagues in Tokyo, since you will be, regrettably, absent?"

"I don't think so, David, but I would like to ask you a question."

Weiss smiled. "The one you always ask?"

"Yes. Why do you denigrate my work here?"

Weiss set the brandy balloon down and leaned forward. Just before dinner he had had a very satisfactory conversation with a friend in the security business in London, and a similar one with a man in the same line who operated out of Brussels, and he felt a great deal better about the mysterious Dennis and about giving him ten thousand quid in cash. Whatever game Chambers was playing would soon be winkled out by the investigator, Weiss thought, and then I will use the information to bring dear Holden sharply to heel, or if it is nasty enough, get him sacked for cause, driving him not only from Traders Bank and Trust but right out of the banking business. In the meantime I may even try to be nice to him. He waits across the table, his expression that of a petulant child, at once angry at Daddy and hurt that Daddy won't praise him. Weiss's grin broadened as he resisted an urge to reach across the table and pat Chambers's hand. "Holden, dear, I think for once I may try to answer that question. I beat on you because you are arrogant and sometimes inflexible, and because you very often fail to keep me fully informed." Holden's eyes glazed, tuning out. "But there is much more to it than that. You and I are much more alike than you know, and in many respects I envy you."

Chambers laughed loudly, without mirth. "Oh, David, good Lord—"

Weiss held up both hands, palms outward. "Let me go on. You are not as clever as I am, and you don't know the business as well, but you do have dash and daring, which I admire. But what I truly envy is your job in this marketplace. When I started syndicating deals for Traders in 1969, London had deals and dealmakers, and I was the best. London 'grew up' as a market—which meant it got civilized and orderly and dull, and every bank in the world set up an office and wanted to be a player. Now the deals get done by committees or clubs, and nobody stands out as a gunslinger, a market mover.

"Hong Kong and Asia are where London was ten years ago. Dash and daring count here more than technical skill, and you are having the time of your life." Weiss paused and sipped his cognac, studying his junior. Chambers's expression continued to register disbelief. Good, thought Weiss. Be wary, it will improve the quality of the game. "I wish I knew how you do it, but you won't tell me."

"I have no secret, David." You do, but not for much longer,

thought Weiss, enjoying himself immensely. "You don't believe it, but I actually work at the business."

Weiss laughed his strange single bark. "Of course you do, Holdy. And don't feel you are unloved! The irony—and one should always find pleasure in irony—is that I love you at least as much as I loathe you."

Chambers flinched backward, then shifted uneasily in his chair. "Well, David, that is a candid statement, if confusing."

Weiss leaned back and spread his arms in a gathering, embracing gesture. "Holdy, don't you see? Our fates are completely intertwined! I have often wished that you and I could have met, working for rival institutions, on a level playing field—London in '69 or Hong Kong of today—and found out for once and all who really was the best."

"You are telling me you intend to destroy me."

"Yes—with finesse, of course." Weiss sipped his cognac. "After all, destroying you by itself is no real challenge. I must destroy you without losing the edge you have given Traders in this marketplace."

Chambers fidgeted despite himself. "Sounds as though I should look to updating my resume."

Weiss relit his cigar, smiling and nodding all the while. "But you won't, bubby, because you still think you can win the game, and you want that."

"Frankly, David, I would just like to do my job without constant harassment from you."

"So you won't quit, will you?"

"Not right away." Chambers was very angry, and he felt his face flush. He could tell Weiss had seen his cheeks color, as David's grin once again broadened. "But neither will I guarantee to sit quietly, waiting for you to spring something awful on me when I least expect it."

Weiss laughed. "Never! It will come, I promise you, when you *most* expect it."

Chambers slapped his folded napkin on the tablecloth and stood up. "So there is no chance you and I can just do business and quit screwing around?"

Weiss leaned forward and rested his chin on his folded hands. His expression was serene. "None, dear boy."

"Then I bid you good evening and a pleasant flight to Tokyo." Chambers turned away, his face and ears burning, pursued from the room by Weiss's clipped laughter.

7

16 April

SIXTY-TWO YACHTS, RANGING IN size from eighty-foot maxiraters to three-quarter tonners barely thirty-two feet overall, started to the noon gun in Junk Bay, just east of Hong Kong Harbour. The China Sea Race began with wind out of the northeast, light but gusty in the confined waters, and light rain showers that kept the racing crews in brightly colored rain gear. Fog hung low on the cliffs, low enough so that only the shorelines could be seen. Wang Lan Island, the first mark of the course, was the faintest smudge of darkness where the gray sky met the gray sea.

Golondrina made a good start, between the American maxi *Kialoa II* and Hamish MacDougal's *Sea Bird*. Holden Chambers had wanted to get under *Kialoa*'s stern, to get into the wind and water shadow of the giant sloop and be sucked along in her wake. His stratagem worked for about two hundred yards, pulling *Golondrina* well ahead of *Sea Bird* and the other two-tonners, but then Jim Kilroy, *Kialoa*'s skipper, bore off in a gust of clear air and shook the smaller yacht off her tail with a burst of pure speed.

Some fifty other craft followed the yachts out into the eastern approaches. Most were pleasure junks or motor yachts, but there were a few smaller motorboats loaded with still and video cameramen, which darted closer to the yachts as the first few began to tack to the north to get searoom to clear Wang Lan. The First New York Bank junk, *Lucky III*, rolled gently in the chop in the middle of the spectator fleet, with a party of thirty-five people on board. There were many more women than men, since most of the guests were wives of men taking part in the race. Richard van Courtland circulated around the large open deck on the aft end of the junk, where the guests were protected from the rain by a blue-and-white-striped canvas awning. A serving bar was set up next to the companionway, which led to the grand saloon below decks, where many guests who were not sailing enthusiasts were seated. The bar was doing a brisk business, and two waiters in

black trousers and starched white coats carried trays of hors
d'oeuvres up from the galley below.

Barbara Ramsay sat on a bench on the foredeck with Mary
Leach, watching the boats maneuver in the narrow slot off
Shek-O rock. The foredeck was protected by a smaller awning
of the same colors as the one aft. The women had a good view
of the start, but the two-tonners soon drew away from the smaller
boats and were swallowed by the fog. Barbara had brought a
whole bottle of champagne up from the bar, which she and Mary
were drinking from plastic glasses. Both women wore rain slickers
but were getting chilled.

"Well, Barbara, they are well and truly off, the lucky bastards."

Barbara laughed and filled both glasses. "Would you go along
if you could?"

Mary shrugged. "I just might. Some years the sailing is brilliant,
and some years it is storms or calms, but usually it is a little of
everything over the four or so days and the 640 miles. The race
is the social event of the season, both here and in Manila; a
combination Easter ball and carnival. Will you be flying down to
Manila for the parties?"

"Why, no," said Barbara, a little startled. "Richard is off to
Tokyo and Seoul for two weeks, and I have my work."

"Oh, nonsense, come down with Mummy and me," said Mary,
taking Barbara's arm. "I can assure you that you will get absolutely nothing done in the financial community in the ten days to
come."

"But, well, Richard—"

"You won't need him, Barbara. The race crews are filled with
unclaimed, dishy young men. Mummy and I will see you don't
get into any more trouble than you want to."

"Well," said Barbara. She would love to get away from the
dripping fog for the sun of Manila, a city she had not visited, and
to enjoy a week of parties. But I shouldn't. Richard would be
furious. "I'd like to, but really, Mary—"

"Then it is all settled. Carol is flying back to college earlier
than we expected, so we have an extra air ticket booked and have
rented a large house; both very hard to get, I can tell you." Mary
stood up, looking immensely pleased. "Let's go find Mummy in
this crush, and get warmed up. Barbara, we will have so much
fun!"

Why not? thought Barbara as she followed Mary along the
narrow side deck back to the party.

18 April

Holden Chambers felt a hand on his shoulder and was instantly awake. "Everything all right, John?"

John Malcolm's large head, surmounted by a rather flashy ski hat, was silhouetted against the red light burning over the chart table, the only light on inside the cabin. "Just foine, Captain, sor," growled Malcolm in his Long John Silver voice. "Just come do'n to wish yer top o' the morning."

Holden wriggled out of the narrow pipe-cot and sat up, rubbing his face with his fingers and prying his eyes open. "You are suggesting I take a turn of watch?"

"Well, and a fine morning you have. It's just come on oh-four hundred."

"Okay," said Chambers, pulling on a long-sleeved shirt and reaching for his heavy roll-neck sweater. "Brief me while I dress, John."

"Aye. The watch has been relieved; Bruces Maxwell and Moore and Chris have their heads down. Ginny is steering with Bruce Carraway watching, and Kevin. We have been changing helmsmen every twenty minutes; it isn't physically difficult, but it takes concentration in the following seas. Wind has continued to back into the north, and is blowing Force Seven to Eight."

"Highest gust?" asked Holden, pulling on his yellow nylon rain overalls.

"Forty-five knots, a half-hour ago. We are on a broad reach, and *Golondrina* is handling it like a racehorse. Good steady eight and a half knots of boatspeed, with some delightful long slides down waves at ten."

"Great. We still carrying the number-three genoa?"

"Yes. My Bruces cleared the number two off the foredeck; it was underwater half the time. It is in the bag, on deck lashed to the weather rail outside the shrouds. The main is still double-reefed, with the third reef rigged and ready."

"Where is the working jib, if we need it?"

"Amidships, squire, ready to go."

Holden donned his yellow coat and pulled a white woolen watch cap down over his brow. The outside temperature was at least twenty degrees Celsius—shirt-sleeve weather, absent the wind and the spray, but bloody cold with them. "Anything else, John? Estimated position?"

"Perhaps ten miles south of the rhumb line, just over two

hundred seventy miles out from Wang Lan. Keep a sharp watch; you will be crossing the shipping lanes from Japan to the Strait of Malacca on your watch." John turned away and started stripping off his own gear as Holden tightened his safety harness and reached out into the cockpit to clip it to the deadeye. "And there is fresh coffee in the starboard thermos, and chicken soup with a touch of sherry in the port."

"Very well, Navigator John, I relieve you."

"I have been properly relieved," said Malcolm, rolling into his cot with a yawn. "Wake me in an hour if you think I can get a morning star sight. Otherwise, breakfast at eight would be lovely."

"Okay, mate. Get some kip." Chambers looked at his burly friend, who was already snoring lightly. He mounted the companionway ladder and stuck his head out into the roaring wind.

"The captain is on deck," intoned Kevin with mock solemnity.

Holden waited for a moment with just his head and shoulders outside the companionway, getting the feel of the sea and the night, and adjusting his night vision and balance. He knew that many man-overboard incidents occurred in the first few moments after a sleepy crewman came up on deck. It was for this reason that Holden insisted that crewmen clip on to the deadeye bolted just outside the companionway before coming up in rough weather, and always before coming up at night.

Holden timed the slight rolling movement of the yacht crossing the waves, and pulled himself into the cockpit. He sat on the bench near the helm. Ginny was concentrating on her steering, one eye on the green-lighted compass and one on the following seas. A full moon showed gauzy-bright through the thinning cloud cover. The loudest sound was the hiss of the water rushing by. The wake behind the boat glowed brightly in two phosphorescent streams. The wind chilled his ears, and Holden pulled his watch cap down.

"Coffee, Skipper?" asked Bruce Carraway.

"Yes, thanks," said Holden. He unclipped his harness from the deadeye and stepped around behind Ginny. He clipped the long pennant to the spinnaker turning block and took the cup offered by Bruce. He stood up on the poopdeck and looked at the night through three-hundred-sixty degrees. He swallowed the last of the lukewarm coffee, jumped down, and placed a hand on Ginny's shoulder. "I think I'll have a turn, old girl."

"Aw, Cap, I'm just getting in the groove."

"I know. You're steering well, but I want to get a feel of it."

Ginny slipped out of the way, taking her harness clip to the starboard safety line. Holden widened his stance and gripped the leather-covered wheel, which was fully four feet in diameter, and began to make slight, timed corrections to the motion induced by the ten-foot swells. Anticipate, he thought, find the groove. A touch to starboard just before each swell lifted the counter, back to port as the wave passed, making hollow, gurgling sounds as it slipped away. Holden thought he heard the hiss of passing water grow louder.

"Skipper's making a half knot better than you were, Ginny," said Kevin.

"Get stuffed," said Ginny amiably. Her voice was muffled by her heavy sweater, which she had pulled up over her chin.

"Hey, look," cried Bruce, standing up and pointing to the wake. "Porpoises! Look at the buggers come."

Ginny and Kevin joined Bruce on the windward quarter. Holden corrected for a slightly oversized wave, then allowed himself a quick look aft. Two large black porpoises, one on either side of the wake, surfed along in the boiling phosphorescence of the quarter-wakes, keeping pace with *Golondrina* as she raced through the night at nine knots.

19 April

Iris announced the call from Mary Leach. Barbara punched the lighted button on her phone. "Hello, Mary?"

"Barbara. I wondered if you could have lunch, and we can review our little trip to the sun."

Barbara glanced at her calendar. It was nearly blank; Hong Kong during the China Sea Race was as dead as Mary had predicted. "I'd love to. Today?"

"Yes. I'm calling from Colin's office; I just dropped off some papers he left at home. Why don't we try the new restaurant on top of the Mandarin? Pierrot, I think it is called."

Barbara had heard of the opening of Pierrot, dedicated to the trendy nouvelle cuisine. "Fine. I'll have my secretary call. One o'clock?"

"Let's just go; I am sure it will be empty. Besides, I'm hungry."

Barbara glanced at her watch. Twelve-twenty. "I'll meet you there."

Mary and Barbara were seated at a corner banquette. The restaurant's new decor was tasteful and muted. Reproductions of

Picasso's many paintings of a ballet dancer costumed as Pierrot were hung on the softly lighted walls.

Mary was wearing a man-tailored cotton shirt, a full tan linen skirt, and low-heeled shoes. The look was very much a country gentlewoman come to town. Mary ordered a gin and tonic while Barbara asked for a glass of white wine. The drinks came and with them menus. Mary set her menu aside without a glance.

"Barbara, I can't tell you how I am looking forward to this Easter holiday."

Barbara smiled and nodded. She still felt a little guilty about going to Manila, especially since she hadn't told Richard. He had been a little drunk when the junk returned from the race start, and she hadn't wanted a row. The following morning he left for Tokyo. "I am, too. I only hope it doesn't get too rowdy."

"Oh, the stories all grow with the telling. The men, for the most part deprived of drink and female companionship for four or five whole days, get drunk and do funny things. But it is like a masked ball; all is forgiven and forgotten afterward. You will be entertained more than shocked, I'm sure."

"When do we go?" asked Barbara, catching some of the other woman's enthusiasm.

Mary reached into her purse, beside her on the banquette. "Here is your ticket. We fly Friday the twenty-first. Shall we pick you up at your flat?"

"No, don't come out of your way. I'll meet you at Kai Tak." Barbara looked at the ticket. The noon Cathay flight first class. She made a mental note to send Mary a check for the fare. "Won't the boats finish Thursday? The radio says they are well along already."

"The fast boats probably will, but that is also part of the contract. The first boats' crews will be in the bar at the Manila Yacht Club all day Thursday, waiting for the smaller boats to finish so they can determine who wins on corrected time."

"How does the time correction work?"

"The handicapping rule is so complicated only engineers can decipher it, but basically bigger boats give time to smaller ones, so the first boats to arrive have to wait for the smaller ones to know who won. Anyway, the truly swinish behavior may be expected to occur Thursday evening, so, by unspoken agreement, wives and girlfriends don't arrive until Friday. It's great fun, really, watching the men exchange worried and knowing glances as the most bizarre stories are whispered."

Barbara laughed. So this is how the stuffy Europeans of Hong Kong let off the tension. I can't wait to see it.

The captain appeared. "Would you ladies like to order lunch, or perhaps another drink?" he asked, smiling.

"Oh, we haven't even looked!" said Mary. "Bring us some more drinks, and then we will decide." The captain bowed and slipped away.

Barbara opened the menu. She glanced around the restaurant, barely a third full at one o'clock. I really shouldn't be running off to a raucous party in Manila without my husband, she thought. But fuck it. I am here to be me, not just Mrs. Him.

20 April

Holden lay stretched out in his berth with his eyes closed but wide awake. He listened to the sounds as the crew tweaked the boat to maximum speed, hard on the wind. They had been becalmed for four hours after midnight, in the famous Black Hole off Mayagao Point south of Subic Bay, as the sea breeze died. As dawn approached, the breeze had filled in from the southeast, warm and fragrant with the scent of flowers and warm earth, and *Golondrina* went to a light number-one genoa and the full main for the beat to the finish. Holden had been up all night, struggling to find a way out of the damp, warm calm. He was very tired, but much too keyed up to sleep. They were no more than twenty miles from the finish, and even with the wind on the nose, they should cross the finish line off Corregidor Rock at the entrance to Manila Bay before noon. After noon the wind would surely die and hopefully trap boats behind them until evening. Holden wondered where the other two-tonners were. They had not seen any yachts at all since the afternoon of Monday, the second day of the race, which meant *Golondrina* was either way ahead of the fleet, or way behind. Holden heard the whisper of the sheets and the popping of the winches as Malcolm's watch tacked the boat. He emptied his mind and dozed.

"Skip," said Bruce Maxwell, shaking his shoulder. "Skipper."

Holden pulled himself back from the depths. He looked at his watch as he rolled out of the cot. He had been sound asleep for more than three hours, and once he shook the cobwebs out of his head, he felt better than he had in days. "Bruce. Where are we?"

"About two miles from Corregidor, still hard on the wind. We just spotted the committee boat, and also a yacht coming in from south of us we think is *Welsh Dragon*."

"Good, I am coming up." He saw that Bruce was shirtless. "Hot?"

"Fine and hot," said Bruce, darting back up the companionway as John Malcolm called, "Ready about!"

Holden climbed into the cockpit just as Bruce and Bruce finished grinding in the genoa. Chris Marston-Evans had the helm, and John was taking a fix with a hand-bearing compass. "Morning, all," said Holden, putting on his dark glasses against the bright sun. At last, the tropics. Ginny pushed up past him, clad only in a bikini bottom, and found a place in the sun. The ugly cliffs of Corregidor loomed ahead, and the hundred-foot motor yacht *Van Triumph*, displaying the race committee flags, flashed as the sun glinted off her glass portlights. "Where away *Welsh Dragon?*"

"There," said Malcolm, pointing off to starboard. The mast and sails could be clearly seen, and when both boats rose to the tops of waves, *Welsh Dragon*'s red hull. "The good news is we should beat her to the line. The bad news is we give her time."

Holden shrugged. "At least we have company at last. Finishing close to Reg Lloyd is certainly no disgrace."

"If we'd a cannon we could sink the barstard," growled Long John. "But hear, hear. We are going fast, I can smell the beer, and it's high time we got a lick of work from the skipper."

Holden smiled and relieved Chris on the helm. "Time to tack, John?"

"One minute. We will cross the line at the windward end."

"Get Bruce and Kevin up, please, Ginny," called Holden as he steered the boat, feeling for the light wind. "All up for the finish."

Golondrina crossed the line at 1021, one hour and thirty-nine minutes short of four days after the start. The committee boat fired a gun as they crossed, and then the crew dropped the genoa and Holden luffed up next to the gleaming white side of *Van Triumph*. A crewman tossed down a chilled case of San Miguel beer, the traditional finish-line greeting. Bruce Halls caught it on the foredeck and passed it back to the cockpit. Soon eight cans were open, and not long after, eight more.

"Why the gun?" shouted Malcolm. Only the first yacht to finish normally got a gun, the rest a blast of the ship's horn as they crossed the line. *Golondrina*'s crew were under no illusions that they could have beaten the maxis.

Christian van Nordholm, the seventy-year-old Swede who was

Honorary Chairman of the Race Committee and who had organized the first China Sea Race eighteen years before, shouted back. "You get a gun, dear boys, because by our rough calculation, you are presently the leader on corrected time."

Holden glanced back at *Welsh Dragon*, half a mile away and gliding toward the finish in the dying breeze. "Who has finished, Chris?" he shouted to the white-haired man on *Van Triumph*'s bridge.

"The maxis, last evening, *Kialoa* ahead of *Passage* by two hours. An hour ago, Hamish MacDougal and *Sea Bird*," von Nordholm roared back. "And now, you had best clear off the line so we can give Reg a gun of his own. Well done, lads, you held the lead for nearly twenty minutes." Chris von Nordholm laughed enormously and toasted with a tankard.

Holden grinned and lifted his beer can as he steered away from *Van Triumph*. The wind was beginning to die.

"Ahem," said John Malcolm. "We might at least win the race to the bar."

"Good thought," said Chambers, handing the wheel off to Kevin. "Start the engine, please, and engage the freezer compressor."

"Aye," said Malcolm, flipping the freezer and battery switches, and turning the key. The diesel caught immediately and *Golondrina* surged away from the committee boat and south to round the island of Corregidor. "We'd best hurry, sor, one more tinny apiece and this slave ship be as dry as the desert."

"Break out the cooler with the remains of the fresh food, John," said Holden. "I believe there may be a few beers under the dry ice."

"Hm." John Malcolm grinned as Ginny passed out the last of the race committee's beers. "There is another case in the sail locker under the storm jib, if you must know. I'll just be putting those on ice if Bruce will look to the cooler."

"Navigator!" called Kevin from the helm. "Course to the bar?"

"Zero niner zero, lad," intoned Malcolm. "And mind your helm for a swift passage."

Barbara Ramsay arrived in Manila with Alice MacDougal and Mary Leach at two in the afternoon on Good Friday, the 21st of April. The day was deliciously hot and quite windy, and the city was fragrant with flowers, especially sampanguita and bouganvillea. Barbara loved the feeling of Manila at first sight. The people were brown and handsome and friendly, the traffic smoky and chaotic, and the heat, the *heat* felt so invigorating after the misty spring in Hong Kong.

Barbara would later remember her Easter trip to Manila as a collage of images, many seen through a mild alcoholic haze. The gaiety swept around her, but she felt more a spectator than a participant. She wasn't disturbed by this feeling of separation; after all, nearly all the celebrants knew each other well. Besides, she was glad for the opportunity to observe the revel of Hong Kong's powerful, especially the Lion, Holden Chambers.

The MacDougals were staying in a large house in Urdaneta Village, near Makati, and Holden and his mob had a house borrowed from his bank's Manila branch manager, who had flown home to the States for the Easter holiday. The *Golondrina* house was just down the street from *Sea Bird*'s, so the crews and their friends flowed together, sharing rides and gathering up strays and temporarily incapacitated members for each other in the endless three-day celebration.

There were, of course, discreet events. There was a dinner on Friday at the Manila Yacht Club, sort of a disorganized barbecue. The yachts went out on Saturday to compete in the Manila Inshore Race, which, with the Hong Kong Inshore and the China Sea Race itself, constituted the series. Yachts were thoroughly cleaned by their crews and then showed off during a moving cocktail party Saturday afternoon. On Sunday Barbara went with Alice and Mary to Easter Mass at the sixteenth-century Spanish cathedral. The China Sea Race Ball was held at the beautifully refurbished Manila Hotel Sunday evening, and then the yachts departed Monday afternoon for yet another party at the privately owned island of Hermana Mayor, one-hundred-twenty miles to the north, leaving the Manila Yacht Club, and seemingly the entire city, to return abruptly to its tropical torpor. From Hermana Mayor, the yachts would face the long slog back to Hong Kong, mostly to windward and into the rain and the fog.

To Barbara, however, the whole three days ran together in a series of chaotically joined scenes.

She had first seen Holden as she and Alice and Mary entered the bar at the yacht club around four o'clock Friday afternoon. He was locked in a bear hug with a man easily four inches taller than him, a man with a radiant blonde afro and a bushy beard around his twinkling blue eyes. "Oh, Holden, oh, Holden," the blonde giant said. "You shat on us, you shat on us!"

"Why," replied Holden, swaying in the big man's embrace, "do South Africans always say everything twice?" He disengaged an arm and took a long pull from his pint mug.

"Who on earth is that?" whispered Barbara to Mary. Alice had drifted off with Joanne von Nordholm.

"David Bonkers, a professional yacht racer. Daddy had him on his crew," said Mary. "He is a very fine helm, but otherwise unreliable at best."

"We don't, we don't," roared Bonkers, shaking Holden by his shoulders and spilling beer on his shoes. "You shat on us, you shat on us!"

"Holden beat Daddy," Mary translated. "Come on, let's meet some people."

The MacDougal ladies plus Barbara had drinks and dinner at the yacht club Friday night with most of the crew of *Sea Bird*. The navigator, Jackie Haver, sat next to Alice, and kept up a running patter about the many twists and turns of the race. Hamish MacDougal had not been seen since he had taken a Philippine television crew onto his yacht on Thursday evening, and then gone off to have drinks with them. David Bonkers had volunteered to go and look for him in the bars and "clubs" of Mabini Street. Colin Leach offered to go along and help, but Mary had dissuaded him with a look. Alice laughed a lot during the evening, but her face looked taut.

Colin escorted Mary and Barbara down to look at *Sea Bird*, the third-place finisher. Barbara had never been aboard an ocean racer, and was amazed at the spartan interior: just sails and an engine box and pipe-cots folded up. Colin and Mary, both well along with the wine, began looking at each other with large eyes, so Barbara excused herself and took a short stroll down the narrow dock. Three slips down she came on the gleaming white shape of *Golondrina*, dressed with her signal flags and wearing the U.S. ensign even at night. Foul-weather gear and towels were pinned to the boom and the lifelines forward, but the cockpit was empty. "Hello," she called, noting a light in the cabin below. No answer came, but she saw the shadow of someone moving. Barbara was just high enough to want another drink, but she didn't feel she could go back to *Sea Bird*. She took off her high-heeled shoes and stepped over the stern pulpit into the cockpit of *Golondrina*. "Hello?" she called hopefully.

Barbara took a step down the companionway into the cabin of *Golondrina*. The interior was only slightly less unadorned than *Sea Bird*, with a teak chart table and a folding table in the saloon. "Hello." She stepped down into the cabin, seeing no one and hearing nothing. A pair of arms wrapped around her from behind and she yelped.

"Who be you come on my vessel?" said Holden Chambers,

releasing his hold enough so she could turn and face him. He was grinning broadly and she guessed he was at least a bit drunk. His breath smelled of beer, but not unpleasantly.

"Holden, it's Barbara Ramsay. You startled me." She tried to shrug off his relaxed embrace, but not very hard.

"Thought you might be a pirate." He tilted her chin up and kissed her deeply. She felt paralyzed and suddenly warm. "Maybe not." He smiled and kissed her nose playfully. "Like a drink?"

"Y-yes," she said, slipping free as he went to the galley sink and withdrew a bottle of champagne with an orange label. He pushed dirty glasses around and found two plastic throwaways. Barbara sat on a pipe-cot, watching. Holden swayed slightly, as though adjusting to waves which were no longer there.

Holden sat next to her, very close. She felt she should move away, but didn't. "Ms. Ramsay," he breathed. "Welcome." He handed her her glass and touched it with his own.

"Thank you," said Barbara, watching his blue eyes flash in the soft glow of the ship's oil lamp. "I didn't mean to intrude; I just wanted to see your boat."

"Danger here be," intoned Holden, shaking his head sorrowfully.

"What do you mean?" Barbara laughed, but she felt uneasy alone with this man.

Holden leaned over very slowly and kissed her again. She knew she should push him away, but she didn't. "I be drunk, Ms. Ramsay," he said, matter-of-factly. She stiffened in his arms, and he quickly released her and held his hands before him. "Oh, not *dangerous* drunk, or mean drunk. Just randy, *sexy* drunk, and no harm meant!" His blue eyes caressed her, head to foot. "Yacht *Golondrina* be a *perilous* place for a pretty *married* lady this evening."

He bent to kiss her again, but this time Barbara pushed him away and clambered up the companionway ladder. She retrieved her shoes and climbed back to the dock. Her face burned as she heard Holden Chambers's rich laugh float up from the boat below her.

Saturday morning *Sea Bird*'s crew, plus most of *Golondrina*'s, gathered for brunch at the house rented by the MacDougals. The boats would leave for the race at three in the afternoon, so brunch began at eleven. Hamish appeared, full of good cheer, and passed the Bloody Marys prepared in great quantities by the servants of the people who owned the house. As brunch was announced, Hamish stood, and declaimed: "There is no truth to the rumor that two young and beautiful Filipinas were seen running down the dock from *Sea Bird*'s slip at four A.M. Friday, clad only in *Sea Bird* crew shirts, and pursued by young Bonkers, here, and another unidentified large man." Everybody laughed. Barbara saw that Alice's expression was pained beneath her smile. In Asia, she mused, even fun is deadly serious.

Holden Chambers smiled at her from across the room. He looked faintly amused as he raised his glass to her. Barbara felt anger and shame, though she knew she had no reason.

The ball on Sunday night was billed as an elegant affair, with the uniform for the men black tie or dark slacks and the traditional Philippine formal shirt, the *Barong Tagalog*. Most of the yachties wore barongs, since cheap ones were easily available, and no one in a right mind would carry good dinner clothes on a racing sailboat. The women wore long gowns.

Each yacht had its own table, or in some cases, two, surrounding the large figure-of-eight-shaped swimming pool. The party began badly when it was found that the bar was to be cash, and not included in the tickets. The yachties didn't care about paying, but the waiters had been instructed to take orders, then queue up for only two cashiers in the room with four hundred seated, then return to the tables to collect the cash, and only then go for the drinks. Bruce Halls slipped away from the *Golondrina* table and bought a liter of scotch from the shop in the lobby, and then began sharing out small drinks to the *Sea Bird* table next to *Golondrina*'s. The rest of the room bubbled in near riot. The Commodore of the Manila Yacht Club finally convinced the manager of banquet facilities for the Manila Hotel that property damage was an imminent danger, and the manager declared the bar open, on the promise of the commodore to negotiate later.

Barbara had worn a gown of rich yellow silk, cut low between her breasts and nipped tight at the waist. She chatted with the *Sea Bird* crew, but felt her attention drawn to the *Golondrina* table, waiting for the appearance of Holden Chambers. Holden arrived at his table to cheers from his crew and their friends with a slim Chinese girl who never left his side all evening. The girl was dark-skinned and exotically beautiful, dressed in a long dress of white satin that left her shoulders bare. Barbara watched them dance after dinner, growing angry despite herself at the tender way Holden led the woman through the dance. Barbara brushed off several invitations to dance from yachties in various stages of inebriation, finally accepting a dance with the leering David Bonkers, and dancing a round with him in spite of the fact that he several times fondled her ass.

Toward the end of the evening, an argument began between the crew at *Sea Bird*'s second table and the crew of *Black Knight*, a two-tonner that had finished toward the back of the fleet. Bonkers and two others of Hamish MacDougal's crew had taken it upon themselves to throw the *Black Knight* crew—and their table, with food, china, napery and cutlery—into the pool.

General mayhem ensued. Bonkers and his mob did manage to get the *Black Knight* crew and their table into the pool, though not without retaliation. *Sea Bird*'s tables were lost, as were *Golondrina*'s. Barbara shrank into a passageway along with Holden Chambers's dark Chinese beauty. Barbara smiled at the girl and was about to speak to her, but the melee followed them into the passage and the girl disappeared. Barbara watched in horror and amazement as Alice MacDougal, Mary Leach, and Joanne von Nordholm were dragged into the fray.

Barbara changed into shorts and a cotton shirt for the impromptu rally-up of the *Sea Bird* crew at their house in Urdaneta Village. Alice and Joanne had arrived, none the worse for humor, dressed in togas they had made from table cloths stolen from the Manila Hotel laundry adjacent to the ballroom. Hamish arrived at two A.M. with two black eyes and carrying David Bonkers, fast asleep, across his broad shoulders. Holden Chambers sent one of the shocked servants down from his house to announce swimming and water polo in his pool. All trooped off joyfully up the street, and even more alcohol was served and consumed.

Never, thought Barbara, have I seen such as this. Playful lions, conquerors of the sea and then the game.

24 *April*

Holden Chambers woke at eight Monday morning, listening to a bronze bell tolling inside his head. His tongue felt as though an entire Arabian camel corps had trod over it. He struggled up and made it to the bathroom before he was sick. A toothbrush and paste helped, followed by three aspirins and two glasses of water. He weaved unsteadily back toward the bed.

May-Ling sat in a chair in the corner, bathed in golden morning light. She was reading one of her fat law books. Holden took a ragged deep breath and sat on the bed, wondering where he should begin to apologize.

"How do you feel, my love?" asked May-Ling, setting the book aside.

"Bloody awful, thanks," rasped Holden. At least I am alive, and with the right woman, he thought, ashamed.

"Do you want anything?"

He thought about it. No, at this point, nothing else could shock poor May-Ling. "Could you find me a cold beer?"

"Of course," May-Ling said coolly. She swept from the room, gossamer-gold in a sheer peignoir.

Holden stretched back on the bed, fighting dizzyness. Just let me live to get onto the sea again, he thought through his headache and stomach ache. Sea air will cure and bring forgetfulness.

May-Ling returned with two cold bottles of San Miguel and a glass. Not like her to start the day with a cold one, thought Holden. She poured the glass full, and he drained it gratefully. She refilled the glass from the second bottle. Oh, what a rogue and peasant slave am I, he thought whimsically.

"Holden," said May-Ling, softly touching his aching forehead. "Why do you put up with me?"

Holden sipped the second beer, feeling benefit in both head and stomach. "Why do *I* put up with *you?* Christ, love, it's me who has been legless drunk for three days."

"But that is your release. It is justified by the tension of your work." May-Ling looked sad. "But I don't share it with you. I don't like parties, I don't sail with you. I am no use; just a grindy student of law."

"May-Ling." Holden's voice was a croak. He sipped some more beer. "I love you."

"But you shouldn't. You should have a flash European bird like that Barbara Ramsay who swarmed around you these last three days."

Swarmed around me? thought Holden. "She is married, love. It is you I need."

"But why?" asked May-Ling, stroking his aching head with gentle fingers.

Holden sat up and swallowed the last of his beer. "May-Ling, I'm sure this isn't the time I can be eloquent. Everything in Hong Kong is transient, like smoke and mirrors in a magic show. The power we have, the money we spend, the honors we give ourselves, all are illusory, foolish, and cheap. I love you because you are the only thing in my life which is true, and real, and honest."

May-Ling brushed a tear from one large brown eye, and crawled into bed beside him, and hugged him. "Then I will stay with you awhile longer, my love."

8
Malaysia, 24 April

THE PRIME MINISTER OF Singapore, Lee But Yang, and the President of Malaysia, Tunku Syed Abdul Rahman, walked along the manicured paths of the President's private park in Cameron Highlands, ninety miles north of the Malaysian capital of Kuala Lumpur. During the colonial period the British had built elaborate summer "bungalows" in the highlands to escape the limpid heat of Kuala Lumpur and the other coastal cities. Most of these very large houses had been converted to inns since independence, but some had been purchased by weathy local businessmen, and the largest was the official summer residence of the President. The highlands were at altitudes up to two thousand meters, and in the evenings the air was deliciously cool.

The two leaders were old political adversaries and more recently friends. The elderly Malay prince's position was largely ceremonial, but Lee always called on him when he went to Malaysia to do business with its own Prime Minister, and when the Tunku went to Singapore, as he did often to shop, Lee always greeted him with full honors as head of state.

Various aides to the two men straggled along behind out of earshot of the two leaders as they walked slowly through the elaborate and brilliantly colorful formal gardens. Behind all of the aides, and watching them all carefully while pretending not to, walked Singapore's Minister of Home Affairs, Colonel Abdul Raza, and the Deputy Chief of the Army of Malaysia General Staff, Major General Ibrahim Mohamdir. The two men were distantly related by marriage and had grown up together in a small village outside the nearby city of Ipoh.

"How is your boy, Abdul?" General Mohamdir asked softly.

"Well, Ibrahim. He is back in school and studying hard." Raza looked at the taller Malay. "Thank you for getting him released."

"A pleasant duty, my cousin," the general said, nodding. "He looks so like dear departed Fatimah." Mohamdir paused, and

Raza stopped beside him. "He won't do anything foolish again?"

"He gave me his word."

General Mohamdir started forward. "Nuff said, then, what? Look, the old boys have started back toward the house."

Mohamdir and Raza picked up the pace and approached the two leaders as they reached the steps of the mansion. General Mohamdir paused again, still out of earshot of the gathering advisers, and stooped to admire a hybrid rose. "Well, my cousin," he said, "you still grow fat in the service of the Chinese."

"Of Singapore, my cousin," said Raza evenly. "In the service of the Republic of Singapore."

"Call it what you like," said the general with a snort of distaste. "I must say it still galls me that we let the shifty yellow bastards slip away with that rich little island."

"When Singapore was part of Malaysia, my cousin, the Chinese were a majority in the whole country," said Raza, smiling. "And I remember *that* galled you then."

"Touché, Abdul. But you aren't up to believing that crap about Singaporeans, if there is such an animal, managing better than we could?"

"Singapore has no natural resources but is rich and growing richer. Malaysia is rich in oil, gas, tin, rubber—"

"And remains backward, Abdul," interrupted the general. "I admit it, the chinks work bloody hard. Still in all, I'd like to kick the lot of them—in your country and mine, Abdul—the hell back to Peking or Canton or wherever the buggers came from."

Raza laughed. "Ibrahim, you never change."

The general smiled. "Still the dinosaur, eh, cousin? But off the record—and we are way off the record—doesn't it bother you when the godless bastards grow fat while allowing our people nothing but menial jobs in their own land?"

Raza faced his cousin and winked. "I am never that far off the record, cousin."

The general smiled and clapped the police colonel on his shoulder. "Nuff said, Abdul."

Singapore, 25 April

Colonel Abdul Raza steepled his fingers on the blotter on his elaborately carved Indonesian rosewood desk. The Singapore police chief waited patiently while the nervous Englishman fumbled a cigarette from his case and lit it. Raza studied the banker, noting his waxy pale skin and dark hair damp at the edges from sweat. Raza felt quite comfortable in the heat of the afternoon, dressed as he was in a short-sleeved safari suit of starched khaki cotton, his shirt open at the neck. He regarded the boyish Englishman in his tight collar and tie and his heavy woolen suit with amusement, enjoying his discomfort. Before admitting the banker to his large office in the old wooden police barracks on Bukit Timah Road, he had instructed his secretary to turn off the air conditioner, open the window, and start the ancient ceiling fans, which stirred the thick, humid air.

Chris Marston-Evans fought an urge to tug at his damp collar. He had flown to Singapore directly from the parties in Manila, and he felt the queasiness and lightheadedness of a massive, enduring hangover. Moreover, this police chief made him nervous, and he hated being forced by his bank to deal with the slimy bastard. Bloody wog looks cool enough, thought Marston-Evans. The colonel was a stocky man, with muscular arms and torso. He wasn't above medium height, but the breadth of his shoulders and his deep chest made one think of him as a big man. A slight smile at the corners of his mouth betrayed amusement. He knows what I bloody want, thought Marston-Evans, feeling ill and overheated, and he knows I am afraid to bring it up. He could accommodate the Bank, or he could throw me in jail under the republic's broad sedition laws, or he could agree to help me today and jail me tomorrow. The very fact that the colonel had insisted the meeting take place in the barracks rather than in his modern office in the Ministry of Home Affairs's section of the government block on Boat Quay seemed ominous. Marston-Evans didn't trust the colonel any more than he really trusted any Asian. After a while, he thought, gathering his courage to speak, they all looked like niggers.

"The chairman of the Bank asked me to come and see you, Colonel, to convey his congratulations upon your appointment to the Cabinet," began Marston-Evans, trying to put some warmth into his voice.

The colonel smiled slightly, showing a gold tooth against his full lower lip. "Sir William is kind to remember me. What is it, eighteen years ago we served together in the British Army in Malaya? We were both corporals, and now he is *Tai-Pan* of the Imperial Bank of Hong Kong, and I am still a simple policeman."

Bugger wants his praise, thought Chris grimly. He tried a charming smile as he inclined his head forward in submission. "Surely the Minister of Home Affairs is far from a simple policeman, Colonel!"

Raza waved his hand dismissively, already tiring of the game with the dull European. Westerners had absolutely no talent for the prebargaining maneuvers so necessary in the Orient, where people were used to conducting business across vast differences of culture and even the lack of common language, with the face of all parties preserved. The bloody British just blunder up to you and bluster, and if that doesn't work, offer money. Raza kept his contempt within while keeping his little smile for the sweating youth. *I wonder why Sir William McQuarry would send such a feckless boy to see me. He knows me better than that. I wonder if he is even really involved.* "You are very kind, Mr. Marston-Evans, but the job is just that of a policeman: to maintain the public order. My appointment as minister is just the Prime Minister's way of confirming the importance of public order and security to his government." *There is your opening, puppy,* thought Raza with distaste. *I am close to power, get it?*

Marston-Evans relaxed a little. *He is telling me he is an insider. It means if he deals, he will cost more.* Chris was far more comfortable with money than with danger. "Well, Minister, Sir William asked me to stop and see you first, in remembrance of your service together, before continuing on my business with the government."

"Ah, you have business with the government, then?" said the colonel, smiling broadly and leaning back, his hands clasped across his small stomach bulge. *A posture of devious Oriental avarice,* he hoped.

Marston-Evans felt his confidence soaring. He became, quite unconsciously, the bluff English colonial, instructing a native retainer. "Yes. The matter of the Bank's wanting a full banking license here. Meetings with the Monetary Authority and the Finance Minister. We hope—that is, the Bank's directors hope—that since Singapore has admitted so many of our European and American competitors with limited licenses, that the Bank might finally have the full license we have sought since Singapore became an independent state." *Independence financed by a large loan from us,* thought Marston-Evans, *plus a few "gifts" to quiet the hotheads in Kuala Lumpur.*

Raza looked sympathetic. "Surely the Monetary Authority will be helpful? Elizabeth Sun is very professional."

"Oh, yes, indeed," replied Marston-Evans, charming. "But frankly, we feel the MAS have been told to delay. We fear there is opposition . . . higher up."

"Surely not," said Raza. "The Bank has always been a friend of Singapore." *And done very nicely out of that friendship too,* he thought.

"Well, one can't be sure, Colonel. I will be seeing Miss Sun later today. Still, Sir William hopes you will be his friend in the Cabinet." There, it's said, at least part of it. Chris felt his face flush as he waited for the police chief's response.

What a dull boy, thought the colonel. He gives away everything and learns nothing. He smiled as he thought of the cutting wit of his old comrade, William McQuarry, should the Bank's chairman actually examine the lad as to this conversation. "Well, I am not well versed in banking matters, Mr. Marston-Evans, but you may tell my old friend that I will endeavor to get up to speed."

Marston-Evans got up quickly, stretching his long frame. He was relieved the interview was over and that he had planted the seed as he had been instructed. "Thank you so much for seeing me, Minister," he said with his best smile.

"Not at all," said the minister, trying very hard to look servile and grasping despite his anger. "I have found our conversation interesting, Mr. Marston-Evans, and I hope you will call on me again."

"Ah, yes, sir. I shall be delighted . . . to keep you informed?"

"That should be perfect."

Got him, thought Marston-Evans as he swept from the oven-hot office.

Hong Kong, 29 April

Holden Chambers sat on the dais in one of the small banquet rooms in the Furama Hotel on Connaught Road. He was fighting to keep his eyes open during the long remarks of the Chairman of the State Bank of India, which the old man read from a yellow pad in a sibilant monotone. The signing ceremony was nearly over.

Chambers was tired from the China Sea Race, the parties in Manila, and the long, slow sail home, but he felt relaxed. Two weeks of sailing were far more restful than twice that much time doing nothing. Sailing engaged the mind as well as the body, and it allowed the poisonous thoughts of business dealings and related anxiety to be purged. Now, back in Hong Kong, back in the game and needing something to think about to stay awake, he found himself thinking about David Weiss, his strange visit nearly three weeks before, and his even stranger comments over dinner. Weiss had made it clear that no matter how successful Holden was in the business, he would eventually destroy him if he could. Why does he hate me so? Because I am better than he ever was, he answered his own question. And David is right about another thing: If I had any brains, I would cross over to one of the many struggling merchant banks just to get away from him. Many firms (and their London and New York parents) had offered him managing directorships, and he was sure he could get a substantial increase in compensation. But I won't leave, and I will beat him, given time. I built Traders Asia from nothing to market importance with no help from bloody David Weiss, and I will leave it only when I want to. As long as we exceed our income goals every year, and as long as the bank's important clients in the region are happy, he can't touch me without hurting himself.

David thinks I have a secret advantage, mused Holden, staring straight ahead at the room full of nodding stuffees as the chairman droned on. In a way I do, but it is nothing David would ever understand. My edge is that I try to understand Asia and Asian values, and also that I know that no European can ever understand Asians fully. Asia was nuance, subtlety, *feel*. David Weiss was about as subtle as a thrown brick.

Most Europeans never got the rhythm of Asia, even ones who had lived in its various countries far longer than had Holden. Business was conducted in English, and European communities in the various capitals tended to keep to themselves. Ironically, Holden credited his time traveling in Latin America with having given him an important key to the puzzle. Traders had a policy that calling officers in Latin America be fluent in Spanish or Portuguese, and in time Chambers spoke both well. Facility with the languages opened the countries to him; he could talk to vendors on the beaches of Rio, go to plays in Buenos Aires, and read local newspapers. In Asia, English was the language of business, even among Asians from different countries—Koreans sold to Indonesians in English, for example. Chambers had learned some Japanese and was being tutored in Mandarin Chinese, though he spoke neither language well enough to conduct business. When he traveled around the region, he always tried to get away from the crowded capital cities and see how the people lived. He had visited Ke San and Kwangju in Korea, Nikko and Kyoto in Japan, Cebu and Baguio in the Philippines, Bali and Sumatra in Indonesia, and Korat in Thailand.

He read and he listened and he *felt*. And yes, David, he thought, I work at it. You couldn't expect to deal with Japanese bankers and businessmen if you displayed no interest in their country and its art, of which they were intensely proud. You couldn't expect the Minister of Finance of Indonesia to listen to your views on the development of his nation if you knew nothing of the country

lamp, the room was rather dark and cool. Sir William waited until his secretary had departed before speaking.

"Sit down, Chris. I am just finishing reading your report."

"Thank you, Sir William," said Marston-Evans, perching on the edge of another ancient leather chair, directly in front of the chairman's desk.

Sir William took off his reading glasses and rubbed the dents they had left on his nose. He picked up the papers of Marston-Evans's report and carefully set them aside, leaving the leather surface of the desk in front of him clear. He folded his hands on the desk and looked at the young merchant banker. Because of his height, Marston-Evans's face was largely in shadow. Sir William pressed a switch under the desk and the overhead lights brightened.

"Chris, your report is fine, very complete," began Sir William. "There are one or two more details I need. First, you have concluded that the Monetary Authority will continue to stall? You really don't think they will proceed with the application, once we answer all these infernal questions?"

Chris leaned forward, bringing his head down level with the chairman's and into the pool of light from the lamp. "No, Sir William, I don't, and I will tell you why. I see a pattern in these questions. They're very like the questions we began getting from the New York Banking Commission, shortly before they put the whole Mariner Bank acquisition on hold 'to study carefully our very complete responses.' "

"A pattern?"

"Yes, sir. After that awful Muriel Siegal and her staff of bumblers had been plodding along for months, not understanding even what questions to ask about our published financial statements, they suddenly began to ask very shrewd questions indeed—especially about hidden reserves we hold. Quite legal here, but not in America."

"Information we could not very well give them, since we don't give it to Hong Kong government or to our own shareholders."

"Precisely, Sir William."

The older man nodded slowly. Nothing of this was in the boy's report, nor should it have been. "Do you think Elizabeth Sun could have gotten hold of a copy of our submission to the New York Banking Commission?"

"She could have, but I doubt that she did. I see another fine hand in all this."

"Go on."

"Well, sir, as I was saying, I see a pattern. Whilst I was working with Mrs. Siegal's people in New York, one of the accountants let me see a memorandum in which Mrs. Siegal had asked most of the major New York banks to comment upon our request to buy Mariner. That in itself is not unusual, and most of the replies were fairly bland, given that Hong Kong allows many American banks to operate here, either as branches or through control of local banks. The only bank to reply at length was First New York, and they raised, very specifically, several issues which they must have known would be difficult for us to deal with, including questions about the hidden reserves and the perfectly absurd suggestion that if Hong Kong were to be taken over by China the life savings of Americans deposited in Mariner Bank would be taken away by the communists."

Sir William nodded. "And shortly thereafter the whole business was put on hold."

"Yes, sir. The First NY brief was signed by the vice-president in charge of some special planning unit. His name, I remember distinctly, was Richard van Courtland."

The chairman looked up quickly. "Van Courtland? Isn't he—"

"Yes, sir. The newly arrived managing director of Pacific Capital Corporation."

Sir William rose and began to pace. Chris leaned back and smiled. This meeting was going well. Sir William raised a long finger like a dagger in front of his nose as he walked, and he stabbed the air as he spoke. "First New York stuck the boot into us with the New York authorities because we hold them back here by denying them access to cheap interbank Hong Kong dollars. We half expected that, and we will even get 'round them in time. Now you think you see the same thing happening in Singapore?"

Chris leaned forward and tapped his report on the chairman's desk. "Look at Miss Sun's questions, Sir William. Hidden reserves. How is primary capital calculated? How does the Bank function as a central bank in Hong Kong and a commercial bank at the same time? Who is lender of last resort to the Bank?"

"The same questions were broached in New York?" Sir William returned to his chair and sank into it.

"Practically word for word."

"And you suspect First New York of once again pissing in the soup?"

Chris smiled and rubbed his bony hands in his lap. He had saved the best for last. "My appointment with Elizabeth Sun was for eleven o'clock. I arrived at a quarter after ten; I like to be early for appointments, especially with government officials. It helps to know who else they are consulting about whatever problem we have been asked to address. Guess who popped out of the lovely Miss Sun's office at exactly half past ten?"

"Not this van Courtland?"

"Richard Bloody van Courtland himself," said Chris, savoring his surprise.

The chairman sat silently, knitting and unknitting his fingers on the cool surface of the desk. A damn clever lad, this Marston-Evans. This was a whole new problem. "I don't suppose he spoke to you?"

"No, not with Dragon Lady Elizabeth standing in her doorway, all resplendent in French silk. But he knew me right enough. He tipped me a wink as he swept fatly past."

The chairman looked carefully at the younger man. Marston-Evans's voice ordinarily dripped with sarcasm, but Sir William thought he heard a deeper hatred. "You seem to feel a special animus toward this van Courtland, Chris," he said softly.

"I am sorry, Sir William, but I do. His snide little memo halted the Bank's takeover of Mariner, and that derailed my posting to New York; you may recall I was to be Assistant Chief Manager of Trading. I wanted that post very badly, Sir William, and my wife, Celia, more than me."

"Well, you may still get it, once we get 'round the Banking Commission. We have friends in New York and Washington, just as do First New York."

"Well, sir, I certainly hope the board will want me to go to New York. But you have me working on Singapore now, sir, and here comes this van Courtland at me again. I hardly think the board would give me such a good job in New York if the second project in a row that I work on gets put off the rails."

Sir William smiled, thinking, our young Chris is a very smart lad indeed. Another setback after New York and the boy would be lucky to manage a branch in Lai Chi Kok, a grimy industrial section of Kowloon. Sir William leaned back and studied the twitching scowl on the other man's face. He looked close to rage. "Well, I am sure you will continue to represent us well in Singapore. And you may be sure your overseas posting will have my support when the matter of Singapore is settled. New York, or, if that is further delayed, perhaps London."

Chris felt his heart pounding as different emotions fought within him. When the matter of Singapore is settled. That is the carrot and the stick. But the reward! To live in London with a salary and expatriate benefits from the Bank might even be better than

New York. "I shall certainly try my level best, Sir William. But what of van Courtland? Aren't we entitled to give him back a bit of his own tricks?"

The chairman's eyes were half closed as he watched Marston-Evans. That is the key to this nasty little man, he thought. He allowed himself a slight smile and an even slighter nod, which seemed to satisfy Marston-Evans and to calm him down. The chairman waited a full minute before speaking, and then he changed the subject.

"Your report makes no mention of your interview with the Minister of Home Affairs."

Chris bobbed in his chair, momentarily confused. Good, thought Sir William. When he leaves this meeting he won't remember whether I assented to his going after Richard van Courtland or not.

Marston-Evans found his voice. "I, uh, assumed, Sir William, that you would not want that mentioned in my written remarks, due to the rather special nature of—"

Of trying to suborn a high public official, thought Sir William as he cut the young man off. "Quite, Chris. But tell me what transpired."

"Well, sir, I told him of the trouble we were having with the government about the banking license. He mouthed the usual platitudes about having no knowledge of financial matters, and little influence beyond his own ministry, but I am sure he took my meaning right enough. Whether he will do anything about it I just couldn't say."

"He is a cautious man. I remember him well from Malaya."

"Perhaps he will get in touch with you directly, Sir William."

The chairman shook his head. "No, Chris, you are still thinking like a European. That is the last thing Minister Raza will do. If he wants to increase his power in the government, or simply to profit from it, and if he wants our support, he will get in touch with me through my appointed intermediary—you. Which means you had better spend as much time in Singapore this summer as possible."

Chris hid his disappointment. Singapore was even more oppressive in summer than Hong Kong and far less interesting socially. "Do you really think he would call me?"

"He will use his intermediary to contact mine. It won't be obvious, and it certainly won't be direct, so you will have to be bloody subtle to see it when it comes. How soon can you get back down there?"

Marston-Evans shrugged. "I suppose I could get the answers

to Elizabeth's questions, at least the ones that can be answered, in a week to ten days, including framing them as a report. That will give me an excuse to make another appointment with the MAS, and then I can just hang about and see if anyone calls."

"Good. I want you on this exclusively until further notice, Chris. Don't be disappointed if you don't hear from Raza for months. Let yourself be seen around the town and the clubs. Take your wife on at least some of the trips; she is quite pretty, as I recall."

"She will be glad to hear you said so, sir."

Sir William rose, and Chris jumped to his feet. "Very well, then, young Marston-Evans. You are handling this well. Continue to report to me personally on the confidential aspects of this matter."

"Yes, Sir William. And thank you."

"Good afternoon, Chris." Sir William extended his hand.

"Good afternoon, sir." Marston-Evans turned and walked quickly from the room. Now it is my game to win, he thought. I will get that branch license, and I will get to New York or London. Watching Mr. Richard Bloody van Courtland go down along the way will add spice to the porridge of revenge. Marston-Evans grinned broadly at the two receptionists and tipped an imaginary hat, then strode to the lifts. I am twenty-nine years old, he thought. I could sit in that old man's chair before I am forty.

Sir William sat down and once again leafed through Marston-Evans's report. A clever lad, clear-sighted, utterly ruthless, he thought, reading again the bland words of the report and thinking of the angry intensity of its author. A powerful weapon, this Chris, to be managed with great care to do the difficult tasks, especially those that could not stand the full light of day. Managed and controlled and then one day discarded. Sir William nodded to himself. The longer he stays in the Bank, the more dangerous he could become to the people around him. It will be best to use him to get this Singapore business settled and then indeed to ship him overseas. A very dangerous man indeed.

10

2 May

CHAMBERS RETURNED FROM THE long managers' meeting for the Indonesian credit at three-fifteen and sat down next to Margaret's desk to give her his marked-up copy of the draft-offer telex for the general syndication and to walk her through his terrible handwriting. Margaret was talking on the phone in Cantonese, so he waited.

The large closet in which all the electrical services for Traders, as well as the telephone and telex switchboards, was across the hallway from Chambers's office, and he noted absently that the door was ajar. A European man in a dark-blue boiler suit with "CABLE AND WIRELESS" stenciled on it backed out, pulling a large metal tool box and a blue canvas hold-all with him. He set his tools down, mopped his sweating face with a bandanna, and locked the closet. He smiled at Chambers. "All set, Guv," he said with a pronounced cockney accent.

"What was the trouble?" asked Chambers. Telex problems were frequent, but Cable and Wireless was efficient about repairing them.

"Just replaced a line we were told was playing up, Guv," said the man. "Should be right now. Shall I just leave your keys with the lovely receptionist?"

"Fine, and thanks," said Chambers. The man went out to the reception area, closing the door behind him. Holden thought there was something odd about the engineer; he seemed to stare at Chambers with rather more interest than one might expect.

Margaret finished her call, apologized, and reached for the telex in Chambers's hand. "Margaret, isn't it a bit odd for Cable and Wireless to send a European engineer around for a routine line repair?"

She frowned. "Nearly all their staff are Chinese."

"Did Hannah check his identity card when he came in?"

"I am sure she did. Do you want me to get her log?"

He stood up. "I'll have a look. Try to work your way through my scribbles on the offer telex." He walked into reception and asked Hannah Chu for the log of visitors.

Hannah favored him with her glorious smile and handed him the book. Tiny, with large, luminous eyes, she was easily the prettiest Chinese girl he had ever met. If she were a bit above eighteen years old and didn't work for me, he mused. He returned her smile and took the log into his office.

The Cable and Wireless man was logged as one Tom Small-bridge, design engineer, ID number 98876. Chambers buzzed for Margaret, who came in immediately. "Margaret, please give a call over to Cable and Wireless. Check that this man was sent here today."

"Is there something wrong, Mr. Chambers?"

"No, I am just curious." The man's look at him had been decidedly odd.

"Right away, sir." Margaret departed to make the call. In two minutes, she buzzed through.

"Mr. Tom Smallbridge is on the staff as an engineer, sir, and the ID number is correct. The dispatcher told me she wouldn't be able to say what jobs he had been sent to today until the logs were turned in tomorrow, but if I write a letter, she can send a transcript of the service-call record."

"That's fine, Margaret, thank you."

"Shall I write a letter, Mr. Chambers?"

"No. I am sure it is all right. I need you to get that telex out."

"Very good, sir."

The man known to David Weiss as Mr. Dennis unlocked the tiny flat he rented in Yun Ping Road in Causeway Bay, which he had equipped for electronic surveillance. He took off the boiler suit and packed it along with the ID card he had stolen three months before from an unguarded Cable and Wireless van. He knew from his legitimate business as a security consultant that the theft of Engineer Smallbridge's uniform, tools, and equipment would not have been reported to the police; a new ID in the same number would simply have been issued, not that he expected his papers would ever be checked. Cable and Wireless technicians were in and out of the international banks all the time.

Dennis took a bottle of San Miguel beer from the small fridge and sat in the flat's only chair, which was in front of the purpose-built switching panel for the electronic equipment. Damn fine job, he thought. In three weeks he had located and rented a flat near both the telephone and telex substations that served the central business district, fabricated and installed the required cable busses and bridges, bought all this shiny new gear, and hooked everything up. He had reported his rapid progress to Weiss the previous week in a letter and received a cable back complaining about the delay and the cost, but also reporting that he had been paid. Dennis smiled and sipped his beer. Right fuckwit, that Weiss. No wonder Chambers won't tell him what's going on.

Two of the five telex machines in the flat were already chattering. Dennis had bugged all the telex lines from Traders Asia, as well as the telephone lines. He glanced at the telexes rolling off the printers: some long bloody thing about a Eurodollar syndication for Indonesia. Two of the three voice-tapes were running as well. He took the tape from the third and ran the reel until he heard the voice of the man he had spoken to, Holden Chambers. He ran the voice slowly through a delicate Japanese scanner, giving the machine enough to recognize the voice, much as a voiceprint. He entered the digital code the scanner displayed into all three voice recorders, which would enable him to search electronically through all conversations on the Traders lines to find the ones in which Chambers participated among all the rest. He yawned at the prospect of hours of listening to boring tapes. It was the expensive way to do the surveillance, but Mr. Weiss wanted results and he had the brass to pay for it.

Holden Chambers arrived late at Piggy and Pamela Martin's party that evening. He was disappointed to see that most of the guests had apparently been drinking heavily and resigned himself to a dull evening with no hope of escape until after dinner, which Pamela inevitably caused to be served late.

The Martin flat was large, in the Strawberry Hill development on the Peak, but oddly furnished with softly padded sectionals and clusters of hassocks in trendy earth tones, and brightly colored oversized pillows strewn about on the carpet. Chambers supposed the furniture was meant to encourage the formation of intimate conversational groups, but he always felt wary of tripping over the low hassocks and pillows. He noticed that most of the guests who were seated sat on the heavy white shag carpet.

He greeted other guests as he passed into the sitting room. Pamela Martin, a fat, unattractive woman, welcomed him with a squeal of delight, followed by a wet kiss on the mouth, which tasted of gin. She directed him to the den in the rear of the flat, where the bar had been set up. Chambers shook hands with Piggy, who did something in government but had his own money and never spoke of his work, and with Ray Adams, May-Ling's boss, and then entered the den to get himself a drink.

He found Celia Marston-Evans pouring herself a generous glass of gin. Surprised to see him, she looked quickly toward the door to see if anyone else were around, then threw her arms around him, kissing him deeply and grinding her belly urgently into his groin.

He held her lightly around her slim hips, enjoying the kiss. She could look beautiful or merely ordinary, depending on her mood. She was tall and slender with pale skin, tightly curled blond hair, and startlingly green eyes, now half closed. Her full lips were soft and her tongue probed inside his mouth. He felt the movement of her hips against him and let her feel his quickly growing erection. Celia gave a little moan in her throat and pushed him away and pouted, flashing her incredible eyes.

"I never see you," she accused, picking up her drink from the bar.

He poured a scotch over ice and added soda from a syphon. "Is Chris here this evening? I didn't see him."

"No. He may come later. Who cares? I only came because Pamela promised me you would come."

He looked at her without speaking. Poor Celia, to be married to the sexless Chris. "Celia, this isn't doing us any good."

She took a large pull of her drink. She had a temper when she drank, and he feared a scene. "Holden, I just want to see you. That's all. I am not asking you to change your life for me, just to make love to me."

"Celia, you are a lovely woman and you know I like you, but you are married, and you know I don't play around with married women."

"Oh, rubbish! Chris doesn't bloody care. This is Hong Kong, not Ohio or whatever dreary province you come from. And you liked me well enough in bed on Warren's junk!"

He leaned against the bar and glanced toward the door of the den, wishing someone would come in and end the scene, yet not at all sure Celia would stop talking if someone did join them. "Celia, darling, that was one time, and over two years ago. We had both had too much champagne and run into each other in the master suite practically naked after swimming. It just happened. It was lovely, but it wasn't meant to continue." His voice trailed off as he remembered how wild she had been and how his own excitement had been perversely enhanced by the fact that Chris Marston-Evans had been immediately above them on the main deck, entertaining his guests. Holden had been new in the colony then and not used to the freewheeling sexual mores of the British. By now he knew she was right: Chris didn't care who his lonely wife slept with and barely cared who knew.

Celia drained her glass and rattled the ice cubes in irritation. He picked up the Tanqueray bottle and poured for her as she held the glass at the end of a stiff arm. Her face twisted into a sullen, spoiled-child pout. "Rather go native, then, virtuous Holden?" she hissed. "The lovely Miss Wong has quite taken our naive American heart?"

He felt the rush of color to his cheeks. May-Ling almost never came to parties, preferring her law studies and her Chinese calligraphy. She was shy and rarely drank alcohol, and he realized the social life of European Hong Kong was pretty deadly without a buzz between the ears, so he never insisted. He resented the fact that many talked behind his back that he kept May-Ling as a secret concubine, but he had hoped her appearance with him in Manila had ended at least that element of the gossip.

His relations with her family were prickly as well. She would have been living with him, but her parents forbade it. Her father was a sergeant in the Royal Hong Kong Police, an evil, obsequious man who ill concealed his distaste for Chambers. Her mother had come from Singapore and appeared to have Malay blood; she had given her daughter the smooth brown skin, which the lighter Cantonese had told Marylin made her ugly since her earliest days in school.

Chambers felt that the purity and simplicity of the love he held for May-Ling was damaged by the fact that it had become discussed derisively in the European community, and at times like these he felt that perhaps her father was right: that he had shamed the girl in the eyes of her own people.

He felt a mental shrug as he smiled tautly at Celia. May-Ling was strong-willed and independent and she cared for him; it was her business that she didn't enjoy parties and indeed found most Europeans shallow and uninteresting. Yet there was nothing whatever he could say, and he was glad of a commotion as Pamela swept into the room, full of loud giggles and with Richard van Courtland and his wife, Barbara, in tow.

"You two deserve each other," spat Celia at Holden, loudly enough to stifle Pamela's giggling. Celia strode from the room, sloshing gin on the carpet. Pamela looked puzzled, Barbara Ramsay looked pretty and unconcerned, and Richard was obviously very drunk.

Richard shook hands with Chambers, saying nothing and apparently not remembering his name. Holden moved aside to let the heavyset man get to the bar, where he poured himself an enormous whiskey with one hand while continuing to hold Pamela around her shoulders with his other arm. Holden thought for a moment that Richard might actually fall, and he moved to support him. Richard looked at him strangely and shook off Holden's hand from his elbow, then was dragged from the den by Pamela, who whooped again with high-pitched laughter. Holden felt acutely embarrassed as he looked at Barbara.

She smiled, a slight questioning look on her face. "What did she mean, Holden, that we deserve each other?"

"I'm sorry?" He felt confusion added to his embarrassment.

"The woman who just left. Celia Evans, I think, said we deserve each other. It seemed an odd remark." Barbara picked up a wine glass and studied the drinks table.

Amused, he felt his calm returning. How intriguing that this woman would think Celia's contemptuous remark about his relationship with May-Ling was intended to link him with herself. He moved closer to her and took the wine glass from her hand. "Here, what can I get you?"

She turned to him, one finger touching the corner of her mouth to reinforce the questioning gesture. "Just some champagne, if you can find any."

He withdrew a bottle from a silver bucket of ice water and carefully filled a champagne flute. She continued to smile at him, her face still carrying its question and a look of faint amusement. He thought she looked radiant and confident.

He would have guessed her height at about five-feet five-inches and her age at twenty-eight or -nine. She was slender, with nicely shaped arms and legs revealed by her simple white sleeveless knitted dress. Her nicely rounded, wide-spaced breasts curved beneath the deep V-neck of the dress and were undisguised by a bra. She took the champagne from him in a slim hand with long fingers unadorned by rings, and she sipped it slowly, holding him with her eyes, which were a lustrous brown in color and very large. Her oval face was lightly suntanned, freckled across the prominent cheekbones, and framed by rich dark hair—its color undecided between brown and black—which she wore loose to the shoulders. The whole effect was softness, self-assurance, and perhaps invitation. How lovely, he thought. How desirable and how very dangerous.

She lowered the glass from her lips. She reached up and touched the collar of his shirt with her short laquered nails: a soft, stroking touch near his throat. He felt electrified, but he held his ground against twin urges to flee and to take her in his arms. "Why did that woman say we deserved each other?"

He struggled to control his face. He managed a smile. "P-prescience, one might hope?" He reddened. He never stammered! Why did this woman have such an effect on him?

She linked her arm in his and led him back into the sitting

room. His self-consciousness increased as they moved among the crowd. He made a point of introducing her to the others, noting the appreciative glances of the men and the rigid smiles of the women. He noticed as well Richard van Courtland in a boisterous group on the terrace, with Piggy and Ray Adams. Celia stood by herself in a corner and watched him intently, her gin glass held tightly to her teeth. Holden took Barbara to her husband's side and asked for a private word with Ray Adams. Barbara gave his arm a light squeeze as she released it. Holden moved back into the sitting room with his lawyer and made up conversation. He hoped his discomfiture was not as obvious as he felt it must be.

Dinner was served an hour later, and Chambers found himself seated next to Barbara. He wondered if Pamela Martin had arranged that and decided, after exchanging glances with Pamela and Celia, that she definitely had not. Chris Marston-Evans arrived just as dinner was served and seated himself between his wife and his hostess.

Barbara leaned close to him as the entree was being served, and he could not help looking down the neck of her dress at her breasts. "Holden, do you have much business in Singapore?"

He almost missed her words entirely and choked a bit on his wine before answering. "Q-quite a lot, B-barbara," he stammered, once again reddening. She did not appear to notice.

She smiled with evident pleasure and touched his arm. He once again felt the tingling shock. "I would love to pick your brain. I have to go there next Thursday. Could I take you to lunch?"

His mind tossed up the immediate arrogant Hong Kong response: Have your secretary call mine. He heard himself say, as from outside his body, "I'd be delighted. I'll check my calendar tomorrow and call you." She graced him with another smile and turned to talk to Ray Adams, seated on her left. Chambers felt chilled when she withdrew her hand from his arm.

Coffee was served in the sitting room, among the dangerous hassocks and pillows. Richard van Courtland had disappeared immediately after dinner, bouncing twice off the door jamb to peals of laughter from Pamela, until his driver came forward, took his arm firmly, and led him to his car. Holden lingered, sipping coffee and later Armangac, avoiding Barbara, yet hoping she might approach him yet again. At midnight the crowd had mostly gone, and Barbara suddenly said good-bye to Pamela and was immediately led to her own chauffeured Mercedes. Holden gave himself another glass of Armangac from the trolley, even though he knew it was making him drunk and morose.

Chris Marston-Evans appeared at his elbow and held up his

snifter to be refilled. "How are you, old boy? One couldn't help noticing you devoted a good part of the evening to the lovely Barbara."

Chambers looked hard at the younger man. He was flushed and sweating, more from drink than from the closeness of the evening. Chambers would like to have splattered his long nose with a quick punch. God, this has been a long evening, he thought. "She is in the business, Chris. We talked about business." He managed a smile.

"Oh, balls! She doesn't have any business here. Who in Asia is going to do business with a woman?"

"She may have more going for her than you think," said Chambers patiently. "And she is a vice-president of the biggest investment bank in New York. That will open doors."

Chris laughed and leaned closer. Conspiratorially he said, "Come on, man, be serious. Roland, Archer gave her that title and some made-up job when her husband transferred out. We both know that American firms coddle women to fill their bloody quotas."

Holden could smell Chris's sweat through his expensive cologne. He felt repelled and fought a desire to back away. "Well, Chris old boy, I think she is going to do some business, and I may just help her do it."

Chris winked, thinking he was getting the joke at last. "Well, call it what you like, Holden old lad, but I shouldn't think you would have too much trouble. Her husband is not the most charming of your countrymen I have ever met."

"He is a pig," said Holden. And you are an ass. You really don't see these people as anything beyond bit players in a game ordained and controlled by the almighty Bank. I wonder if the Bank trains its young executives in blind arrogance or selects for it when hiring?

Chris's face flushed as he leaned forward. "So why don't you have her?"

"Honor. She is a married woman, and I don't sleep with married women."

Chris took a long drink of wine. "What is it, anyway, that lets you be such a prig?"

Chambers smiled. "I have never gotten used to your English unconcern."

"You want to call it *immorality*." Marston-Evans drew out the last word as though tasting it.

"What do you care, anyway?"

"I don't. Well, I do, but I am not going to tell you why, because you are not going to do anything about it anyway." He gestured with his whole body, like a cat. His fingers stretched and clawed, his torso twisted, and his long, ginger-haired head made pushing-upward movements. Chambers recognized these gestures as signing agitation. Why? he wondered.

"Asshole," hissed Marston-Evans. "Stupid, provincial, American asshole."

Chambers grinned. "The best there is, Chris. Besides, why do you care?"

Chris stood, then sat back down. "Okay, Yank, I'll admit it, far off the record. I want van Courtland taken down."

Chambers grinned. "Why him?"

"Thy mother, American. I have my reasons."

"And doubtless your means. I am not your means."

"No, I guess you aren't," he said, an ugly snarl crossing his face.

Chris put his empty glass on the trolley and took his dinner jacket from the back of a chair. When he turned around, though, he looked perfectly composed. "Well, this party is all done. I think I'll drop down to the Foreign Correspondents Club for a final snifter. Why don't you join me? Perhaps I can talk sense into you."

"No thanks, Chris. I'm tired. I am going home."

"Well, do as you like. Celia, darling, join me?"

Celia had been sitting on a hassock across the room, drinking steadily and staring out at the lights of the harbor below with a look of bored indifference. She turned slowly to look at her husband and, without speaking, shook her head.

Chris shrugged into his jacket, then crossed the room to his wife's side and leaned over. She had returned her attention to the window. "Drop you home, then?" he asked softly.

"I have my car," she said.

He was forced to speak to her profile. He straightened up, looking somewhat ill at ease, waved to Holden, and went to find his hosts saying good night to the last remaining guests by the door. Celia waited until Chris was gone, then got up, favored Holden with an angry pout, and followed.

God, the things Hong Kong living does to ordinary people, thought Holden, moving toward the door and his giggling hosts. Like a pressure cooker made of clear glass, Hong Kong magnified and intensified every flaw in people's characters. Easy money and easy power and easy corruption.

Holden thanked Pamela for the lovely dinner and exchanged some vague promise about golf at Shek-O with Piggy. He walked across the darkened carpark to the white Triumph TR-6 he drove when not being chauffeured in Traders Asia's Mercedes. The top was down, and he could see Celia already seated in the left seat. He opened the door on the driver's side and looked across at her. Her expression was pleading.

"Please take me home," she said, barely above a whisper.

"You told Chris you had your car."

"Well, I don't. I forgot I came up with Sylvia Adams."

Holden slid into the car and switched on the ignition. The big six-cylinder engine roared, then settled to a throaty rumble. He reversed out of the carpark and turned toward the block of flats on Peak Road that the Bank kept for its married junior officers. He flicked his headlights on high beam and pushed the little car through the curves of the narrow road, shifting quickly from second gear to third and back.

He knew what would happen next, and he felt strangely resigned. He knew that the flat would be empty when they arrived. He knew, and Celia knew, that Chris would be drinking with his poofter playmates at the FCC for hours or, worse, they might go to Wan Chai to one of the sex-show clubs. He knew Celia would invite him in "for a drink," and he would go. He knew they would make love. Suddenly he realized he wanted it to happen, although he could hardly imagine a more foolish mistake.

Holden parked expertly in the space where Chris's car should have been. He got out and opened the car door for Celia. "Safe at home, Celia."

She got out and handed him her keys. "Come up for a moment, won't you?"

"Thanks, but I really am ready to drop."

She grasped him by the collar and kissed him. "Come *on*, damn you!"

Their sex was urgent, almost violent. The release was from pain, rather than into love. She cried out like an animal when she came, then collapsed on his sweaty chest and wept. He never spoke once he was inside the flat, until after he had showered and dressed, when he bid her a soft good night from the door of her bedroom. She didn't respond. When she heard the front door close behind him, she got up and went into the shower. I suppose I really should change the sheets, she thought, but Chris will be so swinish drunk he won't notice. A grimace crossed her face as she realized she would have to get a taxi in the morning to retrieve her car from the park next to Pamela and Piggy's flat.

Holden roared up the double switchback of the drive of his block of flats on Magazine Gap Road. The watchman in his little hut recognized the sound of the motor and raised the barrier at the top of the drive with a sleepy wave. Chambers swung the Triumph wide on the deck and reversed into his covered parking space. He unlocked his flat and felt the cool air from the laboring air conditioners, walked into the master bedroom, and turned on the overhead light. Marylin Wong rolled over in his bed, blinking at the sudden light. He immediately turned it off and turned on a weaker lamp in the dressing alcove near the bath. Feelings of shame and guilt rose up over him like a flood. He threw his dinner jacket over the chair in the alcove and ripped off his bowtie and silk pleated shirt. Compulsively he rolled up his sleeves and washed his hands and face in the cold water from the basin tap.

Then she was standing at his side, dressed in a nearly transparent nightgown. She was still not fully awake, and her almond-shaped eyes appeared as dark slits in the dusky smoothness of her face. She smiled at him gently and caressed his shoulders as he dried his hands and face. He felt rage, even hatred, that she should be there in his space to confront him when he already felt utterly disgusted with himself.

"Darling, I didn't expect you this evening. You said you would go to visit your sister." Keep the anger out of your voice, he thought. It is not her fault you are a perfect shit.

"The baby wouldn't stop crying, Holden, and I missed you. Should I have stayed away?"

You could at least bloody well call, he thought. "No, of course not, May-Ling. You can come here whenever you like; you know that."

She nuzzled his shoulder, accepting him as she always did. "How was the party, love?"

He took her by the shoulders and held her away from him. He just couldn't help it. She looked up at him, more puzzled than hurt. "Darling, the party was dreadful, and I have a very early meeting. Could we just go to sleep?"

She smiled and backed up a step, then nodded, almost like a curtsy. "Of course, love. Come."

He felt so guilty that he took another shower. He crawled into the cool bed and she cuddled next to him, running her fingers through the hair on his chest and down his stomach in little circles. He knew that when her hand found his penis it would be flaccid and impossibly small, as embarrassed as he was. "May-Ling?"

"Yes, my love?" She kissed his nipple.

"Darling, I really am desperately tired. I am sorry."

She raised herself above him and looked at him. Her face was in deep shadow, and he hoped her expression did not show the contempt he felt he deserved. She bent down and kissed him, first lightly and then deeply, probing his mouth with her tiny tongue. "Good night, then, my love."

She settled into the silk pillows, her head next to his shoulder. For his part, he stared at the ceiling as her breathing became regular against his skin. He felt his mind boiling with a mixture of powerful angers. He hated Celia Marston-Evans for using him to vent her anger at her wretched husband, a despicable man in many ways but nonetheless a friend. He hated himself for being so willingly used, and worse, for enjoying fucking Celia precisely because he despised Chris's attempts to manipulate him. He hated the lovely, gentle May-Ling for being so trusting, so joyful just to lie next to him when he must stink of another woman's lust despite two showers.

He closed his eyes and fell immediately into a dream. He was lying on his back, immobilized. His penis rose above him, enormously engorged. Three women had attached ribbons to its tip, and they danced in a circle around him, their backs to him. He recognized Celia's cap of tight blond curls and the shiny jet of May-Ling's shoulder-length hair. The other head was sheathed in shiny dark black-brown hair that swayed with the skipping movement of the dance, flashing with highlights. The women turned inward as they circled. Celia wore a pout of triumph and anger; May-Ling's face was downcast in guileless sorrow. The third woman, Barbara Ramsay, laughed and laughed, her brown eyes beckoning.

11

Singapore, 10 May

AT 10:00 A.M., COLONEL ABDUL RAZA held a meeting with heads of the several branches of the Police Department in the Ministry of the Interior Building. The weekly meetings were his chief management tool to keep the heads of widely different activities aware of each other's problems and progress. Chief Superintendent Ong, the head of Traffic, the department's largest branch, was just finishing a presentation of his branch's evaluation of a new electronic traffic-control system under consideration to reduce the near-gridlock congestion in the business district when a policewoman knocked and opened the door. She was one of the women who worked directly for Raza, and she beckoned to him.

Raza was annoyed, but he knew Iashiah would not disturb him unless the matter were urgent. He rose, apologized to Chief Superintendent Ong, and went to the door. "Yes, Iashiah?"

"Telephone, Colonel. So sorry, it is your cousin."

Raza nodded and strode off toward his office. He had many cousins, but only one who could have urgent business: General Mohamdir of the Malaysian Army. Raza swung behind his desk and punched the flashing button. "Raza here," he said.

"Abdul, I have a bit of bad news," said the general without preamble. "I thought you should know right away."

"Yes, Ibrahim. What is it?"

"The boy arrested with your son six weeks ago, Jarid Khan, is dead. Sorry, Abdul. I hope he and your boy weren't close."

Raza closed his eyes and saw Yusef in the interrogation room in Johor. He remembered his son's plea for his friend—and remembered as well the promise he had made in reply. "How did it happen?"

"Hanged himself in his cell last night. Report is the lad was a bit fey, and the old lags made rather too much sport with him."

"Cousin, don't you remember I asked you to treat him as a protected prisoner? I promised my son."

"Of course I remember, Abdul. I spoke to the governor of the prison myself, and the lad was confined as a youthful offender. But when we finally found out the boy's true name, he turned out to be twenty years old rather than seventeen, as the university records held. That would not have been a problem in itself; seventeen is already too old for youthful-offender status, but the governor fiddled it for me. But then we ran the revolver down and traced it to the policeman from whom it was taken by three youths last December. The man was badly beaten during the robbery and was nearly two months recovering. Anyway, he picked our lad out of a lineup, first go, dead certain. The boy was confronted and broke down, and eventually pleaded guilty. Magistrate gave him eight years; there was no way I could keep him protected after that."

Raza took the phone away from his ear and stared at it, willing it to change its tale. He balled his left hand into a fist and struck his desk, hard. "Of course you couldn't, Ibrahim. I just wish you had told me so I could have told Yusef."

"Only just happened, Abdul. Kid's trial ended day before yesterday."

"I see. Well, thank you, cousin, for doing what you could. I had better call Yusef at the university straight away."

"Ah, Abdul, hang on a tic."

Raza gripped the phone. Something had happened to Yusef! "Yes?"

"I went down to the campus myself, Abdul; couldn't find the lad anywhere. He turned in his thesis on time two weeks ago but didn't turn up this morning for his oral exam."

"Damn!" said Raza, once again pounding his desk.

"I had rather hoped he might be on his way down to you," said Mohamdir gently.

Not bloody likely, thought Raza, feeling a physical pain in his guts. "Try to find him, cousin. I will search for him in Singapore, but I think he has more friends in Kuala Lumpur."

"Bulletin's already gone out. Also alerted the causeway. We'll probably have him before nightfall."

"I hope so, cousin. I'll ring off then and set things up here."

Yusef Raza crossed the Johor Causeway into Singapore just after noon on a bus crowded with shoppers. Identity papers of all passengers were checked at both the Malaysian and Singaporean sides of the bridge. Raza tried to keep his eyes on the back of the head of the person seated in front of him as the Malay guard checked his forged Malaysia ID card in the name of Mahmoud Assad, and his letter from the Alsagoff Arab School on Aliwal Street in the old Muslim quarter of Singapore, which described his employment as a teaching assistant. These papers had been given to him by the Malay Students' League in Kuala Lumpur after the Yusef bin Sirdar identity had been blown when he was arrested. Yusef knew the forgeries were much too crude to stand any careful scrutiny, but he had guessed that the frontier would be crowded at noon, and he had been right. The Malay guard handed him back the papers, glanced at the other passengers' documents, and left the bus. At the Singapore end of the causeway the inspection was even swifter. The inspecting officers who boarded the bus were both Chinese, and Yusef faced them boldly. We all look the same to them, as they do to us, he thought.

The bus continued south on the four-lane road, its borders parklike with many planted trees. Singapore's almost daily rains kept the carefully tended forest a brilliant green; Yusef had heard the Prime Minister liked the effect of order. Yusef smiled to himself. He preferred the variety and riot of colors in Johor's untended jungle.

The bus made stops at various crossroads on Woodlands Road and at large shopping centers in Dunearn and Orchard roads nearer the center of the city. At each stop the coach disgorged clots of loudly chattering people, bent on enjoying their day. Sari-clad Indians, Tamils in long white shifts, Malay men in long plain sarongs, short black jackets, and pillbox hats, and many Chinese, mostly in Western dress, but a few old men in long surcoats of heavily brocaded silk paraded off the air-conditioned coach. By the time the bus had reached its last stop before its terminus, Beach Road near the Raffles Hotel, there were only two other passengers on the bus. Yusef decided not to chance the terminal, thinking his father's police might be on the alert there, so he left the bus on Beach Road and walked rapidly east into the old Arab Street district.

Yusef had been shocked to learn of Jarid's death. A knock on his door in the dormitory at three in the morning had roused him, and he had opened it to the organizer of the dormitory for the Malay Students' League. Yusef had been overwhelmed by powerful emotions the likes of which he had not experienced since his mother died, and the emotions were much the same: grief for the loss of one so loved and anger at his father for letting it happen. He raged around his tiny room, knocking over his only lamp and throwing his precious books against the walls. The little man from the MSL chased Yusef around the room and finally tackled him onto his bed, and then he gave in to sobs so racking that he thrashed around the bed and finally curled himself into a fetal ball and cried. The messenger, thinking him calmed down, turned out the overhead light in the room and departed.

Yusef lay in the dark, breathing in short gasps. He remembered how terribly afraid he had been when his mother died. He was afraid again now. He had seen Jarid just two days before when he had been led away from the courtroom, his head up and proud even though he knew of the horrors that lay before him in prison. Could my father have known? Yusef asked himself. Could he even have caused Jarid to be convicted and sent to the hard-labor prison? Why? As a warning, thought Yusef. A warning to me!

He jumped out of bed and turned on the overhead light. The harsh brightness pressed back the demons of rage and panic into the dusty corners of the room as he sat back on his bed. He hated his father, but in an odd way he had always trusted him. Colonel Abdul Raza had always been a symbol of harsh rectitude to the boy, of unforgiving justice. His father had given his word, and he would have kept it, and yet it hadn't been kept. Who, then, had wanted Jarid dead? The police? They had said that Jarid and others had beaten a policeman and taken the revolver found in Jarid's pack, but Yusef hadn't believed it. Jarid was a shy and gentle boy, and he never owned anything, not even the rucksack in which the police had found, or planted, the revolver. If the police had killed Jarid, they might take Yusef next. But no, his father would protect him, even in Malaysia. Yusef smiled, but then his guts churned. He closed his eyes tight and formed a picture of Jarid, tortured and then hanged by a group of masked men in police uniforms. Colonel Raza had friends high in the police and a cousin on the Army General Staff, but could he protect Yusef if some rank-and-file death squads wanted to terrorize the MSL? Such things had been rumored for months. Yusef staggered across his room to the small sink and was violently sick.

He didn't sleep again that night, and by morning he had resolved to flee. He wouldn't go to his father until he was sure his hands were not stained with Jarid's blood, but he would go to Singapore. He doubted any Malaysian hit squad would dare hunt him down in Colonel Abdul Raza's Singapore. The campus was just beginning to stir when Yusef saw an official government car preceded by two policemen on motorcycles swing into the fore-court and stop before his entrance. The boy picked up his Singapore Airlines holdall with his clothes, stuffed all his money in the pockets of his jeans, and fled down the fire escape. He was lucky to catch a ride to the bus station on a newspaper delivery truck, and by nine he had begun his long, slow journey to Singapore.

Yusef walked through the narrow lanes of the Muslim quarter. Most of the people were brown like him, and they smiled at him. He began to feel better: so far, at least, so good. The MSL had given him a short list of Singaporean members he could go to for shelter and assistance, and the first name on the list was one Elias, no last name, who could be found in a night club called the New Malacca on Bugis Street. Yusef smiled to himself. What would his father think if he knew his son had gone to ground in his own back yard?

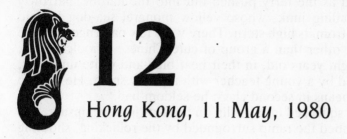

12

Hong Kong, 11 May, 1980

HOLDEN CHAMBERS LEFT HIS office in Gloucester Tower at 12:15. Margaret had given him a note at 11:30 stating simply that his lunch with Mrs. Ramsay of Roland, Archer and Company (HK) Ltd. was confirmed, at the Chesa at 12:45. Margaret asked whether Ah Wong should bring the car around, but Chambers said he would make his own way. The drive to Kowloon via the Harbour Tunnel could easily take forty-five minutes to an hour in the middle of the day. Chambers decided to take the ferry. It was a warm day but breezy, and the old Star Ferry made him feel more the native, more in tune with Hong Kong.

He felt sure that Barbara was going to ask him a lot of questions about Singapore, and likely about the rest of Asia as well. He wanted to be impressive, and not only because of his position as one of the Lions of the marketplace. He had dressed carefully this morning in a white silk-linen suit, light-blue cotton shirt, and pale-blue and yellow-figured Hermes silk tie. He told himself the outfit was not unusual, which it was not, at least among the non-English Europeans, and that the suit, which was his favorite, was due in rotation anyway. He didn't often wear his broad-brimmed Panama hat into Central, but today he had, and he had to hold it in the gusty wind as he approached the Star Ferry pier.

The Star Ferry offered first- and second-class decks. If he had been with someone, or if he had been crossing during rush hour, Holden would have ridden in the enclosed first-class upper deck. At midday the ferry was not crowded, so he went into the second-class deck, which was closer to the choppy waters of the harbor and open to the wind. He liked the feel of the wind and the smell of the salty spray, and he liked to watch the deck sailors warp the green ferries in and out of slips at either side of the harbor. The trip was so short that the ferries were built double-ended; they just shuttled back and forth, never turning around.

He sat in a wooden bench near the bow and looked around,

feeling good as the ferry pushed out into the harbor, narrowly missing a sailing junk, whose yellow mongrel sea-dog barked menacingly from its high stern. There were few passengers on the lower deck, other than a group of cute Chinese schoolchildren, all about eight years old, in their neat blue-and-white uniforms, accompanied by a young teacher with a pretty smile. He saw no other Europeans in second class; he seldom had.

The ferry squeezed into its slip on the Kowloon peninsula, and Holden climbed the ramp surrounded by the rollicking, shouting children. He strolled past the taxi rank and past the old clock tower into Salisbury Road, into the forecourt of the elegant Peninsula Hotel. A small boy stood at either side of the brass-trimmed glass doors leading into the lobby, each dressed all in white in a starched mess jacket and trousers and wearing a pillbox hat with a blue chinstrap. The boys, just beginning their life-long service at the hotel (if they made the grade), pulled open the heavy glass doors into the lobby. The smaller lad needed all his weight to manage the heavy door. Holden nodded his thanks and passed through.

The lobby of the Peninsula stretched the full width of the central part of the H-shaped building, and the ceiling was at least thirty feet high, supported by square columns with elaborately carved capitals. The ceiling itself was decorated with rococo cherubs in pale blue, gilt, and white, and the floor was white marble, which clicked against his heels. Crowds of people were having lunch in the lobby.

He crossed the lobby quickly and mounted the blue-carpeted stairs at the back to the first floor above the mezzanine. Then he turned into the Chesa, the small restaurant known for its rich Swiss cuisine, its even richer desserts, and the highest prices in Hong Kong.

Raymond Chow, the maître d'hôtel, greeted Chambers at the door of the restaurant, which was decorated and furnished in the heavy style of central Europe, all in red plush and dark woods and highly polished brass serving trolleys. Raymond took Holden's hat and handed it to a waiting girl, who bowed and carried it to a shelf, returning with a ticket. The maître consulted his reservation book and turned back to Chambers, who was looking around the room for Barbara Ramsay. "Are you someone's guest today, Mr. Chambers?" he asked.

Holden hadn't spotted Barbara among the diners. The restaurant was fairly full. "Yes, Raymond. A Mrs. Ramsay. She made the booking."

Raymond ticked the name in his book. Holden looked at his

watch: 12:55. People were punctual in Hong Kong, especially at lunchtime, and it was considered rude to let one's guests arrive first. Holden felt a slight twinge of irritation. *I suppose I should be grateful she remembered to book.*

"Well, Mr. Chambers, may I give you your usual corner? It is free."

"Yes, fine, Raymond, if the lady hasn't expressed another preference."

Raymond heard the pique in Chambers's voice and bowed him to the corner booth without speaking. Chambers sat down, and the maître stopped a scurrying captain and spoke to him rapidly in Cantonese. In a moment a waiter appeared and placed a chilled glass of champagne in front of Chambers.

He was amused. *Raymond knew how to smooth ruffled feathers. How silly we Europeans must seem, with our odd rules and our self-importance. Relax, maybe she is stuck in traffic or held up by a phone call (in which case her secretary should have left word and apologies with Raymond). Face is face, and Raymond has seen me lose a bit. Why should I be concerned about how I am regarded by the maître of the Chesa?* Chambers sipped the champagne and recognized it: Tattinger Blanc des Blancs. *Not great, definitely not bad. Still, she really shouldn't keep me waiting, she—*

His thought collided with his senses. He realized that he was very anxious to see Barbara Ramsay, and that *not* seeing her was disturbing his *hua*, his harmony, much more than any petty loss of face.

He sensed and then heard a flurry of activity behind him, as a breathless Barbara Ramsay was ushered to his table by the expressionless Raymond. He rose as best he could, constrained by the table, and she slid into the banquette around the corner from his seat. He felt his attention riveted by her smile, which warmed him and drew him. She looked radiant, as if she had run to the rendezvous, except she showed no signs of heat. She wore a simple dress of pale green linen and tossed her head of fine dark hair behind her shoulders as she sat. She looked at him, concentrating on his face as though he were the center of her universe. He was entirely enraptured, and he felt his face open in a grin of pure happiness.

She moved close to him, her knee just touching his at the corner of the banquette. He held his right hand out toward her, just above the tablecloth, and she placed her left hand on his forearm and leaned toward him. It seemed an intimate gesture, far different from the formal handshake he expected. "Holden, I am so sorry to be late." Her voice was low and musical, and her eyes smiled at him. "Thank God you have a drink."

"I should have waited, Barbara, but they know me here, so they just brought it."

"It looks delicious. Champagne?"

"Yes. Would you like some?"

"Please. Oh, I have been rushing so!"

He inclined his head, and the captain rushed to the table. "Oui, monsieur?"

"Une bouteille de la Veuve, s'il vous plaît," he said, praying his rusty accent wouldn't betray him.

"*Mais bien sur*, monsieur." The captain translated the order into Cantonese, and a waiter scurried into the bar.

"The waiters speak French here, Holden?" she asked, looking around the elegant restaurant.

"Most of the captains. It is a conceit of the place." He was showing off like a schoolboy, but he didn't care.

"It is very grand. I haven't been here before."

"What made you choose the Chesa, Barbara?"

She turned back and favored him with her soft, luminous smile. "I had my secretary call yours to find out which was your favorite."

He smiled as the waiter returned with a bottle of Veuve Cliquot Ponsardin, 1969. He nodded at the gold label, and the waiter carefully uncorked the wine and poured some into a fresh glass for him to taste. He nodded, and the waiter filled Barbara's glass, then his own, and withdrew. Holden raised his glass to her, aware that he could see nothing outside the aura of her smile and eyes and radiant color. "Thank you. The Chesa is indeed a favorite of mine."

She clinked her glass against his, at the same time studying him. Far and away the most interesting man I have met since I arrived in Hong Kong. She had found the bankers in Hong Kong to be generally less clever than the ones she had known in London and New York, though younger and often bolder in their approach to deals. Holden was a good-looking man, a bit under six feet, with regular features dominated by large blue-gray eyes. His hair was brown but lightened by the sun, and his skin was smooth and deeply tanned. He is comfortable here in his little world and anxious to show off his position to me. I think he likes me, she thought, thinking of how she had flirted with him a little more each time they had met. She remembered how he had kissed her in Manila, wondering at the same time how much he recalled of that evening. She decided she wanted him as a friend, at the very

least. "I hope you don't mind if I pick your brain over lunch."
She pushed her knee against his thigh. "I feel I need an adviser."
She inclined her head slightly, letting her hair tilt over her shoulder, knowing the light behind her would shine through.

He smiled, then turned to look out over the room. He was
fascinated, delighted, and flattered by her attention, but he wasn't
so besotted as to fail to notice he was being hustled. He smiled
to himself. Steady, lad, he thought as he turned slowly back
toward her. Be cold, he said to himself. Look at her; find a flaw,
a blemish. When she tries that on you, concentrate on the fault.
His eyes flicked rapidly over her face and torso. Hair eyes skin
features posture shoulders arms breasts voice. He turned away
as the waiter filled their glasses. Damn! The woman is stunning!
The flaw was not in her appearance. "If I can help you get going
out here, Barbara, I will. Perhaps it would be best if you told me
exactly what your assignment entails."

Barbara studied her glass, turning it in her long, tapered fingers.
I wonder what he really thinks I am here to do. Richard tells me
the gossip; apparently I am here on a sinecure, my career on hold
until we return to New York in two or three years. "Holden, I
am going to trust you, because I like you, but more important,
because I think we can do some business. I am here to open
certain select Asian-government borrowers to the Eurobond
market."

Holden looked carefully at his companion. That fitted with the
gist of the general rumor that she was just holding a place while
her husband did his tour. Roland, Archer had no capacity in Hong
Kong to underwrite Eurobonds or anything else. Their three
Asian offices—in Tokyo, Singapore, and Hong Kong—sold U.S.
securities to Asian individuals and institutions, full stop. Holden
also knew that many strong houses, including Traders and Richard
van Courtland's Pacific Capital, had tried to interest the Euromarkets in Asian borrowers (and vice versa) without success. But
I am too old a dog, he thought. As infatuated as I am in danger
of becoming with this woman, I do not believe she is here with
nothing to do. "Let's order lunch, and then we will talk."

She asked him to order for her, and when the captain appeared
with menus, Holden waved them away. He ordered vichyssoise,
Quenelles de Brochet Nantua, and spinach salads to be served
afterward. He looked at her for her approval, and she smiled and
nodded happily. They finished the champagne through the vichyssoise, which was creamy and flavored with fresh chives and
pepper, then drank a young Pouilly-Fuisse with the mousse dumplings of pike in their rich lobster sauce. The salad was just tart

enough to cleanse the palate and to prepare them for the enormous four-layer dessert trolley. He smiled as her eyes widened. The Chesa employed a full-time chef des desserts, who had apprenticed under the great Didier at the Hotel Le Richemond in Geneva.

"What will you have, Holden?" she asked, looking at the fruit tarts, mousses of black and white chocolate, cakes so moist they seemed to drip. Above them all were the sauces: fresh cream, ice cream, purées of raspberries and strawberries laden with Kirsch, and sauce vendome.

He sipped his wine. "I don't normally have anything, Barbara. I haven't time to play the number of squash games each of those represents."

She looked at him with her luminous "you are the center of my universe" smile, steepling her long, tapered fingers under her chin. Her cheeks were slightly flushed. Sexual arousal? he thought, then dismissed the idea as wishful thinking. He wondered if she were unused to drinking so much wine.

"But you must share something with me, we are having such fun," she said, her smile becoming a coquettish pout.

"All right, Barbara," he said. I want to kiss her, he thought. "But you must choose."

"No. I want you to choose. This is your restaurant, and I want to know all the very best things to order when I come back."

He felt a tightness in his throat at the thought of her coming to the Chesa without him, and to his utter surprise, he said so. "If you come back, it must be with me. Then you will never need to know at all."

She looked away suddenly, her smile fading for just a second. What a strange man, she thought. Undeniably the most influential of all the Lions, despite the presence of much larger banks in the colony. Well known and well respected, if not universally liked, but then powerful men in a competitive business needed enemies as well as friends to display their power. Yet he struts with confidence and pride of place, then blushes like a schoolboy on a first date. She had been pouring on her best charm, because she wanted him to tell her the secrets of the Hong Kong game the others would not let her learn. She had been surprised how easy it had been to be charming, to listen to his small-talk through the excellent lunch. Normally she found flattering a man tedious and most men's conversation boring. Holden was different; as strong and confident as he should be, but vulnerable to her. The thought thrilled her, made her feel both powerful and vulnerable herself. If I want Holden Chambers, I can have him. Do I want him to love me? She carefully adjusted her smile. His own face was stiff, awaiting apprehensively her reaction to his last remark. "What a lovely thought, Holden. But you choose something small we can share."

Holden emptied his wine glass with a gulp, surprised at his agitation. Get a grip on yourself, he thought desperately. This woman is married, and a colleague. This is a business lunch, and you are acting like a love-struck teenager about to fall down a flight of stairs.

He ordered a meringue with ice cream and chocolate sauce, topped with shaved fresh coconut. They ate the dessert in near silence, then they ordered coffee. The restaurant was rapidly emptying as the hour passed two-thirty. "Well, Barbara, that was a superb lunch, and I have enjoyed our conversation." He took a deep breath, realizing he had done virtually all the talking, much of it about himself, as she had listened in rapt attention. Am I really that clever, or am I just being hustled? He tried to make himself feel angry and threatened, to break through the pink fog of his infatuation, but he couldn't summon the energy. If she is trying to catch me, she has done so, and I will have to wait until later to break the spell. He relaxed, giving in to her magic, at least for the moment. "But now I feel I should earn my lunch. You said you had some questions for me about your business."

She reached across the corner of the table and placed her hand on his forearm: the same intimate gesture as when she had first sat down. He felt his arm tingle and warm, and once again he fought the desire to lean over and kiss her. She looked into his eyes, and her expression became more businesslike. "Tell me about Singapore. I am going there in two days to try to interest them in a bond offering."

He smiled and tried to forget her hand on his arm. "Many others have tried that, without success."

"Including Traders Bank International of London," she said.

"True. I had TBI's Capital Markets whiz kids out last year. No interest."

"Did they say why not?"

He shrugged. Why not tell her? The people at the MAS would, anyway. "Elizabeth Sun, who heads the Monetary Authority of Singapore and who, doubtless, you will be seeing, was pleased that we felt that Singapore was the quality borrower in Asia and thus the first to be brought to the Eurobond market. She felt, however, that putting that prestige at risk was dangerous, for a failure in the market could damage them much more than a success would help."

"But surely your offer was fully underwritten—it couldn't fail."

"It was. Strangely, that gave Elizabeth little comfort. She said that an offer swallowed by its underwriters might well be viewed as a market failure."

Barbara smiled and sipped her coffee. "This Elizabeth sounds like a pretty sharp lady."

"Huh!" he laughed, remembering the several encounters he had had with the chief of the MAS. "She has a well-earned reputation as one of the finest minds in any finance ministry in Asia, and she is surely the toughest negotiator."

"Incorruptible?"

He paused and raised his empty coffee cup to his lips. Her voice had taken on an edge of calculation. *I had better weigh these questions before I go too far in being helpful,* he thought. "I have never heard otherwise. We made no effort to test her in that way."

Barbara nodded and sipped her wine. "How much did you offer to underwrite?"

"Seventy-five million. She remarked that that didn't seem enough to establish Singapore's prestige and name in the market." He chuckled. "She reminded us that both the Swedes and the Italians are on the same year's London calendar for a hundred million each."

"But the Singaporeans don't really need the money, do they?"

He shook his head. "Some talk of applying the funds to the construction-cost overruns of the new airport, but no."

Barbara leaned back. The warm touch of her hand left his arm. Self-consciously, he pulled the arm back, masking the movement by pouring some cold coffee from the filtre pot into his cup.

"So the key to success will be to offer them a much larger amount than they can reasonably use and guarantee the broadest possible distribution." She smiled at the difficulty of the task.

"At, of course, the finest possible terms," he said.

"Do you think an offer of a hundred million would be enough?" The calculating edge crept back into her silky voice.

"Last year, maybe. That would have been a good-sized offering for an established borrower. This year, with the market still growing, she might want even more, even one-fifty. But do you believe there is that big a market for a Singapore straight bond?"

"Not all in Europe, perhaps." She paused and looked at him, studying his expression. *He is doing business now; the spell has broken.* "But I would hope to put together at least some of the distribution in Asia, and I would also hope to have the help of some of the commercial-bank-owned merchants, Holden."

"Do you have a deal with Pacific Capital?"

A shadow crossed her face as she looked away and then back. "I don't think PCC would be interested. First New York considers themselves as much competitors for the investment banks as for the commercial banks." Her smile returned. "I had hoped Traders Asia might have an interest. Confidentially, of course."

He smiled. "Are you making me an offer? For a senior position in the deal?"

"Yes, and yes," she said crisply.

Now, that is interesting, he thought. No one had put together a major fixed-rate (straight) bond issue in Asia. Floating-rate deals had been done at ten to fifty million each, but those were considered far easier for the underwriting banks to keep on their own books when distribution to investors failed. Straights of blue-chip European entities had been sold to some of the Japanese banks and funds, but they all had offices in Europe. Does Barbara really have the authority to try something like this?

"Enough of detail," she said, sipping at the end of her wine. "What I would really like you to tell me about is the flavor of the place—Singapore as you see it." She bathed him with her special-for-you-alone smile.

He smiled and looked away. Stay wary, he reminded himself. The wine was at last wearing off. He looked at his watch: 2:45. "How much time do you have?"

She looked suddenly pained. "Oh! I have all afternoon, but if I am keeping you from something important . . ." She drew the last word out, making it a plea.

"No, I'd like to give you my thoughts. And I would like to see you crack the MAS. I think I am free until four, but I had better just phone my office to be sure." She smiled her thanks as he rose and went into the entry hall.

Margaret read him his messages and reminded him of his four o'clock meeting. When he returned to the table, he found Barbara with a fresh pot of coffee and two balloon glasses. "What's all this? Would you have me drunk, madam?" he asked, sliding into the bench and feeling her knee press against his thigh.

"I'm sorry," she said with an impish grin. She had added lipstick while he was telephoning, and her lips shone, liquid and tempting. "I am having such fun with you, and I felt naughty." She raised the huge glass to him. "Armagnac. I hope you approve."

He picked up his glass and sniffed it. Excellent. "Well, certainly. Bit strong for lunchtime, but we have coffee as well. How did you know I favored Armagnac?"

She grinned and clinked his glass with hers. "Raymond told me."

So she has charmed the maître as well! She held his eyes as

she sipped the brandy, and he began to think again about kissing her. He knew the Armagnac was a mistake even before he tasted it. "It's lovely. Do you really want my impressions of Singapore?"

"Oh, please. I am all ears."

Holden cleared his throat. "Well then, from the very beginning: The name Singapore comes from the Sanskrit words *Singa Pura*: Lion City. Some call it the Sea Lion City, because the unofficial logo is a lion with a fish's tale, something like a mermaid. There is a fountain-statue in a park along the harbor of this animal, officially called the Merlion, but everyone calls it the Sea Lion. For whatever reason, the Malay people regard the Sea Lion statue as a symbol of Malay ownership of the territory." He hitched himself up in his seat.

Barbara nodded to encourage him, so he plunged on, feeling a little silly but warmed by her attention. "The first settlements on the island were probably founded by Malay traders around the thirteenth century. It was a haven for merchants and later pirates because of its good harbor and superb location astride the sea routes from India and Africa to the Spice Islands, China, and Japan." He looked at Barbara. She looked rapt, her chin resting in one hand while the other toyed with her glass. "Sir Stamford Raffles of the British East India Company arrived in 1819 and found a population of a hundred and fifty or so, nearly all Malays. As the port grew, the Chinese arrived in great numbers, attracted by the riches of the trade. The Malays still regard the Chinese as temporary residents; intruders, even. Malays regard themselves as Sons of the Soil—*Bumi-Putra*, in their language—yet the Chinese dominate the commerce of Singapore as well as its politics."

"Are the Chinese a majority?"

"Ethnic Chinese make up about seventy-five percent of the population, but that figure is misleading, for two reasons. First, because the Chinese go out of their way to make you forget their overwhelming numbers, largely to placate their Malay neighbors in both Malaysia and Indonesia. The national language of Singapore is Malay, although almost no non-Malay Singaporean speaks it. The flag is unmistakably Malay and Muslim. There are four official languages—English and Tamil in addition to Mandarin Chinese and Malay—but virtually all business is conducted in English or Chinese. Roughly fifteen percent of the population is Malay, some seven percent Indian, and the rest are the usual hodgepodge of other peoples you find in any great seaport." He stopped to sip his cooling coffee and then his Armagnac.

Barbara twirled her glass. Holden observed that she wasn't

drinking, and knew he shouldn't, but he was enjoying the light buzz. Barbara looked up, as though she had been taking mental notes and had just caught up. "You said there were two reasons why the figure of seventy-five percent for the Chinese population was deceiving?"

Chambers smiled. He had begun to suspect he was being patronized as the old China hand, but Barbara was evidently paying close attention. "Right. The Chinese community is far from monolithic. A major subgroup is the so-called Straits Chinese, who are, or were, British-oriented. They are English-speaking, often to the point of not speaking Mandarin well. Premier Lee is from a Straits Chinese family, as are most of the top business leaders and many senior officials of government. The rest of the ethnic Chinese population tends to look to Beijing for guidance, or in the case of a minority, Taipei. They have branches of clan societies from China, as well as the Tongs, the secret societies, just as we have here in Hong Kong."

Barbara nodded. Her face was set in serious concentration. "The government is controlled by the Chinese?"

"Lee But Yang has been prime minister since independence. His People's Action Party, which is officially multiracial but in fact dominated by Chinese, controls every seat in Parliament. The government is omnipresent, authoritarian, and paternalistic. Young men with hair the authorities consider too long may have it cut by police, but all social welfare and all government power flows through the party and the bureaucracy, so for a shopkeeper or a farmer or a property owner—even for a taxi driver—to speak against the party would be economic suicide."

"How does Lee justify all that control?"

Holden shrugged and sipped his Armagnac. "To the outside world, he speaks of the need for order in an ethnically divided, culturally diverse community. To Singaporeans, I suspect he doesn't have to justify it at all. Most Asian societies seem to require a strong father figure or tribal chief. The Confucian tradition remains very strong in China, Japan and Korea, and among ethnic Chinese populations throughout the region. Malaysia is a federation of hereditary rulers. Thailand has a turbulent multiparty system, but all under the king. No effective opposition exists in China, Taiwan, Korea, the Philippines, or Indonesia. Singapore probably comes closer to a functioning democracy than any country in East Asia with the exception of Japan, whose constitution was, after all, imposed by General MacArthur after World War II."

"But there is opposition?" she asked.

Holden shrugged and drank the last of his Armagnac. He was getting bored at playing schoolmaster, for all Barbara's flattering attention. "The opposition in Singapore is always described in the press, when it is mentioned at all, as 'divided and weak.' Lee tells foreign journalists he would like to see the emergence of a 'loyal opposition,' but he doesn't mean it."

"What about the communists?"

"Maybe one hundred, most of them closely watched by the police. They get a little support from over the Johor Causeway, from the Communist Party of Malaya. Mostly secondary-school students; no support among the economically active population."

"Are the communists Malays? What did you call them, Bumi-Putra?"

Holden shook his head. "Ethnic Chinese, as are the communists in Malaysia and Thailand."

"Why are the communists so few?" asked Barbara. "They seem to be active everywhere else in Asia."

Holden leaned back and smiled at Barbara. Just a kiss, nothing further, he thought. "Largely co-opted, twenty years ago. Premier Lee and the People's Action Party grew up in the Straits Chinese community. In the fifties and early sixties, communist influence was strong among the China-oriented Chinese, many of whom had come from China to work and had some vague idea of going back. The PAP moved close to the communists to gain influence and acceptance in the larger Chinese community. After independence, Lee broke with the communists, and the ones not already embraced by the PAP were driven out of the country. Lee is said to have 'ridden the tiger' of the communists, and then managed the more difficult maneuver of sliding off his back without being eaten."

"And there is no real Malay opposition?" she asked.

"They grumble. Recently Malaysian state television, which is seen in Singapore, has taken on a fundamentalist Muslim cant, and selling a lot of Malay pride. There is a substantial Chinese minority within Malaysia, and they tend to be the wealthy ones, so there is resentment. In Malaysia, Bumi Putras have all sorts of economic and social privileges conferred upon them that they don't get in Singapore. So the Malays in Singapore bitch a lot, but they stay because the better jobs are there."

Barbara shook her head. "It is hard to believe a developing country in modern Asia with absolute political stability. What about the Right?"

Holden spread his hands above the table, palms upward. "The PAP is the right, and the left, and the center. The party and the government are so pervasive as to be viewed as universal. There are no rival institutions. The army is small, well disciplined, and a creature of the bureaucracy. All religions are tolerated, so there are no militant priests or monks or mullahs. The education system is part of the bureaucracy. In fact, Singapore's biggest drawback from my own personal point of view is that it is so buttoned-up that it is excruciatingly dull.''

Barbara smiled. "My questions must seem dull as well.''

You could have got all this from two hours in a library, thought Holden, but what the hell. "I told you, I am glad to earn my lunch. And I could look at you all day.''

Barbara smiled slightly and looked away. Dumb remark, Holden, he thought to himself. Shouldn't drink so much at lunch. Barbara's expression took on its look of concentration again. "Just a couple more questions, then? Your impressions make the place seem familiar to me.''

"Of course.'' Forgiven, he thought.

"What about the police force? Is it as integrated into the PAP as everything else?''

"The police?'' Holden was taken aback. Perhaps she had already spent those hours in a library.

"I have been told the police are viewed with suspicion by the Chinese population.''

Holden looked at Barbara carefully, seeing intelligence in her large brown eyes, and for the first time, a cool hardness. "The police force was established by the British, and originally it had British senior officers and mostly Malay and Indian other ranks. It was viewed as a colonial force, and it was mistrusted by the Chinese especially, but in recent years efforts have been made to recruit Chinese, so I doubt much of the old suspicion still exists.'' But it is a damn good question for someone who has lived in Asia less than two months, he thought.

"Who controls the police? I mean, what member of the cabinet?''

"Abdul Raza, the Minister of Home Affairs.''

"Malay,'' said Barbara.

"Right. Probably the most influential Malay in the government. Barbara, what are you getting at?''

"Nothing specific. I told you, we want to do a bond for them. I will have to answer these sorts of questions all over Europe when we go to sell the issue.''

"Well, you will sure be ready! But I don't think the police could ever be used against the government or the party, especially since the army is three times as large, and much better equipped.''

"Good. As you know, stability is what sells to Eurobond buyers."

Holden looked at his watch: 3:15. "Barbara, this has been a truly wonderful lunch, and I have enjoyed showing off my little knowledge of Singaporean history and politics, but I had best be getting back for my four o'clock."

Once again she placed her hand on his arm. "Just a few more minutes. One more question."

Holden smiled. He turned his arm under her touch and found himself holding her hand. Her fingers felt cool and dry and perfectly smooth. He felt his own hand suddenly hot, and the heat ran through him and up to his face. He knew he must be flushing bright red, but Barbara appeared to take no notice in the soft, dim light of the restaurant. "Of course," he said, his voice cracking.

Barbara put the slightest pressure through her fingers into his slightly moist palm. "Richard tells me that many banks might not support an entry of Singapore into the Eurobond market, unless Singapore opens more of her own financial markets to them."

"That isn't likely to happen, but it shouldn't bother Richard. First New York has a full license."

"I know, along with First Chicago, Bank of America, and most of the British clearers."

"Right," said Holden, holding her hand like a fragile living thing, afraid the slightest pressure might frighten it away. "The rest of the major international banks have limited offshore banking branches. For most of us, these are useful in supporting our trade banking activities, especially the oil trade from Indonesia and Malaysia. We don't have a great deal of interest in the internal Singapore market, although most of us would take a full branch license if it were offered."

"What about the Imperial Bank of Hong Kong?"

"The Bank? Well, they want a full branch for sure, because of all the business flowing between their Chinese clients in Hong Kong and elsewhere and other clients in Singapore."

"Richard says they won't get a full license."

Holden grinned. "I am sure he whispers such advice into the ears of Elizabeth Sun at every opportunity."

Barbara picked up her brandy balloon, swirling the amber liquid. "Richard says the Prime Minister is opposed, that he fears the Bank with a full license would exercise too much power over the local financial markets."

"Well, he ought to be! The Bank dominates Hong Kong, even to the extent of issuing most of its currency. As Hong Kong

competes more fiercely with Singapore to be the banking, insurance, and communications center of Southeast Asia, Singapore
government would have to be bloody stupid to allow the Bank
that speaks with Hong Kong's voice to grow its power in Singapore's much smaller market."

Barbara smiled and sipped her Armagnac. "I wonder: Does
the Bank speak for Hong Kong, or vice versa?"

"You are learning quickly, Barbara. To those of us who live
in the shadows of the great Bank, it hardly seems to matter. But
the point is the same: Prime Minister Lee will never grant the
Bank a full license."

"Yet the Bank will pursue it?"

"Of course. Did you meet Chris Marston-Evans at Piggy and
Pamela's party last week?"

"I think so. Tall, pale man with long hair, rather effeminate
looking?"

"Just so. Chris is a director of Warrens' Limited, the merchant-
banking subsidiary of the Bank. I believe he is now working full-
time on trying to crack into Singapore."

"He must be frustrated."

"Indeed. Chris is intelligent and really quite clever, if not always
pleasant. He was looking forward to an assignment to New York
after the Mariner takeover was completed. He will want to show
some real progress in the Singapore matter to make sure he isn't
forgotten when the Bank finally gets Mariner."

Barbara looked calculating, and she ventured a tiny smile.
"Maybe he could bring Warrens' into my bond issue. Maybe the
Singapore government might see that as helpful."

He gave her hand a little squeeze and then released it. Starting
to slide out of the banquette, he said, "Anything is possible, but
I really must get back."

She slipped out the other end. "Yes, of course. I have kept
you much too long, but it has been so interesting and so helpful!"

Holden smiled. Anyone can be flattered by being asked questions to which he knows the answers, he thought. And I may be
flattered, young lady, but I know when I am being hustled.

She took his arm and they made their way down the broad,
carpeted stairway and through the lobby, which was now nearly
deserted. When they reached the curb, she waved to her driver,
waiting at the corner, and he ran off and reappeared moments
later, driving the dark-blue Mercedes into the curved driveway.
The doorman stepped to the car and opened the rear door.

"Do you have your car or can I give you a ride?" she asked,
turning close to him and still holding his arm.

"No, thanks. I'll catch the ferry. I need the walk and the air to shake off that lovely Armagnac."

She reached up with her other arm and caught him around his neck, drew him to her, and kissed him on the mouth. Caught completely by surprise, he almost drew back. Being kissed by someone else's wife on the steps of the Peninsula Hotel was indiscreet even by Hong Kong standards. He felt her tongue move quickly inside his mouth, and then it was over and she released him.

"Thank you so much, Holden," she said, backing away and sliding into the rear of the car. He stood rooted to the spot. He glanced at the doorman, who held the door open, expecting him to follow her into the car. The doorman's eyes seemed focused on a spot a thousand yards behind Holden's left shoulder. She reached out and pulled at the door, and the doorman closed it. She wound down the window and leaned out, and he managed an awkward step to the side of the car.

"Let's get together when I get back. Have lunch, I mean," she said quietly.

"Of course," he rasped. The car started forward and he waved, then regained sufficient control of his body to begin the short walk back to the Star Ferry.

13

Hong Kong and Singapore, 13 May, 1980

BARBARA DID A LOT of thinking on the three-and-a-half-hour flight to Singapore. The seat next to her in the first-class section of the Singapore Airlines 747 was vacant, and she had spread out her worksheets on the structure of pricing and trading on the Eurobond market, choosing carefully the points to stress to make the strongest possible first impression on Elizabeth Sun. She managed to concentrate until lunch was served: a collage of shrimp and seafood, served by pretty, attentive girls in batik *sarong kebayas*—clinging blue skirts and loose, brightly patterned overblouses. After lunch, Barbara found herself staring out the window at the coast of Vietnam far below, sipping champagne and thinking of Holden Chambers.

The man was a puzzle. Bright, sexy, powerful, and yet strangely vulnerable. She knew how difficult many men, even those who had superb confidence and presence with their male peers, found dealing with women in the business. Any man who told you he could deal with a woman exactly as he would with a man in the same position was a fool—as was any woman who expected such would be the case. Barbara had learned well how easily men and women could misread signals. If anything, she thought the men had the harder time of it, especially if the woman were also junior to the man. How *should* he act? Protective? Gallant? Those two impulses usually led to condescension. Should he embarrass a woman by noticing her efforts to look her best or hurt her feelings by ignoring them?

Barbara was pleased that she had gotten Holden Chambers's attention, although she felt she had been clumsy and obvious at times. She didn't mind flattering a man to get him to help her, but she rarely flirted. Since she had been married she had never flirted with any man the way she had with Holden. She fretted at her motives. She knew she was good at the business, and she would have felt better if she had dazzled him with her command of the bond markets, but what bothered her more was that she didn't really know how she felt about him. In the business, everybody hustled everybody else, and it was easy to convince oneself that a self-serving action was genuine and vice versa. She knew she was hustling Holden, but did she want more than access to his power? Did he want her, or was he just being kind? Or did he simply dismiss her professional ambitions as of no consequence in the male-dominated market, perhaps more amused by her earnestness than attracted by her shameless advances? She frowned again, gathered up the papers on the seat beside her, rearranged them, and packed them carefully in her briefcase. The plane began its descent toward the old Paya Lebar Airport. She smiled at the thought that the bond she sought might be used to fund construction of the new international airport at Changi, now a year away from completion.

I really don't have the experience for this high-stakes game, she thought. In London and New York she had had the support and the protection of powerful male colleagues; in Asia she was alone, and no one cared to see her succeed. The fact that all those men expected her to do nothing, or fall on her face if she tried, might buy her a little time, but if she got her mandate to do a bond issue, she would have to convince the men, and especially the Lions, that she *could* succeed. Only then would they help her. She shuddered, suddenly afraid. It would be so easy just to go through the motions at the office and just to be Mrs. Richard van Courtland at the Ladies' Recreation Club. Mightn't that be wiser? Mightn't such a course allow her a little time to find herself and her place in the game? But no, she thought, setting her jaw. I want to be as good as they are, and better. And if I wait, I will lose my novelty factor, and *they* will forget I exist.

The plane touched down with a shuddering thump and taxied toward the terminal. Barbara gathered her briefcase and her hand luggage and was first off the plane when it nosed up to the gate.

At ten o'clock the following morning, Barbara was ushered into the offices of the Executive Vice-President of the Monetary Authority of Singapore, located in the brand-new black-glass CPF Building in Robinson Road. The office was long and narrow, and as Barbara marched the length of it toward a large desk backed by a window filled with the sun's glare, she could barely see the woman who rose to meet her. The woman was talking on the telephone in rapid Chinese, and a man stood beside her, apparently taking notes. The woman smiled at Barbara and waved her toward a group of soft chairs, making a gesture that Barbara took to mean the conversation was nearly over. Once seated, Barbara could see Elizabeth Sun clearly, and she took the last few moments of her telephone conversation to study the woman who was said to control all of Singapore's dealings in international finance.

Elizabeth Sun was about Barbara's height, and she was thin, even for a Chinese, with a graceful curve to her hips and small, rounded breasts. Barbara guessed her age at about forty. Elizabeth wore a dress of heavy silk, a pattern of gray and iridescent green. Barbara recognized the dress by its exquisite style and fit: She was sure it had come from one of the best shops on the Rue du Faubourg Saint-Honoré. Barbara respected a woman who wore good clothes well; her own white linen dress and indeed most of her clothes came from the same fashionable shopping street in Paris.

Barbara stood up as Elizabeth put the phone down with a clatter and moved around her desk. They shook hands briefly, and Elizabeth ushered Barbara to a narrow couch. Barbara sat and Elizabeth sat next to her, chatting rapidly, saying she hoped Barbara would find her stay in Singapore interesting and amusing. Barbara found Elizabeth's manner feminine and strangely intimate. Elizabeth's assistant, a grinning Chinese man with bad skin and greasy hair, introduced as Raymond Lo, fluttered about, trying to decide where he should sit, until Elizabeth pointedly told him to go and see about tea for "my guest." Barbara did not know why Elizabeth had thus decided to see her alone, but she thought it a good omen.

The Chinese woman opened a carved silver box on the coffee table in front of the couch and offered cigarettes to Barbara. Barbara refused with thanks, and Elizabeth immediately extracted a cigarette with long, laquered fingernails. It was a swift movement, almost as though she had snatched it. She lit it impatiently with a silver Ronson table lighter. The thick smoke smelled strongly of cloves.

"*Kretak*," said Elizabeth, watching Barbara's expression. "Clove cigarettes from Indonesia. I hope the smoke does not bother you."

"No, Elizabeth—may I call you Elizabeth?"

"Of course," said Elizabeth Sun, patting Barbara on her knee while inhaling deeply of the pungent smoke. "We are going to be friends, Barbara."

Elizabeth continued to chat while tea was brought and set before them by a Malay man in a blue uniform buttoned to the neck. The tea was yellowish green, served in tiny porcelain cups with gold-leaf rims and handles. Barbara tasted hers; it was luke-warm and nearly flavorless, but it had a faint jasmine scent.

Elizabeth continued to lead the conversation, asking Barbara how she liked living in Hong Kong, what she had seen of Singapore, etc. She occasionally asked a question about Barbara's personal life, which seemed embarrassingly intimate. When did she plan to have children? Was she happy in her marriage? In all, Elizabeth's questions were not unlike the conversation of the women she had met in Hong Kong. Barbara had expected to be patronized as a wife and a housewife by Hong Kong's bores, but to hear the same thing from the first prominent and successful woman she had met in Asia surprised and puzzled her.

Suddenly she realized it shouldn't. Elizabeth Sun's world was no less male dominated for her own singular success. Elizabeth was used to dealing with men as equals, and probably had no reason to believe that another woman could be equal with men just because she herself had become so. Barbara's spirits fell as Elizabeth chattered on about the wonderful shopping on Orchard Road. She knew that in Asia a guest does not turn a conversation to business before the host, but she decided to take a chance, rather than lose the entire half-hour she had been granted in small-talk. Elizabeth leaned forward to stub out her cigarette and immediately snatched another from the box and lit it. Barbara took advantage of the break in Elizabeth's patter to speak.

"Elizabeth, forgive me, but I know your time is precious. Could we perhaps discuss a bit of the MAS's plans for entering the foreign capital markets?"

Elizabeth took a deep drag on the clove cigarette, which glowed and crackled in her fingers. She smiled slightly and studied her guest. Her amusing, animated chatter ended abruptly. Barbara noticed that every time she brought the cigarette to her lips, her pointed pink tongue darted out to meet it. The effect—along with the quickness of her movements, the shimmering green-and-gray dress, and the flat black expressionlessness of her eyes, was faintly reptilian. Barbara remembered stories of the Green Bamboo Snake of Southeast Asia, whose bite was fatal in a matter of minutes. God, say *something*, thought Barbara.

Elizabeth continued to smoke vigorously, filling the room with the sweet, nauseating smoke. She nodded, as though she had reached an affirmative decision. "I was testing you, of course. I shouldn't do that." Her face became softer. Without her brittle intensity she was austerely pretty.

"I, well, I think I understand that, Elizabeth."

"All the American banks send a female calling officer to see me at some point. Usually some bright young thing from Marketing or some other staff department. I find that patronizing." Her tone was not unfriendly.

Of course you do, thought Barbara, angered nonetheless. American banks used to send black officers to African countries until they found out the Africans held American blacks in contempt because they came from the tribes the stronger tribes now governing African countries had previously enslaved and sold.

"What in particular are you interested in, in respect of our funding plans, Barbara?" asked Elizabeth softly, lighting yet another cigarette.

Go for it, thought Barbara. You have been told this is your only shot. "We believe Roland, Archer has very strong placing power in the European markets, especially for a fixed-rate debt."

"As strong as the commercial banks?"

"In some important respects stronger. The commercial banks prefer to underwrite floating-rate notes, because if they don't sell them—and they usually don't—they can carry the notes on their own books and fund them just like a floating-rate loan. The investment banks are set up for true distribution of bonds and, frankly, do a better job of it. If we have to hold an issue, it goes directly against our capital; we can't buy cheap deposits like the banks can."

Elizabeth smiled. "You are aware that several commercial banks have asked us for a mandate for a Eurobond issue?"

"Yes, I am." Leave it at that, thought Barbara. If Holden gave me the right information, I also know why you turned it down.

"Why would we be better off with you than with one of them, or a group of them?"

Carefully, now. "First, distribution. We will see to it that the bonds are placed in the hands of genuine investors, not held in portfolio by the underwriters. You need your big commercial banks' credit for trade finance, and for both public- and private-sector projects. If they do an issue and then hold it, their ability to fund the republic's other needs will be reduced." Barbara tapped her left palm with the first two fingers of her right hand, emphasizing the point. Elizabeth nodded slowly and smoked.

"Second, with the right underwriting group and the right presentation, we will raise an important amount of money, which will reflect the economic and political success and stability of—"

"How much would you try to raise?" Elizabeth interrupted, quickly. She put out the cigarette and did not light another.

"I would have to go into that with my colleagues at Roland,

Archer Limited in London, to discuss timing, actual distribution, other issues on the calendar—"

"Roughly," smiled Elizabeth. "As you Americans say, ballpark."

Barbara paused as if to consider. She had her number in mind, but she wanted to sound like the market mover and not like a messenger from London. "Certainly one hundred." She paused to see if interest showed on Elizabeth's face. It hadn't. "Possibly as much as one-fifty."

Elizabeth cocked her head. "Two hundred?"

Barbara almost choked. "Is that the amount that would get the deal?"

Elizabeth shrugged. "It is a matter of face—prestige, if you will. European agencies—and not all of the first rank—raise two hundred, even more."

Barbara nodded. She knew that two Italian state agencies had issues larger than two hundred in the works. "Let me try."

Elizabeth gave a tiny nod and reached for the cigarette box. She plucked up another *kretak* and the heavy lighter, seemed to measure them together. She sat silent for what seemed like minutes, then slowly lit the cigarette and put the lighter down. "Barbara, I want to think about this. Of course I know of your bank, and I know how big it is and how many issues it has done, but it has done little in Asia. The question I am going to ask you when next I see you is how much of Roland, Archer's capital would be behind such an issue, should my government decide to launch one."

"Of course. Our underwriting commitment will be spelled out in our formal offer, as soon as you tell me you will entertain it. May I make an appointment to spell out an offer, say in two weeks?" Too soon, thought Barbara. Too pushy. "Or whenever you might feel ready—"

"Tomorrow." Elizabeth rose swiftly to her feet, smoothing the silk dress across her thighs. Barbara rose and shook the extended hand. "Not a full offer—just an underwriting commitment, rough terms, selling strategy." Elizabeth jerked her wrist to her face and looked at a watch. "Right now I am late for a meeting with some very stupid bankers from Germany. Can you return tomorrow, say at four o'clock?"

"Of course! I am in Singapore to do business with the MAS. I am at your complete disposal." And not to go bloody shopping, thought Barbara, elated at Elizabeth's interest.

Elizabeth smiled and escorted Barbara to the door of her office. "Excellent, Barbara. I have enjoyed meeting you so much."

"I have enjoyed meeting you too, Elizabeth. I hope we can do some business."

"Exactly. Until four o'clock tomorrow, then."

Barbara flew out of the CPF building and hailed a taxi. "Shangri-La Hotel, Orange Grove Road," she said as she slid into the back seat, pushing her briefcase in front of her.

"Reeght away, ma'am," said the very black Indian driver as he guided the new pale-blue Datsun into the heavy traffic.

Barbara sat back, feeling the heat wash over her. Her heart tripped with exhilaration as her mind raced. I have a real shot at a mandate! She knew she had to call Nigel Cross, her managing director in London, as soon as they opened, early evening Singapore time. She had to get his approval for a major underwriting commitment from Roland. Two-hundred million was a small, almost trivial commitment amount for Roland in the U.S. market, but it was a large offering for any borrower in the straight, or fixed-rate, Eurobond market, and certainly a very aggressive number for a brand-new and non-European borrower. The risk to Roland, Archer in making a major underwriting commitment for a new name was that investors used to the tried and true might shy away, and the issue could sit on the underwriter's books, tying up capital and reducing profit. Singapore was a long way from Sweden, a triple-A rated issuer. Yet Singapore was stable, both its politics and its economics. Hong Kong was probably a stronger economy, but its future was clouded by the possibility, always in the background, that the government of China in Beijing might simply walk in and take it over. If Barbara was to make a name for herself and a place for Roland by doing a bond issue in Asia, she knew the borrower had to be Singapore.

Barbara left the taxi in front of the gaudy Shangri-La and raced to her room. She stripped off her dress and her underwear, stopping briefly to admire her body as she did so. Hands encircling her waist, she looked herself up and down in the full-length mirror on the wall. I feel sexy, she thought. Power is sexy. She touched herself between her legs, feeling the moisture. I am as smart as any of those male-chauvinist pigs, and now I have to prove I am as bold. That I have the balls, she thought, grinning at herself. She sat on the bed and spread her legs, still watching herself in the mirror. Her finger probed deeper, finding the smooth, slick pearl of her clitoris, circling it softly as it swelled. She pitched backward onto the bed, rubbing harder and touching her nipples with her other hand, pinching them as they grew hard. She raised her knees and began to breathe in sharp little barks, feeling her orgasm forming like a warm pool in her belly, then bursting throughout her body in a splash of heat. She bit the knuckles of her left hand and let out a stifled moan, then she put both hands in her soaking crotch and moaned aloud, the cry trailing off into delighted laughter. "I have the balls!" she shouted to the ceiling. She brought her hands to her lips and tasted her wetness, and again she laughed. For two minutes, she slept.

Barbara awoke with a start. The warm feeling of pleasure had subsided, and she felt sticky and cold in the hotel's air conditioning. She got up and went into the bathroom and turned on the shower. I am going to have to wash my hair, she thought, to get the stink of those awful cigarettes out. She stepped into the shower and lathered slowly, enjoying the flowery fragrance of the body shampoo. Her hands lingered in her sex, and again she felt the stirring of pleasure. Self-consciously she drew her hands away and rubbed shampoo into her long, thick hair.

Who am I going to get as comanagers for the underwriting? she thought. I should have a plan before I speak to Nigel. First New York was the biggest gun in the market but out of the question for Barbara. She knew Richard would scoff, and even if he had wanted in, she could not let the market think her deal needed her husband or his all-powerful bank to get done. She needed another big multinational. I wonder if Holden would come in? He would have to convince Traders Bank International in London. I wonder how much influence he has with TBI? And Europeans? If I could get a Brit or a Frog—best of all a Swiss! But how? Nobody stuck his neck out in the Euro-straight market. Two hundred million hadn't often been tried, even for first-tier European borrowers.

Barbara stepped from the shower, wrapped herself in one of the hotel's thick full-length towels, and bound her hair in a smaller one. She went back into the bedroom, smelling immediately the scent of her juices in the chill air. She picked up the linen dress and sniffed it, wrinkling her nose. I will have to get this dress cleaned to rid it of the sour clove smell of Elizabeth's cigarettes. She put the dress in a dry-cleaning bag, then picked up her bra and panties, and thrust them into a bag marked "laundry." No, she thought, the laundry will ruin these. She took her underwear out of the bag and tossed them into the bathroom sink, running cold water and adding a capful of shampoo.

She returned to the bedroom, discarding the towels and rubbing her hair. I'll set it later, she thought, dressing quickly in a sleeveless top and a short cotton skirt, both in a pale yellow. First, I'll go down to the terrace and have some lunch.

* * *

Barbara's sandals clicked on the marble floor of the lobby as she crossed to the terrace and asked for a table. Her wet hair felt cool on her shoulders. The captain seated her at a table by the window. She smiled at him and took the menu. I can do this, she thought, but I must be right at every turn.

"Madame would like a cocktail before lunch?" sighed the Malay waiter, his voice silky, unctuous.

"What champagne do you have?" said Barbara, feeling again the rush of power.

"I will bring the list." The waiter bowed low and scuttled away.

Barbara selected Veuve Cliquot Ponsardin. She realized as she tasted it that she wished Holden were with her. He would help me, she thought. He is Lion enough to help and ask nothing.

"Excuse me. Mrs. van Courtland, isn't it?"

Barbara looked up and saw a woman, vaguely familiar. Blond, young, pretty. Pink from a morning by the pool, she guessed. "I'm Barbara Ramsay. Richard van Courtland is my husband."

"You don't remember me. Celia Marston-Evans. We met at Piggy and Pamela's, about a week ago."

Barbara didn't remember. "Oh, yes, I'm sorry. One meets so many people so quickly." Barbara hoped her smile was friendly without being too inviting. "Won't you join me?" Please don't, she thought, I have thinking to do.

Celia seemed to hesitate, as though she didn't really want to sit down, but felt she should. "Well, for a moment, if it is no trouble. I've just finished lunch myself, but I wouldn't mind a glass of that lovely champers." She sat across from Barbara, and the hovering waiter brought another glass and filled it.

The two women smiled and clinked glasses. They realized they had nothing to say to each other, and so each felt pressed to speak. Celia said, "Are you here with your husband?"

"No," said Barbara. "I am here on business. Richard is in Hong Kong—no, I think he might be in Tokyo." Why do I go out of my way to make it sound like I don't care? she thought. "His business and mine are totally separate, of course."

"Well, la!" said Celia with a little giggle. "So you get to travel all on your own! That must be fun!"

"Well, it is business," said Barbara, feeling defensive. Why do I have to justify myself as a legitimate business person, especially to this girlish twit? The male chauvinists are getting to me, and I cannot let that happen, especially now. "But I do like the independent feel of traveling alone. What are you doing in Singapore?"

Celia seemed to frown for a moment, then she smiled brightly. "Oh, I am here with my husband. Chris Marston-Evans, he is a director of Warrens'; I think you met him at the same party."

Barbara remembered Chris: a tall, thin Englishman with exaggerated mannerisms and a sarcastic demeanor. The man Holden said was working on the application for the Bank's branch license for Singapore. Interesting. "Have you been here long?"

"A week. Singers is bloody boring for much more than that, I can tell you. Chris has been here off and on for weeks, mostly just hanging about various government offices. The Bank sent me down to cheer him up." Celia wrinkled her nose with exaggerated distaste.

What is that supposed to mean? wondered Barbara, irritated. Since it was obvious that this silly *wife* could not tell Barbara what Chris was really doing, Barbara wished she would be off. "So you will be returning to Hong Kong soon?"

"I am going back at the weekend. I have no idea how long Chris will stay, though he is as bored as I am." Celia put her glass down with a thud, nearly upsetting it, and stood. She seemed to sway a little, and Barbara realized she was drunk. "Oops," said Celia, touching the glass to steady it. "But I must leave you to enjoy your lunch. I am going to have a swim, and then do a bit of shopping." A thought seemed to come suddenly to Celia, and she smiled with genuine warmth. "But why don't you come with me? There are some delightful shops along the Orchard Road—marvelous clothes made of Indonesian batik, beautiful carvings—things you never see in glittery, plastic Hong Kong."

Barbara smiled automatically. "I have some work to do after lunch—but I'd like to go, for a little while, if that wouldn't inconvenience you."

"Oh no," smiled Celia. "I'd love to show you. We could go for just an hour; all the best shops are within an easy walk from the hotel."

"What time were you thinking—"

"Say around four? It will be a little cooler then." Celia picked Barbara's room key up off the table and read the number. "Shall I telephone your room around four?"

"That will be lovely." An hour's walk through the shops would be pleasant, thought Barbara, and Celia seems to want some company. An hour to unwind before I phone London with my plan, which I had better think about during lunch. She glanced at the menu and immediately summoned the waiter.

Barbara and Celia decided to take a taxi from the hotel to the market area near Cuppage Road and walk back toward the hotel.

They walked slowly in and out of shops and stalls selling everything from skewers of pungent, unidentifiable meat to tie-died
batiks, Chinese silks, gold, jewelry, leather goods, and ornate
Balinese and Javanese wood carvings. Large shopping malls al-
ternated with blocks of shabby shop-houses; two-story stucco
buildings painted in peeling pastel colors. Celia preferred the
shiny new malls, but Barbara liked the dark coolness of the
ground-floor shops in the houses. She supposed the people lived
upstairs.

"I suppose all these grotty shop-houses will be gone soon,"
said Celia.

I hope not, thought Barbara, examining a carved wooden Garuda, the half man, half eagle of Hindu mythology, offered by a
tiny Indian woman with many gold teeth. I hope Singapore has
the sense to preserve a bit of its past, even as Hong Kong did
not.

Celia chatted gaily, pointing to this attraction and that as crowds
of children, mostly offering food or chewing gum or flowers for
sale, but a few simply begging, tugged at their skirts. Barbara
hadn't really felt like shopping and was more interested in getting
a walk outside the hotel, but she bought a blouse of unbleached
silk Celia thought would look pretty, and a small, carved Buddha
which the hawker had insisted was jade and very old, and which
Barbara was quite sure was nephrite and very new. Barbara tried
a few tentative questions about Chris's business in Singapore, but
Celia grew silent and surly, so she gave it up. They had browsed
nearly two-thirds of the way along Orchard Road back to the
Shangri-La, to the vast, crowded Far East Shopping Centre, when
the sky grew very black and fat raindrops began to spatter in the
dust.

"Oh dear, we are going to get drenched!" said Celia.

"We had better get a taxi," said Barbara, glancing at her watch.
It was nearly five o'clock, Nigel Cross would be getting into his
office in London in half an hour.

"We'll be bloody lucky to find one now," said Celia, looking
along the crowded street. "With offices letting out, and the rain
coming. Look, let's make a dash for the Hilton. We might get a
cab, and if not, we can at least get a drink. These afternoon
showers never last long."

They ran toward the Hilton, just a few yards from the Far East
Shopping Centre. The sky seemed to get lower and blacker by
the moment, and lightning flashed thickly, reflected in the upper
windows of the taller buildings. By the time they reached the
driveway of the Hilton, the rain was falling in opaque, wind-blown
sheets, and they were quite wet. In front of the Hilton was a

queue of perhaps twenty people, and no taxis. The wind blew
rain and bits of palm fronds into the entryway of the hotel, scattering the queue momentarily.

"Oh, bugger it," said Celia, clutching her skirt and pushing her
wet hair out of her face as the wind moaned and the rain became
a solid curtain. "Let's get a drink. This will be over in a few
minutes, and then we can walk to the Shangri-La."

She led off toward the bar. Barbara glanced at her watch and
shrugged, and then followed.

With a flurry of hand signals, and a bit of what Barbara thought
overloud commands, Celia had a table and two gin slings organized in less than a minute. Celia took a gulp of hers, and Barbara
a tentative sip. Good, she thought. Smooth and strong.

"Do you recall Holden Chambers?" said Celia, smiling a bit
crookedly. "He was at the party where we met."

"Yes," said Barbara, holding her drink up to conceal her
expression. Why this, straight out of the blue? Or the black, she
thought wryly, watching the rain lash at the windows of the bar.
"The Managing Director of Traders Asia."

Celia lit a cigarette and waved the smoke away, and took another gulp of her drink. Barbara could see Celia was very agitated.
"Bother his employment! He is one of the Lions, and I could see
you and he had taken a great interest in each other."

"We talked," said Barbara dryly.

"Yes, I could *see* that!" Celia was nearly down to the bottom
of her drink, and she flagged a waiter and demanded two more.
Barbara started to protest, but thought better of it. Celia's face
was becoming flushed, and her eyes had taken on a narrow, cunning look. She leaned forward and whispered, much too loudly,
"Have you slept with him yet?"

Barbara was taken aback, not by the suggestion, but by such
a question from a woman she hardly knew. "Celia, I hardly
think—"

"Well," Celia interrupted. "If you haven't you will. I know
that look in dear Holden's eyes."

So this is the reason for our little shopping trip, so kindly
conducted by Celia. A bitch and a gossip, decided Barbara, and
therefore doubly dangerous. She took a long look at her watch
and reached for her purse. She put on her sweetest smile, sup-
pressing her anger. "Celia, this has been a lovely outing, but the
rain is letting up, and I have to make an urgent call."

Celia got up quickly, if a bit unsteadily, swallowing her second
drink whole. She threw some notes on the table and caught up
with Barbara. "Oh, don't be cross, Barbara. Come on, we'll run

back together. I have to dress for some dreary reception Chris is dragging me to at the MAS."

The mention of the MAS, *her* prize, froze Barbara for a split second. I wonder why I wasn't invited? Probably planned weeks ago, she thought. At least, I hope it was.

The two women walked rapidly up Orange Grove Road to the Shangri-La. The rain had lessened to showers, and the wind had gone, but by the time they reached the hotel, they were both soaked. Celia waved gaily as they separated at the lifts, apparently unaware or unconcerned that she had touched a nerve in her companion. There are so many people watching me, waiting for me to fail, thought Barbara, and I have no one to trust.

Barbara unlocked her room and stepped into the chilly interior. She stripped off her sodden clothes and took a two-minute hot shower. She called the hotel switchboard and booked her call to London, then wrapped herself in one of the huge towels and called room service for a pot of tea while she waited for the call to go through. The key to my underwriting group will be Traders Asia, she thought, and if that fails, the Imperial Bank of Hong Kong. Holden Chambers and Chris Marston-Evans. What the hell is this Celia playing at, in love with one, or so it seemed, and yet married to the other?

The phone jangled and she picked it up. "Your call to London is on, Madam," said the hotel operator.

14

Hong Kong, 14 May

MARYLIN WONG LEFT THE offices of Danger, Close and hurried up Ice House Street to Des Voeux Road Central, where she boarded a westbound tram to Wan Chai. The old double-decked trams were rickety and slow, but in busy times like the middle of the day they were less vulnerable to traffic jams than the busses. May-Ling was using her lunch hour to buy the fresh supplies she would need to cook the special dinner she had promised Holden Chambers. She had planned a simple meal by Cantonese standards: steamed fish and shark's fin soup. Holden's servant, Ah King, wanted to learn the two dishes since her master so enjoyed them, but she was originally from a village just west of Beijing, where the cooking was entirely different. Ah King would cook and May-Ling would offer meek suggestions; everyone's face would be preserved.

And Holden will get a bloody good meal, thought May-Ling with a grin as she dropped off the clanging tram on Hennessy Road in the heart of Wan Chai. Most of the ingredients she needed could be purchased in the narrow streets and alleys which laced the square described by Hennessy and Lockhart Roads and Stewart and Fleming Streets. Some of the alleys were so narrow that the awnings shading the fragrant tiny stalls of produce and meats and fish and poultry met overhead, giving the streets a twilight quality in the middle of the day. The press of people was complete; it wasn't possible to move through the crowd without touching and being touched, and the smells of bodies and breath mingled with the sharp odors of spices and fish and soy and oil in the damp heat. May-Ling moved through the alleys at an unhurried pace, discussing quality and bargaining for price as she added one small parcel after another to the two plastic shopping bags she had brought with her from her office.

I'm at home here, she thought, considering a musk melon for dessert and then putting it back on the pile to the anguished wail

of the tiny crone in black pajamas minding the stall. This was
China as it had always been, or at least until the communists took
power: rich and fragrant, boisterous and loud. Perhaps I should
bring Holden here, she thought, stepping over a skinny yellow
dog sleeping partially beneath a stand that supported a precarious
pile of durian fruit. But no, she thought. He would see only a
dark, smelly place too crowded for him to move through, too
claustrophobic for him to breathe. To him, she mused, this is an
Asia for servants and coolies and hawkers and even thieves. This
was Hong Kong for Ah King and never for him.

And probably not for me if I lived with him. She looked into
the next alley.

Different alleys or parts of alleys were reserved to different
kinds of products. May-Ling bought special long-grain rice from
an ancient Hakka woman with a sunny smile punctuated by only
two teeth in one alley, fresh scallions, leeks, snow peas, and
bamboo shoots in another. In the next she bought spices: red-
pepper oil, garlic, sage, thyme, coriander, and several more she
knew no English names for. In the same alley with the spice sellers
were the stalls of the dried-food sellers, who sold dried mushrooms, fungus, and other delicacies, and shark's fin. All the wares
were displayed in large jars, and there were four or even five
grades of shark's fin in some stalls. She stopped at several stalls
and started several arguments before she found the right one.
She selected small, whitish fins—not the highest grade, which she
would have needed to make her own favorite dish, red-cooked
shark's fin—but good. Red-cooked shark's fin was a dish of great
delicacy, but Ah King could not master it in one try, and the best
fins could cost HK$ 400 per catty: a waste for soup. Ah King
would spend much of the afternoon soaking and pounding the
fins, and then she would begin the first of several steamings in
wine, ginger, and green onion. Any shark's fin dish took a lot of
time and effort.

The next alley over was the fishmongers'. The fish, all from
local waters, were of every size and hue, packed in shaved ice.
There were also crabs, small and large shrimps, and giant scallops
from the Taiwan Straits. Each stall was shaded by special low
awnings of black crepe that May-Ling had to duck under to examine the catch. She wanted a snapper or one of the fine-grained
white fish known by the Portuguese name of *garoupa*. She bought
some scallops to steam with the fish but couldn't find the main
dish itself. None of the fish was fresh enough. She knew they
would be all right for baking or frying, but for steaming, the fish
had to be absolutely fresh, caught the same day. Holden liked

his fish steamed and so did she. She would have to go to the fresh-fish market in Sheung Wan, all the way back across Central. She looked at her watch and saw that more than half of her lunch hour had already gone, so she walked to Lockhart Road and hailed a taxi.

The fish market in Sheung Wan was housed in one vast concrete building, cool and with tile floors wet from constant washing. As in the market in Wan Chai, each stall was operated by an individual owner. The variety was as staggering as the din with which the fish were being offered. As May-Ling's taxi stopped, carts and lorries and even bicycles were being unloaded with baskets of fish just in from the docks. Many of the fish were still alive as the baskets were dumped into holding tanks with circulation pumps.

May-Ling left her purchases in the taxi, curtly telling the driver to wait and promising him a five-dollar tip. The driver threw up his hands and said, "Aye, yah," the universal Cantonese wail of frustration. She dashed inside, wondering if Holden would have left his briefcase in a taxi like that; or, if he did, whether the taxi would still be there when he returned. All the rules were different for Chinese and *gwai-lo*, the foreign devils. How would she find a bridge if she stayed with Holden, even married him? Chairman Mao Zedong had once said the only possible combination of communism and capitalism was capitalism; a single taint of capitalism would destroy communism utterly. Was that Holden's idea of Asia and even of May-Ling? The girl could look Chinese, but must she eventually learn to live as a European?

May-Ling found a perfect *garoupa* in the fourth stall. She forced its mouth open and sniffed inside. The stall owner smiled his approval. The fish was perfectly fresh. The man weighed the fish: three catties, just under two kilograms; plenty for May-Ling and Holden and plenty more for Ah King to savor in the kitchen. May-Ling rushed out and jumped into her taxi and gave him Chambers's address in Mid-levels. The driver grunted and started off through the crowded streets. May-Ling looked at her watch. She had only five minutes left of her lunch hour and hoped the other girl in her office, Emily Wu, wouldn't be cross with her when she returned.

When the taxi reached Chambers's block on Magazine Gap Road, May-Ling once again told the driver to wait. She gathered her bundles and raced to the lift, ignoring the stream of colorful Cantonese invective from the driver. Ah King met her at the door of the flat, clapping and giggling happily, and took the packages. May-Ling spent only a few minutes instructing Ah King on the preparations to be begun and once again hurried out into the taxi. The driver complained bitterly as he drove back down to the road. Cantonese love to complain, thought May-Ling, tuning him out. This man is bloody lucky to get a long fare at midday.

She sat back as the driver droned on. She was tired and hot and would be twenty minutes late by the time she reached her office. With the food and the taxi together, she had spent close to a day's pay and all of her lunch hour with nothing to eat. A Chinese man would cherish her for producing such a meal, but would Holden?

It didn't matter, she thought, as she paid the driver outside St. George's Building and rode the lift to the offices of Danger, Close. She was famished already and would enjoy the meal immensely.

When Chambers unlocked the door to his flat and stepped inside, he found his *amah* standing in the hall, holding the telephone. She looked at him and grinned, showing the two gold teeth of which she was so proud. She held the telephone in both hands and shouted at it merrily.

"No hang! No hang! Masta here now! Masta come home!" She held the phone out to him, shaking it emphatically and bobbing up and down, as near to jumping for joy as a fifty-year-old woman plump from her own good cooking could.

Holden shrugged out of his suit jacket and handed it to Ah King. May-Ling emerged from the kitchen, wiping her hands on a cloth. He remembered that she had promised to teach Ah King her Shanghainese recipe for shark's fin soup tonight. He waved away the offered phone and pushed gently past Ah King to kiss May-Ling. Ah King giggled and followed, still holding the magic instrument at arms' length.

"I will take the call in the living room, Ah King," he said. "Wait until I pick it up, please."

"Masta! Long distance!" She pronounced it "wrong distance." Like as not it was, he thought sourly.

He fell into his leather easy chair, swung his legs up onto the ottoman, and picked up the receiver on the coffee table. Ah King hung up the phone in the hall with a crash and fled into the kitchen, still giggling. "Hello?" he said, hearing the hiss of the overseas connection.

"Where the hell have you been? And why did it take two minutes after your *amah* announced your presence before you deigned to pick up the phone?" David Weiss's voice dripped sarcasm.

Chambers closed his eyes and kneaded his temples with his

fingertips. May-Ling placed a tall scotch and soda and a box of cigarettes on the coffee table, and then touched his forehead lightly. He glanced at his watch: eight o'clock—seven A.M. in New York. "David, good morning. You are moving early."

"I'm in London, asshole. And I would like an answer to my previous questions."

What a world-class prick, thought Holden. Authority balanced upon insecurity. "Well, David, let's see: I left the office around six and then I played squash for an hour. As to your second question, I entered my apartment, took off my jacket, and then, I sat down. Sorry!" He lilted the last word with mock contrition. Not smart, he thought. I have no doubt the bastard is standing up to yell at me; he always did, whether in person or over the phone. And doubtless he expects me to take his call standing at attention like a good Prussian *leutnant*. Weiss had spent a few years in the army as a helicopter pilot and considered himself a warrior, though he had never left Germany, despite the warriors' proving ground of Vietnam having been readily available at the time. Holden took a swig of the whiskey and soda and grinned at May-Ling, who had seated herself across the living room and was sipping a cup of tea.

"Very funny, smartass. While you have been playing squash, or more likely drinking champagne at Traders's expense, Frank Portas here has received a very curious call from his opposite number at Roland, Archer Limited: one Nigel Cross." Weiss's voice became muffled. "Frank, we finally located the Prince of Asia. Could you pick up, please?"

Holden thought of Frank Portas, the East Londoner who had risen far above his working-class roots to become head of Securities Trading at TBI. Portas was cocky and pushy, qualities often essential to success in the rough-and-tumble world of high-stakes securities trading. Chambers admired Portas's balls and his market savvy but found him abrasive and often rude. Portas, in turn, thought Chambers pompous and overly cautious. The two men had exchanged these views during a drunken lunch at Jimmy's Kitchen, just up the road from Traders Asia's offices, during Portas's only visit to Hong Kong just over a year before. The end result of the lunch was that they agreed they detested each other but that they were bound together in alliance by their mutual contempt for their common boss, David Weiss. Once the alliance had been drunk, they were both surprised to find many things to like about each other, and Portas always entertained Chambers in his home on Chambers's frequent trips to London.

"Good day, mate," said Portas, broadening his Cockney accent for Chambers's benefit.

"Good morning, Frank. How is Anne?" Anne was Portas's bawdy, buxom wife, easily the funniest woman Chambers had ever known.

"Never better, mate. She misses you, of course!"

"Give her my love."

"Yeah, fine, guys," Weiss broke in. "Perhaps we could get to the point of this jolly little chat."

"Okay," said Portas. Chambers smiled, and he bet Portas was smiling if Weiss couldn't see him. Weiss hated chitchat unless it was his own.

"Please tell Chambers of your discussion with Nigel Cross," said Weiss, plainly growing impatient.

"Oh, right," said Portas. "Nigel runs bond underwriting and trading over at RAL. Says he had a call from a bird who works for him out there, name of—shit, where'd I put that note?"

"Barbara Ramsay," supplied Holden.

"Sounds right. Anyway, seems she is angling for the elusive Euro-straight mandate from the Republic of Singapore, and she mentioned your name as a potential comanager."

Holden kept silent. He knew that if he replied, Weiss would start an argument that could last an hour. Better to wait for Weiss to spell out which apology he wanted, then get on to the shark's fin. Perhaps ten seconds passed with no sound except the hissing background noise.

"Well, Chambers?" bellowed Weiss. "Did you or didn't you agree to work with Roland, Archer on a straight bond for Singapore?"

This shouldn't take long, thought Holden, thankfully. "Of course not, David," he said, trying to sound serene and reasonable. "First, Roland, Archer haven't a mandate, and I doubt they will get one, though they may be aggressive on terms and especially amount." He thought back to his lunch with Barbara Ramsay. What else did I tell her to do? What else would she have told Nigel Cross? "Second, Roland, Archer have not asked us to participate in a potential deal, nor have we asked to be invited into one." Technically correct, he thought, remembering Barbara's offer at lunch. The deal could only be offered from London.

"Then why would she single Traders Asia out as her top candidate?" asked Portas.

Holden grinned. "Well, Frank, Traders Asia is big in this marketplace," he said gently. That was for Weiss. Traders Asia was a top player in Hong Kong and Asia, far more influential than TBI in London or, for that matter, Traders Bank and Trust in New York. Weiss hated to be reminded of Traders Asia's success since he had no way to claim credit for it, having devoted all his attention to the European network, most of which lost money. Chambers knew Portas had fed him a fat pitch. Portas didn't give a shit about rankings: TBI's trading operations were hugely profitable, and he was fast becoming a rich man.

"Yeah," Weiss's voice came over the line carrying a sneer. "I am glad you are such a fucking big gun. Tell him what else your pal said, Portas."

Portas continued with the same tone of amusement in his voice. "Well, the bird asked Nigel if you had influence here at TBI, Holden. Whether you could convince us here to support the bond issue for Singapore."

"I just finished telling you there is nothing to support," said Chambers warily.

"Yeah," said Weiss. "Good boy. Very smart, keep it up. As far as your influence here, if I had taken the call, I'd have told this guy you didn't have squat."

"Very kind, as always, David," said Holden, seething within. Weiss delighted in taking one subordinate down in front of another. Which is what made him loved, thought Chambers, calming himself.

"Don't worry, lad," said Portas. "I lied. I told him you were a first-rate chap and all that."

Holden grinned, his sense of humor returning. Weiss had often played his two subordinates off against each other, fomenting their previous animosity. He didn't likely know of their rapprochement and would therefore completely misinterpret Portas's remark.

"Yeah," grunted Weiss. "Anyway, listen up, Chambers. Eurobonds are outside your jurisdiction. You don't know dick about the fixed-rate market. So if something does come up, you call it in to Frank here and don't even bother to attach your opinion. Clear?"

"*Jawohl, Herr Leutnant*," said Chambers cheerfully.

"I was a *hauptmann*, asshole. If you want to play German, at least get that right. And another thing, before we end this tedious conversation, I don't like hearing about deals in Asia, especially deals with Traders's name attached, howsoever tenuously, from Roland, Archer!"

Nor do I, thought Chambers, resolving to have a talk with Barbara when next he saw her. How nice I have an excuse to call her, he thought. "Point taken, Chief. Consider me properly chastised."

Frank Portas snorted. Weiss's voice went low with menace. "Just keep up the good work, asshole." The connection clicked and died.

Chambers looked at the silent phone in disbelief. How could *anyone* be so rude? How could anyone so rude have become an executive vice-president of a major bank? He put the phone into its cradle and stood, picking up his drink. Why do I take this shit? he wondered. Maybe I should just walk out and come roaring back at Weiss from a safe seat at First Chicago or Wells Fargo; give him the battle he wants. But this is my goddamn bank!

He looked around the living room of his apartment. He liked the flat. It was big, but not fancy, as were the generally newer dwellings on the Peak and in Pok Fu Lam. The master bedroom and bath were near the front door, with the kitchen and servant's quarters across the hall. Two smaller bedrooms and a bath were at the other end of the flat. In between was one great room, fully twenty-five feet by thirty-five. A balcony and glass sliding doors ran the entire width of the north wall facing Victoria Harbour.

The room was furnished simply, with groups of rattan chairs and couches with beige cotton-covered cushions and plain teak end and coffee tables. The couch upon which May-Ling sat, sipping tea and watching him unwind, was backed by an antique tapestry, green and brown and other earth colors, a fanciful jungle full of wild birds and beasts that he had inherited from his grandmother. Chinese vases made into large lamps provided soft light, and rich dark-patterned Persian rugs on the light-colored parquet floor added warmth. On the high ceiling, wood-bladed fans with brass fittings pushed the air-conditioned air around.

May-Ling caught his eye and smiled at him. He smiled back and nodded. She knew to let him ease off by himself when he was upset, and she knew calls from overseas frequently left him upset.

The south side of the room contained the dining area, with its table and chairs and sideboard of plain rubbed teak. He reflected that it had been difficult to get plain furniture; the local cabinet-makers couldn't understand how a piece could be "finished" without carved dragons. Next to the dining area was his "library"— the easy chair, in which he sat, and a bookshelf containing his stereo components as well as books. The library was separated from the dining area by a planter containing a huge and strange plant, so heavy it needed support from a network of bamboo sticks, which had been in the apartment when he had first rented it. It wasn't pretty, but it made a good divider.

Damn! he thought, breathing deeply and trying to regain his shattered harmony. I like this room! And I like my life, and my friends, and May-Ling, and even moody old Ah King with her penguin shape and her appropriately old-fashioned black-and-white uniform. I like my job, and I do it well. So why does my boss, the supposed beneficiary of my well-publicized and immensely profitable successes, give me nothing but shit?

Maybe the game is turning bad, he thought. Maybe it is time to move on; maybe Weiss *will* destroy me, just because he can, and even though it would hurt the bank.

He closed his eyes tightly and continued to breathe deeply. He clenched his fists and pounded the padded arms of the chair softly. Fuck him, he thought.

May-Ling touched his forehead with her smooth, dry hands, then reached and took one of his fists in both her hands. "The shark's fin is ready when you are, Holden," she said.

He jumped up and kissed her, feeling the tension of his conversation with London vanish. "I am looking forward to it, love." He rang the silver bell that had been his mother's, and Ah King burst from the kitchen, bearing the bowl of fragrant soup and giggling happily.

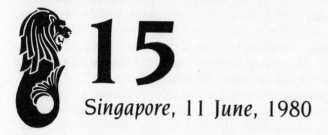

15

Singapore, 11 June, 1980

YUSEF RAZA, FULLY ACCEPTED by his new neighbors as Mahmoud Assad, marveled at the tiny enclave of merriment and frivolity in the middle of strict, stodgy Singapore that was Bugis Street. Yusef had never been to Bugis before fleeing from Malaysia a month before; it was not the sort of place a Muslim boy of good family ever went, but he knew the history. Bugis Street had been the street of the transvestites, the girl-boys who strutted and preened in the wall-to-wall bars and nightclubs and made homosexual assignations with sailors from the port, businessmen from the city, and rich old Chinese merchants. The height of the street had been in the late sixties and early seventies, when absolutely anything could be had in the crazy nightclubs with names like the Zanzibar, the Harem-Harem, the Black Rose, and the Pussy Cat. Later, when the People's Action Party and the puritanical Prime Minister Lee But Yang had consolidated their power, the homosexuals and other kinkies had been driven at least partly underground. Homosexuality had been proscribed in Singapore under the Public Morals Act of 1977 and did not officially exist. Of the riotous clubs that had existed in the two-block-long fleshpot that was Bugis Street but four remained: two at either end of the street, which were visited by gawking American tourists in loud polyester clothes, balding or blue haired and who arrived by tour bus, and by slim young men from Europe, especially Germany, who always traveled in pairs. The smaller nightclubs that remained sold colorful drinks in enormous glasses at exorbitant prices, and each had one or two tame girl-boys dressed like improbable tropical birds lounging in the shadows, paid to titillate the curious. Bugis Street had not been entirely suppressed by the stern eye of Prime Minister Lee and the PAP, but it had grown shabby.

The Club New Malacca, to which Yusef had gone his first night on the run and where he still lived, had never been one of the famous dives on the strip, and though the bar upstairs still did a pretty brisk business, the restaurant downstairs had evolved into something of a low-priced coffeehouse, frequented mostly by students in the Malay-stream schools and their young teachers. The men sat together in small groups or pairs and discussed politics, usually of a violent radical bent. Yusef had been thrilled at first by the talk; it was so much more activist than the tame manifestoes of the Malay Students' League in Kuala Lumpur. After a week, though, Yusef realized that the talk could afford to be more radical because while the MSL in Kuala Lumpur had little chance of changing the society around them, these *bumi* nationalists in Singapore had none at all.

The leading citizen of the New Malacca was the man Elias the MSL had told Yusef to contact. At first Yusef had thought Elias owned the place; his every gesture seemed to possess his surroundings. Yusef learned that Elias had some job or other in government and was in fact desperately poor, since he spent every penny he got on his elaborate wardrobe. Elias was as close to being openly gay as a Muslim Malay could be and still live in the community. He was rumored to have several lovers, all Europeans in the city. He was a tall man with clear brown skin stretched over fine high cheekbones. His liquid brown eyes were enormous, and his mouth was full lipped and feminine. His body was as painfully thin as a fashion model's, and his hair was long and permanently waved. He dressed like a peacock, in skintight trousers of satin or leather, invariably black, black soft-leather riding boots, and silk blouses with huge sleeves in flamboyant colors from rose to indigo, always open to show off his smooth, muscular chest. He had no beard, and Yusef had once seen him plucking the hairs out of his chin with tweezers in the squalid toilet they all shared. Yusef thought Elias was the most exotic, most beautiful human being he had ever seen.

Yusef stayed hidden inside the New Malacca for his first week there while Elias and others watched for police pursuit. There was always a police car at either end of the Bugis Street enclave, but that was routine: puritan Singapore's *cordon sanitaire* around the tiny bohemian community. No police other than routine patrols entered Bugis Street, and the patroling officers, who knew all the regulars, made no inquiries. At the end of the week, Yusef ventured out and began to explore his surroundings, and even to teach at the Alsagoff School, though he never ventured outside the Arab Quarter. Yusef had survived a month undetected in the midst of his father's police state, and he felt proud of himself for that. He also felt he was learning about life and about the shallowness of the Malay fulminations, which after many repetitions sounded like so much useless bitching. Yusef realized his life needed more than Malay pride and endless conversation. At the end of his first month in Singapore, Yusef was becoming bored.

On the evening of June 11, Yusef returned to the New Malacca to find a small party being organized. One of the regulars, Saddam—no one used last names in the New Malacca—a proctor at one of the Malay schools, had seized some hashish from a student and brought it to the club. Sweetened tea was supplied by the club, and the hash was cooked in bowls of a primitive water pipe fashioned from a wine jug and tubes and plugs boosted from the chemistry lab of Saddam's school. Yusef, who had never tried hash or any other drug, was a little frightened, but the camaraderie of the others infected him and he joined in, taking first short tokes and then, when he realized the others were watching him, deeper draws. The smoke, even when cooled through the lemon water of the hookah, felt harsh in his throat, but after a short while he felt the delicious release of the drug and became more relaxed than he had in any moment since his mother had died. Elias sat close to him on a broken couch with a stained cover and whispered to him as he passed the mouthpiece of the pipe. Elias's hands touched him lightly, on Yusef's cheeks and arms and then his thighs. Yusef thought little of this as he smoked and giggled; Malay men touched each other during conversation as a matter of course. The first plug of hash dissolved, and Saddam prepared another.

Yusef drifted through the evening with no awareness of passing time. The young men talked and argued and smoked and giggled. Elias swooped and danced around the gathering, flashing brilliant in his flowing azure blouse and a new gold necklace, which he said was a gift from a new friend. Enormous wink. Yusef coughed from the raw smoke and sucked down the weak tea. His head floated and soon his bladder did, too. He disengaged Elias's hand from his thigh and struggled up from the couch and made his way to the gents'. Elias got up and followed him.

Once he was standing and walking, Yusef's head began to clear rapidly. He pushed open the door of a stall and aimed a stream of piss into the bowl. Elias pressed into the same stall beside him and began to piss as well, playing his stream through Yusef's and giggling shrilly at the mess the spray made. Yusef grinned at his friend as Elias put his arm around the younger man's shoulders. The two finished pissing at the same time, and Yusef began to button up his flies. Elias pulled him close and kissed him on the mouth. At the same time he pushed Yusef's hand away and cupped and caressed his genitals. Yusef was aware of Elias's scent, sweat, smoke, and an overpowering sweet cologne he always wore. Elias kissed his neck and mouth. Yusef was surprised but not repelled. Neither was he attracted, and he pushed Elias away and backed quickly out of the stall, buttoning his trousers hurriedly.

"Mahmoud, darling, don't you like Elias?" the other man whined.

"I do. Of course I do, but I am not . . . like that."

"Like what?" said Elias archly. "Queer? But you are, my sweet. You are too pretty to be otherwise." Elias moved quickly to embrace Yusef. "Let me teach you what you are."

Yusef backed away, his hands in front of him. "But I'm not, Elias," he said, and as he said it, Yusef realized for the first time in his life that he was sure that it was true. "I like you, Elias, but I'm not gay."

Elias tossed his hair and pouted. "You are, my sweet Mahmoud, and one day you will recognize that and then you will beg me to love you." He whirled and stalked out of the toilet.

Yusef went to the sink and washed his face and hands. He grinned at himself in the mirror, because he now knew what he had previously only hoped. He *wasn't* gay, and he never would be. He wanted to shout it from the rooftops or, better yet, go to his father and tell him. He wasn't gay!

Yusef Raza began to think about going home.

II
SOUTHWEST MONSOON
The Heat and the Rains
of Summer

16

Singapore, 4 July, 1980

BARBARA RAMSAY GOT OUT of the taxi in front of the C.P.F. building on Robinson Road, which housed the Monetary Authority of Singapore. It was nine-thirty in the morning, and already the heat and humidity had become suffocating. She pulled at the neck of her sleeveless cotton blouse to free it from her back where it had become stuck from perspiration. She felt sticky and dirty, only an hour after stepping from the shower in her room in the Mandarin Hotel on Orchard Road. Perspiration dripped under her arms and between her breasts. A tiny rain shower burst from the low, black clouds above, just enough to plaster her hair to her forehead. She pushed her hair back angrily as she mounted the steps to the building.

God, I hate this city, she thought, and yet today could be payday. Almost two months of gentle pushing and pulling, trying to get the go-ahead from Elizabeth, whose interest in the Eurobond seemed to surge at some times and then suddenly vanish at others. Two months in this crowded, gritty sauna of a city.

She carried in her briefcase the third version of the offer telex from Roland, Archer Limited for the Eurobond offering. She had sat in her room until two in the morning, discussing with London the final changes to the offer, which Elizabeth had requested the past two days. Barbara had gotten Nigel Cross and his boss, Philip Meyer, the chairman of RAL, to agree to all the changes Elizabeth wanted, but Meyer had stood firm that the offer should be made for $120 million, to be expanded only as comanagers were brought on board. Barbara knew the mandate would be awarded immediately if they went in at $200 million firm, but Meyer had overruled both Barbara and Nigel Cross. Meyer, a stuffy Englishman of the old school, distrusted all foreigners, especially foreigners who had once been British subjects and who had the gall to give up Britain's benign guidance. He probably thinks doing a bond for a bunch of wogs is foolish at best, she thought as she waited in a queue for the lift in the hot, crowded lobby. If I lose this deal because Singapore government holds out for the $200 million I originally mentioned as *possible*, Meyer will probably be relieved.

Barbara pressed into the lift car with at least forty sweating people, all colors from white to black in all sorts of costumes. The liquid heat and the smells of sweat and dirt and breath from bad stomachs was nearly overpowering. Barbara tried to breathe as shallowly as possible, clutching her briefcase to her breasts to avoid being touched up by the grinning, strong-smelling Indian who had turned around in the crowded car to stare at her. When the doors finally popped open on the fifteenth floor, she pushed past the Indian with a muttered "excuse me" and was rewarded with a pinch on her ass, which caused her to leap out. She lashed back at the Indian with her briefcase, which struck the door of the lift as it closed, prompting giggles from the other passengers.

I have to pull myself together before I see Elizabeth, she thought. She had gotten to know Elizabeth's secretary, Mary Lim, quite well, because her boss usually ran behind schedule, and so Barbara had often talked to Mary while she waited. Making friends with secretaries of important people was always a good practice, but Barbara genuinely liked the bright, earnest, and very plain girl who guarded access to the Executive Vice-President of the MAS.

Barbara found Mary on the phone and set the heavy briefcase on her desk. Mary said something rapidly into the phone in Chinese, then set it down and smiled at Barbara.

"Good morning, Mrs. Ramsay. Miss Sun and Raymond are waiting for you."

"God," said Barbara. "I know I am late. The traffic was awful, Mary, but I need to freshen up first."

Mary rose, taking the key to the senior-ladies' washroom from her top drawer. "Of course. You know where the ladies' is? I will explain to Miss Sun."

"Thanks, Mary, you're a friend in need. Keep my briefcase, please?"

Barbara raced to the washroom and locked herself into one of the cubicles. She stripped off her blouse and her bra, and washed her face and dried her torso with a damp towel. The cool water felt delicious, and she felt her calm returning. I have to do this exactly right, she thought. I won't get another inch from Meyer. In fact, if I ask again, he is likely to walk away from the offer entirely, leaving me with nothing. I must make this sound to Elizabeth like the best offer possible.

Offering the full $200 million was the key. Elizabeth had not pushed on the interest rate, a slight but important premium over EEC country issues, nor, more important, on the underwriting and management fees. The deal was priced just above what was going in Europe, and Roland, Archer stood to make a handsome profit if it were successful. Barbara wished she could have lined up her comanagers for a full underwrite of $200 million, but timing and the need for secrecy had made that impossible. The beauty would be to go to the pompous pricks who ran the merchant-banking houses in Hong Kong and even in London, with a mandate in hand for the deal everyone wanted, and well priced at that. She would get her comanagers, if she could just get the bloody mandate!

Barbara dressed quickly and reapplied her makeup. She brushed her damp hair, which still looked limp but better. She picked up her purse and half walked, half ran back down the hall. Mary rose, handed her the briefcase, and led her to the familiar corner office.

"Barbara, how nice to see you! I understand you were delayed in traffic." Elizabeth rose from behind her desk and crossed the room to take both of her guest's hands. Barbara put the briefcase down quickly and accepted the handshake, aware of the dampness of her hands against the cool, papery dryness of Elizabeth's. Raymond Lo rose from his chair in front of his superior's desk and bobbed his head, his oily face shining in the overhead fluorescent lights. "Please sit down," said Elizabeth. "Mary will bring tea."

Barbara picked up the briefcase and sat in the low couch. She opened the case and withdrew the offer telex, covered by a blue folder printed boldly with the Roland, Archer logo, a running bull, and placed it on the table. Elizabeth sat next to her on the couch, taking no apparent notice of the folder. Raymond pulled his chair to the opposite side of the table and sat down. Mary Lim entered with a tray bearing three cups of Chinese tea, placed them on the table, and withdrew. Barbara felt breathless and hot, despite her quick washup.

"Barbara, I know you like to get right to business," said Elizabeth, smiling and lighting a cigarette. "Did you have a chance to discuss with London the changes we requested in your offer?"

Barbara smiled. Holden had told her to expect her overseas calls to be monitored, and the line had clicked throughout her conversation with Cross and Meyer. She also had no doubt that the telex operator at the Mandarin had passed a copy of the offer telex to the police, if not directly to an agent of the MAS, which was why the telex in her briefcase had blanks where the critical numbers—interest rate, fees, and, most critically, amount of the offer—should have been. She had received the numbers in a very short coded telex, which would make no sense to unauthorized readers. "I had a long and fruitful conversation with the chairman of Roland, Archer Limited, Elizabeth. I have here a revised telex, which takes into account your concerns about distribution of the bonds, as well as the legal questions of sovereign immunity and consent to English law and jurisdiction." She opened the folder and handed the six-foot-long telex to Elizabeth, who immediately passed it to her assistant without a glance. Raymond began to scan the telex rapidly while Elizabeth abruptly squashed out her cigarette and lit another. "I think," Barbara continued, fighting down her nerves, "we have a very fine offer for your first Eurobond, Elizabeth."

Elizabeth nodded but said nothing, continuing to suck in lungfuls of the clove-laced tobacco, while glancing sideways at her assistant, who was nearing the end of the telex. His head nodded slowly as he read the legal changes.

"The numbers are left out," he said. "Why is that?"

"The final offer will be sent directly from Roland, Archer Limited to you, by tested telex," said Barbara. "This is a draft for discussion purposes, to be sure we agree on all the boilerplate. Since it was sent to me through the telex at the Mandarin, the numbers were left out, lest they become public. You may also note that the name of the MAS does not appear."

"But you will tell us, Barbara? The only matter on which we had not agreed was the amount of the issue," said Elizabeth.

Barbara felt her pulse quicken. *We are going straight to the hard sell.* She had hoped to warm up with a discussion of the legal points, but Roland, Archer had agreed to all the changes requested by the MAS. "RAL will underwrite the issue to one hundred and twenty million dollars," she said with as confident a smile as she could manage.

Raymond frowned and put the telex on the table. Elizabeth's expression did not change. "We think, Barbara, that two hundred million is really the minimum the government would consider," said Elizabeth, exhaling a cloud of smoke. Her tone was not unfriendly, but it was firm.

"Of course, we want the issue to be finished at two hundred also, Elizabeth, and by underwriting three-fifths of the issue, we are very sure we can get the full amount done," said Barbara, smiling into Elizabeth's opaque black eyes.

"Wouldn't Roland, Archer make more money if they committed for the entire amount?" asked Elizabeth, a hint of shrewdness in her voice.

"Yes," admitted Barbara. No point denying it. "But two hundred million is a large issue for a straight bond; there are few issuers in Europe who could issue as much. London feels that the issue will be best received by comanagers if we can offer them an opportunity to underwrite in the truest sense. If we make a bit less that way but assure a success, we will be happy."

"Perhaps you should get commitments from other managers and make us a joint offer for the full amount," said Raymond, smiling and showing his bad teeth.

"There are several reasons why we don't want to do that," said Barbara gently but firmly, holding eye contact with Elizabeth. "First, if we talk to others without having your mandate, we open the terms and conditions to discussion amongst the banks, and we might not be able to meet all of your objectives as to structure, price, et cetera. Second, a commitment we could get without a mandate from you would not be as firm; banks could find excuses to back out right up until the joint mandate was awarded. If we show a firm deal, already agreed by you, comanagers' commitments will be firm. Third, and perhaps most important, the deal would be public knowledge and subject to public comment; if we had trouble, for any reason, in getting the underwriting commitments, the deal could fail. With your mandate for one hundred and twenty million firm, we can approach the market with a done deal, one your friends in the banking community could support with little risk to themselves." And fourth, she thought, if we have to go to the established Asian banks without a mandate, we would have to share the fees a lot more generously than we intend.

Elizabeth nodded slowly, seemingly sympathetic. Raymond tapped the telex in front of him with a stubby finger. "I assure you we understand your points," he said, an edge of sarcasm in his voice. "However, should the government insist that we have an offer, fully underwritten, of not less than two hundred million, would Roland, Archer be willing to attempt to form a group and bring it to us?"

Barbara felt she could see the door inching shut. Elizabeth and Raymond are playing good cop, bad cop. If that suggestion had come from Elizabeth, Barbara would have believed the government had indeed taken the position Raymond suggested. Time for balls, thought Barbara, and for the first time she looked directly at Raymond. I have to protect Elizabeth's face, she thought, liking her growing savvy; give Elizabeth the chance to overrule her subordinate. "I honestly don't know, Raymond. I think possibly not. You see, we don't set these conditions up just to benefit ourselves. Roland, Archer Limited consider themselves experts in handling Eurobond issues and in making them successful. We are losers, perhaps more than you, if a deal flops, which is why we stress broad distribution. We honestly believe the structure we suggest is the best for the deal and for Singapore." And Mom and apple pie, she thought, favoring first Raymond and then Elizabeth with a smile at once confident and humble. If only that clubby Englishman Meyer had a little more guts, I would have my deal, she thought, grinding her teeth. Come on, Elizabeth, give me a sign!

Elizabeth stubbed out her cigarette with one of her rapid movements, scattering ashes and a still-glowing clove on the surface of the table. "I think we understand your position, Barbara." Abruptly she smiled. "Roland, Archer Limited have a very articulate spokeswoman; I hope they appreciate that. We certainly appreciate how hard you have worked to bring us this offer, and we are confident you will continue to work for us if we can agree on the final package." She rose, straightening her pearl-gray linen skirt and tucking in her white silk blouse. Barbara stood up quickly. Raymond continued to loll in his chair, lumpish and unattractive. He must be a whiz with numbers, thought Barbara. Why else would Elizabeth keep him around?

Elizabeth snatched a look at her watch. "I have to see the minister in ten minutes. We will review the matter and explain your position. If he wishes, he will discuss the matter with the Prime Minister. In any event, I will call you at your hotel this afternoon. Perhaps you could arrange to be available for a meeting with me at about four?"

"Of course, Elizabeth."

"Your London people will be in their offices later, should there be a need for further discussion?" asked Elizabeth, escorting Barbara to the office door.

"Yes. They expect me to call at their opening. With good news, we all hope."

"Of course. So do we. I will call later, then. Have a pleasant day, Barbara. By now you should know Singapore fairly well."

"I will. I have a lunch date, and then I think I will visit the old Arab quarter."

"Good. The Sultan Mosque is quite beautiful. Until later, then, Barbara."

Barbara waved to Mary Lim and hurried out of the building. Now the wait, she thought. But I presented that well; I know I did.

Barbara took a cab to the old colonial Raffles Hotel on Bras Basah Road, on the edge of the old Arab quarter. She walked through the courtyard toward the bar, once again feeling the damp heat. The weather had risen, and there were patches of blue sky among the clouds being driven by a strong southwest wind.

The bar of the colonial-era hotel had twenty-foot-high ceilings and slow-moving ceiling fans. Open to the courtyard on one side and to the lobby on the other, the room seemed airy if seedy and run down. The furniture consisted of simple wooden tables and chairs, and the bar itself filled an entire wall, backed by a tall, tarnished mirror. Barbara swept the room with her gaze, and smiled when she spotted the broad back of a man seated at a corner table. He wore a light-gray suit of silk linen, and his Panama rested on the table in front of his tall glass. As she approached, she could see he was reading the morning *Straits Times*. "Hello, Holden," she said.

Holden Chambers jumped to his feet and pulled out the chair opposite. Ignoring the chair, she placed her hands on his shoulders and kissed him lightly on the mouth. She felt a thrill; she wanted to feel the rush of power that came from her feelings of her morning meeting with the MAS and share it with him, but she knew she could not. He in turn took her into his arms and kissed her, holding her tightly. She pushed him away but gently.

"I am glad I located you," he said huskily. "I am glad you could come to lunch."

She backed away from him and sat down. "Am I forgiven, then, for telling my London that you might be a comanager of the Sing bond?"

He nodded. "Lesson learned." A waiter appeared, and Holden asked her if she would like to try a *stengah*, the traditional gin drink of the old Federated Malay States under the British Raj. She didn't ordinarily drink gin, but she smiled and nodded her head.

She is lovely, thought Holden.

I feel sexy, she thought. It's the power, the feeling of balls. I am going to get the mandate, I just know it! I would like to get a room in this old hotel and drag this Lion of Hong Kong into it and fuck him senseless. Despite herself, she giggled at the thought.

He smiled, enjoying her evident good humor. "Successful trip this time?"

She was bursting to tell him how close she thought she was to the mandate, but held herself back. It was bad luck to talk about it until the issue was final. "I think so, Holden. You know how it is with governments—everything takes forever. I think I have developed a good working relationship with Elizabeth Sun, but there are all the people behind her, people I never see, so I can't tell what they are thinking."

"I think Elizabeth pretty much decides," he said as the *stengahs* arrived. "Cheers." They touched glasses. Either she is very glad to see me, he thought, noting how her eyes shone, or she is not telling all.

"Cheers," said Barbara, and she tasted the tall, iced drink. Tart, she thought; good. She looked at Holden, admiring his clear blue eyes and strong regular features. He was leaning forward, and the muscles of his shoulders and arms bulged smoothly beneath the thin material of his beautifully cut jacket. A handsome man, she thought. Sexy in his powers. Maybe we should get a room and spend the afternoon in bed together. I am sure it would be more interesting than some dusty old mosque.

He saw the color rise in her cheeks and blamed the strong drink. "Best drink that slowly, Barbara," he said, reaching across the table to cover her hand with his.

She turned her hand over, gripped his, and squeezed it. "Oh, Holden, I am so tired of this hot, dreary, dull city! But I do think I am making progress toward a mandate—really I do."

So it isn't just my boyish charm, he thought, liking the way she held his hand. "Well, I hope you get it. You have spent most of the summer down here hustling."

She frowned. "I know. I guess I have missed a lot in Hong Kong."

"Sailing parties, pool parties, long lunches with me," he said lightly.

She nodded and giggled. "At least we have lunch today." And then? she thought and blushed again. And then the Sultan Mosque, she thought firmly. "Let's order."

The kitchen at the Raffles offered traditional English colonial fare. He suggested the Mulligitawny soup, followed by the saddle of roast lamb. She agreed and watched in silence as he discussed with the waiter how the lamb should be cut. Holden then ordered a Margaux, a Chateau Cantenac-Brown.

As lunch progressed, she found herself telling him more and more about her negotiations with the MAS, more than she had intended. He seemed politely interested but asked few questions.

Instead he was thinking how strongly he was attracted to her. There is something different about her, he mused, an unusual combination of vulnerability and great strength. But she couldn't have picked a more unlikely or a more difficult deal to try, especially as a brand-new player.

Elizabeth Sun had flirted with every bank and investment house that ever called on her, wanting to do something special, to make Singapore stand out as the financial center of Asia: safer than Hong Kong, more accessible than Tokyo. But she always wanted a bit more than the market would buy. She could do that, because Singapore did not really need to import capital at the government level. It was a game; she knew it and the Lions knew it. Someday Elizabeth might strike a deal that they all could support, and then the right group would do her deal, and everybody would say nice things and nobody would make or lose any money. Barbara—and indeed Roland, Archer, coming from the outside and not having the all-important feel for Asia—might reach for the prize and overreach. There is no moment so lonely in a merchant-banker's life, he thought, as the moment just after he wins an oversized mandate and before he gets his first commitment from someone real who will take some of the paper off his hands. A Singapore straight bond was one of the region's brass rings, and the sole winner of a deal on Elizabeth Sun's terms might be lonely a long time.

Halfway through the soup course she decided he must be bored. Her first feeling was anger: He is patronizing me; he doesn't think I can do it either. Anger faded into amusement. I will show them *all*, beginning with this handsome, sexy king of beasts. "Holden, I am sorry to burden you with all the details. I just haven't had anyone I could talk with about all this."

He sighed with mock sympathy. "It's a lonely job, that of the intrepid deal-maker."

She flushed, embarrassed. "You think I am becoming obsessed."

"No. Or maybe yes, but we all do when we work on an important deal. But it is just a deal, Barbara, and you can't get so into it that you will be more than professionally disappointed if it doesn't get done." His smile was friendly and concerned.

"It's my first deal in Asia," she replied, tasting the lamb, which was excellent and juicy. He always knew what would be good, wherever he had taken her.

"And you picked a very tough deal to do. You know—and doubtless Elizabeth has reminded you—that many good houses have tried for that mandate, and it has never been awarded."

"I know." Barbara smiled and reached out and patted his hand. "But I had you as a coach. You told me what would work, remember?"

"That is kind, Barbara, but even so, don't let this business get too deep inside you."

"Fine." Barbara nodded vigorously, closing the subject. "Let's talk about you, then. What are you doing here in Singapore?''

He dabbed his lips with his napkin and took a sip of wine, holding his glass to the light and admiring the rich color. Nice, the Brown, he thought. Didn't see it often in Asia. "I have been in Jakarta for four days, seeing Garuda Airways about financing their next three DC-10s. I stopped by to talk to our branch people here, and I will go back to Hong Kong in the morning."

"That's it? Just a visit to your branch?"

"Well, and to have lunch with a friendly competitor."

She felt a twinge of excitement. Maybe we should get a room! "Are you busy this afternoon? We could—see something of the city or something." Would I really do it? she asked herself, once again feeling the color rise in her cheeks. I don't much care for Richard anymore, but I have never been unfaithful.

He smiled broadly. "I would like nothing better than to spend the afternoon with you, but I have been asked to call on a friend of yours."

"Who?"

"Elizabeth Sun."

She felt her smile freeze and her naughty mood evaporate. "How did that come up?"

"A call to the branch. Just before I left to come here. You know how Singapore government keeps tabs on everyone of interest to them who enters and leaves the country. By the way, have you seen much of Chris Marston-Evans? He seems to have spent most of early summer here as well."

"No," said Barbara. She did not want to talk about Marston-Evans. She saw no reason to mention she had abandoned the Shangri-La for the Mandarin at least partly to avoid the man and his strange, clinging wife.

"Hm," said Holden, noting her change of mood. "I ran into him on Collyer Quay this morning. Seems he has been summoned to see Elizabeth right after me."

This has to be about my deal! she thought. "Holden, it is just possible Elizabeth may . . . refer to the negotiations we have been having about the bond issue."

He leaned back and sipped his wine, once again admiring its color in the glass. "Are you getting close, then, Barbara? Very close?"

He looks smug, she thought, fighting anger. What has Elizabeth told him? She thought again of the gap between the $200 million Elizabeth wanted and the $120 million Roland, Archer had on the table, and she gritted her teeth. "I think so. Look, Holden, you know I can't tell you everything, but if I do get that mandate,

Traders Asia will be the first bank I call." If Elizabeth doesn't invite him into the deal before I get the chance, she thought, fighting down a feeling of despair.

He grimaced, remembering the dressing-down he had gotten from David Weiss after Barbara had listed Traders as a probable supporter of the deal without telling him. "I have to say that my flexibility with respect to an offer from you has been somewhat reduced since you told your London you wanted us in."

Barbara took Holden's hand. She looked sad and anxious. "I am sorry about that. I did call you; I just didn't get through. That won't prevent you from coming in with Roland, will it?"

He looked at her, his expression pained. It might, he thought. Weiss would be waiting to stuff the deal right down his throat. But fuck it, I am still the Lion for Traders here in Asia, and I see no reason to show weakness to this beautiful, smart, skillful but still johnny-come-lately lady banker. "If the deal is good, Barbara, I will support it. Straight bonds are not my game, so I will have to enlist the support of my colleagues in London, but I will support it." And Frank Portas will go with me if there is profit enough, he thought.

She nodded slowly. "Please, Holden. You know how much this deal means to me."

"I just got through telling you," he replied sharply, "not to bet your entire self on any one deal."

"Please, Holden." Her hand squeezed his, and her dark-brown eyes begged.

He felt a desire that went way beyond sex. He wanted to hold her, to protect her. He waved at the waiter, who brought the bill immediately. "Barbara, please believe I will do what I can. Right now what I should do, for both our sakes, is not be late for my meeting with Elizabeth." He scribbled his name on the check without looking at it, and it was whisked away.

When they stood up, she embraced him. She thought he looked shaken, so she kissed him, more intimately than she had planned. He took her to the curb and handed her into a taxi, waving down the next one for himself.

"Holden?" she whispered. "Call me later, if you can?"

He smiled and touched her face lightly with his fingertips. "I'll try. I have a reception at the branch."

"Holden," she said, kissing his outstretched fingers, "big kiss!"

He backed away without speaking, and she directed the taxi to drive down Victoria Street toward the Sultan Mosque. What was Elizabeth's game? she thought, biting her lower lip and fighting back tears of frustration. What is she doing to my deal?

17

ELIZABETH SUN SPRAWLED ON the deep leather couch in the Finance Minister's office. She had just finished relating her conversations with Barbara Ramsay, Holden Chambers, and Chris Marston-Evans to her boss and the Prime Minister. The Finance Minister, Woo Mun Kwai, who was called Mickey by his friends and Monkey by his enemies, sat to her left in a low chair. The Prime Minister, Lee But Yang, sat at the Finance Minister's large teak desk. Woo, a portly, jolly Chinese, had asked several questions during her briefing and then, when she had finished, summed it up for the PM's benefit. Showing off, she thought without rancor. Where Singapore's dealings with foreign financial institutions were concerned, she was the boss and everyone in government knew it, including the Finance Minister and the PM.

Lee had sat perfectly erect and still throughout the briefing. He was a spare man, Straits Chinese, and his face showed his mixed Chinese and Malay ancestry. He was thin, with large, intelligent eyes, thin lips, a prominent nose, and slicked-back iron-gray hair. He had the air of being almost too perfectly groomed for this tropical climate. He wore a white linen suit with the jacket buttoned. His shirt was white as well, and his tie was blue silk with a small red figure. French cuffs with jade links surrounded his slender wrists. His hands, folded in front of him on the leather top of the minister's desk, were long, tapered, and well cared for. He had not uttered a word since entering the room and greeting his two advisers.

Elizabeth reached for her purse the fifth time since entering the room, then stopped herself. She wanted a cigarette badly, but she knew the PM hated cigarette smoking and rarely permitted it in his presence.

"Elizabeth, this bond issue," Lee began, choosing his words carefully, "has risks for us. Are you confident Roland's will succeed?"

Elizabeth leaned forward. She was now fully on stage before the only audience in government that mattered. "They have the capital to make it go, Prime Minister. They are clearly anxious to establish themselves in Asia. I believe for them a failure would be unthinkable." She paused; Lee sat as impassive as a statue. "We have their underwriting commitment of one hundred and twenty million U.S. dollars, far more than anyone else has offered, and more than we expected. I believe the Hong Kong houses will support the issue, if only because a straight bond is something they wish to show off to New York and London, to show they have come of age. The banks here will have to support the issue as soon as it appears to be successful."

The PM allowed himself a small smile. "And if Roland falters, I assume we have a plan of our own to avert an embarrassment?"

Elizabeth's throat cried out for nicotine. She fidgeted, shifting in the soft couch. "Yes, Prime Minister. That is why I sounded out the Imperial Bank of Hong Kong and Traders Asia. Holden Chambers is a man we can trust to tell us the truth—not out of altruism, but because he is so proud of his reputation as the grandest Lion in the marketplace. He told me a well-structured deal would be embraced in Hong Kong simply because they could not allow a new player to steal into their market. He is a very ambitious man with much face throughout the region, and I think he will be the first to join the deal, given his terms."

"Which are?" interjected the Finance Minister.

"A role. Not necessarily a major one; perhaps trusteeship. Roland, Archer will live with that as long as they run the book and appear first on the tombstone."

"What is a tombstone?" asked the PM.

"A formal advertisement of the deal, listing the underwriters and comanagers," she answered. "The way it is arranged indicates the pecking order of the managing banks."

"And the Imperial Bank of Hong Kong?" The Prime Minister's voice betrayed his distaste for the region's most powerful financial institution.

"I didn't even mention the bond to Marston-Evans, who is a thoroughly amoral man, guided only by his own mission to get a branch for the Bank here," she said. "I did tell him that his application was proceeding through channels—which, quite frankly, it isn't—and I mentioned that there might soon be an opportunity for the Bank to show, in a tangible way, its support for Singapore."

"You would ask us to give him his branch here in return for his support of this bond issue?" Lee asked quietly.

"I don't think it will come to that. Frankly, I would prefer to freeze him out. I don't want to grant that license just yet, although at some point we will have to. But it is insurance: If we need it, it could get the deal to the two hundred million we want." She sat back, feeling short of breath.

"So you think we should take Roland's offer," said the Finance Minister.

"Yes." She was quite firm. She knew Woo wanted to distance himself from the deal in case it didn't succeed. "Take the offer, but manage it ourselves, should the need arise. I like this American woman; I give her full marks for her knowledge of the structure and workings of the Eurobond market. She is, however, naive where Asian realities are concerned. I can work with her and, if need be, take control of the deal away from her. We will be protected." There, my dear Monkey, she thought, now it is mine to win or lose. I will have this office soon enough.

"Mickey?" said the PM softly.

Minister Woo shrugged, glad the lines had been drawn. "I think we should go with *Elizabeth's* plan, Prime Minister."

The PM grunted and studied his pale, hairless hands. "I concur. Elizabeth, please call the American woman and ask her to come here to receive our mandate."

"At once, Prime Minister." Elizabeth leapt to her feet and raced for the door, as glad to get outside and have a cigarette as to see her plan accepted.

Barbara sat in the darkness of her hotel room, staring dully out the rain-streaked window at the *son-et-lumière* provided by the violent thunderstorm, which lashed the potted palms on the small balcony into whirling dervishes. The window was cracked open, admitting the cool, damp, fresh-smelling air, and the air conditioning was turned off.

She brushed out her thick brown hair methodically, without thinking. Elizabeth had said she would call by four, and it was nearing five. Barbara's brain had ceased to torture her with all the ways the mandate she had sought for nearly three months could be snatched away from her, and she felt drained, numb. Holden was right, she thought bleakly. I should not invest so much of myself in one deal. But it is my only deal.

The telephone rang, shrill and urgent. The phone was across the room, on the table on the other side of the bed. Clad only in bra and panties, she dove onto the bed and snatched up the receiver. The first sound she heard was loud static, and she thought with dread, It's Nigel in London.

"Barbara? Are you there? It's Elizabeth Sun."

The static grew worse, and Barbara realized the storm was causing it. Her heart was bouncing around inside her chest like a frightened animal. She took a deep breath and tried to calm herself. "Elizabeth! How kind of you to call!" Her voice was breathless, almost strident. What an inane thing to say, she thought.

"I am sorry I didn't call earlier. My meeting with the minister took longer to organize than I expected. Barbara, I know it is late, and the weather is foul, but would it be possible for you to come to see me now?"

Barbara rolled off the bed, still clutching the phone. She touched the pale-green Shantung-silk dress that was hanging on the knob of the closet door, fresh from the hotel's cleaning plant. "Of course, Elizabeth! I will just throw something on and then try to find a taxi."

"You won't get a taxi in this rain, Barbara. A Finance Ministry car will be at the Mandarin in fifteen minutes. The driver will make himself known to the doorman, and he will wait if you need more time."

"No! Oh, thank you, Elizabeth! I will be ready when he gets here!"

"Good. I will be in my office. We will have much to discuss, Barbara."

"Yes, I—I hope so! Until then, Elizabeth."

"Until then." Elizabeth rang off.

Damn! thought Barbara, crossing to the bathroom in little hops, grinning and clapping her hands with glee. I've got it! I have the fucking mandate!

The ride to the MAS was slow. Most of the traffic was flowing out of the city, but the heavy rain had overwhelmed the oversized storm drains and there was much flooding. Barbara was impatient to see Elizabeth and get the news she had so long waited for, but she sat back in the comfortable seat of the government car, a large black Datsun with white cotton slipcovers and pleasant, efficient air conditioning, and savored the sights and sounds of Singapore's polyglot millions hurrying home in the driving rain. The dominant sound was the din of auto horns, softened by the rain and the rhythmic slap of the Datsun's windshield wipers. Workers from the central city passed by the car, some on foot and already drenched, some in taxis, which advanced at a crawl in the heavy traffic through hubcap-deep water, and many in scooters and trishaws, at least as wet as the pedestrians. The lights of the many stores and hotels along Orchard Road seemed softer and less garish in the rain than they had on clear nights, and Barbara realized she was beginning to feel at home in Singapore. She felt she had picked up at least a bit of the rhythm of the place, its heartbeat. She felt relaxed, sure of herself and ready to join the Lions of Hong Kong on their own ground as soon as she had her mandate.

The driver turned off Orchard Road into Bras Basah Street, passing the Raffles Hotel, where Barbara had met Holden Chambers for lunch four hours before. It seemed ages ago. The driver turned into the Nicoll Highway, then followed Connaught Drive across the Anderson Bridge, its double arches of wrought iron gleaming wetly as they passed under. Fullerton Road and Collyer Quay were nearly deserted, and the car proceeded swiftly into Shenton Way and around into Robinson Road and stopped in front of the CPF Building. The driver got out and opened a large black umbrella before opening the rear door and helping Barbara out. Barbara favored the slim Chinese with her most brilliant smile and thanked him. She strode toward the entrance of the building, swinging her briefcase in time with her long strides. The small Chinese scuttled along beside her, protecting her with the umbrella. Barbara savored every moment, every impression, and she recalled how she had pulled up to this very building early that morning in a hot, dirty taxi with her clothes sticking to her and her hair wet and blown.

The driver opened the door to the lobby for her and gave a little bow. Barbara thanked him again and went to the lift lobby. Mary Lim was waiting with the guard. She rushed forward when she saw Barbara, a smile of welcome on her pale, plain face, and guided her into a waiting lift. Barbara and Mary were the only passengers in the lift as it rose without stopping to the fifteenth floor. The doors opened, and Mary led off down the familiar corridor. Barbara followed, still swinging the briefcase and thinking of the contrasts with this morning's journey.

Elizabeth waited alone in her office. She rose as Barbara entered, stubbing out a cigarette. Barbara noted Elizabeth had changed her dress since the morning meeting; now she wore a dress of dark-blue linen, accented by an Hermes scarf tied around her slender waist.

Elizabeth greeted Barbara warmly and ushered her to her usual seat on the low couch before the glass coffee table. Elizabeth sat next to her, perched as usual on the very edge of the seat. She flipped up the lid of the cigarette box and grasped a cigarette, lighting it with her quick, jerky movements and inhaling deeply.

Barbara noted the cigarette was an English Silk Cut and not one of the awful *kretaks*.

"By evening, the clove cigarettes are too rough even for me," said Elizabeth, smiling, doing her mind-reading trick.

Barbara smiled back, unperturbed and perfectly content to wait for Elizabeth to come to the point. How different I feel from the first time I came into this room barely two months ago, she thought.

Elizabeth smoked, inhaling deeply and acting as though she had been deprived, lighting one cigarette from the end of the one before. She punctuated her smoking with blasts of rapid speech, talking of the worry of her job and the politics. After fifteen minutes, she became silent, as though her overwound motor had run down. Barbara felt sympathy for this powerful, driven woman and, for the first time, felt that they were more alike than different.

Elizabeth stubbed out her cigarette, stood up, and turned to her desk. She picked up a long sheet of paper, which Barbara recognized immediately as being the draft telex from RAL that she had brought in that morning. Barbara sat up straight, tingling with anticipation.

"Barbara," said Elizabeth softly, a conspiratorial tone in her husky voice, "I have convinced the cabinet to accept your proposal to do a Eurobond for us. It was not easy, but we have won."

Barbara stood up, clasping her hands in front of her breasts. "Elizabeth, I am so glad! I am sure we will have a great success—"

"Barbara, there will be a few minor conditions. Please sit down; relax. The Finance Minister is absolutely set on the notion that we must have two hundred million."

Barbara's heart flipped in her chest. "I am sure we will get there, Elizabeth."

The Chinese woman nodded. "So am I. But you must understand something. *We*—you and I—must have an agreement. The minister will approve my accepting your offer, which your London can send to me for my opening tomorrow, with all the numbers filled in." She dropped the draft telex on the coffee table, sat down, and took both of Barbara's hands in hers. "But if underwriting commitments totalling at least two hundred million are not secured, the Finance Minister may cancel the mandate before issue."

Barbara felt her smile freeze on her face. She forced herself to breathe deeply, conscious of the gentle kneading pressure of Elizabeth's hands on hers. "Elizabeth, surely—surely the minister understands that a mandate with an option to cancel the issue is not really a mandate?"

"Of course. The mandate we will give will be for one hundred and twenty million. But you must gather enough other banks to make the full two hundred before the bond can be issued."

Barbara nodded, her heart slowed. Philip will be furious. Suddenly she felt very cold, yet very powerful. I won't tell him. The decision thrilled and shocked her. This is what the Lions do, she thought. This is what *we* do. "I will get you the full two hundred, Elizabeth. But this condition remains just between us? It must."

"It will." Elizabeth released Barbara's hands and pressed the buzzer under the table. Mary Lim entered, listened to a burst of rapid-fire Chinese from her boss, and withdrew, reappearing with a bottle of Mumm's champagne and two glasses. Elizabeth poured and raised her glass. "To our success, Barbara. To two hundred million."

Barbara picked up the glass. She knew she was trapped, and yet she was glad. This will show them all!

They drank the champagne quickly. Barbara thought Elizabeth drank most of it, but she felt a decided buzz as Elizabeth escorted her to the elevator. Elizabeth seemed unsteady herself, and a long ash from her cigarette fell unnoticed on the beautiful Chinese rug in her outer office.

"The driver is waiting in the underground carpark to take you back to your hotel," said Elizabeth, handing Barbara off to Mary in the lift lobby. "Mary will show you."

"Why the carpark, Elizabeth?"

Elizabeth shrugged. It was a sinuous, quick movement. "There is a demonstration at the container port across the way. Dockworkers threatening to strike."

Barbara stopped dead. "Is it serious?" If Philip Meyer hears of serious labor trouble here, he will tear up the offer.

Elizabeth smiled, but her face was taut. "A strike would be illegal, but I think the party can control the situation."

Barbara smiled and forced a laugh. "I certainly hope nothing gets out of hand. We will need a quiet, stable image for Singapore to get the right reception for our bond issue."

Elizabeth looked at Barbara, a strange, cold expression on her face. "Not to worry, Barbara. Singapore is a stable country. Singaporeans are very disciplined people. The bond will not fail because of anything which might happen here."

18

COLONEL ABDUL RAZA WAS weary when he reached his home a little after eight. He had sat through a rancorous cabinet meeting during which the threatened dock strike had been discussed. The Labor Minister, a feisty Chinese named Eng, had shouted at Raza, demanding the police arrest the ringleaders. Raza had advised caution; the summer's oppressive heat always caused minor unrest. After the meeting broke up at six, he dragged himself to a dreary cocktail reception at the American Embassy for a celebration of their national day. As a token Muslim in the cabinet, Raza never drank in public, but he wanted a drink now.

Raza still lived in the modest bungalow in Bukit Timah that he had bought as a wedding present for his wife. The furniture and rugs were worn and stained, but he didn't care. He could still feel his wife's presence in the place and his son's. It was a place of rest, so shabby that the cabinet minister never felt compelled to entertain anyone there.

Lasa, the old Dyak woman that Fatimah had hired as a baby *ayah* as soon as she knew she was pregnant, met Raza at the door and smiled at him with her gap-toothed smile. "Some tea, Master?" she asked.

"Whiskey," he said, walking into his library and flopping into a soft leather chair, putting his feet up on the matching ottoman. Lasa brought a large whiskey and soda on a silver tray and, with it, his mail.

"There are two letters here for the young master," she said. "When will he be coming home?"

Raza sighed and tried to smile at the old woman. "Yusef is a man now, Lasa. He will come and go as he likes."

"I miss him," she said, handing Raza his drink and placing the letters on the table beside him.

"So do I," said the colonel.

All of his own mail was routine and he tossed it aside. He would not ordinarily have considered opening his son's mail, but under the circumstances he felt he should. The first was from Yusef's university in Kuala Lumpur. Raza slit it open and read the single sheet. The writer expressed regret that Yusef had been called home before he could be examined on his thesis: ethnic discrimination in the countries of the former British Empire. Raza smiled at that. The writer went on to say the examiners felt they had lost an opportunity to discuss with Yusef his work of exceptional clarity and merit and to see into what other areas Yusef's painstaking research might lead; in any event, the board was so impressed by the written work that it had waived permanently the requirement for an oral examination. Yusef's degree was therefore awarded with honors and would follow in a later post.

Raza read the letter a second time. I'll be damned, he thought, smiling. He raised his glass to his absent son and took a long pull.

The second envelope was of a very heavy vellum bond with a tiny blue crest where the return address might have been and a colorful clutch of stamps from the United Kingdom. Raza slit it open and withdrew a thick sheaf of paper. He scanned the top sheet, poring through the orotund academic phrases. The heart of the matter was that Yusef Raza was invited by the fellows of Balliol College, Oxford, to read political economics, beginning in the fall.

Raza laughed aloud and again raised his glass. The silly bugger actually pulled his finger out and did it!

He finished his drink, put the two letters in his briefcase, then went upstairs to shower and change for dinner, feeling better than he had in weeks.

Raza strode into his office early. He scanned the situation reports of nighttime police activity, reading carefully the reports of surveillance of the dockworkers. The policewoman on duty outside his office, a tiny Chinese woman with a pretty smile, brought him a cup of strong black tea. "Connie," he said, taking the tea, "would you ask Chief Superintendent Al-Habshi to come in?"

"Straight away, Colonel," said the woman, withdrawing.

Chief Superintendent Daoud Al-Habshi, head of the Special Branch, entered Raza's office a minute later and closed the door behind him. "Sit, Chief," said Raza. "Where is my son?"

The chief superintendent sat down and crossed his legs. "Still in Bugis Street, Colonel."

"The same dive?"

"Yes. The Club New Malacca."

Raza nodded. Bloody nice company the lad keeps, he thought. "Are you sure his playmates have no idea of his true identity?"

"Certainly no sign of it, Colonel," said Al-Habshi. "The MSL brat who gave him his new papers is an informant of the Kuala Lumpur police. He lost the records, as instructed."

"So you don't believe Yusef is in any danger?"

"I doubt it, Colonel. None of those people are exactly dangerous, but one can't be sure." Al-Habshi shifted in his seat. "I would still like to bring him in so you could talk to him."

Raza shook his head emphatically. He had had this conversation with the head of the Special Branch before. "No, Daoud. The boy knows where I am if he wants to talk. He is trying to sort out some things, and if I pull him in and blow his cover, he will just hate me more than he does."

Al-Habshi frowned. The colonel was torturing himself over his son. "I'm sure he doesn't hate—"

Raza waved the rest of the thought away and took the two letters from his briefcase. "Have some of your people go and see him, Daoud. Arrange it so he is a witness to a crime of some sort, a snatch-and-grab or something, so his pals won't be suspicious." He handed Yusef's letters across to Al-Habshi. "Show him these."

Al-Habshi took the two letters and read them. He looked up and smiled at Raza, who smiled back. "With your permission, Colonel, I'll look after this myself."

"Thank you, Chief." Raza went back to the papers on his desk, and Al-Habshi stood up and departed.

Yusef walked slowly from the Alsagoff School through the narrow streets of the Arab quarter toward Bugis Street. The heat was stifling, and the brassy sky held no promise of an evening shower. He passed rows of faded and peeling shop-houses, some falling down and crudely roofed with tin sheets. Yusef noted as he walked that while this was the district of mosques, Arab street names, and Malay-stream schools, many of the businesses—and most of the well-kept shop-houses—had the names of Chinese on them and even a few Indians. The Malay shops sold mostly spices and tropical woods, the Indians textiles, and the Chinese everything. The most prosperous shop-houses were all medical or dental clinics and all Chinese. Are there no Malay doctors, even here? wondered Yusef. Must we pay *them* for absolutely everything?

Whole families lolled on doorsteps, many fanning themselves with dried pandannus leaves. Their upstairs bedrooms would be ovens this night, as would his corner in the basement of the New Malacca. Young Raza decided he quite liked Singapore, despite the heat and the oppressed condition of the Malays. The university and Kuala Lumpur seemed long ago and faraway, a simpler, more provincial place and time.

Near the intersection of Bugis Street and Victoria Street, Yusef was passed on the sidewalk by a hurrying Chinese man, quite old and dressed in a long blue gown, carrying a large case held against his chest with both hands. A slim Malay boy stepped out of a shop stall and blocked the man's path, then grabbed the case from his grip and knocked him to the pavement. The elderly man screamed and the Malay ran, barrelling full tilt into Yusef and knocking him to the street as well before running into the crowd in Bugis Street. Yusef heard a police siren immediately as a police car pulled to the curb in front of him. One constable bolted from the car and pursued the thief into Bugis Street while a second helped the old Chinese man to his feet. Another car pulled up, its blue roof lights flashing. The police held a hasty conference on the street. The driver of the first car pointed to Yusef, just now getting to his feet. A sergeant with white traffic-detail sleeves walked over to Yusef. He was Chinese and addressed Yusef in English. "Are you all right, sir?"

"Yes, fine," said Yusef. "Just got knocked down."

The sergeant took Yusef by the elbow and steered him toward the second police car. "Come give a statement to the inspector, please. Description of the assailant and all that."

Yusef's heart sank and then began to pound. He could see there was a man in plainclothes seated next to the uniformed driver. The sergeant opened the rear door and Yusef got in.

"May I see your identity card, please?" asked the sergeant pleasantly.

Yusef gave it to him. I'm nicked for sure, he thought. The MSL ID card had been none too good to begin with, and time and sweat had caused it to fade and smear.

"Mahmoud Assad," said the sergeant, handing the card over the seat to the man in plainclothes. The man did not turn to look at Yusef.

"Indeed, from Kuala Lumpur," said the man. "Hello, Yusef."

"M-my name is Mahmoud," said Yusef, his head bowed. "I have a job—"

The man in plainclothes twisted around, putting his arm across the back of the front seat. He seemed glad to see Yusef. "Come on, Yusef, I bounced you on my knee."

Yusef looked up. "Hello, Superintendent Al-Habshi," he said miserably. "How long have you known I was in Singapore?"

"Since the day you arrived, I'm afraid. And by the by, it's chief superintendent now."

Yusef was puzzled and a little hurt. "But if you knew I was here, why didn't my father . . ." His voice trailed off.

"Arrest you? You have committed no crime in Singapore of which we are aware, Yusef, other than giving a false name to a police officer." Al-Habshi handed the boy his bogus ID card. "I myself would have liked to have brought you in for a talk, but your father was, and is, dead set against that. He seems to think you need some time to yourself."

Yusef nodded slowly, savoring his father's trust. "Then what is all this about?"

"Just a statement about that robbery," said Al-Habshi.

"And then I can go?"

"Free as a bird, and with no one wondering why you were seen talking to the police." Al-Habshi produced the two letters. "Your father wanted you to have a look at these."

Yusef read the letter from the university in Kuala Lumpur and smiled. He took a little longer with the letter from England. Like his father, he had a little difficulty in plowing through the formal, convoluted phrasing. "I have been admitted to Oxford!"

"So it seems, Yusef. Your father sends his heartiest congratulations, and I add my own. Bloody well done." The chief superintendent reached his hand out, and Yusef shook it firmly. "You had best let me have those letters, since they don't match your chosen identity. Your father will keep them for you."

Yusef handed over the letters. If they had driven him straight to his father, he would not have protested, but something in his father's expression of trust told him to stay away a little longer, to learn a little bit more.

"Just sign my notebook, sir, if you would, and then you can be on your way," said the traffic sergeant who had brought him to the car. The "statement" said nothing more than "witness to daylight robbery, Bugis Street." Yusef scribbled "Mahmoud Assad" just to see if they would let him get away with it. The sergeant glanced at the signature and put the book in his pocket.

"That mugging was a setup, wasn't it?" asked Yusef. "A sham for my benefit?"

"Did it look set up, Yusef?" asked Al-Habshi, grinning.

"No," said Yusef. "But I know what you Special Branch lot are capable of."

"Well, you should," the chief inspector said. "You are your father's son."

Yusef pushed the car door open. No one moved to stop him; he almost wished they would. "Chief Superintendent, please tell my father I will come and see him very soon."

"Good lad," said Al-Habshi. The police car pulled smoothly into the heavy evening traffic and was gone.

19
New York, 5 July

DAVID WEISS SAT IN his office at seven-thirty in the morning, reading again the thin report from "Mr. Dennis" that detailed his surveillance and investigation of Holden Chambers over the past three months. Although the report didn't say so explicitly, it was apparent that Dennis had recorded Chambers's telex and telephone communications from his office and his telephone conversations from his flat. It was also apparent that Dennis had monitored Chambers's direct conversations with friends, colleagues, and clients in offices, restaurants, and even on his yacht. Weiss supposed he had some sort of sensitive directional microphones. Dennis's report covered Chambers's activities in Hong Kong and on trips he had made during the period to Seoul, Taipei, Manila twice, Singapore, Jakarta, and Bangkok. The report was complete, detailed, and contained absolutely nothing of value.

Damn! thought Weiss, pacing around his large corner office on the twenty-second floor of Traders Bank and Trust Company's headquarters, a black-glass tower on Park Avenue. Chambers came through in the report as thoroughly prepared with his clients and well regarded, if not universally liked, by his colleagues. He seemed relaxed, confident, and competent. He had lots of friends, went to lots of parties, and had too much fun, but as much as Weiss hated drinkers and partyers, he had long before decided that such flaws were not actionable in the entertainment-intensive world of international banking. Three months under investigation, during which Chambers had finished a highly successful deal for Indonesia, landed another there, and locked up important mandates in Korea and the Philippines, and nothing to suggest where he got his angle!

The report had been delivered to Weiss at his home in Greenwich, Connecticut, on Saturday, the 2nd of July. Weiss had read it and reread it through the long weekend while his wife and sons splashed in the backyard pool and their neighbors came in Sat-

urday evening and cooked and ate and drank. Nothing! Dennis
had concluded his report with a recommendation that surveillance
be terminated. He also wrote that he would call Weiss in his office
at eight o'clock on Tuesday, today, to answer any questions. He
asked for yet another payment of ten thousand pounds.

The phone warbled. Weiss picked it up immediately; his secretary wouldn't be in for another hour. "Weiss," he barked.

"Good morning, Mr. Weiss. It's Mr. Dennis. I hope you received the package."

"I did. I must say I had hoped for rather more."

"It's sold as is, Mr. Weiss. You know my firm makes the best.
If it's embellishment you want, you can add that yourself."

The remark irritated Weiss, and he supposed it was meant to.
"You found nothing of special interest among our clients?"

"I have very good contacts in all of the countries in which you
do business out here, Mr. Weiss, including people who would
have received part of any sales incentives, had any been offered.
As detailed in previous reports, I even went back to major buyers
of the prior three months."

Weiss boiled at the man's tone of scornful confidence. He would
love to tell Dennis to fuck off and stiff him his final payment, but
Weiss knew that not paying such people generally had disagree-
able consequences. "I want you to keep on a bit longer, Dennis.
There is one more place to look."

"Yes?"

"I want you to have a look at his private files."

There was a long pause. Weiss was about to speak again when
Dennis said, "I would have to go in after the office was closed."

"Do as you like. That office belongs to me; nothing in it should
be kept from me."

Another pause. "You are specifically authorizing me to enter
that office and a locked file cabinet as your representative?"

"Yes, and I want it done quickly. Look also for anything at all
related to Singapore, especially new transactions."

"I can begin as soon as your account is brought current."

"Which will be within two hours."

"Done. Anything further?"

"No. But you should call me each Monday at this time, and
on any day if anything important breaks."

"It's your *jeton*, Mr. Weiss. Good morning."

Weiss hung up without replying.

Dennis hung up the phone in the flat in Yun Ping Road and
shut off the equipment. I will charge him a pretty premium for

breaking and entering, he thought, smiling. I have to go in anyway to remove the taps from the telephone and telex lines, and my Cable and Wireless cover is wearing thin. Whether Mr. Weiss likes it or not, I intend to shut this operation down. It has gone on too long, and that is always dangerous.

20
Hong Kong, 6 July

THE TELEPHONE ON CHAMBERS'S desk buzzed, and he punched the intercom button. "Yes, Margaret?"

"Mrs. Ramsay," she said.

"Okay," he said, pushing the button for the incoming line. "Barbara? How are you?"

"Fine," she bubbled. "Great! Holden, I just got in from Singapore. I got the mandate!"

"That's wonderful!" he cheered, hoping that it really was. "How much?"

"One hundred twenty million, to be increased to two hundred in the management group."

Jesus, that is big, he thought. She can't be trying to do this all by herself. "Do you have any other banks lined up?"

"I just got back, Holden. I just got my copies of the offer telex and the acceptance from RAL." Her voice was a little sharp, a little tense. "And I did promise to call you first."

He found it hard to believe that Roland, Archer had committed one hundred and twenty million to the underwriting; and even if they had, where would they get the other eighty? An issue of seventy-five or eighty would be reasonable at the right terms, *maybe* one hundred, but to do two hundred she would need a powerful group—really a consensus team of all the major players. "Well, that's bold, Barbara. How do you intend to fill out the underwriting group?"

"We will be looking for comanagers, two or perhaps three at forty million each. Subunderwriters at twenty each to ensure broad distribution."

He frowned. She is trying to do too much. Nobody big enough in Euro-straights to underwrite forty million is going to come in on a second line, at least not in Hong Kong, and not likely in London following a newcomer to Hong Kong with no Asian distribution network. "Barbara, bonds aren't really my business, and I wouldn't presume to advise you, but don't you think you should bring banks in as co*lead* managers? Two hundred million is a hell of a lot to sell, and you are going to need some powerful friends." He listened to the silence on the line for perhaps ten seconds. It really is none of my business, he thought.

"Holden"—her voice was suddenly tired—"it is structured as a sole lead. It's our deal, and the MAS didn't ask us to bring in anyone else at the top, although they did of course mention several banks, which they regard as special friends and which they wished to see offered prominent positions in the deal."

He smiled at that. She had learned the standard formula: Come in on my terms now, or the borrower will hammer you in on any terms later. All the same, he doubted whether Singapore had much in the way of markers from the big players in Eurobonds, and his smile faded.

She continued rapidly, her words almost tumbling over each other. "Holden, the Sing government is very interested in this deal, and they want it out quickly. A joint-lead manager approach would be just too cumbersome. Look, I am not playing games with you. There will be credit and profit for everyone, and the tombstone and other publicity will be balanced. Holden, I need you. I need you for this deal."

"You know I will have to go to London on this. I told you that." He had a sick feeling that he had puffed up his influence with TBI in London, and in doing so he may have deceived Barbara. At the same time he laid himself open for a real punishing by David Weiss. "I am flattered, and I want to be helpful. Why do you want us particularly?"

She sighed. "We want a prominent Hong Kong merchant bank to give the deal credibility in the region. My London wants you or Chase Asia or Pacific Capital. I don't like the new man at Chase, and PCC would be personally difficult for me. I want *you*. Traders is respected, and you are the Lion of the syndicated-loan market; people listen to you. The other managers will be one or two Europeans and one Japanese. I can get them, Holden, but if I don't get a real Hong Kong name, a *Lion*, people will say this is a London deal. You remember how the Lions broke away from their London masters in the syndicated-loan market. You don't want London and New York tramping back into Hong Kong with hobnail boots." Her voice seemed to wind down like a record spinning too slowly. The last words were very soft.

Holden felt a tightness in his jaw and in his chest. She is so far out on a limb, at least as far as John Carroll and Bob Burleigh and I were in our Philippine deal, which opened this market and made us Lions. At least we had the comfort of each other as we waited for the axes to fall; she is truly all alone. "How are the terms, Barbara?"

She told him. He wasn't involved directly in Euro-straights, but he read the *Agefi* newsletter, plus the more influential *Euromarket Insider*, and Barbara's bond seemed well priced and well structured in what was a very competitive market. The actual yield on the instrument would depend on the issue price, which was normally set at par or a fraction below, a few days before the issue was marketed. Normal practice allowed the issue to come at or under par only to reflect upward movements in underlying interest rates. The Singapore issue's coupon gave it a slight premium over first-rate Western European credits recently issued, enough to interest investors in a less-familiar name yet small enough to make the Singaporeans very proud indeed. But two hundred million! "Send me the offer telex as soon as it's ready, Barbara. I will go over it with London, and I will do my best for you." He glanced at his watch: ten after five. "In the meantime, congratulations. Could I buy you a bottle of champagne?"

"The offer is ready now. I'll have the telex operator send it right out. Holden, you really will be the first to see it."

"Good, then. I will get it off to London, and then we shall see. Would you like that drink, then?"

"Holden, I am absolutely drained from the negotiations, and besides, I won't likely be out of here before late."

"Well, soon, then, I hope," he said, understanding but nonetheless feeling let down.

"Very soon. Good-bye, Holden; big kiss!"

"Good-bye, darling." He punched the intercom button, and Margaret answered immediately. "Margaret, would you make sure the telex operator has the tape-cutter turned on on the local telex machine? We will be getting a long one, and we'll have to retransmit it to TBI."

"At once, Mr. Chambers."

Thank god for Margaret, he thought idly, staring at the ceiling. Two hundred million! Can it possibly be done? he wondered. I only pray that Weiss is not in London. If this idea is cracked, Portas will tell me and that will be that. But what will I tell Barbara?

Nigel Cross was in his office early, and Barbara reached him at a quarter past five, Hong Kong time. "Good morning, Nigel.

God, I am glad you are in early. I am about ready to collapse from exhaustion.''

"You are doing a lot by yourself, Barbara. Do you want me to come out for a couple of weeks?"

She considered that for a moment. Nigel would be a tremendous asset. He was a tireless worker, he knew every angle of documentation, and he was a friend. But if he came out, the deal would become RAL's and she would be viewed as just a sales rep on a prolonged trip out of London. "No, Nigel, that's kind of you, but I'll be fine. I just need a night's sleep or two."

"Okay, just don't hesitate to call me if you need me." He sounded as if he understood. "I would like to send out one of my new people, a very clever young lad named Iain McIntyre, to help you with the grunt work. He is very good with documents." He paused, and she thought about it. "He'd report to you, of course," he said gently. "I really think he could help—unless, of course, you think he would get underfoot."

At this her wariness relaxed. "Nigel, you are a prince. If you say the man is good, by all means send him. He can act as liaison with your legal people in getting the prospectus and the indenture together, and then he can help me negotiate the documents with the MAS."

"Quite," he said, a little stiffly.

She hoped she wasn't pushing, but she wanted to settle once and for all that all negotiations would take place in Asia and she would lead them. "Of course, Nigel, I will want to be in daily contact with you, and perhaps you can come out for the signing."

"Well, we'll see, of course." His voice lost its chill. They both knew that signings of bond indentures were not the big deal that signings of syndicated loans were, since loan signings took place after syndication was complete and were therefore victory celebrations, while indentures were signed before a single bond was sold and no one knew whether the issue would be successful or not. But he knew that she wanted to be the point on her deal, and so far she had handled the transaction well. "Tell me, then, how went the first day of calling on potential managers?"

"Well, I think," she said, glad a tense moment had passed. "I called Traders Asia. I told Holden Chambers he was *the* Asian merchant we wanted. I think he wants to do the deal, although he suggested we look for coleads rather than just other managers."

"I thought he would do that. What did you say?"

"I stalled. I told him that the MAS had given us a sole mandate and that he could be expected to get his arm twisted."

"Good," he said. "I recommended Traders to you because, while they are strong in Asia, they are much weaker in underwriting straight Eurobonds than either Chase Limited or Nibble." He nodded to himself. "They ought to be able to swallow being on the second line."

"I hope you are right," she said. "He seemed a little staggered by the amount of the offer."

"One hundred twenty million? It's big, but not outsized. One hundred twenty can be done."

But it is one hundred twenty to get two hundred, she thought with a chill. I haven't told you, Nigel, but by now you should have guessed. And I am asking managers for forty million apiece, not the thirty we discussed two weeks ago. You will hear about that soon enough, but by then I should have at least some of my managers. "Well, anyway, that's Traders. I spoke to Mr. Nishimura of Nakamura Securities; as expected, he is very interested." She heard her voice racing and forced herself to relax. The next days, and maybe the next hours, were all she had to bring this off, and she was acutely aware that if she failed, she would likely bring Nigel Cross down with her. Balls, she thought. Lions' balls. "I spoke to the representative of Credit Genevois; he was noncommittal, very Swiss. I will need your help to bring them in. I also spoke to Henri du Lac at Banque Française du Commerce. He is also only a rep, but he has been in Asia for twenty years and may have some influence."

"Good, Barbara. I think the price is right. The Jap will come, although he doesn't do us a hell of a lot of good; he will demand all the Japanese orders at least until he clears his allotment, but it's a good name. I think I can do something with the frogs and the Swiss. You get Traders, and we have a lock."

Oh, God, Holden, she thought, I need you on this! "I will do the best I can. Give a good word to your friend at TBI, won't you?"

"Of course. I have set a lunch with him this afternoon. His secretary just called to confirm—at nine in the morning, mind you. That means he is in early and reading our telex."

"Excellent, Nigel. Send me a telex for my opening."

"Will do. And Barbara, jolly well done, so far, but don't forget we've a long way to go."

"I know, Nigel, but we will get there. Good morning."

"Good night, Barbara."

Holden Chambers got through to Frank Portas at 8:00 P.M. Hong Kong time—noon in London. "Well, Frank, what do you think of it?"

"First, old man, tell me how important this is to you," said Portas, cupping his hand around the phone.

Chambers frowned. This thing grows around me like a poisonous plant. "It isn't, Frank, unless it is successful. If we—sorry, if you—think the deal will go, I would hate not to have a piece of it."

"Cut the crap, Holden. It's just you and me on the phone, mate."

"No, I mean it. If the awful Weiss is right about anything, he is right about my ignorance of the Eurobond market. If this issue is going to be successful, Traders Asia—and frankly, Frank, I—cannot have it succeed without me, done either by my rivals here or done all in Europe."

"I understand, of course, and you're right. So you are asking me if the issue will go or not?"

"Yes. If it does, there will be money to be made." Holden's thin confidence was rapidly dissipating. But if Portas said the issue wouldn't fly, then he could tell Barbara with a clear conscience—well, almost clear—that he couldn't support it.

"It's priced dead on, Holden," said Portas. "Even a bit fat, depending upon how you or anyone measures Singapore as a credit compared to, say, Belgium and Italy, which both just issued."

Holden swallowed. "So you think—"

"We might even buy some, Holden, for private clients in T-BAG." T-BAG was Traders Bank, A.G. Traders's highly unprofitable Swiss subsidiary. "Because it might fit. But whether we should buy forty million!" Portas laughed, a light, musical trill. "Dear boy! And without even a lead position? Holden, more than the pride and face of our beloved David Weiss's equally beloved Prince of Asia must have to be at stake."

Holden wanted to laugh, but his face burned. He sipped his drink and nodded to the telephone. "You are telling me that the bond won't really be distributed."

"Old man, that is exactly what I think. Terms are bang on. Timing is good; there isn't much quality paper in the offing. But at two hundred million, the issue is enormous, Holden. If we took the forty we are offered, how much do you reckon you could place in Asia?"

Chambers took a quick mental tally of his clients who invested in Eurobonds and who might take the issue from him as an accommodation. "About two million," he said bleakly.

"Then we end up booking thirty-eight, Holden." Portas's voice seemed solicitous yet final. "With a Swiss in the deal, and maybe a Brit or a Frog, we will sell nothing. We just don't have the clout. I assume RAL will get the duty Jap, so we wouldn't even have a crack at them. Holden, I am sorry, but I just don't see Belgian dentists and offshore mutual funds absorbing more than forty million of a new issue for Singapore, maybe fifty. We would be stuffed, and you-know-who would have our guts for garters."

"Have you discussed this with Weiss?"

"No. So far this is between you and me. So far neither you nor I have taken a position on the offer."

"Thanks. When I made the call, I was praying David wasn't in London."

"You were in luck, but he arrives in two days, from Frankfurt." Portas chuckled. "Still pouring good money after bad there, I guess. We can rely on his being in a foul humor when he gets here. He always is after visiting the scene of his earliest triumph."

Holden nodded and smiled himself. Traders Bankverein in Frankfurt had been Weiss's first management position, and it had never made money. Yet he runs the department, and Portas and I both have to report to him. "Right. Strength built upon strength, eh, Frank? Anyway, to sum up, you think this issue has no chance?"

"I didn't say that, Holden. It could go, over time. The Swiss manager will get first crack at Swiss banks and, of course, will stuff their managed accounts. The Japs won't do badly, or at least they will spread it among their countrymen. A German manager won't mind holding, although I doubt RAL can get anybody good. RAL and we or any other American, Brit, or Canadian who has to actually sell this deal to willing but unstuffable buyers won't sell a bean. It's just too exotic."

"So you think it will just sit on the managers' books," said Chambers.

" 'Fraid so, old son. And all the above assumes nothing negative on Singapore or Asia generally comes up in the meantime." Portas paused, listening to the wavering hiss of the satellite hookup. "If you don't mind my asking, you seem to have something more of an interest in this transaction than your usual ruthless profit motive."

Holden leaned back in his chair and picked up his drink; nothing left but ice water. He felt a little guilty. "I guess I don't want RAL to bring a beauty of a deal without me in it. It could be a new market."

"Fine, mate, and that's what I will tell the lovely Mr. Weiss. I have to talk to him about this, of course."

"Sure. Just say I forwarded it without endorsement." Sorry,

Barbara, but Portas would prevail no matter what I said, as well he should on any Eurobond deal.

"It's not the bird, is it?" asked Portas softly. "Not poking her, are we?"

"No." Holden laughed. At least that is true. "But I do like her, and I think she knows her stuff." He stretched to reach the decanter on the bookshelf, then slopped a couple of ounces of scotch into the icy water in the bottom of his glass. "Though I might like to if she weren't heavily married. But there is one other thing which makes me curious. I never thought she would get the mandate; every merchant banker in Asia and his dog has tried for it and gotten knocked back. Okay, let's say you are right, and the deal is too big, and the Belgian dentists don't buy it. Who suffers? Who looks dumb?"

"Besides RAL, and whatever plungers they get to comanage?"

"Right," said Holden, taking a swallow of scotch. "Who else?"

"Singapore government, I suppose." Portas's voice had lost a bit of its sureness.

"Just so, Frank. Singapore government, an outfit not commonly known to handle itself badly in the world of international finance."

"What's your point?"

"Suppose the issue starts to drop in price. Singapore has plenty of cash: Perhaps they might support the issue even if the managers didn't."

Portas chuckled. "Why would they buy their own bonds? Pay RAL and friends huge fees and end up owning their own paper?" He frowned. "Unless—"

"Bingo," said Chambers.

"To preserve their market reputation?"

"Out here, we call it *face*, Frank, and it is a very serious business."

"But everyone would know! If they were seen to be buying their own issue to rescue it—"

"They might not be seen."

"Come on, mate! They couldn't buy without people in the market knowing it."

"Can you buy and sell without the market knowing it is you?"

"Well, of course, to some extent, through friends, nominees, but—"

"Then why can't they?"

"Holden, I can move in and out of the market through the kindness of friends. Even central banks do it, but *somebody* has to know, if only the nominees, and they talk, after a time. Eventually everyone finds out. It can work, say, if the Bundesbank wants to sell dollars to support the mark and the market doesn't know who did it until the intervention is complete—a matter of hours, Holden, or at the most days—but eventually everybody *knows!* No, for something like this, the Sing government would lose face, and indeed money, once it came out."

"Maybe," said Chambers. "Maybe. You are the expert, and I will rely on you. But even if they did lose, would the managers?"

Portas thought about it as he lit a cigarette. "It's preposterous. The Singaporeans would look foolish at best, and the managers, especially Roland, Archer, would look like pirates."

"Maybe no one would want to talk about it," said Chambers.

"No, Holden, I just don't believe it. It is too Byzantine."

"But you will think about it?"

"Yes. Yes, I will."

"Good friend. Good morning, Frank."

"Good night, Holden. Sweet dreams." Portas set the phone in its cradle. An Asian issue, by a new player, in a wide-open market, he thought, stubbing out his cigarette and reaching for another. Was *anything* too Byzantine?

21

Singapore, 7 July

SADDAM AL-SELIM RECEIVED THE message in the usual way, by hand-delivered letter at his office, just after the noon prayer. The message wasn't signed, but they never were. Saddam was instructed to rouse his students to demonstrate in the streets against Chinese dominance of Singapore's society and their repression of the Malay people, to whom the land rightfully belonged. Saddam tore the note into thin strips and burned them in his ashtray while nodding his head slowly. He felt his anger gathering, melting into hatred at the arrogant, spiritless Chinese interlopers. A devout Muslim, Saddam was a proctor at the Al-Halim High School on Sarangoon Road. He was twenty-four years old, studying law at the National University and doing poorly, largely because his English was not fluent and all the law courses were taught in the language of the colonial master, even the few courses on the *Sharia*, the law of Islam.

Saddam knew the note he had received would be delivered to organizers at all of Singapore's Malay-language high schools. The schools were a cruel joke: Set up by the dominant Chinese ostensibly to give the Malay minority the "freedom" to pursue studies in their own language and culture, they served to prevent Malays from entering the mainstream of Singaporean business and government. Saddam himself had tried to transfer from Al-Halim to nearby Raffles High School in each of his four years of high school, but each time he had been refused because his English was not good enough. The English instruction in the Malay-language schools was rudimentary, and he was sure that this was done purposely to ensure that Malays remained second-class citizens in their own land.

Saddam left his tiny office, locking the door carefully, and then walked quickly toward the giant rubber tree in the central courtyard where the students gathered to talk after the end of classes.

* * *

The Malay students marched in solid phalanxes, arms linked, filling the narrow streets of the Muslim quarter, and then expanding and broadening as the roads became wider. They marched along Beach Road, chanting and singing, then swirled around the War Memorial into Connaught Drive, past the Cricket Club with its carefully manicured great lawn, and then to Parliament House. To Prime Minister Lee, watching them crowd the streets and swell into the Cricket Club grounds from his second-floor office, they looked like an army of boisterous children, nearly uniform in their dark slacks and skirts and their short-sleeved white shirts open at the neck, revealing arms and necks and faces of uniform brown skin.

Lee turned to Dr. Fong, the aging Cabinet Secretary. "What brought this on, Fong?"

"No way to know," the old man rasped, joining Lee at the window. "The heat, probably. Police activity on one of the Malay campuses, possibly."

The PM grunted, looking up at the brassy, nearly cloudless sky. The heat in the street would be stifling. He looked down at the three police constables in their light-green uniforms who guarded the front steps of Parliament House, now being joined by another from traffic duty who wore white sleeves over his uniform shirt. "The police don't seem to have anticipated this demonstration the way they normally do," Lee said, watching as the students behind forced the ones on the steps to press the four constables backward.

"Here come the reinforcements," said Dr. Fong, pointing from the other window, which overlooked the Elgin Bridge and North Bridge Road. Police with riot helmets and plastic face guards and long, springy staves called *lathis* were getting out of cars and blue vans and forming up into squads. The police vehicles blocked the Elgin Bridge beyond, their roof lights flickering. Lee could see other roof lights reflected on the tower of the Victoria Memorial Hall, just south of Parliament House, and he knew the police would be blocking the Cavenagh and Anderson bridges into the central city as well. When the students were done demonstrating, they would be given room to retreat into the Muslim quarter but denied access to either the central city or to Chinatown, just to the north.

Yusef Raza watched as the man he knew only as Saddam exhorted his students to confront the fascist Chinese police. Yusef was very uncomfortable being in the demonstration, but his students at the Alsagoff Arab School had asked him to lead them, and since he had been lecturing them on the importance of Malay pride for months, he thought it would look odd if he refused. He knew that 99 percent of the kids thought of the demonstration as a lark or a chance to let off a little frustration, and he was afraid they could be in danger if ranting blockheads like Saddam provoked a real confrontation. He knew his father's crowd-control officers were well trained and disciplined, but anyone might panic if pushed too far. Yusef halted his small contingent well short of the doors of Parliament House and told them to watch.

Near the front of the mass of demonstrators, Saddam al-Selim waved and encouraged his students to taunt the policemen, now standing with their backs to the great doors to Parliament House and looking very uncomfortable, despite their long clubs held in front of their chests and their revolvers in their buttoned black-leather holsters. The crowd of students around Saddam seemed to be in a festive mood, not at all in keeping with the big banners demanding the end to Chinese infidel domination and reunification with the rest of Malaysia. These students demonstrate because they are bored, he thought. They don't really hate the Chinese, who grow fat eating the pork that the Prophet forbade and sucking the blood of the *bumi-putras*. Saddam felt his anger rising, and he began to tremble. Something must be done to make these young Malays see what is being done to them!

Saddam pressed toward the front row of students and came face to face with the four policemen. He scanned their faces, Chinese pig-fat and pale. But no! The one on the end, a slight man with silver sergeant's chevrons pinned to the white oversleeves of a traffic-duty officer, had brown skin and round eyes.

Saddam pressed himself against the Malay policeman. Saddam was taller by at least a foot. "Pig-eater!" he shouted in Bahasa Malay. "House-nigger! Chink lap-dog!"

The policeman's face remained a mask, but he pushed back at Saddam with his baton, first gently and then with increasing force as Saddam continued to rage. "Move along," the policeman said quietly in English.

"So, *brother*, you even talk the talk of your masters? Have you learned Chinese as well, cunt-face?" Saddam felt the crowd behind him begin to pick up the pace of its shouting as he continued to rail at the policeman in Malay.

The policeman's face burned with the insult. He drew back his baton to strike, but Saddam was quick and he grasped the swinging club, nearly dragging the little sergeant off his feet. Saddam felt a sharp pain on his shoulder as the policeman beside the Malay struck him a glancing blow. Saddam roared with pain and rage and grappled with the Malay sergeant, getting his arms around the smaller man's waist and driving his head into his stomach so the other officers couldn't get a good swing at his head. The two rolled to the ground, and the crowd parted as more policemen struggled to reach the doors of Parliament House. The Malay sergeant had his baton behind Saddam's neck and was applying great pressure. Saddam heard a roaring in his head and began to see red. He tried to reach the policeman's groin, to hurt him and make him release the awful pressure on his own head. He touched something cold, metallic. Before he knew what it was, he was holding the policeman's service revolver in his hands. He heard a deafening explosion and felt burning powder on his face. The pressure on his neck was suddenly released.

Saddam stood and stared at the revolver in his hand, then at the badly wounded officer writhing on the stone steps below him. The officer next to him shouted something, but Saddam didn't understand him. He turned toward the crowd, which had grown silent and fallen back. The officer next to him shouted again, and Saddam turned to look at him, swinging the gun around as he did so, without thinking about it. The officer's pasty Chinese face was contorted with fear, and he held his own revolver in both hands, pointed at Saddam's heart. Saddam started to speak, but the officer shouted again. Saddam realized he was shouting in Mandarin. "I am sorry, I never meant to hurt—" The Chinese officer fired twice in rapid succession. Saddam spun around, feeling the revolver fly from his hand, then sank slowly to the steps next to the policeman he had shot. Saddam al-Selim was dead before he hit the ground.

The police reinforcements reached the steps in front of Parliament House, parting and scattering demonstrators. Many officers had drawn their service revolvers. An ambulance pushed its way down High Street, guarded as it came by a squad of police in riot gear. The crowd fluttered with hushed voices, both frightened and angry, as news of what had taken place flowed back away from the bloody steps. The demonstrators began to move away, back into the Muslim quarter, tramping across the Cricket Club grounds as they went. The demonstrators broke into smaller groups as they dispersed, and the students began to talk of Saddam and what he had done. They were sullen, and they were angry. Some shouted of going back to Parliament House and having it out with the police then and there. More cautious heads counseled patience: The police were too many and had all the arms. The crowd continued to disperse.

The leaders of the shadowy movement that had convoked the demonstration met that night in a small house on Aliwal Street, near the Hajjah Fatimah Mosque. This itself was unprecedented; the leaders never gathered together all at once, for fear of being taken together by the police. There was a great deal of violent talk of rooting out police informants, and Yusef, standing in the shadows near the door of the house, knew his days in the Muslim quarter were numbered. The leaders agreed that Saddam's death should not be in vain. They agreed that the rest of the summer would be dedicated to Saddam the Martyr, and then they dispersed to plan individual acts of violence for their individual cells. They did not plan to meet again.

22

Hong Kong, 7 July

DENNIS HAD STATIONED HIMSELF across Pedder Street from Gloucester Tower at four-thirty in the afternoon, to watch from behind a news stall as the workers began to depart the office block. Each time one of the workers or officers from Traders Asia departed, he ticked his or her name off on the roster he had stolen during his prior visit as an engineer from Cable and Wireless. He knew many would enter the Metro station below the building without his seeing them, but the more he could count, the better. He especially wanted to see Holden Chambers depart, and he was sure Chambers would wait at the curb for his white Mercedes or, if not, walk away to one of the nearby pubs or bars. Dennis acknowledged that Chambers might cross the above-ground walkways to the Mandarin, but he couldn't cover both egresses, and this late in the game it was far too risky either to stand in the lift lobby and risk recognition or to bring in an untrusted confederate. Dennis preferred to work alone, and if he missed Chambers, he would just have to wait until very late to break into Traders Asia.

Dennis had gone to Chambers's flat in the early afternoon, dressed in a boiler suit stolen from Hong Kong Telephone, and retrieved the bugs from the central telephone box in the kitchen. Chambers's *amah* had stood over him as he worked, arms folded and scowling, but Dennis had gotten the switch and the microphone out and palmed them into a pocket without arousing the old woman's suspicion. He hadn't even shown her the ID card he carried; just as well, since it didn't look much like him, but then, to Chinese, all *gwai-los* looked pretty much the same.

Chambers emerged at a quarter to six and entered the Mercedes as it drew up. Dennis hailed the taxi he had engaged two hours before and followed. The meter already read HK$160, but Dennis didn't care; it was Weiss's money, and he doubted the little man would even look at the receipt, much less keep it. Chambers's driver took him to the Hilton, barely three blocks away, and then turned into the adjoining multistory carpark. Dennis paid off his cab driver, who laughed uproariously at his good fortune. Dennis followed Chambers to the fifth floor and into a reception being given by the Royal Bank of Canada to introduce its new representative. No way he can stay here less than an hour, thought Dennis, who exited the hotel rapidly and then walked back to Gloucester Tower, carrying his large blue holdall.

Dennis rode alone in the lift to the thirteenth floor: Traders Asia. The hall was lighted, and he could hear the sounds of cleaners on the side of the floor away from Chambers's office. Dennis moved close to the door to Chambers's side and listened for five measured minutes. Silence. The lock on the outer door took two minutes with shim and spacer and he was in. Once again he paused and listened. Satisfied he was alone, he pulled his Cable and Wireless coverall out of the bag and donned it over his suit. It would certainly fool the cleaning staff, should he be discovered. He took a small jar of lanolin cream and smeared his fingers. He could work much more quickly and deftly without the rubber gloves favored by amateurs; the cream would assure that all of the many fingerprints he left would be smudged and useless.

The lock on the electrical closet was even less trouble than the one on the front door: Dennis snapped it open with a single stroke of a credit card. He stepped inside, lit a flashlight, and quickly removed the bugs from the telephone and telex cables. He relocked the closet by pushing it to, then turned to the locked door of Holden Chambers's office.

Chambers was enjoying the chatter at the Royal Bank of Canada reception, most of which centered on Roland, Archer's coup in getting the mandate for the bond for Singapore. Many of the players sought him out, and most were confused. Naturally, we want to be there, they said, but isn't it too large? He declined to offer an opinion and kept moving, hoping he might see Barbara, but she didn't appear. Must be working like hell, he thought. Few of Hong Kong's players missed a chance to bask and preen when they had won a big deal.

John Malcolm appeared at his side and took his elbow firmly. Excusing them both from two Australian bankers, he guided Chambers to a quiet corner.

"What is it, John? You look like you lost a friend."

"Might have, squire," said Malcolm. "I passed by the Reuters machine in the lobby on the way up. Singapore's had a bloody riot; at least one man killed."

Jesus, thought Holden. "John, did you know that the Singapore government just gave Roland, Archer a bond deal?"

"I do. And then this, the first real violence in a decade."

"Let's go down and take a look." Holden felt disoriented, slightly sick.

"You won't get near that machine now, laddie. You had best go back to your office and read your own."

"What are you going to do?"

"Go check my own machine, then call London. Meet me at the Captain's Bar in an hour or so. I'd like your advice."

"Done."

They made a hurried apology to their Canadian hosts and ran for the lifts. The news had apparently spread, for the lobby was already crowded with bankers from the Royal Bank party and two others in other banquet rooms on the same floor.

Dennis slipped the lock on the office door and stepped inside, closing the door behind him. He lit only the desk lamp and knelt before the two-drawer steel filing cabinet labeled "Holden Chambers—Private Correspondence." The lock was the simple press-in type, and it yielded to the first touch of the pick. The top drawer held hanging files, all neatly labeled, with such exciting titles as "Flat Records," "Insurance Policies," "Club Bills," and "Golondrina," which proved to contain shipyard bills and various registrations for a sailboat. The lower drawer held financial and tax records, and Dennis decided to start with those. Each year's tax file had a neatly typed note stapled to the first page—"copy sent to New York Personnel"—and a date. God, thought Dennis. This guy is so clean and orderly he squeaks. Still, I guess I have at least to look through the dreary stuff; any one of the labels could be an intentional deception.

Chambers looked at his watch as he rode up the lift in Glouces-ter Tower to his office. Just a quarter past six, he noted, plenty of time to read the reports and to call Frank Portas in London. He stopped as he entered the reception area. The door to the executive side of the office was ajar; he would have Margaret speak to the cleaners in the morning. He entered, his steps silent on the thick carpeting, and stopped again. There was a light on inside his office, and once again the door was not completely closed. He heard the rustle of papers from within.

I should call the building security guards in the lobby, he thought, but they would take too long. His pulse tingled. Too much weird shit is happening, he thought. He pushed the door open in one swift movement and found a European man in a boiler suit kneeling on the carpet, with Chambers's personal records strewn around him.

Dennis sprang to his feet. Chambers shouted angrily, "Who the hell are you?"

The man scooped up his open holdall and rushed for the door. Chambers blocked his way and grabbed his arm, but Dennis dropped the bag and twisted away, aiming a punch at Chambers's head as he did so. Chambers ducked the punch and tackled the man around his waist, wrestling him to the carpet. He felt the shoulder of his jacket tear as the man popped him under the chin with the heel of his hand. Chambers held the man down with his weight and punched him in the solar plexus. The man lost his breath with a whoosh and stopped struggling. Chambers held the man pinned beneath him and looked him full in the face. He was sure he had seen him before, and in this office. "Tell me who you are, mate," he said, "and then we will have the police."

The man seemed quite serene. "You win, Guv," he said, his tone friendly and resigned. He pulled an arm free and landed an expert blow on Chambers's jaw, sending him backward. Then he rolled over him and locked his elbow under Chambers's neck, pulling his fist back and down with his other hand, blocking Chambers's windpipe and compressing the carotid arteries which sent blood to his brain. Chambers heard a roaring inside his head and his vision blurred. He pulled the man's elbow with both hands but couldn't loosen the grip. He twisted his body, and they rolled together across the carpet.

As Dennis rolled, he struck his head against the corner of the desk. Chambers felt the grip loosen a fraction, and with what was left of his strength he lashed backward with an elbow and felt the blow strike the other man's ribs. The man grasped him across the mouth with his right hand. Chambers opened his mouth to the pressure and the hand tightened. He bit down hard on the web between the man's first finger and thumb and tasted salty blood. The man screamed and the hand was snatched away.

Chambers twisted free and stood, swaying and backing away, shaking his head to clear his vision. The other man got up slowly and bent over, clutching his injured hand to his gut. Chambers moved in, his hands raised in a boxing stance. His breath rasped painfully in his throat. The man raised himself on one leg, waving the other toward Chambers. He was wobbly, and his face was contorted with pain. *I must have hit the same spot on the solar plexus again*, thought Chambers. *I had better finish him off before he gets his wind.* He moved in quickly and jabbed with his left hand.

Dennis took the blow glancing off his temple and kicked Chambers in the thigh, missing his balls but knocking him down. "Bastard!" he rasped, and he kicked Chambers viciously in the stomach and then in the head. Chambers moaned and lay still. Dennis bent over, touched him under the ear and felt a pulse, then peeled off the boiler suit and stuffed it into the holdall and ran from the office. Chambers didn't move.

Dennis left Gloucester Tower and walked up Pedder Street to the taxi rank midway in the block, forcing himself not to hurry. He joined the queue and got a taxi in under a minute. He threw his holdall into the back seat and climbed in. "Kai Tak Airport," he said. The taxi moved off, turned right into Connaught Road, and headed for the Cross Harbour tunnel.

Dennis examined his right hand. The web of skin was badly torn and bleeding freely. Have to get that looked at as soon as I get someplace, he thought. Human bites were usually more toxic than animal bites. He wrapped the hand with his pocket hand-kerchief, tying it as tightly as he could with his left hand and his teeth. Still using his left hand, he pried open the hidden com-partment in the bottom of the holdall and removed a New Zealand passport in the name of Richard Winstead, a pocket edition of the *Official Airline Guide*, and a thick wad of money in various currencies. He opened the passport and looked at the photo: Richard Winstead had a dark mustache. He took a false mustache from the theatrical makeup kit in the compartment and applied it to his lip with gum adhesive. That ought to get me through the airport even if the alarm gets right out, he thought.

He opened the *Official Airline Guide* as the taxi entered the tunnel and scanned the Hong Kong departures table. Qantas had a flight leaving for Sydney in forty minutes, with a stop in Manila. Manila would be just fine; he knew a doctor there who asked no questions. Then he would call bloody Weiss and tell him the operation was blown and that he was out of it.

Chambers woke up slowly, coming up as from a deep dive. As he grew closer to consciousness, he felt more and more pain from his injuries. He got to his knees, and the room spun. He waited until it slowed, then stood up and moved behind his desk and dropped into his chair. He pulled the wastebasket from under the desk and vomited into it. His head cleared, but the smell sickened him again, so he picked up the basket and ran as best he could to the men's room, where he vomited again. After rinsing his mouth, he stuck his head under the tap and ran cold water over the bruise on his left temple. He left the basket in the utility sink with water flowing into it, then returned to his office and phoned the Royal Hong Kong Police.

He looked at the records spread out on the floor. Better leave them as they are until the police come, he thought. Why would anyone want to go through my personal files? His head ached, as did his gut and his leg where he had been kicked, and his throat felt raw and sore from the choking. He phoned the police again and asked them to send a surgeon.

Two uniformed constables arrived in five minutes, each with a holstered revolver and a radio slung from his Sam Browne belt. Bruce Maxwell arrived two minutes later, along with the police surgeon. The doctor made Chambers look up and down and side to side, asked him to count fingers held up before his eyes, and said that he might have a mild concussion. Maxwell waited until he had finished bandaging the bleeding bruise on Chambers's temple before pulling out his notebook. A fingerprint team arrived and went to work.

"Well, Skipper, how did all this come about?" began Maxwell. "Did you get the number off the lorry that ran you down?"

Holden tried to smile, but his throat hurt. "It was one man, Superintendent. A European. I am sure I have seen him before."

"Get a good look?"

"Very. An inch shorter than me, thin build, brown curly hair, blue eyes, wide mouth. Early thirties; looked English."

Maxwell picked up the phone on the desk. "Hang on a tick. I'll get that description out to the radio units, as well as to the airport and the ferry piers."

Chambers racked his bruised brain while Maxwell spoke to headquarters. Maxwell was Special Branch; he must have heard the radio call. Good to have a copper on one's yacht, Holden mused. Suddenly an image clicked into sharp focus in his brain: the *gwai-lo* engineer from Cable and Wireless who had been in the office to change a line two months before.

Maxwell hung up the phone and glanced at his notes. "Well now, Skipper, how's a little bloke like this get the best of you? You and me stood back to back in a bar in Manila two years ago, and you gave a good account of yourself."

"He fought like a trained man, Bruce. And I just remembered where I saw him before. He is an engineer from Cable and Wireless, or said he was. His name and ID number will be in the receptionist's log."

"Good, we will get to that. I will also have a police artist up here shortly to do a sketch. Now, tell me, in as much detail as you can, how you encountered the man, what he said, and what seems to be missing."

Chambers told him. It was precious little.

23

Manila, 7 July

DENNIS CHECKED INTO A suite in the Manila Hotel, using a credit card in the name of Philip Russell of Melbourne. He called Dr. Rosario and induced him to shut his clinic on Mabini Street and come at once with a promise of $500 U.S.

He then took a very hot shower and examined the large purple bruise just under his sternum. That bugger Chambers had power if little skill, he thought. His hand continued to throb and ooze blood. It was red, very swollen, and doubtless already infected.

He dressed in one of the long white terrycloth robes provided by the hotel, then phoned down for scotch and ice and a roast-beef sandwich. Dr. Rosario arrived and examined the hand, clucking and chattering about the danger of human bites and the risk of infection in the complex bone and sinews of the hand. He recommended that Dennis go to the hospital, where drains could be installed and massive doses of antibiotics administered intravenously. Dennis told him irritably to clean it and sew it up. Dr. Rosario shrugged and did the best he could. He told Dennis to soak the hand in very hot water at least twice a day until the swelling disappeared. He then gave Dennis a large injection of penicillin and left some tablets. He took his $500 and departed.

Dennis topped up his drink and placed a call to Weiss's office in New York. His secretary called back and gave him a number in Frankfurt. The hotel operator had Weiss in ten minutes.

"What's happened?" barked Weiss, as soon as Dennis had identified himself. "Did you get in?"

"Yes. Unfortunately, while I was going through totally innocuous records, our friend walked in."

"Shit! What happened?"

"I scarpered. I am afraid I had to knock him around a bit. Game lad."

"But you got out? The receptionist here said you were calling from Manila."

"Right," said Dennis, sipping his drink. "I went directly to the airport and caught the first available flight."

"What do we do now?" Weiss's voice had an irritating whine.

"*We*, or rather *I*, dear man, send you a final rendering of my accounts, and *you* pay me off."

"But I am not through with you!" bellowed Weiss. "You have found nothing I can use!"

"Most likely because it isn't there. But no matter. The point is, this operation is blown. Our friend got a very good look at me, and serious charges await me in Hong Kong. I won't be able to go back there for years, if ever."

"But you can't just walk away."

"I can."

"Then perhaps you should walk away as well from whatever expense money you think you have coming," sneered Weiss.

He is brave enough over a telephone, thought Dennis. "I can still operate with impunity in London, and New York, and in Greenwich, Connecticut, Mr. Weiss."

"Oh, don't worry, I'll pay as agreed," Weiss said hastily. "But I need you to do one more thing. Are you known in Singapore?"

"Not well," said Dennis. It is another place with a bloody good police force, he thought gloomily, and, like Hong Kong's since the work of the Independent Commission Against Corruption, nearly impossible to bribe if one did get nicked.

"Go there," said Weiss in a tone of royal command. "I think the game may well come to you. Singapore is about to launch a bond issue, and I think our friend may be dealing with the underwriter without telling me. The underwriter's rep is Barbara Ramsay. You ought to be able to find out something following her; can't be too many American women hanging around the Monetary Authority. And I am sure that Chambers will be returning to Singapore soon."

"Mr. Weiss," said Dennis slowly, fighting his anger at the rude American. "You are not listening to me. This op is *over*, and even if Chambers weren't now in a position to identify me on sight, sending a *gwai-lo* to conduct a surveillance in a Chinese city—"

"What's a *gwai-lo?*" Weiss interrupted.

"A foreign devil," said Dennis, wrapping his throbbing bandaged hand around the iced drink. "A bloody European, Mr. Weiss. You'd as likely send a black man to follow someone through Copenhagen."

"All right, find someone else to do the actual tailing. But I want you there."

"And I am not bloody going!"

Weiss chuckled. "Twenty thousand quid additional change your mind?"

Dennis thought about the danger but also about the fact that all of his special equipment and all his clothes save what he stood up in were in Hong Kong, by now secure behind a police lock. Maybe I'll just go over to Singers, have some suits made by the expensive tailor in Shenton Way, and then bugger off. "All right, Mr. Weiss, I'll go. Have the money in my account today?"

"Of course." Weiss laughed. Power was making people do what they didn't want to. "And Mr. Dennis, do you recall the second code word I gave you?"

"Committed to memory, Mr. Weiss."

Weiss caught the man's insolent tone. He is beginning to irritate me as much as Chambers. It would be nice to find a way to bury them both in the same hole. "Keep it in mind, sweetheart. You may soon have need of it."

Weiss allowed himself a chuckle. What an absurd little shit was dear Mr. Weiss. "I'll fly down to Singers tomorrow morning."

24

Hong Kong, 8 July

BARBARA SAT IN HER office with her feet propped on her desk. The clock on her desk said 20:30. Her short woolen skirt fell about two-thirds of the way up her thighs. She felt decidedly unladylike, and she didn't care. Her head pounded, and besides, there was no one left in the office except her secretary, Iris Wu, who sat at her desk outside Barbara's cramped office, trying to get a call through to London. The securities salesmen and the office staff had gone home at five o'clock, as always.

Barbara wished for a cold cloth to put on her head, which boomed with pain. She wished for aspirin. She wished for a good stiff drink. None of these things would be hers until her call went through to Nigel; then at last she could get off home.

She felt profoundly sad. What was she becoming? Was she truly ruthless enough to play with the Lions? Was she becoming *too* ruthless? She felt she was using Holden, whom she thought she could love, for the sake of the deal. She was lying to Nigel, who had his neck on the block along with hers, and was glad to be there, because he trusted her. How far would she go? Could she stop if she wanted to? Simply back off, save herself, and be a real person again? Or was the deal *everything*, and if so, what would *she* be, even if she won?

She had spent the day reassuring Nakamura Securities' Hong Kong branch manager about the Singapore situation, feeding him information she was getting from Elizabeth Sun over the telephone. Yes, there had been a "disturbance"—Elizabeth's word. A man had been killed. One man. A policeman had been injured but would recover fully. One policeman. Several demonstrators had been arrested, but only seven were being held, mostly as witnesses to the shooting. Singapore was calm.

Mr. Nishimura called several times to check on new rumors. Elizabeth admitted that the striking dockworkers had been more aggressive toward police since the "incident," and a few arrests had been made. But the city was calm, and shipments were moving across the docks, loaded by dockworkers who had ignored or abandoned the illegal strike and, in a very few cases, Elizabeth had asserted, by soldiers. There was nothing in any of this that should concern the bond's underwriters. Singapore was an ethnically diverse society, and frictions occurred. Stability would return, said Elizabeth to Barbara, and Barbara to Nishimura-san, probably when the heat broke and the rains returned.

Nishimura said he would try to reassure Tokyo, but Barbara knew he was unconvinced. She fretted with a tendril of her hair in the quiet of her office. Another "incident," and she was sure the Japanese would bolt.

Barbara had gathered her management group after four days of frantic dealing by herself in Hong Kong and Nigel in London. It wasn't the group she might have wished, lacking any of the power players of Asia. After Traders had turned down the co-manager's position, Credit Genevois, Chase, and First New York had each refused the offer in quick succession, citing existing commitments to the borrower and wishing her luck. Only Holden had told her the truth: They were all afraid of the amount, afraid of having to swallow their entire allotments.

Nigel Cross had been able to deliver Banque Suisse d'Investissement. BSI was not a major player and it added little prestige to the underwriting, but at least it could be expected to stuff the bonds into private client portfolios. Both Credit Suisse and Union des Banques Suisses had turned Nigel down, citing "other commitments in the market" and "the heavy fall calendar." What bullshit, thought Barbara. If the big guys supported a deal, it sold. RAL was a new player and the big guys were perfectly happy to see them hung out to dry. Next time she thought the big guys would chuckle, the upstart Yanks would get it right and invite everyone who mattered to share the top line and all the fees.

After Nakamura and BSI had committed, Barbara had petitioned Philip Meyer to take the issue up to the two hundred million the Singaporeans required. Meyer had curtly refused, saying that since the Japanese would corner the Japan market and the Swiss their own, nothing had really been accomplished to sell RAL's huge position. Barbara didn't tell Meyer that the Singaporeans might cancel the issue if the amount weren't raised; she was afraid he might gladly accept such an outcome. But then Nigel had performed a minor miracle and convinced Canadian Bank of Commerce to join in. CBC had never been a player in Eurobonds and probably wouldn't be able to sell a bean, but they had the cash and they would book their allotment if they had to. Barbara declared her profound gratitude and promised him the best dinner in London or Hong Kong as soon as the deal was sold and done, and Philip Meyer had grudgingly agreed to increase the issue.

Nigel's junior man had spent a fast three days in Hong Kong and Singapore gathering economic information for the prospectus and running drafts of the indenture to the MAS and the managers, and had returned to London. The deal would have been ready to sign, price, and market in three weeks or less, but then some stupid schoolteacher had managed to turn a routine high school frustration march into something of international interest by getting himself killed. Barbara rubbed her forehead with one hand and pounded her desk with the other.

Iris buzzed the intercom. "Mr. Nigel Cross is on, Mrs. Ramsay."

"Fine, Iris. You might as well go; it's late."

"I will wait," said Iris, and put the call through.

"Nigel?" said Barbara, hoping at least for no more bad news.

"Evening, love," he said. He sounded cheery enough. "How are our friends? Gutters running with blood?"

Barbara bit back an angry retort. She took a slow breath before replying. "That isn't funny, Nigel. The incident was minor. The man was shot by accident. Nothing has changed."

"Okay, sorry. But no need to get testy with me. I am in this as deeply as you are."

"I am sorry, Nigel," she said wearily. "It is just that I have spent the entire day trying to calm a very jittery Japanese manager, and I am not sure I fully succeeded."

"Do you think they might pull out?"

"So far they are just nervous. If things stay calm, they will be all right."

"Too bad the Singaporeans took this moment to shed their reputation for labor peace and racial harmony," said Nigel, his voice depressed.

"Oh, Nigel," said Barbara, dropping her feet to the floor and leaning over her desk. Two large tears plopped on the green blotter in front of her, staining it dark. "Not you, too. One strike, for the most part orderly. A demonstration which everybody who knows Singapore expects in the heat of midsummer; a single death. Christ, the bloody Japanese have enormous demonstrations and huge strikes every spring, and whenever a nuclear-powered warship makes a port call."

"Nobody seems to get killed."

"I know, and they aren't supposed to in Singapore either, Nigel! But how many died the last time the blacks and Asians rioted in Brixton, or Manchester, or Liverpool? Was the United Kingdom's credit affected? There was rioting and looting in New York a month ago during a blackout: did Treasuries collapse?"

"Okay, I know, Barbara. Perhaps it isn't fair, but what is? Singapore is an untested issuer, and we have an awful lot to sell."

He was right, and there was no point in arguing it. "How is Philip holding up?"

"If he could cancel it, he would. I am afraid if we lose our Japanese friends, or indeed any of the others, he will reach for the Material Adverse Change clause."

"Can you hold BSI and CBC?"

"I think so. They are in this because they owe me, and they still owe me. Unless the issue really bombs, I doubt the Swiss will have any qualms about stuffing the paper into their managed investment accounts, and the Canadians weren't expecting to make many sales other than through us."

"How is your order book?"

"Not bad, not great. But it is early days, yet." Nigel's voice was soft, encouraging. "We need a little calm, Barbara, and we will get there."

"Philip will have our asses if we don't," she said bitterly.

"Hm. Well, at least yours is cute. But this is what we get those big bonuses for, my love."

Barbara smiled, ever so slightly. She felt the tension ebb from her face, and she wiped away the next two tears. "Nigel, no matter what happens, and no matter how far they throw us if they throw us out, I will never forget how you have stood by me."

"Nothing at all, Barbara. It's instincts. Yours are good, and mine are to trust you."

Barbara winced. I should have told him everything, but now I can't. "Well, anyway, thanks. If there is no more news, I think I will get home. I need a shower and a drink."

"Sweet dreams. And pray for peace." The line went dead.

Iris stood in the doorway, her steno pad in her hand. She looked distressed, even anguished. "What is it, Iris?" asked Barbara, as she put down the phone.

"I was listening to the news on Radio Three," said Iris. "There was another incident in Singapore."

"My God," said Barbara. She felt as though she had been hit as all her breath rushed out. "What happened?" she whispered.

Iris read from her notebook. "A police substation was fire-bombed. No policemen were injured. The report said a new group

called the *Straits Times* to claim responsibility, one calling itself
the Brigade of Saddam the Martyr."

Barbara felt her body go limp. She struggled to sit upright. I
must think this out, I will not just give up. "Iris, call London
back for me, and then I insist that you go home."

# 25
16 July

FOUR YACHTS LAY RAFTED together, anchored two hundred yards
from the jetty in Sam A Wan, a quiet cove in the New Territories
only a few miles from the border with mainland China. The cove
was surrounded by high hills and small rice farms run by the
Hakka people, using methods of hand cultivation unchanged in
a thousand years. The sailors liked the spot because it was well
protected from the weather and because it couldn't be reached
by road from metropolitan Hong Kong and therefore was always
quiet. There were walking paths among the paddies and through
the hills and a waterfall that could be climbed to a deliciously
cool fresh-water pool.

Joanne von Nordholm was serving canapes aboard *Daydream*,
a classically beautiful wooden yawl now thirty years old, while
her husband, Chris, passed up drinks. Holden Chambers, John
Malcolm, John's wife, Sharon, and Marylin Wong were alongside
in *Golondrina*. Hamish and Alice MacDougal and Colin and Mary
Leach had crossed over from *Sea Bird* and sat in *Daydream*'s
small cockpit, and Eric and Jocelyn Jones, from *Mercury*, moored
outboard of *Golondrina*, sat in that boat's cockpit. Eric was drinking beer from his own boat, since he had refitted the icebox to
his own design and boasted rightfully of the coldest beer on the
water. The rest of the sailors gradually moved to white wine, with
chilled bottles collected from all four yachts, as snacks of stuffed
mushrooms, crab, shrimps, and caviar came up from the galleys
of *Daydream* and *Sea Bird*. The sun had dropped behind the high
island to the west, and the day was beginning to cool. In an hour
Holden would start the crown roast in *Golondrina*'s gas oven,
vegetables and salads would be assembled from the other yachts,
and dinner would be served as night fell. Sam A Wan was so still
they could hear the putt-putt of the motor of a distant junk.

Eric Jones sat up straight, listening. "Sounds like the bugger is coming in here," he said, angered by the growing beat of the engine.

"I hope it is just the ferry from Tai Po," said Alice.

"Doesn't run this late," said Eric.

Lucky III entered the mill-pond-still waters of Double Haven through the narrow Cruiser Passage. Her wake spread behind her in a long series of parallel Vs, and the sound of her big diesel engine echoed back from the silent wooded hills. Barbara Ramsay sat alone on the foredeck bench reading, while Richard van Courtland stood in the pilothouse next to the coxswain, Dan-Dan. Richard put his gin and tonic down on the chart. "Let's go in here, Dan-Dan; this little cove in the southwest corner of Double Haven. Looks protected, and there is water enough."

Dan-Dan didn't look at the chart. He knew the islands and coves but found the charts baffling, as though picturing the world from above. "There?" he enquired, pointing southwest.

"Yes. Should be just around that steep point of land."

"That Sam A Wan," said Dan-Dan, shaking his head. "No good place for junk. We go *there*." He pointed to a narrow beach between two black crags on the east side of Double Haven. A junk with a yellow awning was anchored right next to the beach.

"What's wrong with this place?" said Richard, jabbing the chart sharply. He considered himself a competent sailor and resented the way Dan-Dan frequently dismissed his expressed desires.

"No good," said the coxswain. "People no like junk in Sam A Wan."

"Well, to hell with them. It looks like a good spot to me, and nobody owns the water. We will go to Sam A Wan."

Dan-Dan looked at Richard coolly, his black eyes showing nothing. "We go, take look-see. No junk there, we go other beach, okay?"

"All right," said Richard, picking up his drink. "Let's go look, anyway." He climbed down the ladder to the open midships deck to replenish his drink.

Barbara set her book aside as the light faded. Richard had suggested they go away for the weekend, just the two of them, on the huge junk. At first she had protested, citing how much work she had to do before the bond could be issued, but he had talked her into it, saying she needed a rest. She knew she did indeed need to get away, and she had found the waters and many coves of the New Territories quiet and lovely. They had spent the previous night in Long Harbour at the entrance to the Tolo Channel under a sky clear and full of stars. It was nearly impossible to believe that mad, greedy, bustling central Hong Kong was only ten miles away as the crow flew.

The sailors sat in silence as the big junk rounded the headland and entered the cove. Its engine seemed deafening as it approached. Scowling, Eric Jones stood up and squinted. "Why, that's the *Lucky III*, belongs to bloody First New York Bank. I know her coxswain. He ought to have sense enough to stay out of here, even if the bloody Yank bankers don't."

"Take it easy, love," said Jocelyn. "Junks don't overnight here."

"I'll say they don't," said Eric. "And I will say so if the bugger anchors."

"Look-see," said Dan-Dan. "No junk here."

"Well, what about all those sailboats there?" asked Richard, looking around and loving the tight cove.

"Sailboat place, not junk place. People no like."

"Well, Dan-Dan," said Richard, in his firm, important boardroom voice. "I like it here. Drop the anchor over there, well away from the bloody sailboats."

"Aye, yah," said Dan-Dan, the universal Cantonese expression of displeasure. He shouted at the boatboy to ready the anchor.

The junk's engine died, and the boat swung to her anchor in the ebbing tide. Barbara looked across and recognized two of the yachts as being *Golondrina* and *Sea Bird*, both of which she had visited in Manila the previous Easter. She waved from the foredeck, but no one waved back. Perhaps they didn't recognize her in the fading light.

"I am going to row over there," said Eric.

"Let's leave it, Eric," said Hamish MacDougal. "Let's just have dinner. They haven't harmed us yet."

Lucky III gave a bark and a puff of blue smoke, followed by the tinny pounding of her diesel generator.

"Well, I am bloody sorry!" shouted Eric. "I am not going to listen to their fucking generator all night just so they can run their air conditioning and watch bloody television!"

Holden stood up. "I'd better go with you, Eric."

"Fine. You can row."

"Eric," said Jocelyn sharply. "Don't get in a row. Be polite."

"Aren't I always, love?" asked Eric with a grin, climbing into the stern of *Daydream*'s dinghy as Holden unshipped the oars.

* * *

Richard was in the saloon, rebuilding his drink and watching the cook lay out prawns and fresh fish for dinner. Barbara popped her head in the companionway. "Someone is rowing over from the yachts, Richard."

"Good," he said, adding a splash of tonic to his glass of gin. "Ask them up for a drink." He heard shouting from outside, and then Dan-Dan answered in Cantonese. The generator suddenly died, and with it the air conditioning and the electric lights over the grill. The cook cursed and slammed his turner down on the counter. "Bloody hell," said Richard, emerging on deck. A small white dinghy, rowed by Holden Chambers and with a red-faced man Richard didn't know in the stern, drifted off the side of the junk. The red-faced man was talking to Dan-Dan in loud Cantonese. Dan-Dan answered angrily and pointed at Richard. "I say, what is all this, Dan-Dan? What has happened to the generator?"

"I told him to shut it off," said the red-faced man evenly.

"What bloody right do you have—" stormed Richard.

"Every right!" yelled Eric. "I'll not have this noisy, smelly barge destroy my evening!"

Fighting for calm, Richard strode to the rail and leaned over. "And who might you be to give orders to my coxswain?"

"I'm Eric Bloody Jones, that's who. And I am telling you to clear off. Junks don't come in here with their bloody racket, as Dan-Dan tells me he informed you."

"What right have you—" Richard choked on his rage.

Eric pointed a long finger like a gun. "You may be some great *tai-pan* of some bloody big American bank, sir, and you may move 'em and shake 'em in Central, but on the waters of Hong Kong, sir, you go where the Royal Hong Kong Yacht Club says or you don't go at all. Now, be off!" Eric turned his face upward and shouted some more to Dan-Dan. Dan-Dan shouted back and then started the main engine. The boatboy ran forward and began to raise the anchor.

Richard clambered heavily up the ladder to the pilothouse, spilling most of his drink. "What the hell are you doing, Dan-Dan?" he roared. "I give the orders on this junk!"

Dan-Dan turned as the junk began to move slowly out of Sam A Wan. His voice was shrill with anger. "Mista Co'ttland, I say you, this place no good for junk! We go now!"

"Damnit! I say when and where we go!"

"I work this boat for First New York five year!" shouted Dan-Dan. "I take you back Hong Kong, then I quit! I quit!"

* * *

Barbara looked at Holden across the widening space between the junk and the dinghy. She thought he looked sorry for her embarrassment.

As he looked at her in turn, she nodded, seeming to understand.

May-Ling watched Holden and the woman on the junk and wondered.

The big junk slowed as it approached the beach on the eastern side of Double Haven. Dan-Dan once again sent the boatboy forward to ready the anchor. Richard came up the ladder, swaying and carrying a fresh drink. "I don't want to stop here."

"Good place," said Dan-Dan, still angry.

"No!" Richard's voice rang with rage. "Take us—take us back to Long Harbour!"

"Long Harbour no good tonight. Wind in night come from north."

"Long Harbour, damnit!"

"Aye, yah," said Dan-Dan, pushing the throttle forward and turning the junk violently toward the north. "Aye yah!"

Eric climbed over *Daydream*'s stern, a grin splitting his features as Holden secured the painter. "Well, now I feel ready for dinner." Chris von Nordholm chuckled and Joanne laughed uneasily.

Holden climbed up into *Golondrina*. "Where is John?" he asked May-Ling.

"He is below, lighting the oven," she replied.

She looks frightened, he thought. He touched her face and whispered, "Sorry about the noise, love. It might have been worse if I hadn't gone with him."

May-Ling nodded and kissed his hand. The crowd on *Daydream* laughed happily as Eric recounted the confrontation. Holden went below, where he found John Malcolm struggling with the balky oven and laughing so hard that tears streamed down his cheeks.

"God, that must have been beautiful," he choked, breaking again into gales of laughter.

"Could have been done with less violence," said Holden, adjusting the gas and getting the oven lit.

John slapped him on the shoulder. "With the likes of our Eric, my captain, there will always be an England." Malcolm sat on the cabin sole and laughed until he was out of breath.

Richard sat in the saloon, pouring from the bottle into his glass, no longer bothering with tonic. Barbara sat across from him, watching the cook preparing their dinner. "God, Barbara, I hate this place," said Richard, his fury smoldering. Tears streamed down his face. "Everything I do, I am thwarted by these bloody colonials, and worse, by that pompous bastard Chambers!"

"Richard, please calm down. Let's just have a nice dinner when we reach Long Harbour. It is a beautiful place."

Richard looked at his wife. His face flashed with hatred, and she was suddenly frightened. "I'm going to bed," he said. He stood up, grasping the gin bottle, and shambled unsteadily toward the aft owner's stateroom.

The yachties went to bed before eleven, John and Eric drunk and the rest just tired from the long, lazy day of sun and wind and good food and drink. John and Sharon slept in separate pipe-cots forward in *Golondrina*'s open hull, while May-Ling and Holden slipped into the owner's aft, a partially closed-off alcove tucked under the starboard quarter. It was the only cushioned berth on the boat, and it was nearly a double bed in size.

They slept spoon fashion, with Holden embracing May-Ling around her tiny waist and breathing through her perfumed hair. "Are you sleepy, love?" she asked.

"A little," he said, kissing her hair. She pressed her buttocks against him with a small circular motion. He pressed back and felt his penis straighten out between her slim thighs. "Maybe not," he added.

She twisted onto her back and hugged him around his neck, kissing him deeply. Then she pushed him away gently. "Was the row with the junk truly awful, Holden?"

He spread his hand on her chest, caressing first one nipple erect and then the other. "An ugly shouting match. Eric might have been a little more tactful, but I doubt van Courtland would have shoved off with just a gentle push."

"The poor man," she said, stretching and relaxing as his fingers toyed with the tiny patch of hair above her sex. She spread her legs and breathed deeply as his hand gently probed into her wetness.

He hitched himself up on an elbow and looked at his lover. Her eyes were closed, and she was chewing her lower lip. She always did that when she became aroused. "Why 'poor man'? Richard van Courtland is a bore, and he had no business bringing his junk into this place. His coxswain had told him that."

"Not van Courtland," she said, opening her eyes. "Dan-Dan, the coxswain. He lost terrible face. I wish I had not been here to see it."

He considered this. The row between van Courtland and Eric

Jones meant little to either of them, but the Chinese coxswain had been shouted at by both *gwai-los* and had indeed lost much face. "Thank you for telling me that," he said, kissing her eyes and her lips. "You are very wise, my sweet."

She spread her legs wider and forced herself beneath his weight. "Just love me now," she said. He picked himself up on his knees and she raised her legs and crossed them over his back. She gave a little gasp of pleasure as he entered her and began his deliciously slow thrusting. Pleasure so close to agony, she thought, twisting beneath him and wishing he would move faster, all the while knowing that his way was so much better for her. She stroked and scratched his muscular back, and soon she lost all control, thrusting up at him and gasping for breath. She felt him slow her with his weight, ever so gently. "Now," she said, nipping his ear with her sharp teeth. "Now."

He reached a big hand underneath, lifted her buttocks off the mattress, and thrust deeply. She felt his explosion deep within her just as her own orgasm flooded through her body, and she saw bright pinpricks of bright red on the insides of her closed eyelids. A long, low moan escaped from her body. It was too loud, but she was powerless to stop it. He finally rolled off and lay quietly beside her. She rolled back into the spoon position, enjoying the slickness of their mingled sweat and the fragrant smells of their lovemaking.

From forward in the boat came the muffled sound of slow applause, followed by a harshly whispered "John!" and the sound of a sharp slap. May-Ling realized she should be terribly embarrassed that John and Sharon had heard the sounds of their loving, but for no reason at all, the muted applause struck her as very funny and she laughed. Holden playfully covered her mouth with his hand and shushed in her ear. She stifled the laughter, but her body shook against his for several minutes.

How silly the *gwai-los* are about sex, she thought. Chinese are used to living close to each other, several generations of a family in the same room. We are not ashamed of or amused by sex or nudity because our privacy is in the mind. She smiled as she snuggled in Holden's arms and drifted toward sleep.

26

Singapore, 20 July

MINISTER ABDUL RAZA ENTERED the Cabinet Room next to the Prime Minister's executive office in City Hall. The PM looked up and favored the police chief with a cold glance. Raza was fifteen minutes late for the meeting, and Lee hated tardiness.

Raza sat at the end of the long table. The other participants at the meeting were the Cabinet Secretary, a small, silent Chinese named Fong who kept the Prime Minister's calendar and took notes at meetings; the Finance Minister, fat, oily Monkey Woo; and Elizabeth Sun, the pale, fidgety head of the MAS foreign department.

Not my usual group, thought Raza warily. He had been elevated to the Ministry of Home Affairs only six months before. The cabinet rank was a nice reward for running an efficient police department, but he didn't feel at all part of the inner circle. The only meetings he had previously attended in this room had been meetings of the full Cabinet, called to ratify some decision already taken by Lee But Yang and his closest advisers.

Raza also felt set apart from the Cabinet by his race. He was certain his appointment had been a sop to the Malay minority, but he hadn't felt it politic to make waves. The only other non-Chinese ministers were the Indian Dr. Gupta, eighty-nine years old and senile, who was Minister of Health, and the Malay Yusef Ibrahim, Minister of Social Affairs, a silly man who maintained the access of Muslims to the official Sharia Court and who presided over the Muslim holiday observances.

Raza, like all ministers, was a People's Action Party member and a member of Parliament, but he was little involved in politics. He was happy just to run an efficient police force. He had been told nothing of the agenda for today's meeting and hadn't asked. He sensed that the four Chinese in the room had started the meeting without him, and not simply because of his tardiness.

Raza did not expect to be consulted; on the contrary, he expected them to give him orders, and he intended to carry them out.

The Cabinet Secretary rose and turned to a sideboard. He brought back a Chinese tea cup on a wooden saucer for Raza and an ornate porcelain pot. As he filled the cups all around the table, Raza noted how frail Fong had become and how his hand shook as he poured from the heavy kettle.

"Abdul," the Prime Minister said quietly but with the usual insistent force in his voice, "thank you for joining us. We have a delicate problem and we need your advice."

Raza sipped his tea, his face expressionless. What problem could involve both the Finance Ministry and Home Affairs? Bank robberies? None in the last quarter. Embezzlement? Government corruption? Raza knew he had to reply to the PM, but he was tempted to wait, to see what Lee's not quite Chinese and not quite inscrutable face might tell him. Anyone other than the PM, and he certainly would have waited silently, the trained interrogator, the confessor to all. "Thank you for inviting me," he said carefully, smiling so slightly as to barely wrinkle his weathered brown face.

The PM returned his cool smile. "The Finance Ministry is concerned, Abdul. The dock strike continues; we had thought it would not. And the students seem more than usually rambunctious in their demonstrations against the summer's heat."

"The affair of the man Saddam al-Selim was most unfortunate," said Minister Woo, looking at the PM. Puppylike, thought Raza. Fat puppylike.

Raza studied the four faces around the table. What was the true reason for the Prime Minister's summons? Over half the dockers had already returned to work, after less than three weeks of the illegal strike. The others picketed, but carefully, watched by a few of his Special Branch detectives and a few more uniformed police. The shooting of the boy Saddam had occurred two weeks before, and demonstrations since had been timid and poorly attended. If anything, it was an unusually quiet August. A few secondary-school students continued to carry placards and daub slogans on the walls of flyovers, those from the Chinese-stream high schools for communist causes, and in the Malay stream for Malay supremacy and reunification with Malaysia. A few Malay kids wore T-shirts with the image of Saddam the Martyr, a spotty kid with an indistinct expression. Students in both groups were watched and occasionally restrained, but nothing unusual had occurred. Two important ringleaders of the so-called Brigade of Saddam the Martyr were under secret arrest, without charge, but Raza saw no reason to reveal that to these finance wallahs. The few angry kids still out there didn't even know how to make a gasoline bomb that would explode and not merely burn.

He framed his reply carefully. "Prime Minister, the dockers have been long without a contract. As you know, they are mostly poor Chinese, and they are infiltrated to a small degree by agents from the Communist Party of Malaysia and perhaps from Beijing. The students are mostly those held in class through the summer; not the best. With due respect, the problems are manageable and under control."

The PM waved his hand in front of his face, as if to dismiss the apparent concern he had previously voiced. "Of course. The police you command are very efficient. Yet my colleagues here"— he indicated Woo and Sun, both of whom leaned forward to listen intently—"are concerned, Abdul. They have a number of initiatives in the markets of Europe and America that could be jeopardized by the slightest hint of instability here at home."

Raza sipped his tea. "Surely, Prime Minister, a crackdown on the dockers would only make such *instability*"—he threw the PM's insult back to him; there was no instability in Raza's Singapore— "appear more than it is."

Again Lee waved his hand. "The dockers do not concern me. They want some wage and rule concessions, and I propose to give them some."

Which means another opening to the left, thought Raza, holding his tongue. That was a political matter, but he did not like it. "Sir," he said simply. "And the students?"

"Abdul," said the PM evenly, steepling his hands in front of him, "I think you must be a bit more firm with the students. Especially, I am afraid, with the noisy ones in the Malay stream. They are getting their views on television in Malaysia and from there to Indonesia."

Raza sat bolt upright. "Prime Minister, it has always been your—been the government's policy not to tread on the minorities, especially the Malays. You yourself have often spoken against the view of us taken by our closest neighbors that Singapore is a third China. I fail to see—"

"Quiet them down, Abdul," said the Prime Minister, his voice as cold and hard as steel. "Get them back in their classes, or if need be, arrest some of the leaders."

"But Prime Minister, their leaders are a few ragged *Bumi-Putra* nationalists running mimeograph machines inside Malaysia. The leaders inside Singapore are young hotheads with big mouths and little brains, and every one is watched. As you yourself have said, these demonstrations come with the summer heat, as regular as power outages."

Lee folded his hands in front of him on the table and seemed to study them. "Abdul, this is not an ordinary summer. What I have to tell you is in the strictest confidence. Very soon we will launch a Eurobond issue, the first of its kind for any Asian borrower and very important to the republic. We will therefore be under scrutiny from the foreign press as well as by the banks and investment houses who will, or *will not*, support the issue. To a very large extent, the ability of Singapore to enter the Eurobond market will depend upon the reputation of our people for stability and discipline. We must have calm through September."

Raza knew just enough about the foreign financial markets to believe that political stability could well affect the outcome of a bond issue. Yet Singapore *was* stable, and surely the foreigners wouldn't think a few students marching to get out of overheated classrooms could change that. Repression of demonstrations, however, could invite meddling from the outside, not only from the tiny and disorganized Communist Party of Malaysia, but from *Bumi-Putra* politicians in Kuala Lumpur and throughout Malaysia. Malaysia's *Bumi* politicians had ranted for Singapore's expulsion from Malaysia in 1965, arguing that Singapore was a poor Chinese sore on the backside of a vigorous emerging Malay nation. After Singapore had grown rich, these same politicians described her as the stolen jewel and hoped to return her to rightful Malay owners. Repression of the Malay students was madness, pure and simple, bond issue or no. "But surely, Prime Minister, restraint has served us well in these matters?"

"A quiet two months, Abdul. Please make it so."

Colonel Raza looked from the set face of the PM to the stony faces of the other three Chinese. He rose to attention. "Of course, Prime Minister. We will, ah, increase our vigilance."

The Prime Minister nodded silently, dismissing him. Raza turned and left the room, his face burning.

Abdul Raza returned to his spacious office at the Ministry of Home Affairs. The room was sparsely furnished and in some respects had more the look of a command post than a cabinet minister's office. His gray-metal desk was pushed against one window, and the opposite wall was lined with radio transceivers by which he could stay in touch with any operation and, indeed, speak directly with any radio-equipped unit. Each frequency in use was attended by a constable–radio-operator, who carefully logged communications of interest for the minister's later review. Raza had another smaller office down the hall, expensively furnished in government chrome-and-glass style, where he received his occasional guests from foreign police forces.

He checked his messages and then spoke to the radio-operator on the end of the line, a young Chinese woman whose dark complexion and first name, Iashiah, indicated Malay blood. "Iashiah, please see if the Head of Special Branch is in his office."

"Yes, sir," said the constable, picking up one of the three telephones on her table.

As Raza waited, he lit a cigarette and watched the smoke rise slowly to the ceiling, pondering the PM's order. Lee was Singapore's most gifted politician; indeed, in some senses he was her only one. He knew better than anyone the fragile nature of the republic's ethnic balance and political stability. Did he call me into that meeting just to reassure his finance people? Does he really expect me to crack down on my people to make that pig Monkey Woo's life easier?

Chief Superintendent Al-Habshi entered the office and halted in front of Raza's desk. "You wished to see me, Colonel?"

Raza waved Al-Habshi to a chair. Few of his policemen called him "minister," and he didn't expect them to. He preferred his professional title to the uncomfortable political one. "Yes, Daoud. I need your advice."

Al-Habshi sat and lit a small cheroot. The smell of cloves drifted on the air. Raza rapped his knuckles on his desk, and the constable named Iashiah turned and looked questioningly. "Take a break, Iashiah. You men, too. Get some tea." Iashiah and the two other radio operators got up and filed out of the room. Iashiah closed the door behind her, leaving the two senior officers alone.

"Something up?" asked Al-Habshi. The minister rarely dismissed his operators, all of whom had the highest operational security clearance and all of whom belonged to Al-Habshi's Special Branch.

"Politics," spat the minister, stubbing out his cigarette. "I have just come from a meeting at City Hall. It seems the PM and the finance people have decided to launch a bond in Europe, and the bankers want to see Singapore spruced up and whitewashed, all of our loyal subjects in clean clothes and keeping off the grass until after the issue is sold."

The Chief Superintendent shifted uneasily. When Raza said "politics," he meant "trouble": a high-level mess the police were expected to clean up or cover up. "What does the PM expect from us?"

Raza smiled. No reason to be gloomy, he thought, just because

Lee Bloody But Yang had fenced him into a corner. "Daoud, let me cut through to the heart of what the PM expects. We will speak as comrades, not as politicians, yes?"

Al-Habshi sat back. "Understood, sir."

"Very well. The PM tells me he will handle the dockers, basically by giving them what they want. The dockers are mostly Chinese, and their union, which government have tolerated but never recognized, reports to Beijing. Government concessions, then, especially in the face of an illegal strike, strengthen the left. Lee has moved left before to get Chinese support." Al-Habshi nodded, remembering the PAP agitation before independence and Lee's successful co-opting of the communists.

Raza continued: "Every time Lee talks with the poor Chinese, and therefore with the communists, his supporters—including, of course, his important financial backers in the Straits Chinese community—get a case of the shits. They panic, fearing to be slain in their beds by their house servants." Raza smiled and lit another cigarette, enjoying his own hyperbole. "Worse, not only do they fear their yellow brethren, who are like them in every respect except for their distressing poverty, they fear as well *any* successful union effort which would drive up their costs. The worst nightmare is a union success among the longshoremen, which would immediately raise the costs of any business that imports or exports. And that, my dear Al-Habshi, is virtually all of them."

Al-Habshi smiled. The colonel liked to become sarcastic and even theatrical when he let off tension. Al-Habshi was proud to be one of the few people trusted enough ever to witness these rare performances. "Then why will the PM run the risk of losing his base of support by settling the dock strike?" he asked. "Why not just let them be for a few more weeks? They will come back."

"The bond issue," said Raza, gesturing with his index figure like a teacher driving home an important lesson. "An illegal strike makes fat Germans and pallid Englishmen and callow Americans who run the big banks afraid of instability and unrest and non-payment—or, worse yet for the bankers, a hard time flogging the paper."

Al-Habshi smiled, almost laughed. "When did you become such an expert on international finance, Colonel?"

"I have had a young man from the Imperial Bank of Hong Kong instructing me, but that is another story. The point is, the PM will settle the dock strike. The Straits Chinese business community must be made to believe Lee continues to merit their support, even while he dances before the tiger's jaws. And how might that come about?"

Al-Habshi frowned. "Another threat?"

Raza smiled like a professor who has elicited a correct answer after infinite patience. "Go on, my friend."

"An external threat to the republic?" Al-Habshi's expression said he clearly thought his suggestion preposterous, even as he offered it. Raza waved his hand before his face, a gesture that implied "sort of." Al-Habshi slapped his forehead with the palm of his hand. "You can't be suggesting he wants us to confront the Malay students!"

Raza's grin became saturnine as he leaned back and compressed his chin onto his neck. "Eureka," he said softly.

Al-Habshi stood up, dropping his dead cheroot into the heavy glass ashtray on the desk. Raza shoved the heavy teak cigarette box, carved in the Balinese style, across his desk. Al-Habshi took a filtered Players and lit it with his own lighter. He walked across the room to the window at the other end. In the distance he could see the dockworker pickets marching in an orderly circle in front of Clifford Pier, watched by a single pair of uniformed constables. Can the PM, he thought, really be asking us to stir up a conflict? He turned back to the minister, who was once again blowing smoke clouds toward the ceiling. "So that is it? We confront the students? Justify this Saddam the Martyr when he has no support among the Malay community and, if anything, frightened them with his insane act? And how should we confront them, Colonel? Invade the campuses and the Muslim streets? Employ firehoses? Baton charges?" He heard anger creep into his voice.

The minister's smile shrank slowly, until only a sad little grin remained. "We will do our duty, Daoud. We will bring tranquillity to the campuses and to the streets." He stood up quickly and placed his hands on the Special Branch chief's shoulders. "What we will *not* do, Daoud, is risk breaking any students' heads, especially"—Al-Habshi opened his mouth to interrupt, but Raza put a finger to his lips—"especially any Malay heads, Daoud. I want you to make sure that the leaders of the students know today that we will be strictly enforcing order tomorrow. I want you to put some of your Special Branch officers in uniform to make sure orders to the riot police are strictly adhered to. And I want you to make sure that the units who will have to face the students are—let us see what our politician-masters would say—racially sensitive."

"Malays," said Al-Habshi, nodding.

"Well, at least not overly Chinese. Another thing, Daoud. We—you and I, no one else—must have our own political initiative. Don't ask me what that means; I couldn't tell you just yet. We must enforce our bankers' calm without rending the republic." He winked broadly.

Al-Habshi smiled. "I am at your order, Colonel."

Raza patted the Chief Superintendent on his shoulders and nodded. "First, on your way out, ask Iashiah to come back. I will tell her to phone my cousin in Kuala Lumpur on my private line."

"General Mohamdir?" asked Al-Habshi, his brows rising.

"The very same. The Deputy Chief of the Malaysian Army General Staff."

"Wh-what will you say to him?" Al-Habshi was plainly shocked. Raza was clearly going beyond his authority if he meant what he said.

"We will discuss cricket, Daoud. It doesn't matter. The second thing you will do is locate the one we call Sea Lion."

"That's easy, Colonel. Sea Lion is in Singapore. Do you wish to get in touch?"

"I wish to consider, Daoud. I wish you to set up communications with Sea Lion that do not lead to you or to me. I may very well have a message after I speak to my dear cousin."

Al-Habshi nodded stiffly and came to attention. "I will have Sea Lion tracked down within the hour. Should I call you?"

"Yes. And remember, Daoud, only you and I will ever know of these things."

"Sir!" said Al-Habshi, pivoting and striding toward the door.

"Don't forget to send in Iashiah," said the minister, feeling one hundred percent better than he had when he left the Cabinet Room one hour before.

Chris Marston-Evans was struggling with his bowtie when the telephone rang. Letting go of the ends of the tie with a curse, he crossed the suite in the Shangri-La toward the phone. Celia normally tied the bloody tie, but she had finished dressing while he was still in the shower and, impatient as always, had gone down to wait in the bar.

"Hullo?" he said, aware of the irritation in his voice.

"Chris?" The voice on the phone was a seductive whisper. "Chris Marston-Evans?"

"Yes, who is that?" he said, annoyed but intrigued. He listened intently, trying to recognize the low, throaty whisper, but he could not.

The voice chuckled musically, infinitely amused. "I am one who has been asked to speak to you, Chris Marston-Evans, on a matter of delicacy."

What could that be? he wondered. Celia playing a joke? But no, he knew Celia's trick voices too well.

"Chris? Are you there, Chris?" The voice seemed to caress him.

"Yes, I'm here. Who is it? What should I call you?" He strained to decipher the magnetic voice. He realized he could not even tell if it belonged to a man or a woman. A homosexual! he thought. A friend of his playing a joke? He didn't consider himself actually gay, but the dimly lighted world of the homosexuals of Asia had a certain . . . attraction.

"You may call me Sea Lion, Chris. I have a message from someone who wishes to help you."

He shivered with excitement despite himself. "Help me do what?" It was a lame question, but he wanted more than anything to keep the apparition talking.

Again the throaty, amused chuckle. "Help you accomplish that for which you came to this city, of course."

A sexual suggestion? he thought. Or, he thought with a shock, the branch! Could this finally be Minister Raza's messenger? "C-could we meet?"

"That would be nice"—the voice acquired a lilting quality—"but unwise, for now. But I have a message for you. You must think about who would send such a message and then act with extreme caution."

He took a deep breath and then another. Calm down, he thought, but he could not. He wanted the voice; he wanted desperately to touch it. "Yes. Tell me."

Chuckle. "There will be more student protests tomorrow, and the police will move to quell them with more force than before. Do you understand me?"

"Yes," he said, though he couldn't see what this news had to do with him.

"Good. There will be violence; students will be hurt and more arrested."

"I understand," he said, mystified.

"And then a high-ranking official in Malaysia will be quoted in the press as saying, 'Malays will not stand idly by whilst Malay brothers are clubbed and shot by Chinese policemen.' Subsequently, the statement will be officially denied."

Chris waited for the voice to continue, but even its breath was silent. "And what should I do with this information, Sea Lion?"

"Nothing," said the voice, seductive, insistent. "Nothing. You must know that I can predict future events. When you know this, we will speak again." The connection was broken with a tinny click.

Marston-Evans listened for a full minute, hoping the voice would return. When it did not, he put the phone back in its cradle and returned to the mirror and the recalcitrant bowtie. His hands trembled, and he made a mess of the knot, but he lacked the will to try again.

If this is Raza's messenger, he thought, he would speak of events the police could indeed predict. If the events proved true, then the voice would have bona fides. He finally got the tie more or less straight, and he grinned at himself in the mirror. Raza will be ours, and then we will have our branch. He held a finger up to his smiling lips and winked at himself, then he picked up his dinner jacket and went to find Celia in the bar.

21 July

Raza entered the drawing room off the large banquet hall in the Peninsula Hotel. The Prime Minister waited, dressed in dinner clothes. Raza was in fatigue uniform, grimy and sweaty from the street. "Prime Minister," he said.

"Abdul, that was a nasty scene in Muscat Street today."

Raza nodded, his face purposely grim. The PM looked genuinely agitated. Good, thought Raza, it was your bloody stupid idea to get tough with student demonstrators. "It was your wish that demonstrations be . . . discouraged, Prime Minister."

"Yes. And you advised against it." The PM tugged at his jaw. "We must have calm, Abdul. We must. Much more than mere prestige is at stake here, please believe that."

"The bond?"

"More than the bond. If I had known this would be a violent summer, I would never have allowed the bond. It has put us in the spotlight in Europe and America and even in Hong Kong at the worst of times."

"But you wanted us to crack down. We cracked down," said Raza firmly.

Lee spread his hands in a gesture of exasperation. "But there was so much blood, Abdul! Right in front of the TV cameras!"

Raza kept his face set, fighting his mixed emotions. He knew the "riot" had been all but staged: Special Branch detectives in plainclothes had provoked a group of surly Malay kids just where the lone TV crew Special Branch had permitted to enter the Muslim quarter was set up. The police had been instructed to thump a few heads in dispersing the kids; superficial head wounds let out a lot of blood. "There were no serious injuries, Prime Minister."

The PM nodded. He looked shaken. "What do you need, Abdul, to restore calm?"

The Minister of Home Affairs was startled. He hadn't expected this opportunity to come so quickly, but he was ready with his answer. Speak slowly, he said to himself. Reasonableness, no anger. "Prime Minister, we could have a domestic emergency in the offing. I don't believe it, but I think we should be prepared." He stopped to let it sink in.

"How prepared, Abdul?" The PM's voice was tired but wary.

Softly, softly, catchee monkee, thought Raza. "I should have temporary command of the army, Prime Minister. I would like the soldiers on alert but confined to their barracks, to move only at my order. No troops in the streets, no tanks, no pressure. But ready in an instant if I need them."

Lee nodded slowly. He seemed relieved. "What else?"

"A sign, from government. A tangible sign that interracial brotherhood will be preserved in Singapore."

The PM smiled and seemed to stand straighter, as though a weight had left him. "You say you are not a politician, Abdul."

"I am a policeman, Prime Minister," said Raza stiffly.

"Just so, Abdul. Very well, I will instruct the Ministry of Defense, and then I will work on your 'tangible sign.' You will trust me to look after that myself, Abdul?"

"Of course, Prime Minister."

27

Hong Kong, 23 July

AS SIR WILLIAM MCQUARRY rose from behind his carved desk, his features indistinct in the dim light of his office, Chris Marston-Evans sprang to his feet. "Thank you for a very complete report, Chris. You were quite right to bring this to my immediate attention and very wise to have done so in person. Now, if you would be so kind as to wait outside, Major Carrington and I will discuss this."

"Of course, Sir William." Chris tugged at his rumpled jacket. He had come in directly from Kai Tak. His flight had been delayed in departing Singapore in the confusion following the attempted hijacking of a Singapore Airlines jet in Bangkok by young people claiming membership in the Brigade of Saddam the Martyr, and he felt sticky and tired. He turned and left the office, closing the door behind him.

McQuarry turned to the other man in the room and motioned him to a group of club chairs in a corner of the large office. "You had better come over here, Charles, and join me in a good think. And I think I will have a drink; I am sure it's late enough. Will you join me?"

"Yes, thanks," said Major Charles Carrington, rising. He was a spare man, ramrod straight, with thinning gray hair and a neat Guards mustache. He wore a flawlessly tailored gray woolen suit, white shirt, and a Guards tie. He had been with the Bank for fourteen years since leaving the British Army, and for the last five years had been chief of trading of foreign securities. "Quite a story, that."

"Quite," agreed McQuarry, dropping into a deep leather chair and picking up the telephone on the table beside him. Carrington sat opposite. "Miss Chu? Would you please send us a steward with whiskey and soda? Thank you." He put the phone down. The steward entered almost immediately; it was McQuarry's custom to serve drinks at late-afternoon meetings with senior staff.

The two bankers sat silently as the steward mixed the drinks in tall Waterford glasses. The interlude gave each man time to go over in his mind the strange tale Chris Marston-Evans had flown up from Singapore especially to tell.

Chris had told them of the first Sea Lion call and its prediction. He had brought a cutting from the *Straits Times* of the previous day. Carrington still held the cutting, plus one other. The first read:

MALAYSIA RATTLES SABRE AS SINGAPORE STREET DISTURBANCES RESUME

Kuala Lumpur, 20 July, 1980, by our own correspondent— A source considered reliable by this newspaper quotes a senior Malaysian Army source as saying, "Malays of other nations could not be expected to stand idly by whilst Malays were clubbed and shot by Chinese policemen in the streets of Singapore."

Carrington spread the second cutting on his knee. It was from this morning's edition of the same Singapore daily:

GOVERNMENT IN KL DENIES INFLAMMATORY REMARKS

Times stands by its source and its story.

The steward placed the tall drinks on coasters on the low table between the two bankers along with a dish of salted nuts and left the office.

The second call had come that morning, Chris had reported. Sea Lion had said that "his master" might soon have to call on "your [Chris's] master as a friend in need" and then had said ominously that steps might have to be taken to curb the abusive power of the Chinese usurpers of Malay soil.

"What do you make of it?" asked Sir William, lifting his drink. "Cheers."

"Cheers," said Carrington, sipping the single-malt Scotch. "What do I think this Sea Lion means by all this? Or whether I believe any of it?"

"First, what does Sea Lion want to tell us?"

Carrington leaned forward and took a handful of nuts from the silver dish. "We are to believe that someone—if Marston-Evans is correct as to source, the Minister of Home Affairs—is planning to take advantage of ethnic clashes to attempt to loosen the grip of the Chinese on the government of Singapore, or even overthrow the Lee government."

"And your assessment of the report's veracity?" asked Sir William, smiling over the rim of his glass.

"Highly unlikely."

"Just unlikely?"

"All right, bloody preposterous. Cloud-cuckoo-land. Daft."

"Hm." McQuarry pursed his lips and seemed to chew the thought. "I am not so sure."

"Surely, William," snorted Major Carrington, "you don't think the entrenched government of Lee But Yang and his one-hundred-percent People's Action Party parliament can be overthrown by a bunch of ragged-arse Malay kids, with or without the aid of the Chief of Police?"

"Even if aided by the Army of Malaysia?"

Carrington laughed, took a cigarette from the silver box on the table, and lit it. "William, even if Malaysia wanted to, the United States would never permit it, nor the U.K., nor in fact Australia."

McQuarry's eyes twinkled as he smiled. "Let us take this thing apart, one step at a time. Point one, let's assume, for the sake of argument, that this Sea Lion is speaking, however indirectly and doubtless untraceably, for Colonel Abdul Raza"—Carrington started to protest, and McQuarry cut him off with a hand held up—"which, by the way, I am inclined to believe."

"But why?" growled Carrington, incredulous.

"Partly the structure of the thing, Charles. First he has this Sea Lion predict the future. The events predicted take place. It wouldn't have been difficult for Raza to ensure a small riot, in front of TV cameras. You may have noted that despite the fact that a fair amount of blood was shown on television, there have been no reports of serious injuries, and none of arrests. And the foreign press were present and have made reports, to all appearances uncensored."

"What about this business of some high Malay army brass threatening to intervene on behalf of his *Bumi-Putra* brothers?"

Sir William raised his finger, and shook it once. "There again I find the very fine hand of the good Colonel Raza, Charles. It isn't generally known that Colonel Raza is a cousin-by-marriage—really no relation at all, in the English sense—of General Mohamdir, the Deputy Chief of the Army of Malaysia General Staff. I have no reason to suppose that Colonel Raza knows that *I* know of that relationship, but given this information, I would wager he does."

"So his cousin leaks the threat, and then the denial?" asked Carrington. "But why?"

"Precisely to give credibility to this Sea Lion and his stories, Charles."

"But why on earth would he pass his message to you via young Marston-Evans?"

"Ah," said Sir William, pointing with his finger toward the ceiling. "As it happens, I sent our young man to see my old comrade-in-arms, the good minister, several months ago, in the faint hope that he might be able to un-jam our branch application from the bureaucracy. Chris was to hint that any favor would be appreciated and reciprocated."

"But, William, you are not seriously suggesting that Raza intends to take over the government, and has just decided to let his old army pal in on the deal?"

"No. In no way do I imagine that there will actually be a coup. But he is trying to tell us *something*."

"Well, now you have me going. Why are you sure the coup threat isn't real if the information is genuinely from Raza?"

"I don't suppose I am *sure*, Charles," said Sir William, his eyes drooping and his mouth again pursed. "But I knew Raza quite well, and in any covert word he would send me, he would expect me to remember him *as he was*. Raza was a very good soldier, and I know he is a very good policeman. Policemen don't overthrow governments, Charles; for one thing, they are too busy. To overthrow a government, you want a general or a colonel with an ego, and troops and equipment under his command and time on his hands. Policemen deal with reality, Charles. For another thing, I served with Raza when we were both young men, during the Emergency in Malaya. He was, and I have no doubt *is*, a very steady lad, and no ranting Malay nationalist."

"And yet you say you can't be sure," said Carrington. He leaned forward for the whiskey decanter and the siphon, and refreshed both drinks.

"Charles, forgive me if I act the pedant," said McQuarry, with a sly smile, "but I have been in Asia, man and boy, for nearly thirty-five years; yourself, a mere fifteen or so. In Asia, one never expects to be absolutely sure of anything. But let us continue to study this problem. If we assume that the message does indeed come from Raza, we have to consider what he means to tell us. Broadly, is it true or untrue? Let's first test the precept that it is true, that he indeed intends a coup. Why would he tell us, and what would he expect us to do?"

Carrington spread his hands in a gesture of helplessness. "I haven't the foggiest. What, then?"

"Well, he would certainly want help, and friends. We are not without influence, Charles, and not just in matters of finance. He would want recognition of the new government by the U.K. and by other countries where the Bank have influence. He would want assurance of uninterrupted access to international credit, especially trade credit. He would want intervention in foreign-exchange markets to prevent panic selling of the Sing dollar. He would want air-service and electronic-communications agreements kept in place. These would all be very important in gaining and maintaining international acceptance of what had taken place."

"And the Bank, plus companies we either influence or control—" said Charles Carrington slowly.

"Cathay Pacific Airways, Cable and Wireless (Far East) Limited," offered McQuarry, sipping his drink.

"Not to mention the great trading *hongs*. The Bank is perhaps uniquely in a position to help," said Carrington, shaking his head, still not believing what he was thinking. "What about the bond they are going to issue?"

"That would be of pretty low priority, I should think."

"But it would surely fall if a coup were to occur."

"Or even if this rumor got out."

"So why does he tell us this, and then swear us to secrecy?"

"Well, Charles, I am trying to think like my friend the policeman. Suppose we were to take a short position against the bond, in the gray market before it is even issued."

"Sell it short on a when-issued basis? We would make a tidy profit—*if* this really happened," said Carrington slowly, touching his mustache. "And be well and truly buggered if this turned out to be so much air."

"Well, if he really is going to do it, he would be well along in the planning by now, and maybe he knows he will strike his blow just before or just after the bond comes out." Sir William smiled. "We make a killing based on what amounts to a tip from him. He might think of that as an advance payment for our help with his post-coup needs."

Carrington shrugged. "I admit it all fits together, William, but it's bloody thin."

"Of course it is thin. Now let's look at the other side of the coin. If Raza *is* telling us this, but is relying on us and our good sense to recognize it is *not* to be taken literally, what *then* is he trying to tell us?"

Carrington took some more salted nuts from the dish and sipped his drink. "I may be seeing this too narrowly, William, blinkered by my own discipline, but I suspect it must have something to do with that bond."

"I agree completely. That huge bond issue sticks out like a sore thumb. The market is already jittery, especially in London, where they really don't know Singapore."

"And might believe this?"

Sir William nodded.

"Jesus, William, do you think he wants the bond to fail? Perhaps to cause embarrassment to some rival in the cabinet?"

"That is sort of what I thought when I was listening to Chris tell his tale. But that assumes Raza is politically ambitious, which I doubt, and reckless, which I doubt even more. No, I think he wants a nervous market to get more nervous. As you pointed out a moment ago, a short position, especially by us or any other bank with no allotment from the lead underwriter, would be highly risky. If the lead had the guts and the capital, he could force the bears to cover their shorts at par or even at a premium."

"Not the sort of risk we would take on the basis of a rumor."

"Not at all. But I don't think Raza would want us to short anyway—assuming there will be no coup and no post-coup needs. Remember, I approached him through Chris for help with our branch application. He now comes back to me via the same channel with this strange tale. I am sure he realizes that if we are found to be, or even suspected to be, mucking up the pet project of the Monetary Authority of Singapore, we would never get our branch license through, with or without his aid. What he would expect us to do, I think, is to step in and support the issue, and receive in grateful exchange our long-sought license."

"Which we probably would do, if a deal could be struck, without this strange message."

"Precisely," said McQuarry, sitting back and folding his hands on his little paunch. He looked contented, as though he had just explained a tricky chess problem. "The profits to be made in that branch are worth far more than what we could get by keeping this tale to ourselves and shorting a bond, and they carry none of the risk."

Carrington gave a short laugh. "You look as though you have solved the puzzle, William, and you do indeed make me feel the new boy in Asia. I am as completely baffled as when we started."

"The message is addressed to Europe," said Sir William simply, as if that explained everything.

"Then why does he tell us, and why does he insist we keep it secret?"

"He tells us because he can confidently expect we will figure out he is the source of the information, without ever being able to prove it." McQuarry ticked the point off on an outstretched finger. "He tells us to keep it secret, first because he knows we wouldn't give the matter five seconds' consideration if he didn't. This information, if true, would be of great value to a speculator. And his telling us could be construed as treason. You might better ask whether he *really* wants, or even expects, that we shall keep his secret."

"We could let someone else take the short position."

"Right. Look, Charles, no matter how clever we are in defining Raza's motive, *if* we really are dealing with Raza, you and I both know that Singapore is about as likely to suffer an overthrow of its government as it is to receive a foot of snow. But in London, they see a riot. Their Asian offices tell them it means nothing. In Geneva, they see a killing. An accident, they are told. The emergence of a new terrorist group. A few kids. A comic-opera hijacking attempt. If they ask us, or their own people out here, we keep saying that these are isolated and unrelated incidents, and that Singapore is as stable as the church. Let's assume they are reassured but nervous. Then, *then*, my friend, they get this rumor. What might the finest minds in Europe do?"

"The comanagers might begin to cut losses by shorting in the gray market," said Carrington. "And plungers might even take naked short positions."

"And then out comes the bond and nothing happens, and Roland, Archer has all the demand it needs to open the issue on a strong up-tick."

"It's brilliant," said Carrington quietly. "It's terrifying."

"It's *Asia*, Charles. Ancient as the Great Wall, and new as tomorrow."

"So we leak it?"

"To the best of friends."

"Who, if your analysis is correct, will get stuffed? Who do you have in mind?"

"I have reason to believe we owe First New York a bit of turnabout," said Sir William, grinning with immense satisfaction. "And I think that young chap from Traders Asia could be taken down a peg or too. He has been far too successful, and he doesn't share with us as a good colonial should."

"But can we afford to be the source of this?"

"Locally, Chris will be the source. We will instruct him to take Holden Chambers into his confidence, to ask his advice. He will tell Chambers everything *except* the source of the rumor, which, after all, is speculation anyway. The two are well acquainted, and it should seem natural enough. Chambers is not much more likely to swallow the story than we are, but Traders in London might, and he will have to report it. You will have to manage the leak to First New York in London, and to the bond's comanagers. If we seem to be doing a favor for First New York here, even Chris will smell a rat, and we want him to continue believing in Sea Lion."

"And whatever happens, the Bank can't lose, William. It's brilliant."

"That is why we are the Bank, dear boy."

Carrington rose. "Shall I sent young Chris back in to you?"

"Yes. I think I will give him a well-deserved drink and a pat on the head. Perhaps you could call a friend or two in London while I am doing that."

Major Carrington saluted his chairman and walked across the carpet and left the office.

28

24 July

"WHO THE FUCK IS Saddam the Martyr?" rasped David Weiss the moment Holden Chambers picked up the phone in his office.

Chambers sighed. Instantly, as if on command, his head began to pound. "Good morning to you, David."

"Howdy. Who is this guy? The papers say the crazies who tried to hijack the Singapore Airlines flight in Bangkok were from the Brigade of Saddam the Martyr."

"Well, David, the man who was killed during a demonstration two weeks ago in Singapore was identified as Saddam al-Selim, a university student. It seems the *Bumi-Putra* underground has decided to make him a hero."

"Other incidents?"

"A police station was firebombed; they smudged the paint. Slogans scrawled on walls. It is mostly high school kids, amateurs. The hijacking attempt in Bangkok was a farce; the would-be hijackers were disarmed by the aircraft's purser."

"None of this has made it into your chatty evening telexes," said Weiss, a sneer in his voice.

"I had no idea you would be interested, David. Why *are* you interested?"

"We will get to that. Next question, bubula: Who the fuck is Sea Lion?"

Chambers sat up straight, suddenly alert. "Sea Lion is supposed to be a closely guarded secret."

"Well, unguard it, asshole."

"Sea Lion is a rumor, or the source of rumors. Speaks to a fellow who is in Singapore for the Imperial Bank. He tells a few others, and it is supposed to stop with them."

"And you saw fit to keep it from me and your colleagues at TBI?"

"Again, I saw no reason for you to be interested, David."

"There is said to be a major Eurobond issue in the offing for Singapore," said Weiss dryly.

"Of course, but we are not in it," said Chambers, puzzled.

"Jesus Christ!" Weiss bellowed. "Do you remember my telling you you know nothing about the bond market? Just because we decided not to underwrite the fucking great whale of an issue doesn't mean we are uninterested!"

Chambers felt angry and keenly interested at the same time. "So please enlighten me."

"The bond is due out any day. We hear the Singapore Finance Ministry is pressing RAL and its exiguous comanagers to price the issue and get it on the market. We hear the comanagers are very nervous and may even be selling their positions in the gray market. What makes them nervous is a couple of ugly incidents that seem, as you say, amateurish and perhaps more comic than serious."

"And?" Chambers was ashamed to admit his ignorance, but he had to know.

"And, dear boy, then along comes this Sea Lion and puts a new spin on these apparently trivial incidents."

"But the Sea Lion rumors are preposterous. He suggests that there could be a general uprising among the Malay population, even an overthrow of the government! David, in regard to political stability, Singapore is closer to being Switzerland than it is Uruguay. The likelihood of anything like that happening is remote."

"Yet some of the Sea Lion rumors have proven true. There was that statement attributed to a high official in the Malaysian army about not standing idly by whilst Malay brothers and sisters are clubbed and shot down by Chinese policemen."

"The Malaysian government denied the statement was ever made. Likely whoever feeds Sea Lion with information also leaked that to the *Straits Times*."

"Be that as it may, Holdy-poo, some here in London, where real markets are made, think Sea Lion could be official or semiofficial."

"I have heard that, and I think it is utter nonsense. Who in government could gain by such a rumor? And besides, if anyone 'official or semiofficial' wanted to leak something, they would hardly go through Chris Marston-Evans, the Bank's man temporarily in Singapore. He is very junior, a staff man, not a market man. He lives here, but he doesn't know Asia. He wouldn't know what questions to ask, and he would most likely get whatever they said wrong."

"Perhaps they want someone who won't ask too many questions."

"It isn't their style. It isn't *Asia*, David."

"So you don't think that Sea Lion speaks with any authority." It was a statement, not a question.

"In a word, no. I am curious, of course, but to one who knows Singapore, the whole idea of a coup or violent change of government is absurd. Government in Singapore is the People's Action Party, and the PAP reaches everywhere. The Malay kids who demonstrate don't represent the Malay people of Singapore, and any that wish to live among their *Bumi-Putra* brothers in Malaysia are free to go there, but they don't."

"So you wouldn't, say, advise us to take a short position against RAL's bond issue?"

"You have told me repeatedly that I am to have no opinion about Eurobonds, but since you ask, no."

"Well put, asshole. Now, will you answer my question? Who the fuck is Sea Lion?"

"No one knows. A voice on the phone, maybe a practical joker."

"But you will find out for me." Once again a statement, not a question.

"And just how would you have me do that, run an ad?"

"Don't be sarcastic with me, it ill becomes you," said Weiss sweetly. "You know, you have never had much sense for the business, but at least you used to keep current on what went on in your market. It seems you may even be losing that small usefulness."

"What does that mean?" asked Chambers angrily, tiring of the game.

"Before I called you, I had a word with Tony Wren—you remember Tony? The manager of our branch in Singers?"

"Yes, David." Fuck you mightily, he thought.

"Well, it seems our Tony has a friend, he says, who could introduce us—introduce *you*, that is—to Sea Lion himself. So, dear boy, get your ass on a plane and go and see Tony's friend."

"Why can't Tony see his own bloody friend? I have a lot to do with the Korea Exchange Bank offering to get out."

"Let your expensive and oversized staff deal with that. Tony is not exactly the right instrument for this, and besides, he is too well known in Singapore. And even if he weren't, given my present mood, you are far more expendable."

"Oh, Christ, David! Just because Tony's—"

"I want you in Singapore tomorrow, laddie, and I don't want to hear anything further from you until you run this Sea Lion to ground."

"And when I get this information, if indeed it can be got?"

"Then you can sit back and watch how a real player in this market can make a lot of money off someone else's fucked-up deal." Weiss hung up abruptly.

This is very strange, thought Chambers, staring at the silent telephone in his hand. There wasn't anything serious going on in Singapore, and he was sure of it. Yet the few scattered incidents could look like major instability to someone thousands of miles away in Europe, especially when stitched together by the clever but certainly groundless Sea Lion rumors. He glanced at his watch; just five-thirty. "Margaret?" he called.

She popped her head in through the doorway. "Yes, sir?"

"Try to reach Captain Kelley at the American Consulate. Tell him I need to speak with him, urgently. I will pick him up there in ten minutes, if possible."

Captain Sean Kelley, USN, the Defense Intelligence Officer attached to the American Consulate, slipped into Traders's white Mercedes in the underground carpark at the Consulate on Garden Road. Kelley was a trim, athletic man who looked much younger than his forty-nine years. He was dressed in an expensive sports jacket of soft gray linen and black woolen slacks. Only the high shine on his shoes and his short haircut suggested his military occupation. He reached across to shake Chambers's hand. "Where are you taking me, all mysterious?"

"My place. I need to talk. There will be no one there. Ah King is with her sisters in the New Territories."

Kelley nodded. His job was to gather intelligence in Hong Kong and to glean what information passed across the Chinese border with the legal and illegal trade. In the course of plying his craft, he consulted with a few of the American businessmen in the colony, especially the ones who traveled frequently and who had contacts with high government officials. Often what these men observed was very useful, and Holden Chambers was an especially acute observer. It was from him that the U.S. intelligence community had first learned of the serious and debilitating illness suffered by the President of the Philippines. From time to time, Chambers would come to him with a question, and if he could answer it, he would. "Just don't ask me anything operational," he always cautioned. It was their little joke. Kelley was the senior "legal" intelligence officer in the consulate, and operational intelligence was not part of the very visible naval officer's job.

Ah Wong moved smoothly into the light traffic heading into Central, then passed over the interchange into the thick, slow-moving uphill traffic aimed at the Peak and Mid-levels along Cotton Tree Drive. "Fair enough," said Chambers. "I wouldn't want to know the violent secrets you protect." They talked about mutual friends until they reached the interior of Holden's flat. Holden made tall drinks and they sat facing each other on the upholstered rattan chairs beneath the tapestry.

Kelley said genially, "Glad you didn't blurt out any secrets in front of Ah Wong the Master Spy."

"Which means you would like me to get to the point," said Chambers with a smile. "Aye-aye, Captain. Have you heard of someone called Sea Lion?"

"Singapore," said Kelley. "We heard, though sadly, not from you."

"Christ, Sean, in retrospect, I'm sorry. When Chris Marston-Evans first came to me with this, I thought he must have been hallucinating. I never believed for a moment that anything could disturb the benevolent authoritarianism of Prime Minister Lee and the PAP."

"Has something caused you to change that opinion?"

"No. But the rumors persist, and some, my own boss not the least among them, believe the source is someone in or near government in Singapore."

"No comment," said Kelley, just above a whisper.

"Fine, Sean, I know the rules. I brought you up here just to confirm that I am not going mad. One question, unofficial, nonoperational."

"Before you ask it," said Kelley, holding up a hand, "and at the risk of sounding melodramatic, has it ever occurred to you to have this flat swept for electronic listening devices?"

Chambers grinned, lop-sided, embarrassed. "I had it done two weeks ago, the office as well, and again this afternoon. I am still a little rattled after the break-in at my office. I felt quite silly."

"Not silly. Who did it?"

"Swire Security Service."

"Okay. They're very good. So ask your question." All the banter had gone out of the officer's voice.

"It is simply this: Is there any possibility that the United States would allow the government of Singapore to be overthrown or the city-state to be reabsorbed into Malaysia?"

Kelley looked at Holden for a minute without speaking. He reached for a silver cigarette box on the table before him and opened it. It was empty. Holden got up quickly and walked to the sideboard, opened his humidor, and extracted an unsealed box of Dunhill's. He returned to his seat and handed them across to Kelley. "Trying to quit again, I see," said the captain, extracting one cigarette, lighting it, and tossing the box on the table. It slid across to Chambers.

He in turn got one out and lit it. "Yeah. But these times are hard for moral initiatives. Can you answer my question, Sean?"

Kelley blew a long stream of smoke straight up into the ceiling fan, which revolved slowly above them. "I shouldn't. I am trying to think of what I can tell you. It wouldn't surprise you to hear that this is a very delicate subject indeed?"

"Actually, it does," said Holden glumly. "I had hoped you would say something to the effect of 'No, no way. Never in a million years.' "

"Well, it might be something like that. Might. But the riots of the summer have gotten people to thinking. People, unlike you and me, old man, who do not have the clearest view of Asia. Let us speculate that Prime Minister Lee makes another vault to the left, as he did just before and just after independence, to get the Chinese firmly back on the reservation."

"The dockworkers," said Holden. He felt suddenly drained.

"And let us further speculate that he thumps a few Malays and infuriates what is becoming an ever more right-wing government in Malaysia in the process."

"But the U.S.—"

Kelley waved his hand through the smoke in front of him. "Suppose, in the eyes of someone faraway, the most important thing for the U.S. in the immediate vicinity of Singapore was a large and very well-equipped former British naval base and repair facility, on the north side of Singapore Island. A base we have wanted since Cam Ranh Bay in Vietnam was regrettably lost to us. How do you think that someone would react to Lee's cozying up to Beijing?"

Holden felt despair rising in waves. He even felt slightly sick. "Lee refuses us access to the base?"

"He does." Kelley sipped his drink, then downed it in one gulp.

"So the United States might be amenable, even pleased, if Lee's government—"

Kelley rose, his finger pressed to his puckered lips. "Thank you for the drink, Holden. Could you have your driver run me back to the Consulate?"

Holden stood up and shook his head. "Of course, Sean. And thank you."

Holden escorted the captain to the door of the flat. "Holden," said Kelley, his voice barely a whisper. "This conversation never took place."

"What conversation?" said Chambers, trying to smile and failing.

* * *

Holden Chambers began packing a bag as soon as Captain
Kelley had departed. Something is very odd here, he thought.
What the hell is Weiss doing? How is he going to profit if Barbara's
deal fails? He picked up the phone and booked a call to Traders
Bank International in London, then mixed himself a drink. The
call went through almost immediately, and Frank Portas came
on.

"Good evening, Holden. David been rattling your cage?"

"Good morning, Frank. Yes, he has, and I am puzzled. I hate
to display such ignorance, but just how does the gray market
work?"

"Don't be ashamed, old boy." Portas chuckled. "Half the bond
gunslingers don't understand the gray, and the ones that do won't
usually go near it."

"How does a short sale on the gray work?" asked Chambers,
picking up a pad and preparing to take notes.

"Well, you know how an ordinary short sale works," said
Portas.

"Sure." Holden shrugged. "You sell a share or a bond you
don't own, in the hopes you can buy it later at a cheaper price."

"Right," said Portas. "But in reality, that is only half the transaction. Your broker has to borrow the security from someone
who does own it and pay interest or a fee for the privilege. Now,
what happens if the price of the instrument rises and the owner
wants it back so he can sell it?"

"I have to buy in. I lose money."

"Well, not necessarily," said Portas. "Say it is General Motors.
There's tons of shares around, so your broker can borrow someone else's shares and give them to the person you originally borrowed from, and you can continue to be short, if you still believe
GM is going down in the future."

"Okay," said Chambers.

"Well, in the when-issued market, which we traders call the
gray market, there is an added risk. Say we short this Singapore
bond, when issued. The bonds do not yet exist, so we can't borrow
them until they do. But nonetheless, we have completed your
half of the transaction—sold, say, at 96. When the bond is actually
issued, we have to deliver at 96."

"Which means we have to close my position. We can't borrow
from someone else."

"Exactly. Now, think: Who is the probable buyer of your short
sale?"

Chambers frowned, sipping his drink. "I have no idea."

"In a normal deal, the buyer is probably the lead underwriter himself, the dealing usually masked by intermediaries. A short position will create demand for his bond when it comes out."

Holden smiled. It was becoming clearer. "And when the bond comes out?"

"Say the bond comes at 100. Your buyer, whoever he is, but especially if he is the lead underwriter, demands you settle immediately, because he wants to sell at 100 and make his four bucks. You must settle, even if you have to buy the bond from the underwriter at 100, or even higher."

"And the only place I can go is to the lead underwriter," said Holden.

"Right as bloody rain, Holden," said Portas. "And if the bond is ticking up, you may find your direct line to the lead underwriter's trading desk is temporarily out of service. If you are the underwriter of an issue which unexpectedly turns hot when it is issued, it can be great fun indeed."

"The underwriter could screw absolutely everyone," said Chambers.

"Too right, lad. It's called a bear squeeze, and a good one is a joy to behold, *if* you are on the right side of it."

"Christ!" breathed Chambers. "Why would Weiss want to run such a risk?"

"Well, of course, if the bond goes down, say to 94, then the short player can make his profit in the usual way, by buying from an underwriter, who in such case is only too glad to get out from under his own position."

"But it is a very high risk. Surely David won't really do it?"

"I only work here, Holden," said Portas. "Have a nice evening."

29
Singapore

YUSEF RAZA DRIFTED ON the edges of the Malay student community, fascinated and yet frightened by the fervor of the talk of confrontation with the Chinese usurpers and revolution in the streets. The talk was intoxicating, and in the nearly all-Malay enclave of the Muslim quarter, it seemed to make sense, but Yusef knew the political realities and was sure nothing could be gained from violent confrontations with the authorities. Yusef, after all, knew his father.

Yet the rumors persisted, flowering and dying each long hot day: rumors of Malay volunteers from across the causeway, or better yet the Malaysian Army disguised as volunteers. Raza even heard the name of his father whispered as the leader of the city-state after the revolution, or of the province if Singapore was to be reabsorbed into Malaysia. It was all great fun in the New Malacca and the other coffeehouses where students and teachers met to gossip, but it was also very silly and, if carried too far, dangerous.

Raza descended the stairs into the basement of the New Malacca just after 8:00 P.M. He had been kept late at the school preparing statements for students arrested in the big demonstration of nearly three weeks before, statements they would take to Magistrates' Court. As Raza went down the stairs, he heard shouting and the scrape of furniture. He entered the room quietly and saw several groups of men staring at Elias, who whirled and ranted on the narrow stage, an impromptu one-man show. Elias's face and chest were slick with sweat and his lips were wet. Yusef approached the stage cautiously; Elias frightened him when he was stoned. Elias's eyes were wild as he leapt about in some kind of frenzy, like the monkey-god puppet in the Ramanayama plays in the Hindu temples. Must be whacked out of his skull on something, Raza thought, taking a seat near the back of the room.

"Why hello, sweet Mahmoud!" shouted Elias, throwing out his

arms in greeting. Yusef smiled and waved. "Elias is just telling these dullards the good news of the coming revolution, but they *don't believe!*"

"Tell Mahmoud," said Sayed, one of the older regulars at the New Malacca. "He has a level head."

"Yes, try to convince Mahmoud," said another.

"Elias has found a spy," said Elias, pointing a thumb at his chest and spinning around. He lost his balance and almost fell. "A spy," he said, grabbing the edge of the stage and sitting heavily, "who talks to foreigners to gain support for the glorious new day!"

Yusef grinned and nodded. Today's rumor. "Why does the spy talk to foreigners?"

"Foreign bankers," said Elias. His wild eyes looked cunning. "To gain support when our brothers cross the causeway and the streets run deep with Chinese blood."

The statement chilled Yusef, even though it was preposterous. "If you believe what you hear, Elias, you should go to the police."

"The police!" Elias pouted. "The police don't *like* poor Elias, and besides, who knows where the police will stand?"

"That's absurd, Elias," said Yusef. "The police stand with the government."

Elias grinned and clapped his hands. A peal of drugged-out laughter burst from him, high pitched and joyous. "And what if I told sweet Mahmoud that my spy may belong to the highest Malay in the land?"

Yusef laughed with the others, sharing the enormity of the joke. What does Elias really know, and how does it threaten my father? he thought. And what should *I* do? He would laugh at me if I took to him the ravings of a drug-addicted homosexual and doubtless have Elias arrested and charged. Yet if *any* of this were true, Singapore was in danger and so was his father.

30

25 July

HOLDEN CHAMBERS WAS MET by Tony Wren just outside Immigration Control in Singapore's overcrowded Paya Lebar Airport. They shook hands and Wren took one of Chambers's two carry-on bags and led him through the crowd toward his car.

At forty-four, Tony Wren was in some respects considered the dean of Traders's corps of officers scattered around Asia. He was a tall man, with the erect bearing of his former calling, the British Army. He had the loud, mellow voice and the exaggerated gestures of an actor. He always dressed well, although a shade flamboyantly for a banker. Today he was wearing a suit of a rather bright blue linen, a lavender shirt of an almost transparently thin cotton, and a yellow silk bowtie with a tiny blue figure. A handkerchief of the same material as the tie rose like a jungle flower from the breast pocket of his suit jacket, its lower petals hanging down at least eight inches. He kept a large old house in the Hougang suburb, with lots of servants, and he gave wonderful parties. He had been in Singapore for eleven years since leaving the army, first with the British High Commission, and later with Traders, hired to open the marketplace when Traders had opened its first office in any Asian country in 1973. Holden thought Wren a likable man, and there was no doubt he knew everyone in Singapore worth knowing, as well as important people in other countries in the region. He doubted, however, that Tony knew more than the rudiments of the banking business, or that he cared.

They reached the curb, and Wren's driver spotted them and swept grandly up. Wren's car was an old Daimler he had had brought out from England at the bank's expense before there were rules about such things. It was a huge car, painted a creamy off-white. Its cavernous interior could easily accommodate six in the passenger compartment, separated from the driver by a glass panel. Tony had bought the car, built in the midsixties, from an impoverished baron in England. Before shipping it to Singapore, he had the car completely reupholstered in red leather and a modern air-conditioning system installed, all this also at the bank's expense. He proudly told visitors that it was the exact same model as transported the Governor of Hong Kong, although of course the Governor's car (Tony knew Sir Murray MacEachern well, of course) was black and had the Queen's arms on the doors. Holden thought the car a grotesque embarrassment. They both got in, and the uniformed driver put Holden's luggage in the boot.

"Awfully sorry you won't be staying out at the house, Holden," said Tony, crossing his legs and revealing sheer hose that approximately matched his shirt. "I've some wonderful people coming out on Sunday for the afternoon. Young people, mostly artists."

"Thanks, Tony, but given the nature of this trip, I am better off downtown. Besides, David doesn't want you compromised in the community if this little escapade goes awry." Tony always invited Holden to stay at his home, and he always declined. The arrangement suited both of them, as they had little in common.

"Yes, well, I quite understand that, though I am not quite sure what David thinks he will accomplish by your seeing this Sea Lion person. You and I both know that what he is saying is quite preposterous."

"You've heard what he has said?" asked Holden. Christ, if Wren knew, all of Singapore would know soon.

"Only a summary, from David last night. He had some very unpleasant thoughts about using various parts of my body in new ways if I breathed a word."

"Well, that is as it should be. Please be very careful to tell no one, especially while I am snooping around."

"No fear. How are you going to go about your secret mission?"

"The reason I am here is that David is convinced that you have a friend who knows the identity of Sea Lion. But if you hadn't heard of him until David called you—"

"Oh, one hears talk, Holden. I see a lot of senior government people. They tell a tale of a person who is feeding silly lies about Malay uprisings to some foreign banker or bankers. Very little is actually known, and less is said, other than speculation. People talk to me, Holden. I know you think me a somewhat frivolous man, but I hear many people's confidences and I keep them."

Chambers smiled. "Touché. I guess we are all getting paranoid. Still, David thinks you have a friend who claims to know who Sea Lion is."

"It's more I know someone. A junior clerk in the cabinet office until recently; communications, I think. He has many friends among the senior staff and he turned up at a cocktail party given by old Dr. Fong the day before yesterday. He pulled me aside and quite suddenly blurted that he knew who Sea Lion was and could I arrange for some sort of a reward for the information. At first I brushed him off and suggested he go to the police. He's afraid of the police, he tells me, especially since this Saddam the Martyr business. The lad's Malay, by the way; his name's Elias. Very likable but not awfully bright. Then I got to thinking, maybe this information has some value, you know, perhaps to the FX people here and in London. So I told Elias to keep quiet, to give me a few days to see about the reward. Then I phoned David."

And here I am, thought Holden. Fucking brilliant. "Why didn't you just give him some money and have him tell you what he knows?"

"David said no to that. David was very excited, by the way. It seems he thinks this Sea Lion business is very important. David wants you to find Sea Lion and figure out how good his information is. Then he wants you to report back to him and to him alone. He bellowed something about 'having your guts for garters' as well if you either 'fucked up' or told anybody else what you find out."

"It is nice being held in such high regard by one's boss," said Holden grinning. He was seeing Tony in a wholly new light, smarter and more solid than he had ever thought.

"Oh, but that's just David. He is a bore and absolutely without social graces. What I do find irritating—and why I must apologize to you for stirring this up—is that I, who have been here for donkey's years and know what can and cannot happen in this nation's politics if not what actually will, have told David that a Malay rising is nothing more than a Chinese mother's story to frighten her children, and that the government of Lee But Yang is as stable as a billiard table, and yet he insists in disrupting your life and mine to corner the story."

"I have told him the same," said Holden.

"Of course you have—your head's screwed on straight. But David is the boss, as he frequently reminded me last evening."

Holden laughed despite himself. "You seem able to take that better than I do, Tony."

Tony shrugged. "You get shouted at for four years at Sandhurst, and for a year after that as a subaltern. You learn to tune it out."

Good advice, thought Holden. "Do you yourself have any idea who Sea Lion might be?"

"No, just speculation. Perhaps one of the Malay student leaders has found a gullible ear. Perhaps a reporter trying to manufacture news."

Holden nodded. Tony's theory was as good as any other. "What do you intend?"

"First, to get you settled at the Mandarin. Elias insisted on that, by the way, although I have no idea why. Maybe he knows someone on the security staff. Anyway, as dear David took great pains to point out, my only responsibility is to get you into contact with Elias and leave the rest to you."

"How do I contact this Elias?"

"You don't. He will call me and then you this evening and arrange to meet you at a place of his choosing. You should be prepared if he asks for some earnest money. The lad loves to dress and go out, but he is desperately poor. What will happen next I can only guess. Dinner with Sea Lion? Visit to his pirate lair? Watching him plot treason through a one-way glass? It is all just too silly, if you ask me."

Holden nodded, amazed to find so much wit in a man he had considered a useless relic from the days when one got business by connections rather than skill and daring. He found himself actually liking this silly man. "I hope you told David that."

Tony wrinkled his nose in a parody of someone smelling something rotten. "I did. He called me the most *vile* names. Poor David—no breeding at all."

Holden chuckled. "Well, I would like to get this charade over with as quickly as possible. Quite frankly, I don't care what this Sea Lion says, or even if he exists. We will just play the role, and I will be out of here in two days or less. But I will need you to back me up with David."

"Agreed. I repeat, I am sorry I got you into this."

"So what is the drill?"

"We are nearly to the hotel. Relax, freshen up. Elias will call me at seven this evening to see if you have agreed to meet tonight. If yes, he will contact you in your room at eight. If no, he will call me again tomorrow. May I suggest we get this done tonight?"

"Definitely. I have real work to do in Hong Kong."

"Then I will tell him it's a go." Tony handed Holden a business card with his home phone number written on the back. "If for any reason you wish to postpone, call me at home before seven. All right?"

"Good. And thanks, Tony."

"Here's your hotel. I trust you noticed, as we passed through the Muslim quarter, that there were no soldiers, no police beyond traffic detail, and absolutely no demonstrators of any kind on the streets?"

"I noticed."

"Save for the tiny incident last Monday, there has been no trouble for weeks, Holden."

Holden nodded. "I am sure that is true. Do you feel someone is staging a play for London?"

Wren smiled and placed a long finger against the side of his large nose. "If I don't see you before you leave, Double-Oh-Seven, safe home."

Barbara sat with Elizabeth Sun on the couch in her corner office. Elizabeth finished initialing the MAS final changes to the indenture agreement and sat back, lighting a cigarette as she did so. Barbara thought Elizabeth looked drawn and tired. She herself felt edgy and slightly feverish; she hoped she wasn't giving in to the tension and fatigue.

Elizabeth put her hand out, covering Barbara's. "Barbara, what do you know of the gray-market trading in our bond?"

"Down," said Barbara bleakly. "There are always speculators."

"Trading below the fee, our London traders believe."

"Yes." Whenever an issue was traded at a price less than par minus the underwriting fee, it was said to be "trading below the fee." Among other things, it meant that the underwriters would make no profit, and perhaps a loss, on the issue. "We need some good news, Elizabeth."

"The Minister is very concerned. He is considering whether the issue should be postponed or withdrawn." Elizabeth stubbed out her *kretak* and lit a new one.

Barbara sighed. It would almost be a relief, she thought. "Elizabeth, we—and I mean you and I—have worked too hard, gone too far, to drop the issue now. To give up now would be even worse for you and me, and for RAL and the MAS, than to bring it and have it trade down."

"I agree," said Elizabeth, stroking Barbara's hand. "But the Minister wavers. He wishes me to ask you how much of the issue RAL would take back from the comanagers to stabilize the issue."

Barbara's heart bobbled, but she tried to keep her face expressionless. Philip Meyer had told her the previous evening, and not for the first time, that the short position was too big to squeeze unless RAL held the entire issue of two hundred million. Roland's would take its lumps, he said, but only on eighty million—the original underwriting minus Canadian Bank of Commerce's forty. If the other two comanagers wouldn't hold their collective eighty million, the issue could free-fall at opening. But I can't tell Elizabeth that, not now. "We will support the issue at a viable level,

Elizabeth. The open short positions create a demand for the issue, which is why good news is so important."

"Or at least the absence of bad news," said Elizabeth. "So you can assure me—and I can tell the Minister—that Roland, Archer Limited will support the *entire* issue, at a reasonable level, through the distribution period?"

In for a penny, in for a pound, thought Barbara. "Yes, you can tell him that," she lied. She felt her face flush. "But please get us some good news."

Elizabeth nodded, satisfied, withdrawing her hand. "Good. It is curious, Barbara, that while the Minister of Finance is nervous as a cat, the Prime Minister is quite sanguine. 'The weather and the news change alike for a lucky man,' he said. It is an old proverb; a favorite of his. And he says the weather and the news will be good, indeed."

She suckered me, thought Barbara, too tired to be angry. If the PM was happy, they weren't going to pull the issue whatever the gray market told them. And now I am at the very end of the limb, with the bears grinning below, and no help promised from the MAS.

Chambers completed the registration formalities and went to his room. It was three-thirty, and he didn't feel like going into the branch. He took a long shower and then dressed in a short-sleeved safari suit of light khaki drill, since he didn't expect the meeting with the mysterious Sea Lion to be formal. The more he thought about it, the more he thought this Elias character probably had nothing to sell. Grifting Europeans was, after all, something of an Asian tradition.

He telephoned down for tea and the newspapers. The *Straits Times* had another lurid headline: "Minister Lashes Government on Malay Student Policy."

Holden read the article quickly. It seemed that Yusef Ibrahim, the Minister of Social Affairs, had attacked the Prime Minister in a speech outside Parliament for the "continued repression of Malays and insensitivity to Malay values and traditions." At the bottom of the article, an unnamed spokesman for the PM's office had responded blandly, "Dr. Ibrahim was a valued counsellor to the Prime Minister and his views would be carefully considered." Holden shook his head. Why won't this whole Malay business just go away, like it always has in the past?

He phoned Margaret in Hong Kong and got his messages, then spoke for half an hour to Walter Faring, his deputy in charge of the Korea Exchange Bank deal in his absence. At four-thirty, he was tired of the room and decided to have an early cocktail in the downstairs bar. As he entered, he was surprised and pleased to see Barbara Ramsay sitting alone in a corner booth, sipping a cup of tea.

"Barbara, how are you?"

"Holden!" She caught him and held him with her special smile. "Please join me. What are you doing in Singapore?"

Holden sat down. "You probably wouldn't believe me if I told you. A fool's errand, I suspect. But how are you? How goes the Deal of the Year?"

She shrugged and her smile faded a little. "I just left Elizabeth. We are moving well on documentation, almost done, in fact. The comanagers seem pretty relaxed now that the streets have been essentially calm for three weeks and the dock strike is petering out. Singapore GDP and trade figures are both good, both growing. We should have a fine issue."

"Great. I am so glad. May I buy you a drink? Champagne seem appropriate?"

"Well, it's premature, but I am through for the day and flying to Hong Kong tomorrow." She pushed the teacup aside and smiled brightly. "So I would be happy to join you."

Holden nodded to a passing waitress, a pretty Malay girl in the traditional batik *sarong kebaya*, and asked for Veuve Cliquot, 1971 or '75. The girl went to the bar and returned immediately to inform him that neither was available. "Give us the nonvintage, then. The orange label." He turned back to Barbara as the girl left the table. "When do you plan to enter the market?"

Her face took on a pained look. "I am not sure, Holden. The MAS wants us to price the issue and get it on the market early next month. Technically, we are ready, but I don't want to rush." Her voice trailed off uncertainly.

He waited, expecting her to continue. He felt guilty, because he saw she was being brave and he thought he knew why. Suddenly a thought popped into his mind: Maybe debunking Sea Lion would be worth doing. But he couldn't tell her about his "mission."

"Holden," she said, leaning forward and touching the back of his hand. He felt the electric surge her touch always produced. "I need to take you into my confidence once again. Everything *should* be right to launch the bond, but everything isn't. There are rumors floating around London that have begun to get back here as well. Someone here in Singapore and claiming to have a source high in government is telling people that the riots of a few weeks past may result in a general disturbance in the economy and even destroy the political stability of the republic."

He tasted the proffered champagne. He nodded to the waitress, and she filled Barbara's glass and then his own, then placed the bottle in a silver ice bucket. Barbara had fallen silent and took a drink of her wine without apparent interest. The waitress backed away, leaving Holden with a little bow and a fetching smile. He held a brief moral debate with himself while savoring the champagne. Love quickly defeated Reason. He squeezed Barbara's hand and said softly, "I know."

Barbara looked up, startled. "You do?"

"Sea Lion," he said, his throat tight. "The rumor source calls himself Sea Lion."

She was suddenly animated, and a blush of color rose over her high cheekbones. "Yes! That is what Elizabeth told me, though that and the gist of the message were just about all she knew. How did you hear?"

"I—Barbara, I can't tell you that. I've been sworn to secrecy."

She nodded, and he was pleased she didn't press. She knew the rules, knew he was already over the line. "The rumors are absurd, of course, Holden. Singapore government is solidly in control—do you remember how you told me that when we had our first lovely lunch at the Chesa?"

He grinned. "I will always remember that lunch. I have been slightly smitten with you ever since."

She took his hand, and a fraction of her smile returned. "You have been so kind to me, Holden, since the very first time we met."

They sat for a moment in silence, warmed by each other and the memories of first touches. He held another mental debate, and Prudence was the loser. "Sea Lion is creating a bit of a stir in London," he said softly.

"I know. That is my problem. Holden, I want to trust you. Can I, please? I know this is an imposition, and against the rules, but will you swear to bury this information in your heart forever?" Her voice was both pleading and caressing, and he wanted nothing more in the world than to save her.

"Of course. My word." His heart thumped.

"This Sea Lion business has caused some of my comanagers to begin to sell their allotments in the gray market. Speculators"— the word came out in a hiss—"have joined the short-sellers. My bond could very well collapse."

"Barbara, I am sorry."

"Elizabeth told me today the PM might cancel the issue rather than risk a market embarrassment. Oh, Holden! This is a good issue! And I have worked so hard!"

He frowned. "Surely your London wouldn't allow the bond to

fall. They know Singapore is safe. Wouldn't they hold it at issue and crush the bears?''

She looked up at him, her eyes brimming with tears. "I told Elizabeth we would. I had to say that, Holden, to save the bond."

In a flash he saw the truth. He felt as if he had been kicked in the solar plexus, so that he couldn't breathe. "You didn't have authority to make that commitment, did you, Barbara?'' he whispered as soon as he had gathered enough breath to speak.

She shook her head ever so slowly, and her chin quivered. Two large tears spilled from her eyes and raced down her cheeks. "RAL will not support the issue beyond its underwriting commitment,'' she whispered. "I either find buyers for it or it crashes. The only place I can find new money for the deal is in Asia, Holden.'' And I will do anything to get it, she thought. I have gone too far, and a piece of my soul is lost, either way.

He picked up his glass and saluted her. She smiled a small, reckless smile and touched her glass to his. "What a gamble, Barbara! A career, not just at Roland, Archer, but in the *business*, on one roll of the dice!'' He shook his head as fear for her and admiration for her audacity bounced around his brain.

"*Morituri te salutamus*,'' she said. The tear streaks remained on her cheeks, but no other tears followed. He was reminded of a photograph of a filthy soldier after a battle, smiling in victory, with two clear tracks on his grimy cheeks. "Will you help me?''

He nodded slowly. "I think I can. I can't buy your bond, Barbara, I told you that. My boss would never agree. But I might be able to help in another way.''

"How?''

"Barbara, what I am about to tell you must also forever remain our knowledge alone.''

"Of course. What is it?'' Her smile made his treason against David Weiss worth any future pain.

"I have a line on Sea Lion. I may be seeing him as early as tonight. Once I report to London that he is a nobody spouting nonsense, the bears will flee and you will launch your bond. But no one must ever know that I have told you this.''

It was her turn to feel the wind rush out of her. He thought she looked frightened as her eyes shifted and danced. She took a gulp of her champagne and choked. He got up quickly and patted her on the back until she caught her breath. "Tonight? Sea Lion?'' she squeaked.

"Yes. I have a contact. If it pans out, I will demand he prove his information is genuine, which we both know it can't be, or I threaten to expose him. One Sea Lion off the air.''

She was still breathing in shallow gasps. "Won't—won't that be dangerous?"

"I don't see why. Darling, are you all right? A glass of water?"

She shook her head and began to breathe more normally. She wiped her eyes with a handkerchief from her purse and took a tentative sip of champagne. "You would do this for me?"

"I am doing it for my horrid boss in New York, Barbara. But if I actually get to this liar, you should be home free."

"And you won't be able to tell me?"

"Probably not. But the rumors will stop."

"Yes. Oh, Holden, that would be truly wonderful." The smile bloomed, though her eyes were still tense. "But be careful, darling."

He blushed. "More of the widow?" He reached for the bottle.

"No, thank you." She stood up, a little unsteadily. "I have had too much already." He jumped up to take her arm, but she turned away from him. "I think I will lie down for a while. I feel a little faint."

He waved frantically at the waitress. She brought his check and he signed it, then followed Barbara out. "I'll walk you to your room. Are you all right?"

"Fine," she said, but she let him take her arm as far as the lift. When they reached her floor, she kissed him and pushed him back into the car when he tried to follow her. "I am fine, really. But you be careful." He said nothing, and the doors closed.

He unlocked the door to his room. It was five-thirty, still two and a half hours before the earliest possible beginning of the end of the Sea Lion business. On his own, he would have killed more of the time in the bar, rather than return to his room, but having left with Barbara he didn't feel like returning. He removed the shirt-jacket of his safari suit and hung it in the closet. He opened the doors to the small balcony, which overlooked the pool. The evening was warm but dry for July. He took a bottle of Heineken from the minibar in the closet and sat on one of the metal chairs on the balcony, enjoying the sea breeze cooling his bare chest.

Barbara has really sown in the wind, he thought, admiring her daring while being very glad he wasn't in her position. Even if everything worked, she would be hung out to dry if her bosses ever found out she had promised Singapore government that RAL *by itself* would squeeze the bears. Christ, even by the standards of the Lions of years ago, what she was doing was sheer madness. He was thrilled, shocked, and amused all at once.

He took a long pull at the beer and closed his eyes. The lack of sleep over the past few days and the alcohol carried him along in a mild buzz, punctuated by an insistent tapping, like the sound of someone knocking on a door a long way off.

He sat up suddenly, awake but groggy. Someone *was* knocking at his door. Elias, he thought; but no, his watch said five minutes to six. He got up and went to the door, setting the beer bottle on a table as he passed it. The tapping continued, soft but insistent. "Coming," he called, then ran his tongue over his teeth. Nothing made for a more sour mouth than to fall asleep after drinking champagne, he thought. He opened the door. Barbara Ramsay slipped past him into the room without a word.

She had bathed and changed into a simple white cotton dress. The fabric seemed almost transparent across her shoulders. He felt her perfume all around him. His mind became a heated blank.

She reached the end of the king-sized bed and touched the spread lightly with her fingertips. She hadn't looked at him since entering the room and now seemed to look out the balcony doors, or miles beyond. Without turning, she sat on the edge of the bed and carefully removed her shoes.

He came and stood next to her, conscious of his half-nude state. She turned toward him but didn't look up. She bent forward, ever so slowly, and kissed the growing bulge at the crotch of his trousers. He placed his hand on her glossy hair and pressed her to him. She pressed her cheek against him, her eyes closed, and gave a little moan.

"Holden?"

"Yes?"

She unbuckled his belt and pulled his trousers down. He stepped from his shoes and then his trousers while she kissed his sex through his painfully tight underwear. He lifted her up and unzipped her dress, and she pushed it off her shoulders and stepped out of it. He tugged his bikini briefs off clumsily with one hand, freeing his painfully engorged penis.

She was naked and so was he. As gently as he could, he took her in his arms. Her head came up quickly. Her hair brushed across his face, stunning him with her perfume, and she kissed him hard, deeply, her tongue probing urgently. He ran his hands over the smooth skin of her back and shoulders, while kissing her ears and her throat. He held her across her shoulders with his left hand while his right hand stroked slowly down the hollow of her spine to the round, cloven smoothness of her buttocks. With a little cry she gripped him around his neck and fell backward onto the bed, pulling him with her.

He rolled off and began exploring her body with his fingers and his mouth. He traced around her breasts with a finger, watching her nipples darken and stand erect. He kissed each one in turn and let his fingers travel slowly across her belly and tickle her navel. She reached between them and gently grasped his penis. When his hand found the opening of her sex, she gasped. She was already soaking wet. She pulled harder at his aching penis.

"Holden, come inside me," she gasped, her chest heaving. "Now, before I lose my nerve."

He rolled onto her as she raised her legs. They were joined instantly. She wrapped her legs around his hips and began to thrash wildly, keening in a high-pitched warble. He slid his hands beneath her and held her buttocks, holding her to him as he surrendered to her movement. Her head twisted from side to side, and her keening deepened to a moan. He trapped her mouth with his and kissed her. Their breathing mingled, and their sweating bodies sucked and slapped at each other.

Her moaning rose and her movement slowed. She pushed him up and looked at him, her special smile bright as never before. He took over the thrusting movement. She began to shudder violently and pulled him down on top of her, biting his ear. She took a deep breath and let out a single sharp "Oh!" He felt his body tremble as he released himself into the torrent of her orgasm.

He opened his eyes. The room had grown quite dark. Shit, he thought, the time! Barbara was sleeping next to him, purring like a satisfied cat. He slid out of bed, quietly so as not to awaken her, and found his watch where he had dropped it with his clothes by the foot of the bed. Six-forty-five. Damn! He had to get ready for his encounter with Sea Lion.

He looked back at Barbara, who slept on. Poor woman, she has been under a lot of strain, he thought. He tiptoed into the bathroom and closed the door before starting the shower.

He lathered quickly and shampooed his hair. A sharp, stinging sensation on his back and neck greeted the soap. He realized she had scratched him deeply with her fingernails.

She just walked through the door of my room, took off her clothes, took off my clothes, and all but raped me, he mused. He had never known such intensity in a woman, such animal need. This was a woman one could stay with, he thought, could love and share with, equal to equal. The thought made him warm, and the pleasure of their lovemaking flooded back to him, chased away immediately by a wave of sadness, as he realized it was never to be.

He rinsed his hair and then his body, then shut the taps and opened the glass door. Barbara stood on the bathmat, wearing his safari-suit jacket, fastened by one button. She put her arms around his neck and pressed her face into his chest as he put his arms around her waist and held her tight. She tilted her face up to him. Tears were running freely down her cheeks and her chin quivered in a look of shattered hope.

"Where are you going?" she said, her voice halting and squeaky from crying.

"Barbara, I told you this afternoon. I have to go and meet this Sea Lion."

"Oh, no," she wailed, pressing her face into his chest again and pounding his chest lightly with one small fist. "No, no, no, no. You can't leave me, Holden, you just can't!"

"Barbara, it's important to you that I find out—"

"Nothing," she said. She pulled away from him and looked at her feet. The front of the safari jacket was soaked from contact with his wet body. "Nothing."

"Barbara, darling, I don't understand."

She looked up at him. Her face was calmer but still distraught. "Nothing is more important to me in the world than that you spend the night with me, Holden."

He felt his throat tighten and a hot feeling in his gut. With her makeup streaked, her eyes and lips puffy and red, and the front of her hair plastered wet to her forehead, she had never looked more lovely, or more alone. "Barbara, stay here. I'll be gone an hour or two, and then I will come back to you."

"No." She shook her head and more tears fell. "Tonight I want you to hold me. We both know we can never do this again. Just this night, Holden, stay with me."

"But Sea Lion? Don't you want to know?"

"Postpone your meeting. Or forget about it. I need you with me, and Sea Lion is probably nothing anyway." She reached out her hand and stroked his face. "Stay with me just this night." He pulled her back to him, picked up her chin, and kissed her. He felt her heat flowing into him. "Please, Holden."

There is no way I am going to leave this woman to run an errand for David Weiss, he thought, trying to build his resolve.

"I'll stay, Barbara. Of course I'll stay. But let me make a call. Maybe I can postpone the meeting." He released her, and she took a step back. She looked at the floor again and slowly nodded.

He walked quickly back into the bedroom, sweeping Tony Wren's card off the dresser as he passed. He dialed the number on the back. Tony picked up immediately.

"Hello," came his big actor's voice.

"Tony? Holden Chambers here. Listen, about this meeting, Elias—"

"The dear boy is on my other line just now, Holden, keen as mustard to kiss the Sea Lion on the cheek and collect his thirty pieces of silver."

"Tony, something's come up. I can't make it tonight. You said tomorrow was possible?"

"Can't make it tonight?" Tony's voice was thick with amused sarcasm.

"Right," said Holden bluffly.

"Find one of our local lovelies more interesting? Can't say as I blame you." Tony followed his comment with a loud guffaw.

Holden wanted to say something sharp but thought against it. He felt slightly ridiculous, standing buck naked and dripping wet, talking on the phone and listening to another man's wife taking a shower in the bathroom. "Look, Tony, please just fix it so Elias calls me tomorrow and not tonight."

"Anything, my dear man. Hold on a tick, I'll talk to him."

Holden heard the click and then the white-noise void as he was put on hold. Barbara emerged from the bathroom with one of the Mandarin's huge bath towels wrapped around her, covering her from breasts to knees. She looked questioningly, and he nodded and smiled.

"Holden?"

"Tony? Go ahead."

"Well, Elias is disappointed. He is afraid Sea Lion might be about to leave Singapore."

Damn, thought Holden. He looked at Barbara and smiled. What the fuck do I care? "Can he at least agree to try to set something up for tomorrow?"

"He says he will do it. Holden, you are sure you will be able to keep the rendezvous tomorrow? I mean, love and all that—"

"Of course," Holden interrupted. "Just cover it for me, Tony, please."

"You are going to owe me a big one, young lad."

"You'll take care of it, then."

"No fear. And you take care of yourself." Tony laughed, and rang off.

Holden put the phone down. Barbara was drying his back with her towel. I really should go tonight. Barbara is a big girl. I *would* go, if seeing this Sea Lion was really important, he thought. At least I prefer to believe I would. Barbara had started to dry his legs and was paying special attention to his crotch. He felt himself stirring.

"Holden?"

"Yes, love."

"Let's have dinner here. Room service."

He smiled and realized he was quite hungry. "Good. What shall we have? I'll phone it in."

She straightened up and dropped the towel. Her left hand continued to stroke his balls while her right arm went around his neck. He felt his temperature rise as she kissed him.

She teased him with her tongue and giggled. "Maybe just a few more minutes before you call room service, darling." She pushed him backward onto the bed.

In the Celebes Sea, south and slightly east of the southernmost Philippine island of Mindanao and some five degrees north of the equator, the sea-water temperature exceeded 86 degrees. Great columns of moist air rose and joined into a dense black cloud mass. The earth's rotation and the ocean currents caused the mass to spin slowly in an anti-clockwise rotation and to move slightly northwestward. The spin and the continued rising of hot air from the sea caused the barometric pressure within the cloud to drop, and this in turn brought strong winds, laden with moisture and energy of their own, into the rotating mass.

Observation stations noted the formation of the tropical depression and reported it to weather stations around the western Pacific. Each country had its own identification system. In Hong Kong the nascent storm was named Karen.

31

26 July

THE MAN CALLED DENNIS sat in a rented Toyota saloon at the curb opposite the Mandarin Hotel. This is utter madness, he thought, to expose myself to observation by any passing cop or even a suspicious doorman. A European did not sit behind the wheel of a parked car for any length of time in Singapore. They either parked and went about their business or they were driven. There were no European chauffeurs in Singapore.

He had called Weiss in London the previous evening, as instructed. Weiss wanted to know where he was staying, so he told him the Raffles. In fact, he was lodged in a tiny, run-down hotel called the Mayfair but had arranged for the desk men at the Raffles to take messages addressed to either of the two names by which he was known to Weiss. At the Mayfair he was Mr. Philip Russell of Melbourne.

All of which was good and proper tradecraft, except for this idiocy of trying to follow Holden Chambers. Dennis had thought just to hire a local agency and let them fuck the job up any way they wished, but detective agencies in all major cities had to maintain good relations with local police, and Dennis couldn't chance bringing himself to their attention. He was sure that identikit composite drawings of himself, which the police would surely have gotten from Chambers, would be circulating around Asia by now. He had two and a half weeks of heavy beard growth, but a careful observer would see around that, if he had a reason to look closely. Worse, none of his passports showed him with a full beard, so he would have to shave it off to avoid attention at airports. All of which meant he would be much safer in Europe. He was booked to Geneva on Swissair for the following afternoon.

Dennis got out of the car, which was legally parked, and entered the Crown Prince Hotel to get a packet of cigarettes. He stood just inside the glass doors, looking, he hoped, like a businessman or tourist staying in the air conditioning, waiting to be picked up. Bloody stupid, he thought. Next I will have to pretend to look at the shops. Weiss had promised him a final bonus of £10,000 if he would track Chambers for just two more days. Last night he had never emerged from the hotel, and tonight was positively the last night Dennis would stay in Asia.

Holden Chambers sat in the bar of the Mandarin, nursing a long scotch and soda. He glanced at his watch: seven-fifteen. Elias had called twenty minutes before and told him to sit at the bar and wait for another call. This is like a pulp spy novel, he thought, growing impatient. Next he will send me to a phone booth.

Barbara had flown out in the morning, and already he missed her. They had agreed somberly that while the night had been lovely, it could not be repeated. She had cried a little, and he had played at being manly and strong. He knew he hadn't meant it, and he doubted that she did. Do I love her? he wondered, sucking his ice cubes and turning it over in his mind. I don't really know her at all. She told me she had never been unfaithful to her husband before. But I wonder—

"Mr. Chambers?" The barman stood before him. "The call you were expecting. You can take it at the phone at the end of the bar."

"Thank you." Holden slid off the stool. "Best give me the check."

"At once, sir."

He picked up the phone, making sure no one was near him. "This is Holden Chambers."

"Elias, Tuan." It was the same voice, low and sibilant. Malays leaned on their esses. "Leave the hotel now and cross Orchard Road. Pass the Crown Prince Hotel and walk along Bideford Road. I'll collect you there."

"Right. How will you know me?"

"I'll know." The line went dead.

Holden went back to his stool and signed his check, adding a generous tip. He picked up his folding umbrella. He was wearing the same safari suit as the night before, freshly starched and pressed by the hotel laundry. He walked through the lobby into the hot, humid evening and crossed at the corner. He proceeded a hundred yards into the narrow, shop-lined Bideford Road. A tall, thin man dressed in motorcycle riding leathers fell in beside him.

"I am Elias, Tuan."

Holden stopped and looked at the man. He was tall, two inches taller than Chambers, although part of that could be attributed to the black cavalry-style boots that he wore. His leather suit was black as well and very dusty, as though he had ridden a long way over unpaved roads. His face was dark brown and his features were sharp, aquiline. His black eyes were at once intelligent and hard. He wore a white plastic crash helmet with its dark visor raised. He must be suffocating in that outfit, thought Chambers. "What do we do? Where do we meet—"

"We go, Tuan, on my bike. You are not dressed for it, but we will not go fast."

Holden stepped back. "Now, wait a minute. I thought we would meet Sea Lion here in town. My man told me—"

"Sea Lion was in the city last night. Tony told me you were . . . engaged last night." Elias's voice had a menacing cast. "Tonight, Sea Lion is in the north. But it is better. Tonight all your questions will be answered."

Holden shrugged. I have to go for it, he thought. "Where is your bike?"

"There," said Elias, pointing to an alley between two stalls, one selling batik and the other serving Malay barbecue to a small crowd.

The motorcycle was a huge black Kawasaki. "I hope you are a good rider," said Holden. "I don't much like those things."

Elias smiled, then slammed his visor down with a quick movement. "The best, Tuan. I show you Sea Lion, and then you have something for me?"

"As agreed. I'll give it to you as soon as you get me back here in one piece."

Elias took Chambers's arm and guided him through the crowd. "There is a helmet on the pillion, Tuan. Put it on and wait. I will make a phone call in the stall and then we will go."

Elias slipped into the batik stall. There was no telephone. He took a small radio from an inside pocket of his jacket and pressed the transmit key. "Hassan?"

"Here, Elias," said the radio.

"There is a European following our subject. Blue Toyota saloon, plate SMG-3447. Take him off."

"Okay. Safe trip."

Holden strapped on the unfamiliar helmet. In less than a minute Elias returned and started the powerful engine of the motorcycle. He motioned Chambers to climb onto the back seat and hold on. In seconds they had left the crowds in Orchard Road and were racing west. Holden recognized Upper Bukit Timah Road as they turned into it, the bike leaning way over, at the intersection of

Jurong and Bukit Timah roads. My God, he thought. Elias is taking me north, to Malaysia.

Dennis followed the bike at a safe distance. The rider was not going fast, and the Toyota hummed along nearly at the speed limit. As he followed the bike along Upper Bukit Timay Road and into Woodlands Road, two police motorcycles emerged from Choa Chu Kang Road and drew up behind him. He slowed slightly, glancing at the speedometer to make sure he was still under the limit. The motorcycles swept past, and two more took their positions behind him. All four riders turned on their blue flashers, and the driver near his right front fender pointed to the left, motioning him to pull over and stop. Jesus Christ! thought Dennis, pounding the steering wheel as he slowed. Now I am well and truly nicked!

32

27 July

HOLDEN CHAMBERS WAS AWAKENED before dawn by a male nurse who took his temperature and blood pressure and gave him two painkillers. He also left him a paper cup of sweet fruit juice of unidentifiable flavor. The juice had an unpleasant, metallic taste, but he drank it because he was thirsty. All the ripe tropical fruit in the world in the open market just across the road, he mused, and they give me juice from a tin. The nurse told Holden to expect his breakfast in about an hour, after which the doctor would come.

Chambers threw off the starched sheet and thin blanket and inspected his body for damage from the motorcycle crash. He was lightly bandaged on the outside of his left leg from the hip to the ankle. Just cuts and scrapes from sliding across the pavement, he decided, probing the bandages on his thigh with his fingers. When he leaned forward to check the bandages lower down, a sharp pain in his chest stopped him, and he leaned back into the pillows. He tried a deep breath and once again the pain jolted him. He touched the heavy, overlapping tape around his chest just below his nipples. Broken ribs, he thought.

"You were lucky, Mr. Chambers. You could have been seriously injured."

Holden turned his head toward the door. A short, thick-set man was silhouetted in the doorway, back-lit from the hallway. "Are you the doctor?" asked Holden.

"No, the doctor will come later." The man's voice was soft, slightly breathy. He entered the room and closed the door behind him, leaving the room in nearly total darkness. The man found a rattan chair and brought it close to the bed. He reached above Holden and swiveled the reading light until it pointed directly down at Holden's face. The man turned the light on, then backed into the shadows and sat down. "I am a policeman, Mr. Chambers. I have come to discuss with you the unusual events which led us to bring you here last night."

Chambers's mind vaulted back to the motorcycle chase and the crash. He remembered being lifted from the ditch, lying on the road, immobilized more by the drug he had been given than by his injuries. He remembered the faces of the policemen as they had peered down at him, their features and their weapons alternately revealed and concealed in the rotating blue lights on the roofs of police cars. Last, he remembered the helicopter and the man in uniform who had told the policemen to send him to the hospital. That man had had a parade-ground voice with a touch of gravel. The man's name he couldn't quite remember last night, but it was clear enough now: Abdul Raza, the Minister of Home Affairs.

The man sitting back in the shadows had the same deep, gravelly voice. Could it be the minister? He did say he would interrogate me this morning. Should I recognize him? Clearly he doesn't want me to.

"Do you feel up to talking?" asked the policeman. Holden was nearly certain it was Raza's voice. "The doctor assures me that your injuries are minor and that you could even leave hospital today if there are no . . . complications."

Holden wondered if he were talking about political complications, rather than medical. If he is really plotting to overthrow the government, then I am a witness to that plot and decidedly a danger to the plotters. Holden didn't really believe they would harm him, a moderately well-known American, but they could easily keep him locked away in this hospital until the coup had been completed. "Yes, of course," he said. He tried to pull himself more upright in the bed, the better to see his interlocutor, but the pain in his chest defeated him.

"You are well known to government here, Mr. Chambers," the policeman began. "We have verified your bona fides with the MAS. They consider you a sober professional and a friend of Singapore."

Holden smiled. If the MAS know the police have me, they will enquire if I am not released. Or would they? "I am glad—"

"All of which makes it difficult for us to understand why you were found in the company of a known criminal—"

"Now, just a moment! That man was vetted to me—"

"Carrying illegal drugs across the border from Malaysia, failing to stop at the border posts of both countries, failure to obey orders from a police officer." The man in the shadows paused. His voice had lowered to little more than a whisper. He seemed to wait for another protest from Chambers. When Holden remained silent, he nodded slightly. "There could be other charges, of course, once the investigation is completed."

This is a variant of the old badger game, thought Chambers. He had no doubt the charges could be made to stick, false though they would be. "Do you expect me to answer those charges?"

The man chuckled. "We would like your cooperation, as I said, in understanding what happened. We would like you to assist us in our inquiries."

Holden smiled ruefully. When he had first seen that phrase in the Hong Kong press, "So-and-so is assisting the police with their inquiries," it had seemed very simple, almost amicable. He later learned that the innocuous-sounding phrase meant that either so-and-so was selling someone else to the police in order to save his own skin, or that the police were holding off charging the poor sod to give him more rope. Either way, it meant the police had old so-and-so by the balls. "All right." Holden paused. He should address the policeman in some fashion; it was certainly best to be polite. "Minister" would give the game away. "Constable" might be viewed as insulting. He settled on "Inspector." An inspector was about the level of officer who would be handling this case, if it were a simple chase, even across the border. "All right, Inspector—is that your proper title?"

"It will do," said the man in the shadows. His voice revealed neither approval nor disapproval. A skilled interrogator, thought Holden.

"Very well, Inspector. The man who took me into Johor Baru, the man driving the bike, was known to me only as Elias. He was vouched for by my branch manager here as a minor official of the cabinet staff."

The policeman nodded slowly. He gave no sign of taking notes. Ominous, that, thought Holden. British police and their colonial heirs usually wrote absolutely everything down. "Why did you go to Malaysia, Mr. Chambers? Surely a business or tourist visit would have been undertaken at a more conventional hour and by a more comfortable means of transport."

Interrogators always lead with questions the answers to which they already know, thought Holden. I have to stay as close to the truth as I can. "Well, I can tell you, Inspector, it had nothing to do with drugs." Try to get him off the scent.

The silhouette shrugged. "Drugs were found on the driver's person. Both diazepam and alcohol were found in your own blood. That is a dangerous combination, Mr. Chambers."

Chambers waved his hand dismissively, wincing as the movement hurt his ribs. "I was drugged some time that evening. Probably in the tea I was given when first we crossed into Malaysia."

"Ah, yes. We return to your journey and its purpose." Once again the voice of the man in the shadow slipped into a sibilant whisper.

He isn't interested in the drugs, and he won't be led away, thought Holden. How much does he know? Holden was beginning to sweat in the close air of the small room. How much can I tell him without his locking me up? "There have been rumors, Inspector, rumors floating around Hong Kong and even London." Softly, softly, thought Holden. The MAS have heard that much. "Rumors to the effect that hotheads in Malaysia, specifically in Johor, might take advantage of the recent labor unrest and student demonstrations to . . . influence events in Singapore."

"You mean to overthrow the government." The policeman's voice was matter-of-fact, almost bored.

"Yes," said Chambers quickly. "As incredible as that may seem."

The man ignored Holden's attempt to lighten the mood in the room. "And so you went to Malaysia to find out? To find out *what*, Mr. Chambers?" For the first time the policeman's voice had an edge of menace. "And *why* did you go, Mr. Chambers? In the middle of the night, running the border between two sovereign and friendly nations, loaded up with drugs of which you disclaim knowledge, on a *motorcycle?*" The man jumped to his feet, knocking the chair backward to crash into the door. "How stupid do you take us for, Mr. Chambers?" The man's gravelly voice was a suppressed shout. "Answer!"

"M-min," Holden coughed elaborately to cover his slip. He was terrified, and his fear wouldn't let him speak, although he knew that he must. He fought the panic down as the policeman glared at him, his face in shadow but his powerful hands clearly visible, gripping and releasing, a crushing, strangling movement. "The source of the rumor was someone who called himself Sea Lion. My head office instructed me to come here and to try to confirm or deny the rumor—"

"Of an impending coup!" The man picked up the chair and thrust it up against the bed, startling Chambers enough to make him shift away from the blow, causing a sharp pain in his chest. He fought for breath. "And did you find this Sea Lion on your clandestine journey into Johor?"

"No, Inspector," said Holden, gradually gaining control of himself. This is theatrics. I wonder if the whole thing was contrived, presented to me like a melodrama. But to what end? "I was taken to a small roadside camp and given the tea, which must have been drugged. Later we went to a larger camp. There were men in uniforms, some with weapons. I couldn't possibly tell you how many; the drug made me very fuzzy. Then the Malaysian police came. This Elias forced me back to the motorcycle, and off we rode. We had stopped earlier at the border posts going from Singapore to Malaysia; our papers were completely in order. I don't know why Elias ran past the border coming out, but as he never slowed, I had no choice but to hang on. The rest you know."

The man remained standing, his hands squeezing and twisting the back of the rattan chair. "Tell me what I know."

Holden pushed himself back into the pillows. "We were stopped at a roadblock. Elias took the bike down. I was brought here."

The man leaned closer. The light from the lamp almost reached his face. "And you never found your Sea Lion."

"No. It was a wild goose chase, perhaps even a robbery. The nurse gave me my wallet when she brought me in here last night, but my money is gone." Holden built a whine into his voice: the beaten man giving in to his interrogator.

"And the camp in Johor?" the policeman said gently. "What did you make of that?"

Chambers spread his hands in what he hoped was an attitude of abject surrender. "I barely remember it. I am sorry, Inspector. Couldn't you ask the driver?"

"Your Elias was badly hurt. He hasn't regained consciousness, and he may not."

That is a threat, thought Holden, chilled. I could have been seriously injured in that crash or killed. It could still turn out that way. Does anyone outside the police know I am here and not seriously injured? "Foreign Businessman Killed in Motorcycle Accident" would run on page four for one day.

The policeman released the back of the chair and walked around the narrow room, entirely in shadow. After a long pause he returned and once again gripped the back of the chair. "Mr. Chambers, I have enough evidence to charge you with very serious crimes. But do you know what I think, Mr. Chambers? I don't think you are a criminal, but I do think you are a foolish man. A very foolish man. If this crazy story of coups and camps in Malaysia and the like were to get out, it could only make a delicate situation seem more important than it is. So perhaps I should lock you up until events prove your silly rumors false." The policeman paused and seemed to stare from the deep shadows. "But then again, I think not." The man leaned forward, as though to emphasize a point, and his face was faintly illuminated by the penumbra of the light. His eyes were completely obscured by the shadows cast by his brows, but the shape of his head was right and the blade of a nose. Holden thought he could see the roughness of the man's moustache. Abdul Raza without doubt, he thought. Had he showed me his face on purpose? "What I think I will do, Mr. Chambers, is put you on the afternoon Cathay Pacific flight to Hong Kong. I think I can do that, because the highest levels in the Finance Ministry have assured me that you are a respected businessman. A man, in short, who has been foolish but, now that his little drug trip has worn off, will be circumspect enough not to talk of foolish rumors. Could you give me that kind of assurance, Mr. Chambers?"

Holden was elated at the prospect of being released, but he couldn't shake the impression that Raza had meant for him to see what he had seen. Yet he was less and less sure exactly what he had seen. Troops in Malaysia being addressed by Raza? Was it a force to back up a coup by the police against the government? The images that had seemed clear to him the night before had now faded and blended into one another. How much had the drugs clouded his mind? Were the man in the clearing in Johor, the man who came to the crash site in the helicopter and the careful interrogator who stood across the room from him now all the same? And were they really Abdul Raza? The only clear picture left from last night was the wild, skidding ride from Malaysia and the sliding crash of the bike. He could still see the sparks flying past his face as the bike slid across the pavement on its side, still taste the leather of Elias's jacket and the copper of fear in his throat. Yet even that picture, etched so clearly in his mind by terror, seemed to be slipping away.

A tiny thought rose in his mind: They are still giving me drugs!

I have to get out of Singapore! His throat felt dry and his tongue thick. They could make me disappear. Fear enveloped him and he shrank into the pillows, afraid of the man in the shadows, afraid of the drugs in his blood.

"Well, Mr. Chambers?" The policeman's voice had taken on an echo.

"Y-yes," Holden heard himself say. "I have been foolish. I will tell my head office that I could not find this Sea Lion. I-I am sorry to have inconvenienced the police, Inspector."

The man leaned forward over the back of the chair and once again his features were faintly revealed in the edge of the light. "Good. Your kit will be collected from the hotel, Mr. Chambers, and then you will be driven to the airport in time for your flight.

I think it would be best if you did not return to Singapore for a while—let us say, three months." The policeman turned and opened the door. He stopped, once again a silhouette in the light from the corridor. "By the way, your X rays are clear. The doctor will remove the tape from your chest before you go. That should make you feel much better." He slipped through the door and closed it behind him.

The room was strangely silent. Chambers pushed himself up against the pillows, knowing the pain would come, hoping it would clear his head. The juice, he thought. The drug had to be in the juice.

Three months. The minister's words bounced around inside his head. The coup will occur within three months. Holden swung his legs over the side of the bed, leaning into the pain and feeling his head clear. I have to get out of Singapore.

Outside Chambers's room, Minister Raza motioned for the Special Branch superintendent to follow him away from the two armed constables who guarded the door. "He bought it, I am sure, Superintendent."

"I should hope so, sir," said the super, a thin Malay named Habash. "We went to enough trouble."

Raza nodded. "He won't dare go public; the story is just too vague. But he will do *something*."

"Hopefully the right thing, Colonel."

"By the way," said Raza, taking the superintendent's arm. "The driver of the motorcycle. He wasn't really hurt, was he?"

The superintendent chuckled. "No, Minister, not a scratch. Sergeant Rahman is the best rider on the force. He could have done that maneuver blindfolded."

33

Hong Kong, 27 July

BARBARA SAT IN HER darkened office, listening to the phone ring in London over her speaker. She massaged her forehead, fighting the headache that had become a regular nightmare. After more than twenty rings, the phone was answered.

"Roland, Archer Limited. Mr. Cross's office."

"Pamela, it's Barbara Ramsay. Is Nigel in?"

"Yes, surely, Mrs. Ramsay. Hang on a mo'."

We have to price the bond, thought Barbara, listening to the drumming hiss of the line on hold. We must or Elizabeth will pull it. And we have to price it fairly, and then we have to sell it.

"Cross here."

"Nigel. We have to price, Elizabeth insists."

"Damn. Philip is on the warpath."

"Well, shit," she said. "We can't wait. There is no reason to wait."

"Sea Lion," he said softly.

"Sea Lion is bullshit, Nigel." She felt fatigue washing over her, softening but not eliminating the awful pain of the migraine. "There have been no disturbances in the streets of Singapore for weeks, save one tiny push between students and the police which was quickly contained. I have been all over the city, and absolutely nothing is going on. Even the dock strike is dying for lack of interest."

"But the rumors—"

"Persist. I don't know why and neither does Elizabeth. But it will never happen. You are more likely to get a coup in London."

"But Barbara, the market—"

"Nigel, fuck it. Let's show the market. Price the fucking issue!"

"Philip will want a big discount," he said unhappily.

"No way. Nigel, interest rates have ticked up a fraction since we set the coupon. We can price the bond off par only because of that."

Nigel sighed. This woman, much as I like her, could drag me down with her if the bond crashes. "What price do you suggest?"

"Ninety-nine and a quarter," she said without hesitation.

He took a deep breath. "Christ, Barbara, the bond is discounted to ninety-six, when issued, on the gray."

"Naked shorts," she said with as much courage as she could muster. "Buy orders will come; the shorts will get killed."

"God, I love your confidence."

"It will happen. Nigel, I have never been wrong for you."

"Barbara, I have always backed you."

"I know. I'm grateful, Nigel, you know that."

"So tell me how you know this will come right."

"I can't. But it will. Trust me one more time."

Nigel sighed. "Good night, love."

Holden Chambers sat in his leather chair, his lightly bandaged leg propped up on the ottoman. He had his stereo headphones on and was listening to the plaintive songs of the Eagles' *Hotel California* album. He wore only a *yukata*, a lightweight cotton Japanese robe tied with a sash. He held a tall whiskey and soda in both hands on his stomach. His eyes were closed and he was nearly asleep.

May-Ling pinched his bare toe. He cracked open one eye and looked a question. "Telephone," she said very slowly, allowing him to read her lips.

"Who?" he mouthed back silently.

"David Weiss," she said, with a grimace.

Holden hitched himself up in the chair. His bruised ribs gave him a jolt of pain, but he could feel them getting better. He set the headphones aside and punched the stereo off, then put his drink on the end table and picked up the phone. "Hello, David."

"So what happened, Secret Agent Zero?"

Chambers ground his teeth. God, how I loathe the man. "Frankly, David, I am not at all sure exactly what happened."

"Don't take that frosty tone with me, Holdy. Did you see Sea Lion or not?"

"No."

"So what the fuck happened?" David Weiss's voice was rising in pitch and volume as he became irritated. Good, thought Holden, get pissed off. Weiss continued. "I get a call from Tony Wren last night, says you had disappeared. This morning he telexes you have checked out of your hotel. I call your office an hour ago, and they have no idea where you are, and now I find you at home at six o'clock in the evening, talking in monosyllables. *Tell me what happened!*"

"Well, David, I met Tony's friend. He took me into Malaysia on a motorcycle. We saw a bunch of troops exercising."

"Troops?" Weiss interrupted. "Whose troops? Rebels?"

"I couldn't tell. We were only there a few minutes when the police came and Tony's friend Elias insisted we leave." Holden decided he wouldn't tell Weiss about the confusing effect of the drugs he had been given. Weiss was a near teetotaler who thought anyone who drank was an alcoholic, and anyone who so much as took sleeping pills was a dangerous addict.

"What else did you see?" Weiss's voice had become quiet, but the menace remained.

"David, things happened very fast, and I am not at all sure of this, but I think I saw Singapore's Minister of Home Affairs, Abdul Raza, addressing a group of officers at the Malaysian camp. Later, Elias and I were stopped by a police roadblock back in Singapore, and Elias dumped the bike. A helicopter landed, and an official came out who looked like Raza, and he ordered the police to take me to the hospital under guard. And this morning, a policeman interviewed me in the hospital, and he sounded a bit like Raza. I couldn't see his face."

"Jesus. Then it's true," said Weiss. There was a tone of triumph in his voice.

"What is true?"

"We have another source which suggests that the 'master' to whom Sea Lion refers is Raza."

"David, I must emphasize I am really not sure of this. There was a certain staged quality to it—"

"Come on, Holdy! You may be *my* Prince of Asia, but I hardly think a cabinet minister would stage his coup preparations just for you!"

"I am just telling you, it seemed—"

"Oh, bullshit! You just can't admit that you were wrong when you told me Singapore was as safe as Switzerland! Look at the *facts*, bubula! Sea Lion is real. I hope you paid Tony's friend as agreed." Weiss's voice was jubilant.

"In fact, I didn't. I didn't see him after the crash. Later, the police told me he was badly injured." Something tugged at the back of his mind, where the fuzzy impressions of the wild motorcycle ride still lay wrapped in question marks. Elias?

"Well, in any event, good job getting as close as you did. Be ready to return to Singapore if we get another chance to talk directly to Sea Lion."

"Ah, David, the police were rather upset, because Elias ran the border on the way down," said Holden, once again omitting any mention of the drugs. "The inspector told me to stay away for a while, persona non grata."

"Shit. How long?"

"Three months."

"Damn! Still, maybe that tells us you did indeed see too much. One last thing, Holden, be reminded that you are to discuss your adventure with absolutely no one."

Holden sighed. *He hears what he wants to hear.* "As you wish, David. I still think caution should govern us in this."

"Don't strain your tiny little mind. Good night." The phone went dead.

Holden put the phone down, and picked up his drink. The movement elicited a twinge from his ribs. He shook his head in wonder. *I told that son of a bitch I had been in the hospital, and he never even asked how I was.*

34

Singapore, 31 July

CHRIS MARSTON-EVANS UNLOCKED THE door to his room at the Shangri-La. The telephone was ringing. Damn, he thought, I have to change for a dinner being given the Chairman of the Oversea-Chinese Bank, one of the Imperial Bank's biggest customers in Singapore, and I am late as it is. I hope that is not Sir William's razor-voiced secretary, Miss Willows, demanding a report on progress on the branch license application. Progress reports were particularly difficult to write when there was none. Chris threw his umbrella and his case on the bed and wrenched his tie loose. He picked up the phone. "Hello?"

"Chris?"

Marston-Evans sat on the edge of the bed. The silky, androgynous voice thrilled him as always. It was Sea Lion. "I-I didn't expect to hear from you again, Sea Lion. Has something changed?"

"It grows near, Chris. Your master must be prepared to move quickly to help my master."

"Of course. When—"

"Days," said the voice. "Not today, and probably not tomorrow, but soon, very soon."

"Sea Lion, wait," he said, reaching across the bed for his case and dragging it toward him. He took out a small notebook and a gold pencil. "I have a question from my master."

"I can't answer many questions, Chris." The voice seemed to apologize. "The phone is not secure."

Chris found the page with his notes from his last meeting with Sir William McQuarry. "I know. But my master says he must have an answer or two to be sure."

"To be sure of my master?"

"More to be sure of you."

"I see." Sea Lion sounded sad, disappointed. "Your master would withhold his help without this answer?"

"He says he has to know."

The voice sighed. "Very well. Go to St. Andrew's Cathedral. Do you know where it is?"

"Yes. Next to City Hall."

"Good. Go into the cathedral and sit in a pew all the way to the right, and in the second row from the back. Do you understand?"

"Yes. All the way to the right, second row from the back. What if there are other people in that pew?"

"There won't be. Be there in half an hour." The line went dead.

Damn, thought Marston-Evans, there's my dinner knocked into a cocked hat. He phoned the office of the chairman of Oversea-Chinese Bank and explained to an executive assistant that he would be unavoidably delayed, but that he would be along as soon as possible. He then washed his face and tightened his tie. Getting to St. Andrew's in the evening traffic could easily take half an hour. Chris felt a rush of pleasure and excitement. At last I get to meet the man behind the voice. I am still betting he is gay.

The taxi dropped Marston-Evans on Coleman Street, in front of the grayish-white limestone cathedral. Chris noticed there was a police car with three men in it just across the street. It was just six-thirty, nearly half an hour since Sea Lion had called. The colonial heart of the city was nearly deserted. Chris hurried up the steps and into the darkened Gothic church.

Once inside, Chris had to let his eyes grow accustomed to the dim light. Hundreds of candles lit the altar at the far end, and there seemed to be a small service, perhaps a wedding or a funeral, being conducted. The back of the church was virtually empty, with just a few scattered people in the pews. Chris looked around for someone who might be looking for him, but saw no one. He found a seat in the second pew from the back, all the way over on the right, and sat down to wait. By seven o'clock he was getting nervous, and he began to wonder if he had been sent after a wild goose.

"Chris?" The voice came from directly behind him, inches away. He could even feel warm breath on his neck as he twisted his body to see. A hand on his shoulder stopped him. He could see the hand was gloved. "Don't turn around, Chris. You mustn't see me."

"But—" Chris's heart sank. So close!

"You recognize my voice, don't you?"

"Yes," said Chris miserably.

"Then that is enough. Ask your question." The voice was crisp, businesslike. The hand on his shoulder was warm.

"Okay. Sir William—"

"No names, Chris. Not even here."

"Okay, sorry. My master asks how the event you predict can possibly take place when the armed forces are vastly superior in men and equipment to the forces of—your master."

There was a silence. Chris listened for Sea Lion's breathing, but couldn't hear it. Finally the voice spoke. Sea Lion seemed sad. "Chris. Tell your master that my master has nothing to fear from the armed forces, because he controls them. They may not be his allies, but they will not be able to oppose him. Have you another question?"

"N-no. Why can't I see your face?"

"Security. If I become known, I could no longer help you, or help my master."

"I see. It's just that listening to your voice so often in the last weeks, I feel I almost know you, and I have come to care for you."

"That's nice, Chris, but not yet. Perhaps after the event."

"All right. But promise." Chris waited, but the voice did not reply. He stood and turned around quickly, hoping to get even a glimpse. The pew behind him was empty, and there was no one who seemed to be moving away from the spot. Damn, he thought.

Chris rushed outside, but once again there was no one who seemed to be hurrying in the street. He hailed a taxi and went back to the hotel. Before changing into dinner clothes, he rang the travel desk in the lobby and booked the morning flight to Hong Kong.

The police car parked across the road from St. Andrew's Cathedral pulled away from the curb. A slender Malay boy darted from the shrubbery in front of the church and flagged it down. The constable next to the driver lowered the window as the boy approached. "Yes, what is it?" he said.

"My name is Yusef Raza," said the boy. "Could you please take me to my father? He is—"

"Get in the back, next to the sergeant," said the policeman.

Hong Kong, 1 August

Sir William McQuarry and Major Carrington listened in silence while Chris told of his latest conversation with Sea Lion, then asked him to wait outside. They adjourned to the club chairs at the other end of the vast office. "What do you think, Charles?"

Carrington shrugged. "If it's true, it puts a whole new complexion on things."

"Yes, if," said McQuarry, his finger raised in the familiar gesture. "But perhaps more important, Charles, it is something we can check."

"Of course!" said Major Carrington, leaping to his feet. "And if it turns out to be a crock, then Sea Lion is a crock."

"Just so." Sir William folded his hands on his small paunch and smiled. Carrington thought he looked like a contented cat. "You have a man on your U.S.-dollar desk, Richard Li, who hails from Singapore, if I'm not mistaken?"

"Right you are. And he has a nephew in the army, in a mechanized rifle battalion. I wrote a letter to get him into a short armor course in the U.K. last year."

"Have Richard call his nephew. Perhaps some chaff about working for the police but softly. See what he can discover. Meanwhile, we have friends in Singapore government; we'll snoop. Something will tell us."

"I'll go and see Richard now, William."

"Good. We could be in possession of a very valuable tip indeed."

"God, I should say. What will we do with young Marston-Evans?"

"Lock him up in the study down the hall. Literally. Tell Miss Willows he's neither to make nor receive outside calls." McQuarry got to his feet. He was smiling broadly. "Feed him some bumpf about security. We can't have him talking to anyone until we know what we have."

Barbara picked up the phone on the first ring. She was alone in the office except for Iris, who, as always, insisted in waiting with her whenever she worked late. Barbara turned on her desk lamp as she brought the receiver to her ear. She had been sitting in darkness to ease the headache. "Barbara Ramsay."

"It's Nigel. I have just come from going three bruising rounds with dear Philip."

"Oh, God, Nigel. Was he truly awful?"

"No," said Nigel cheerfully. "He was merely rude, obstinate, overbearing, pedantic, and insulting."

"Poor Nigel. Did he agree to price the issue?" Please, oh please, she thought.

"In the end, yes. He reluctantly agreed that Roland, Archer

"And if it isn't? Could Raza possibly command the army to assist him in a coup?"

"I doubt it, William. But if he really has support from over the Johor Causeway, he could just do what he has done: keep Singapore's army in quarters, deny them access to their heavy equipment—neutralize them."

"Sea Lion seems rather more dangerous, then."

"But a coup in Singapore still seems preposterous, William."

"I agree. But isn't it possible we are just too confident of our own expert knowledge?"

"Are you thinking we should take a position against the Sing dollar or against the bond?"

"Perhaps just a modest one," said McQuarry, smiling.

Carrington nodded. "I'll see to it. What do we do with this information?"

"Put it out very quietly to our friends at First New York in London. I hate to think we may actually have done them a favor." He curled his lip as against a bad taste.

"And what of young Chris?"

"He is stood down, out of it as of now. We must make sure this information does not surface in Asia, unless via London."

"I'll see to that, too."

"Good night then, Charles."

"Good night. Ah, William, how modest the short positions?"

"Modest."

Carrington nodded. "I agree. This could still go in any direction."

"I think I shall be going home, Holden," said May-Ling.

Startled, he looked up from his chair. She looked sad and upset. "What is it, love?"

"I've been waiting for this for months. Now it has happened, and you haven't even looked at me since you came home from Singapore." She began to cry.

He swung his legs down from the ottoman and stood up, favoring the bandaged leg. He went to her and tried to take her in his arms, but she backed away. "Darling, I am sorry. I've been distracted. Perhaps—"

"It happened, Holden. You have slept with her, and you are different."

"May-Ling—"

"You have, haven't you?" She took another step backward and brushed the tears away with the back of her hand.

"Yes," he admitted, tasting ashes in his throat.

"Then I want to go home."

"Darling," he said, already feeling helpless, already knowing she would go and not return. "These things happen. She is married, and it won't last—"

May-Ling shook her head. "This woman matters to you, Holden. I think you may even be in love with her. The others didn't matter, and I never complained." She bowed her head and let out a high-pitched sob.

He took a quick step forward and put his arms around her. It seemed an awkward gesture, as though he had never held her before. She leaned against his chest but remained stiff in his arms. He felt her tears soak through the thin cotton *yukata*. "God, May-Ling, I am so sorry. You have been everything for me, patient with all of my failings."

"A Chinese woman expects to suffer to sustain her man, and she expects him to be foolish much of the time." She lifted her head and looked Holden full in the face. "But she never expects him to abandon the bond which joins their souls."

"I'll give her up. I won't see her again." The words stuck in his throat, for he knew he didn't mean them. "But darling, please don't just leave me."

Her expression changed fleetingly to contempt, then back to sadness. Her chin dropped and she stopped crying. He tried to pull her closer, but she pushed him away. "Just call me a taxi."

"I'll drive you."

"A taxi. I will only be a moment." She turned away from him and went into the bedroom. A moment later, she emerged with the few things she left in his flat in her orange duffel bag. He walked with her to the door. She kissed him lightly and pressed the button for the lift. He tried to take her in his arms again, but she pushed him away. The lift came, and she was gone.

By early evening, Typhoon Karen's strength had increased to the point of designation as a super-typhoon. Satellite pictures showed clouds reaching out three hundred miles from the center as the storm filled the Celebes Sea and covered most of Mindanao. The eye of the storm was twenty miles across, with barometric pressure dropping below 28 inches of mercury. The typhoon moved more rapidly north, lashing the islands of Mindanao, Leyte, Samar, and southern Luzon with winds of 150 knots and torrential rains. As Karen passed up the west coast of Luzon, she accelerated and began to turn to the northwest.

35

Singapore

COLONEL ABDUL RAZA SAT in the old leather chair in his study. His son sat in a straight chair opposite, his handsome face illuminated by the light from the setting sun streaming through the window. The colonel himself was completely in shadow.

They sat in silence, comfortable now. When Lasa, chattering with joy, had brought the boy in an hour before, the air between them had been charged, brittle. They had shaken hands. Lasa had brought whiskey for the colonel and a pot of tea with milk for the boy. Then Yusef began to talk. His father listened without comment for forty-five minutes as the boy told what he had heard about the plans for the uprising. Yusef tells the story well, the colonel thought as he listened. Just what he has heard; no embellishments. Told as a concerned citizen, but not as an informant. No names, and no exact places, dates, and times. Just the plans for a rising and an invasion of "volunteers" from across the causeway, which, if carried out, could result only in a bloodbath that, in the end, would change nothing.

When Yusef finished, his father shifted in his chair and took a cigarette from a carved ivory box on the table beside him and lit it. As an afterthought, he offered the box to Yusef, who shook his head. The colonel cleared his throat and took a sip of whiskey. "Thank you for bringing this to me, Yusef," he said. "You did the right thing."

"Can you stop it?" asked the boy.

"It won't happen," said the colonel.

"But Father, can you be sure? There have been so many rumors, but in the last few days they are all becoming the same story." Yusef thought of Elias jerking and twirling around the little stage at the New Malacca and of his unexplained disappearance the following day.

"Rumors feed upon themselves, my son. I am sure you realize the police have informants in all the communities, including the

Muslim quarter." The colonel paused and studied the boy. *He looks five years older than he did in the cell in Johor. He looks confident and mature.* "Neither the means nor the will exists around Arab Street for any serious rising; in fact, I would doubt even another large street protest."

"And what of the Malaysians?" asked Yusef. "Couldn't they create an incident here and then march?"

Raza shook his head. *The lad has thought this through rather well.* "We work very closely with the Malaysians, Son, despite all the enmity and distrust spouted by politicians on both sides. Your uncle, General Mohamdir, and I are in daily contact; nothing will occur we do not wish."

"But can you be sure of the general, cousin or no? He has been a bit of a *Bumi-Putra* ranter for years."

"I can be sure," Raza said. He smiled. *He was sure, but that was a bloody good question from someone who knew as little as Yusef did.*

Raza sipped his whiskey. The silence was pierced by a sharp cry from the macaw Lasa kept in the kitchen. A wild bird in the overgrown garden answered, and a conversation ensued. The colonel got up and closed the door to muffle the din.

"Will you go to England, then, Yusef?"

"Yes, sir. To Oxford and not to Sandhurst, if that's all right."

"Of course it is. I am very proud of you, and I know you worked hard to get that."

"I did work hard, Father," Yusef said. He looked a little sad. "Father, even if there is no violence, and I hope there isn't, can't *you* do something for the Malay people? You have the rank and are respected in Singapore as a whole, and yet some I have heard think the Chinese want a crackdown, even an expulsion of Malays from the republic. These men say the police have become an instrument of the party and not the people."

"I do what I can," the colonel began.

"I know you do, Father," said Yusef, leaning forward, earnest. "And I know you see yourself as above politics, especially politics of race."

The father returned to his chair and sat down heavily. "I will do more, Yusef."

"Yes?" The boy smiled. The colonel saw his wife in the smile, and his chest ached.

"When I saw you in Johor, Yusef, when I *struck* you, I had a realization. I have always believed that the Chinese got where they are because they have worked hard. We Malays are more childlike; we want gifts. We want to share the national bounty just because it is there and we were the first people in these places. I still believe that, Yusef, but since I saw you in Johor and abused you, I have come to see the Chinese as arrogant and as abusers of the Malays and other minorities as a father might abuse his children."

"Father—"

"Just a bit more, Yusef. First, I am profoundly sorry that I struck you in that room in Johor. It was an act of arrogance, and of cowardice. I beg your pardon."

"Father! I provoked you. But that is not what you asked. You have my pardon."

Abdul Raza stared at his bright, handsome son in the gathering shadows of the study. His mother's soft beauty was still in the lad's face, but his jaw had grown firmer. "Thank you, my son. Thank you, Yusef."

"Father," Yusef said softly. Something seemed to catch in his throat.

"Now, Yusef, I have said I will do something to reduce the arrogance of the Chinese in government and to remind them of the importance and worth of the Malays and other minorities, and I shall. But you must trust me to do it in my way."

"Of course, Father. No one could expect you to sweep Lee and his party aside in a single stroke."

Colonel Raza smiled but didn't answer. Dangerous, this man-cub. I am glad he is mine. "Will you be staying here until you leave for England, Yusef?"

"I'd like to, sir. I'm sorry it took me so long to come to see you."

"I am sure you had things of your own you needed to do. You may hate me for saying this, but in addition to your mother's good looks and sensitive soul, you have a bit of your father's stubbornness."

Yusef stood up. "I would call that character, Father. And I could never hate you for reminding me where it came from."

Raza heaved himself out of the chair with a groan, a cry of love for his son too long suppressed. The two men embraced in the center of the dim study, each man's face buried in the other's shoulder. They rocked each other, pushed apart to grin at each other, and then embraced again.

36
Hong Kong, 2 August

BARBARA RODE THE elevator to her flat with a Chinese *amah* who smelled strongly of whatever awful thing she had just eaten. Why will they never use the service lift as they should, thought Barbara, wrinkling her nose in irritation as the woman belched loudly and smacked her lips. The lift stopped at Barbara's floor and she stepped out, fumbling in her purse for her keys. She dropped the purse and then she dropped her briefcase, swore, and then struck the door with her fist. She was dead tired, and she felt close to tears.

She was sweeping things back into her purse, having at last found her keys, when the heavy door swung open. Richard stood in the opening, a cigar in his mouth and a brandy balloon in his hand.

"Barbara, darling, let me help you." He set his glass on the table just inside the door and balanced the cigar across the top of it, then returned to the hall to pick up her briefcase. He took her arm solicitously and led her into the sitting room. She fell into the large easy chair and once again dropped her purse, which disgorged money, keys, dark glasses, and other small items across the carpet. She stared at it venomously but made no move to pick it up.

Richard knelt and swept the stuff into the blue leather bag. He looked up. Barbara felt paralyzed by fatigue. "Drink?" he asked, placing the purse on the end table.

"Oh, yes, please, Richard. Scotch."

He brought the drink and sat in the chair on the other side of the end table. "It's after nine o'clock. Have you had anything to eat?"

"My secretary went out and got some of those awful hamburgers from the McDonald's across Connaught Road." She had never understood how the Chinese, who took food and eating very seriously, had become such enthusiastic patrons of McDonald's.

"Ah Tong fed me an hour ago. She said you called."

"Yes, I knew I would be late. I had a run-through with Nigel in London on a few last-minute changes in the prospectus. They will print the final run today, now that the issue has been priced."

"Still no chance the Singaporeans will pull the issue? It's sure to open at a deep discount." He drained his brandy glass and went to the sideboard to refill it.

No thanks to you, she thought. She was almost certain that Nibble in London was one of the major bears driving the price of her bond down on the gray market. By agreement, she and her husband never discussed the supposedly confidential aspects of their respective businesses. Nibble would not want to be seen trading lest they offend the MAS, but Nigel Cross was sure they were in the market, using brokers and intermediaries.

Richard returned to his chair and sat down heavily. He relit his cigar, which had gone out. Barbara hated his cigars. "We believe we will have a very firm reception for the bond, Richard. I only wish you had decided to support it."

He laughed, a single wheeze that burst up from his fat belly. He had gained a lot of weight since arriving in Hong Kong, and his expensive Savile Row suits no longer fit. "My dear, you know the level of our commitments to Singapore. The last thing *they* would want is for us to swallow this disaster. Elizabeth Sun as much as said so. Your bond is supposed to be new money from new sources."

"The bond will be distributed," she said, trying not to react to his efforts to provoke her. "Bear raiders would be wise to remember Roland, Archer has over a billion dollars in capital."

"Pity your comanagers aren't as strong."

"They are strong enough."

"Or as committed," said Richard, pouring brandy into his smile. A few drops leaked out the corners of his mouth and ran down his chin. She fingered a glass ashtray on the table beside her, fighting the urge to throw it, savoring the image of the shattered balloon glass slashing his slack grin.

She finished her drink and stood up. "I really don't want to spar with you, Richard. I am dead tired. I am going to take a shower and wash my hair, and then I think I will go right to bed."

"Perhaps I'll come in later and rub your back," he said, still grinning. "Might help ease away the tension."

"No, thank you," she said coldly. "I will be just fine." Turning away quickly, she thought she had seen just the slightest look of hurt cross his face. As she crossed to the bedroom door, she heard his heavy tread as he returned to the sideboard for more drink.

A portion of her angry tension slipped away in the hot shower. She regretted being rude to Richard, even if he was acting against her bond. That was business, and they were both professionals. And he was right: The bond was supposed to be money from new sources, not to be absorbed by Singapore's lead banks. Still, he had no reason to belittle her efforts, nor to revel in the possibility that her bond might fail. Was Holden right? she thought. Am I too obsessed with this bond to see the business in perspective? Am I becoming too ruthless? The Lions she admired could take a setback, but could she? She remembered with a shudder the promise she had made that RAL would support the entire issue, and she realized that she could not survive a failure of the issue and remain in the business, much less walk with the Lions. She had to win, but even if she did, what would she have become? Her tears flowed in the hot water of the shower. What have I lost, or given away, for this fucking deal?

An hour later Richard entered the bedroom, holding a full glass of brandy. Barbara was sitting up in bed, trying to concentrate on a paperback mystery and waiting for her hair to dry enough to remove the rollers. He grinned and set the glass down on his bureau with a sharp click. He turned away from her and took off his trousers, tossing them on a chair for Ah Tong to hang up in the morning. He threw his tie on top, then walked unsteadily into the bathroom, pulling at his shirt buttons. Barbara hoped absently that he would put his shirt and underwear in the laundry hamper rather than leave them on the stool by her dressing table as he often did.

He returned from the bathroom, grinning, and flopped on the bed. He was naked. He rolled across the king-sized bed and nuzzled her, pushing her book from her lap with a sweep of one hand. His other hand went under her back as he pushed his face into her nightgown, searching for her breast.

She was disgusted. Her husband smelled of toothpaste, sour cigar smoke, and stale sweat. She tried to push him away, but his weight had her trapped. "Richard, stop. I told you, I'm exhausted."

"Back rub," he giggled into her chest. He found her nipple and licked it. The nipple didn't respond. She pushed him again, and he rolled off onto his back. He had a slack near-erection curving down below his thick belly. "Wan' me to rub you, or you wanna rub me?" He reached down and began to stroke his penis, which began to rise.

She tried to pull free, but his massive thigh was across her legs. She remembered she had once found him worldly and sexy and even the raunchy stories he told when he drank cute and daring. They had made love often, both before and after their wedding, and he had been a thoughtful if not very exciting lover. After a while she had lost interest, though she still let him come to her when he wished, but in Hong Kong, as he drank more and more, he had mostly lost interest as well. "Richard, I don't want to! Oh, God, couldn't you at least go and take a shower first?"

"Wanna make love," he said, rolling on top of her, pawing at her hair and disarranging several of the plastic rollers. "Nothing unusual about a man wan's make love t'is wife."

What about what *I* want? she thought angrily. But she didn't want a scene. Maybe if I just go along with him, this will be over quickly and I can finally get to sleep.

He rose up on his elbows and knees, swaying slightly and still grinning. He grasped the hem of the sheet and pulled the covers all the way off. He reached his fingers under the low-cut neckline of her nightgown and exposed her left breast. The gesture was almost tender, and she relaxed and tried to smile. Just do it and pass out, she thought.

He leaned over her, his lips pursed, but suddenly lost his balance and fell heavily on top of her, knocking the wind out of her. His mouth found the breast and sucked greedily. Once again she felt nothing. He scrabbled around, lifting the hem of the nightgown where it lay across her thighs. With brute force he pushed her thighs apart and pinched her pubic mound with thumb and forefinger. She was completely dry, and it hurt. Her anger flared with her pain. With a little cry she grasped him under his shoulders and threw him off. He looked surprised, and tried to roll back over her, but she leaped out of bed and backed to the wall. She clasped her hands and chewed on a knuckle. The adrenaline rush made her tremble. For a moment she was afraid he would come after her, but he stayed in bed. He raised himself on one elbow and looked at her. His eyes had taken on a cunning cast, and he suddenly looked less drunk.

"Barbara, I'm sorry. Come back to bed."

His voice was soothing, but his eyes still held that cunning look. She shook her head and backed away along the wall. "I just wanted to go to sleep, Richard."

As he sat up and swung his legs over the edge of the bed, she noticed his erection had shriveled. "Barbara, a man has some right to make love to his own wife."

"Oh, sure!" She began to unpin the rollers from her hair, knowing she would have to get up early in the morning and do the whole job over. "I come home late, and all you want to tell me is that my bond issue that I have worked on all summer is going to fail because assholes like you are shorting it to death before birth—"

"Barbara, surely." He stood up, seeming quite steady.

As he advanced, she wrenched out more rollers and hurled the double handful at him. "Oh yes. You piss all over my deal, my efforts, then you stumble in here d-drunk"—she was crying freely now—"and sweaty and reeking of those awful cigars, and then you start pawing me like a sailor with a whore, and you think you have a right?"

"So that's it," he said, staring stupidly at the plastic rollers as they bounced off his chest. "I won't support your deal, so you won't fuck me."

She looked at her husband in disgust. That is what all these pigs think, she thought, suddenly feeling chilled. The only way a woman can get anything done in a man's world is to spread her legs. "Go to hell, Richard," she said coldly, stepping into the dressing room and closing the door behind her.

She ignored her husband's muffled entreaties to come out as she removed the last of the rollers and brushed out her thick, damp hair. The damage wasn't really so bad, she thought. She stripped off the nightgown and stuffed it into the laundry hamper. She took a brief cold shower, which calmed her. She was wide awake now and knew she wouldn't be able to sleep for hours. She brushed her hair again and applied light makeup. Why am I doing this? she thought. Certainly not for Richard, who will doubtless be snoring mightily by now. She put a dab of Opium perfume behind each ear and between her breasts, and then she knew she was going out.

She reentered the bedroom, stepping softly. Richard lay sprawled across most of the bed, his bare ass in the air. He was purring softly into a pillow. With any luck, the air conditioner will freeze him to death before morning, she thought, her anger still burning. She dressed quickly: a white cotton shirt, blue linen skirt, and a wine-colored Thai silk shawl she had bought in Singapore. She left the flat quietly and took the elevator down. She had no idea where she would go, but she needed to get out. She desperately wished she had a friend to whom she could unbend.

She had her car keys, but there was a red-and-silver taxi in front of the building, the fare just paying. On impulse, Barbara got in. The car might be a nuisance.

"Wheah to, Missy?" asked the driver, not turning to look at her.

She still hadn't decided. "Central," she said.

Holden Chambers's telephone rang just after eleven-thirty. He set his book aside and picked up the receiver. "Hello?"

"Holden, it's Barbara." Her voice was a hoarse, cracked whisper, and he sensed she had been crying. He could hear soft music and movement in the background. "Holden? Are you alone?"

"Barbara? Yes, what's happened?"

Her voice broke. "Holden, I am at the Hilton, just outside the Dragon Boat Bar. I have to see you."

Damn, he thought. She had filled his thoughts every minute since their night in Singapore, and more than ever he was sure she was danger. I suppose this is as good a time as any to tell her that I can't see her again.

"Holden, I can't stay here. I have just had the most awful row with Richard. I stormed out of our flat. I just have to talk to someone."

He felt a hitch in his throat. The image of her crying softly in his arms in Singapore nine days before rose in his mind, and he couldn't put it out. "I'll be there in a few minutes. Meet me in the open area just outside the bar." Better at least try not to make this look like a clandestine meeting, he thought.

"Okay, I'll wait right here. Thank you, Holden, and please hurry."

He put the phone down without responding. His throat was suddenly tight. This is easily the dumbest thing I have ever done in Hong Kong, he thought. Why did she have to sound so all alone? He opened a closet door and pulled his blue blazer roughly off the hanger, which clattered to the closet floor. He picked up the keys to his Triumph and the door key and let himself out. While he was waiting for the pokey lift to come up from the lobby, an unfamiliar feeling of warmth came over him. He smiled, accepting his recklessness and the reason for it. He wanted desperately to see Barbara Ramsay, whatever the risk.

He parked the Triumph in the multistory carpark adjacent to the Hilton and took the escalators through the shopping levels to the lobby. The Dragon Boat Bar was at the far end of the lobby, well away from the reception desk, but as always there was considerable traffic. Just about the worst place to be seen at midnight having a drink with another man's wife, he thought grimly, but what the hell, hide it in plain sight.

He spotted her right away, seated in one of the overstuffed banquettes just outside of the bar itself. A small service bar was behind her, and waitresses in the same shimmering blue *cheong sams* as worked the main bar stood there, looking tired and bored. He saw no one he knew; most of the other bar patrons seemed to be tourists.

"Hello, Barbara," he said quietly, slipping into the banquette adjoining hers. She was wearing dark glasses and pretending to read a magazine.

She set the magazine down and removed her glasses. Her eyes were slightly red. She burst into her wonderful smile and snatched his hand in both of hers. "Holden," she whispered.

"Barbara, I came as quickly as I could. What's happened?" He felt his hand burning in hers. "Darling, we can't just hold hands in the Hilton lobby." Once again he glanced around, hating himself both for being dumb enough to walk into this and timid enough not to make the best of it.

She dropped his hand but held him with her smile. A waitress arrived, and she asked for a scotch and soda. He asked for the same and a packet of Dunhill's. He had hardly smoked in two months, but clearly this was a special situation.

"Oh, Holden, I am sorry to drag you out like this in the middle of the night, but I just had to see someone who wouldn't hate me or bully me." She began to cry softly. She dabbed at the tears with a handkerchief she pulled from her purse.

"Barbara, what's happened? What's Richard done?" He spoke gently and reached across for her hand again.

"Richard." She balled the handkerchief in her free hand and caught the last of her tears. "Holden, when I married him, he was the kindest, most thoughtful person imaginable. Our relationship wasn't really passionate, but I don't think either of us wanted that. Richard was enough older that he could be like a teacher to me, and he taught me a lot. He helped me, Holden, helped me get started in investment banking. He was proud of my advancements, and he encouraged me. But deep inside, he wanted a wife who would wait for him at home with his slippers and adore him." Barbara looked at her knees. Holden didn't speak. He was embarrassed to be hearing his lover talk about her husband, yet drawn by her trust. "It was all right until we came here. Here, I felt I was ready to do something, not just carry water for the gunslingers who fought in the front lines. Richard, on the other hand, feels trapped. New York and London are pressing him to do great things, get all the big mandates, etcetera.

The Lions—you, most of all, Holden, but also Malcolm and Ben-teen at the Chase—outmaneuver him, shut him out." She looked up at his face. "He hates you, Holden."

"Fuck him," he said, and he immediately regretted his harsh-ness. "I'm sorry, Barbara. I shouldn't have said that, but this is a tough game in Asia. London and New York are far away and that is the way the Lions—and okay, *I*—like it. Richard shouldn't expect to come along too fast, and he shouldn't expect to be given a slice of the pie just because his calling card says First New York or Pacific Capital."

"I know." Her eyes were so large and so brown as to glow in the dim light. "But New York and London press. You and I both know New York and London press us all, almost hoping we will fail. And to ward them off, we make promises, some of which we can't keep."

He smiled and squeezed her hand gently. "That's why we are Lions and they only gunslingers."

"Everything in Hong Kong has become a threat to Richard," she said, looking away. "Imagine, Holden, how he will feel if my bond issue is a major success."

It could be Euromoney's deal of the year, he thought. But it is a long *if*. "He should be proud."

"You don't mean that. He will be devastated. I never realized it until tonight, but the success of this issue—or, rather, its fail-ure—is even more important to Richard than it is to me." Her voice trailed off, wistful and sad.

"What happened tonight?" he asked gently, stroking her hand ever so lightly and living in the light in her eyes.

"Nothing. He got drunk. He decided he wanted to make love to me. He was rough—more clumsy than rough. I have been working sixteen, seventeen hours a day for a week to put the bond to bed, with pricing and prospectus final only today. I just couldn't deal with it." Her voice and her eyes had grown cold. Holden released her fingers, and she put her hands together in her lap.

As she fell silent, he couldn't think of anything to say. She seemed sad, and he felt a bit of her loss. She was learning the price of being a Lion. She is losing a bit of her humanity, he thought, a part of her she never even knew was to be placed at risk.

The waitress returned and asked if they wanted another round of drinks. Barbara shook her head, and Holden paid the check. When his credit card was returned, Barbara reached forward and grasped his forearm in both hands.

"Holden, take me to your flat. Make love to me."

He felt a flush rising up his neck and a rushing of his heart. When he spoke, his voice was husky, compressed to a whisper. "Barbara, we agreed that what happened in Singapore was wonderful but wouldn't be repeated." She said nothing but began to cry softly. "It is just too dangerous, Barbara."

She looked up at him and her eyes flashed. "Holden, *everything* is dangerous! I need you! I need someone whose concern for me isn't limited just because it's *dangerous!* Do you have any idea how lonely I feel?" She snatched her hands away and looked away. He sat paralyzed. She knew he was right. "I'm sorry. It isn't fair to lay this on you. My problems are my own." She took her purse and stood up.

He banged his shin on the low table as he jumped up to catch her. "Barbara, my car's next door. Come on."

She looked at him with an expression that said he was her last hope. "You're sure?"

"Come on."

They entered Holden's flat quietly. He did not switch on the light in the hall, not wanting to rouse Ah King. Barbara stood, silvery in the abundant moonlight that poured in from the windows overlooking the harbor, as he locked the door. She followed him into the bedroom. Heavy drapes blocked the moonlight, and he switched on the overhead lights. He turned and took her hand in his. She came to him slowly and then pressed against him, kissing him hungrily, forcing her tongue deep into his mouth and making little muffled high-pitched cries. Her arms went up around his neck, and her knees seemed to give way. He wrapped his arms around her and took her weight. He felt heat like a great fever spread through his body and felt the ache of his penis constrained by his jeans as it swelled. Gently he lifted her and sat her on the bed. She released him, and smiled her special smile, and he felt his knees wobble. He reached inside his jeans and freed his erection, then knelt on the bed and bent over her. She grasped him around the neck and pulled him on top of her, once again locking her mouth on his. He felt her hand undo the top button of his jeans and grope for his erection. He rolled onto his stomach away from her hand, knowing that if she got hold of his penis he would lose control immediately. Her hand went around his back and tugged at his shirt-tail. He unbuttoned her blouse with numb fingers, then unfastened the hook between the cups of her bra. He kissed her breasts gently, raising the nipples with his tongue, while trying to detach his mind and slow his heartbeat. He breathed as deeply as he could, and some control returned.

She scratched his back with one hand, pulling his shirt free.

Her other hand softly combed his wavy hair. His kisses on her breasts were soothing, and the heat of her first passion slipped into languor. She felt his breathing slow as he licked each erect nipple in turn. Oh, God, Holden, my love, she thought, enjoying his caressing mouth. Make it last, my love. He found the clasp at her skirt waistband and the zipper beneath it, but her weight and his made the clasp impossible to undo. "I'll do that, darling," she breathed in his ear. He rose up, kissed her softly on her mouth, then stood up and quickly got out of his shirt, jeans, and shoes. He hadn't worn socks. His bikini briefs came last, a little self-consciously, she thought, and there he was, his engorged penis pointing up at an angle toward the ceiling like a spear.

She stood and took off her skirt, watching him as he watched her. His face was flushed and his expression flickered between desire and guilt. She dropped her shirt on top of her skirt on a chair and shrugged off her bra. She had to tug her panties off, for they were damp and clung to her thighs. The guilty look disappeared from his face. He wanted her, and she wanted him to want her. "Aren't you going to pull down the covers, love?" she whispered.

He swept the covers aside and then sat on the edge of the bed, taking in every line of her body. Things had happened so fast in Singapore he really hadn't looked at her carefully, or if he had, he didn't remember. She slid her panties slowly down her slim legs, teasing him, all the time holding him with her eyes and bathing him with the heat of her smile. As she dropped the panties on top of the rest of her clothing, she took a step toward him, and then another, and then stopped. Her full breasts glistened slightly from his saliva, and the nipples were still firmly erect. He could see droplets of moisture on her pubic hair and the shiny pink flesh of the lips of her sex as she took another step toward him. He reached out and placed his hands on the backs of her thighs as she stopped, her feet on either side of his. He stroked her thighs and caressed her buttocks. She leaned forward and put her hands on his neck, stroking his hair. She kissed the top of his head as he pulled her to him and pressed his face into the damp hair. His tongue found the open lips and flicked inside. She shuddered, pushing against him and giving a long, low moan. His tongue found her pearl and circled it, caressing and teasing. She felt her orgasm rushing up from the center of her being in a hot, tingling wave and she came, pushing her sex against his face and soaking him with her juices. She threw back her head and bit back a cry just before her knees buckled and she collapsed in his lap.

He picked her up and put her on the bed. She reached up for

him. He smiled gently, feeling more in love than he had ever been with any woman. He kissed her eyes closed, then very gently kissed her mouth.

"Please," she whispered. "Please."

He rolled between her knees and entered her. Her muscles inside pulled him in deep and her hands gripped his back with sharp nails. He began to stroke inside her, long and gentle, in control and making it last. At the end of each stroke, her breath came out in a little sigh. Her eyes were open and looked a little glazed in the harsh light. Her smile seemed frozen. He felt her begin to move with him, then she tried to quicken the pace. He kept it slow, holding her by his weight. "I want you to come again, Barbara," he whispered, kissing her ear and her neck.

"Oh. I want to!" Her voice was high pitched and breathless. "I've never . . . come . . . twice, darling!"

He felt the movements inside her quicken. Gradually he built the speed of his thrusting, sensing her rhythm and matching it, feeling her nails bite into his ass. "You will, Barbara. This time you will."

"Oh I can't! But I want you to."

"You will." He increased the pace again, and she caught up. She began to move wildly, and the little sighs grew to louder moans.

"Oh, darling!" Her voice trailed off into a keening moan and he held her under her hips as he shuddered through his release, wave on wave in time with her wailing cries.

She felt the orgasm's intensity unlike any she had ever known. She felt it difficult to breathe, as though drowning in a warm, thick liquid. She felt the intensity peak at the moment she felt his release inside her.

They didn't move for what seemed a very long time. Their breathing slowed and synchronized. He kissed her gently and rolled his weight onto his shoulder. She released her grip on his buttocks, and was surprised how stiff her fingers felt. The air-conditioner-chilled air felt cold on his sweat-soaked back, so he pulled the covers over them. She took his face in her hands and looked at him. Her face had a look of wanton satisfaction. "Thanks," she whispered. "You were wonderful. So strong and gentle at the same time."

He felt more than a little pleased with himself. "You bring out the beast in me."

"Lion!" She smiled.

Holden dozed. Barbara rolled next to him and propped herself on one elbow. She ran her hands lightly over his arms and chest, barely touching his skin. He smiled and stretched, fighting a yawn. His slack penis began to awaken.

She moved her cooling, tingling fingers down under the covers and over the skin of his thighs. Her hands stopped when she encountered the dry scabs and smooth new skin along the outside of his left leg. She pulled back the covers and looked at the scar tissue, whiter than his tan skin. She touched the wounds gently. "What happened to your leg?"

"Motorcycle accident," he said. His mind filled with fuzzy images of that strange evening. "Nothing serious."

She continued to touch his legs, and his penis continued to swell, albeit without the urgency of before. It stretched and straightened languidly, and he just felt it lifting clear of his belly when she kissed it and caressed his balls. He smiled broadly, his eyes still closed. He was absolutely sure that making love to Barbara Ramsay was indiscreet, dangerous to them both, and just plain stupid, but he couldn't help how happy he felt with her.

She crawled on top of him and kissed his smile. "What is so funny?" she asked as he kissed her back. She reached back and guided him inside her.

"Nothing, darling. I'm just happy. Are you happy?"

"Yes," she purred, beginning to ride him. "For the first time in months."

They made love slowly, exploring each other, savoring sights and textures and tastes and scents. She moaned a little as she came, and then she giggled and bit his ear. He kissed her through the giggles and told her that he loved her. She kissed him but didn't respond. He wasn't sure she had heard.

"Hold me just a moment," she said. "And then I must go."

Holden awoke with a start. The sheet and down comforter were thrown back and he felt cold. The overhead lights were still on, and he sat up quickly. He heard the shower in the adjacent bathroom. He looked at the radio clock: It was just after four. His earlier fears about the danger of an affair with Barbara flooded back to him.

She emerged from the bathroom and padded across the carved Chinese rug next to the bed, naked and beautiful and glowing pink from the hot shower. She threw her towel at him playfully and began to dress. "Call a taxi, please, love," she said.

Holden dialed the gatehouse down in the carpark and asked the sleepy-voiced guard to get him a taxi. The guard would have far more success with the dispatchers than Holden would. He pulled on his jeans and grabbed a polo shirt from his dresser. She was already dressed when the guard down below rang up to say he had the taxi. Holden pulled the curtain aside and saw the silver roof and red body of the cab in front of the lighted entrance. The sky was lightening rapidly, though all but the tallest towers of Central and all of the harbor were shrouded in fog. He saw that the traffic on Magazine Gap Road was already building toward the morning rush.

She kissed him lightly and picked up her purse. She opened the bedroom door and walked through the hall to the front door, with Holden close behind her. Ah King burst through the kitchen door, just across the hall from the bedroom. "Masta! You go so early? Not have breakfus?" Ah King wore a black padded jacket over her long woolen nightgown, and her hair hung down her back in a long, ragged queue. When she spotted Barbara standing in the open doorway, her questioning expression gave way to shock and then recovered to a tiny frozen smile. "Good morning, Missy," she said sharply.

"Good morning," said Barbara, passing into the hall and pressing the call button for the lift. Holden followed, then turned back at the doorway to say something to Ah King about having breakfast at the regular time. She was standing at the kitchen door, and she gave him a look of utter contempt as she went back into the kitchen and slammed the door. His comment about his breakfast died in his throat. Ah King was very fond of May-Ling, he thought bleakly. Christ, she has been gone barely more than twenty-four hours. Guilt and shame knotted his guts like a kick to the stomach. Even if the rest of this crazy business eventually comes right, I will forever live with how I hurt that innocent girl, whom I never really loved as much as she deserved because she never demanded it of me. Asia teaches us Europeans to take long before it shows us the subtleties of giving. No wonder we are regarded as pirates and barbarians.

He went to Barbara in the small lift lobby, very careful not to let the door lock behind him. The lift arrived, and she threw her arms around his neck and kissed him.

"I'll call you later, Holden. Big kiss!"

He returned to his bedroom, peeled off his jeans and shirt, and tossed them into the laundry basket in the bathroom. He shut off the overhead light and crawled under the covers. I had better think this thing through before it overwhelms me completely, he thought, staring at the dark ceiling. If it hasn't overwhelmed me already.

He fell into a deep sleep and didn't wake up until nearly nine.

37

3 August

WHEN CHAMBERS REACHED HIS office at ten o'clock, Margaret brought him a stack of messages with his tea. He asked her to order up some rolls from the bakery in the basement of Gloucester Tower, since he had left his flat without breakfast. He hadn't been prepared to put up with Ah King's surly conversation or, more likely, lack thereof. When he had first come to the colony three years before, he had been told that Chinese servants had their own personalities and moods, which, unlike servants of other races, they never deigned to conceal. Ah King had always been a handful, but maybe she had now gone too far, he mused. It was none of her business whom he invited to his flat, and it was certainly not her place to prefer one woman over another. He resolved to give her two days and no more to forget her anger, and if she didn't, he would set Margaret about finding a replacement.

He realized he felt pleased about reaching that tiny decision. It suggested to him that he was in charge of his life, in control. He knew that the facts were far different. He was in love with another man's wife. Somehow that still seemed something he could deal with, given time. Love seldom seems truly threatening, at least not in the early going. Barbara and he were adults, and if it came to that, Richard van Courtland probably would be, too. Scandal would harm everyone.

Holden shook the thought off. He doubted that Richard would ever know anything if he could just convince Barbara to be discreet! Better yet, he knew, would be to make a clean break. Somehow that seemed a lot more possible sitting at his desk, buttering one of the sweet scones Margaret had brought him, than it had just hours earlier in his bedroom. He closed his eyes and saw her—touched and tasted and smelled her—and it didn't seem possible at all.

He glanced at the morning papers without interest. The *Asian*

Wall Street Journal and the *Tribune* both had a couple of stories he should read. The *South China Morning Post* and the *Hong Kong Standard* were still busy with lurid dissections of the life of some poor homosexual policeman who had committed suicide.

His more pressing problem was how to gain control of the situation regarding David Weiss's embrace of the rumor of the coup in Singapore and its short position in the bond Roland, Archer was apparently ready to fling in the face of a vicious bear raid. He felt profoundly uneasy to see Traders take such a speculative position against a not-yet-issued security, and he felt sure that Frank Portas was at least partially as uneasy as he was. But Weiss! Weiss absolutely believed in the Sea Lion rumors and had built the short position in anticipation of disaster.

Chambers thought two things prevented Weiss from thinking clearly about the short position. First, he needed what his favorite expensive outside consulting firm called an "early win." All of his European operations were unprofitable, with the exception of Portas's trading operation, but Weiss didn't get full credit for the trading desk, forced as he was to share control and accounting with the head of Bank Resources Management in New York. Second, he wanted Chambers's head on a pike. What could possibly suit him better than to make an enormous profit trading an Asian issue contrary to the advice of "Mr. Asia"? And at the very worst for Weiss, Chambers thought, if he gets it wrong, he'll find a way of placing the blame on me. No one was more skilled in political maneuvering in the softly lighted corridors of Traders Bank and Trust Company than David Weiss.

The telephone on his desk buzzed. He stabbed the intercom button and said, "Yes, Margaret?"

"Mrs. Ramsay is on the line. Shall I put her through?"

"Yes, thank you, Margaret." The next button over began to flash, and he pressed it. "Barbara? How are you?" The new phone system had a neat feature: The center of the white button would show black if anyone else in his office was listening in. It glowed a secure white.

"Morning, Holden. Can you get away for an hour? I have just found out I have to fly off again today, and I need a bit of advice."

"I suppose so," said Holden, watching the button not change color. "What do you propose?"

"Meet me in the lobby of the Mandarin. On the mezzanine level. I'll buy you a coffee."

"Okay. What time?"

"Ten minutes. I'm just leaving now. Are you sure this isn't inconvenient?"

Holden pulled his calendar toward him. Nothing until lunch with John Malcolm at the Yacht Club at one. August wasn't supposed to be a busy month. "That's fine. I'll meet you at the top of the stairs."

"Perfect," she said, her voice cool, even slightly abrupt. She rang off.

Another good opportunity to tell her it's over, he thought, picking up his jacket off the back of the chair in front of his desk. Even better than last night, with the cold light of morning and no alcohol. I wonder if she knows anything about this Sea Lion business which could give me a lever with Weiss? It would be unprofessional as hell to ask her, and equally so for her to answer, but he was beginning to feel desperate. Besides, he noted grimly, my professional conduct of late has been a little sloppy at best.

He told Margaret where he was going and that he would probably be back within the hour; if not he would call. She gave him a slight smile and a bob of her head. He rode the lift down to the first floor of Gloucester Tower, the one above street level, then made his way through the elevated walkways to the back of the Mandarin, glancing idly at shop displays as he went. The covered bridge over Chater Road brought him into the hotel, also on the first floor, which the Mandarin thoughtfully labeled the mezzanine to avoid confusing American and Japanese guests, who expected the first floor to be the one on the ground level. The passage opened out into the upper lobby, where drinks and light snacks were served all day. The upper lobby ringed the lower, with its center open, and was furnished with comfortable couches and chairs and less comfortable hassocks, all in cream-colored leather. It was a bright, airy room and quiet, despite the muted bustle of the main lobby, which floated upward. He found Barbara waiting at the maître's lecturn at the top of the broad staircase leading downstairs. She looked fresh and much better rested than he felt. She wore a sleeveless café-au-lait–colored dress of fine silk, belted at the waist with wide red leather. The belt set off the slimness of her waist and the roundness of her hips. She turned and saw him while he was still coming toward her. He smiled, and she looked back with an expression of agitation, her dark eyes frowning and her teeth worrying her lower lip. A thought hit him with such force as to stop him in his tracks. Suppose she called me here to tell *me* that *she* wants to end the affair? His eyes blurred momentarily, and he fought to catch his breath. He knew suddenly that an end to this insane affair was the last thing in the world he wanted, and he also knew that if she suggested it, he would have to accept without demur. His bright smile collapsed into a look of sudden pain. She looked at him quizzically, then turned to follow the maître to a quiet corner near the windows. They sat opposite each other across a small marble-top table. He folded his hands on his lap and tried to smile. She laid one hand lightly on both of his.

"Holden, what's the matter? When you walked in, you looked as though you had had the most awful shock."

"Nothing. Just a stray thought that passed through my mind—some unpleasantness at work. How are you? You look much more relaxed than you have in weeks."

She smiled brightly and laughed. He thought the laugh might signal a reprieve. "I feel wonderful, and you are the only person in the world who knows why. I really got very little sleep, but it was good sleep."

"You looked a little worried yourself when you first saw me," he said guardedly.

"I have to fly to Singapore. I am taking the noon flight."

"Is that a surprise?" Say it, if you are going to, my love, he thought: And since we won't be able to see each other for a while, this would be a good time to end our little fling, don't you think?

"Not really. I had thought to go tomorrow. RAL priced the bond officially yesterday. Under the terms of the indenture, we have to bring it to market within the next five working days. I want to be in Singapore when the issue is brought." Better there than here, she thought bleakly, and her smile faded. "And I just wanted to see you before I left, my darling."

His heart took a tentative leap off the pit of his stomach. "I'm glad. I wish we could have spent the whole night together."

She looked at her watch. "I have only a few minutes. My driver is picking me up here at eleven. I just had to see you." She leaned forward and captured him with her glowing brown eyes. "I wish I could kiss you."

He felt a lump grow in his throat. He nodded, trying to swallow the lump.

"Holden, last night in bed," she whispered, "you said you loved me. Did you mean that?"

He got most of the lump down this time. "Yes, I did. I do."

"Thank you. I had to know." She waved to the passing waiter and signed the check when he brought it.

Thank you? he thought. But it could have been far worse. "I'll walk you down to your car," he said sadly. "Do you have luggage?"

"Already in the car," she said, suddenly all business. She picked up her red-leather purse. "Let's go."

Her Mercedes was waiting just outside the Mandarin driveway, and the driver pulled it in smoothly between two taxis as soon as he saw her wave. Just before the car reached them, she grabbed Holden's arm and whispered urgently, "Are you sure? You really meant what . . . you said?" Her expression looked fragile, as though she might cry.

"Yes, Barbara," he said, fighting tears of his own.

The car reached them, and the uniformed doorman opened the rear door. She looked at the open door and seemed to hesitate. She turned to him, squeezing his arm and then releasing it. "Holden, tell TBI to get out of their short position. The bond will be successful." She slid into the car and the door was closed behind her. The car inched forward, then had to stop behind a taxi that was unloading luggage. Holden took a step forward, level with Barbara's window. The taxi finished unloading and started to move off. As she opened the window, he put his hand on the window molding and leaned toward her. "Barbara, if you can tell me anything to pass on to TBI, anything concrete, I will insist—"

As the car moved forward, he walked alongside, feeling very conspicuous. "I can't say anymore," she whispered. "Good-bye, darling. Big kiss!"

He watched the car pull into traffic and saw the window go up. What exactly did she mean by saying the bond would be successful? Wishful thinking, or did she know something? And more important, he wondered, why did she warn me? Does she love me? She hadn't really said so, either way. Could she be using me to get TBI to buy in its short? He shook his head, wanting to put this last thought out of his mind, but it stayed there, just a whisper.

Holden sat in his office, the late-afternoon sun warm on his back. He had closed the office door, something he rarely did, signifying he did not wish to be disturbed. He looked at the closed door and it seemed to increase his sense of isolation and despair.

He had a pad of legal paper on his desk. *Sea Lion* was written at the top, double-underlined. Below the name he had drawn a *T* dividing the whole page, the way an accountant does. At the top of the *T* he had written *pro* on one side and *con* on the other. He was attempting to sum up the Sea Lion rumor from its beginning, but his mind was tortured with images of Barbara. She is in danger and so am I, and if I knew what this Sea Lion business really meant, perhaps I could save us both.

He sighed. Drawing the yellow pad toward him, he read the few, inconclusive notes.

Pro:

His first story, about the Malaysians threatening to intervene, and its retraction, played out as he said.

I saw armed men assembled in Johor. Of that I am sure.

I saw Abdul Raza associated with the rebel force, and later at the roadblock, and later in the hospital. I am not sure of any of these sightings, but Raza, as Chief of Police and the most prominent Malay in government, might be the logical choice to build a coup upon.(??)

Con:

The idea that a Malay coup could occur in Singapore defies all logic, even if one postulates Malaysian intervention.

The party would prevent it.

The army would stop it.

Malays are only 15% (!!) of Singapore's population.

Neither the *ASEAN* countries nor the U.S. nor the *ANZUS* pact would allow the Malaysians just to walk in. (But what if Washington sees it as Kelley suggested? An opportunity to stop the PAP's drift to the left and to get the naval base?? What of London? Canberra?)

He picked up a pen and scrawled across the bottom of the page, right through the line dividing the two columns: WHY THE HELL AM I SO CONFUSED ABOUT WHAT I REALLY WITNESSED IN JOHOR? And below that: WHAT HAPPENED TO ELIAS?

He slammed the pen down and buzzed for Margaret.

"Yes?" she said.

"Try to get Tony Wren in Singapore for me, please."

"Right away," she said. He leaned back and rubbed his tired eyes.

"Holden. How are the wounds?"

"Healing, Tony. Nothing serious. Look, have you seen Elias?"

"Just yesterday, in fact. He was arrested, you know, and the police held him for two days."

Chambers lit a cigarette. It tasted harsh, but it calmed him. "How is he?"

"Fine. Scared, I think, but fine. Apparently the police went out of their way to terrify him."

Chambers blew smoke toward the ceiling. "Tony, the police told me he was badly hurt."

"No sign of that. How did they say he was hurt?"

"Not now. But you saw him, and he is all right?"

"Yes. Holden—"

"Go with me on this, Tony, please. What does Elias look like?"

"Dark. Tall and slender. Very young."

That fits, thought Holden. "Does he own a big motorcycle?"

"I don't know, Holden. Quite frankly, he isn't the type. Why do you ask?"

"The man called Elias took me for a ride on a motorcycle, Tony." God, I hope this call isn't being recorded. I could be putting Tony in real danger. "I wonder if it was the right Elias."

There ensued such a long pause that Chambers began to think the connection had been broken. "Holden?"

"Yes."

"It's important?"

"Yes, very."

"Very well. Listen, Holden, I trust you. You are a decent man, not like that fascist troglodyte Weiss. I am going to give you a confidence."

"Go ahead. I promise to keep it." Tony knows the international lines may be monitored as well as I do.

"Well, I have many friends among the gay community here. Social acquaintances, really. Young artists, you understand?"

"I understand." Tony Wren's homosexuality was one of the worst-kept secrets in Traders and in Singapore.

"Elias is gay, Holden. And he has a quirk."

"Yes?"

"He always wears the most awful scent, Holden. Very strong lavender scent. You would surely have noticed it immediately upon meeting him."

Holden forced his mind back to the night of the wild ride. He remembered the smell of Elias's leather and his sweat, and he remembered his own smells and tastes of fear. But he was sure he remembered no smell of lavender, no smell of any cologne at all. He nodded to himself. Now he was certain. "Thank you, Tony."

"Can't tell me anymore?"

"Best I don't, Tony."

"Right. Understood."

"Good-bye, Tony. You're a friend, and I owe you."

"Twice, actually. Take care."

Chambers stared at the yellow pad in front of him. He drew two heavy circles around the name *Elias* and then put an *X* through it. He tore the top sheet off the pad and dropped it in his briefcase, then picked up his jacket and left his office, telling Margaret he was going home as he passed her desk.

III
TYPHOON

38

HOLDEN CHAMBERS PACED THROUGH his living room, out to the balcony overlooking the harbor and back to the cluster of furniture under the muted Belgian tapestry. Each time he turned, he looked intently at the telephone on the end table, waiting for it to ring. He had booked his call to London half an hour ago, thirty minutes before TBI's opening. Frank Portas would be in his office, but the lines were always busy in the period just after Hong Kong's close of business, which coincided with London's opening; traders were passing currency and securities positions. Chambers looked at his watch, sipped his drink, and walked back out onto the balcony, leaving the glass doors open to hear the phone. I hope I am right, he thought, staring out at the harbor, watching the ship traffic and the scudding clouds. The typhoon will come early tomorrow if it doesn't veer away. The financial storm he foresaw could begin tomorrow as well. He looked at his watch again as the phone rang loudly, the double ring that signaled the overseas operator.

He closed the balcony door behind him and crossed the room in four long strides. He set his drink down and snatched up the receiver. "Chambers."

"Hong Kong overseas operator. You are Mr. Chambers?"

"Yes."

"Your call to London. Go ahead."

There was a hiss and a series of clicks. God, don't drop the line, he thought; it will be another half-hour in the queue. "Hello?" he said hopefully.

"TBI trading," said a voice with a strong cockney accent.

"Frank Portas, please. It's Holden Chambers in Hong Kong."

"Hong Kong? Hang on, Frank's on another line. I'll tell him you're on."

"Please tell him it is urgent," said Holden, but he sensed he was already on hold. He waited, hoping no one in London punched the line up and then hit another button, dumping his call into the ether. It happened often.

"Holden? Good evening, old man," said Frank Portas cheerfully.

"Good morning to you, Frank," said Holden, leaning back in relief. "Look, I need to talk to you about your position in the Belgian franc and the when-issued bond." Belgium and its currency were this week's agreed code for Singapore. International lines were monitored and indeed often became crossed. Holden had heard some very confidential information in dim echoes under his own conversations.

"Short and short." Portas's voice dropped an octave and became suddenly attentive. "You know that."

"Okay, Frank, now listen carefully. I think you should square it up. Something is not right, especially with the bond."

"Go on. You realize it will probably be expensive to square against the spot BF, and very difficult to buy back the bonds we sold in the gray market."

"I know. I think there is a good chance that both the currency and the bond will firm. The bond could rise sharply at issue."

"Why? Both have been dropping like rocks since the latest report from you-know-who came out."

"I think the report may be, well, misleading. This is very serious, Frank."

"Damn! I suppose we could get even in the franc, maybe even without loss if the market is still soft. How did Belgian close out there?"

"Down all day but firm at the close." There was no significant trading in Belgian francs in Hong Kong. The longer we talk, the easier it will be for any listener to decipher this silly code, thought Chambers, taking a gulp from his drink and waving at the hovering Ah King to refill it.

"Why do you think the bond may fly? As much as you can tell me."

"Perhaps a bear squeeze." It wasn't the right answer, but it would get Portas thinking.

"Hm. We don't think the underwriter will call the allotments in. The comanagers wouldn't have been willing to push as much out on the gray market if they thought the lead might take it back."

He is telling me he doesn't think Roland, Archer will support the Singapore issue, thought Holden. "Then you should be able to buy more from the comanagers?"

"To the extent they still have any," said Portas very quietly. "Most have been active sellers."

Chambers rubbed his eyes. God, I hope I have finally figured this out. "Frank, I have been looking at this. I have concluded that the events of the summer, which suggested that the bond issuer might be in trouble, were in fact trivial—"

"But the, ah, confidential information—" Portas broke in.

"Made it seem otherwise. That's exactly my point. Ask yourself: Without that confidential information, would you have taken your current positions?"

There was silence, save the hissing in the line. Portas spoke yet more slowly. "Against the franc, no. But we have proprietary information here that the underwriting group for the bond is very nervous."

"How widespread would you guess is the trading against the bond?"

Portas pulled a printout from his briefcase at his feet. "Hard to guess; there are a lot of brokers. Not very, I'd say, by the timing of the trades."

"Is it possible, Frank, that the shorting is confined to the parties to the confidential information, plus the nervous comanagers?"

"Possible. Likely, even. Holden, hold on a tic." Portas placed his hand over the mouthpiece of the phone, sensing a man looming over him. He looked up to see David Weiss, his face pulled into a deep and angry scowl. "Give me a moment, Holden," said Portas, again covering his mouthpiece with his hand. "Good morning, David," he said without cheer.

"What the fuck does Mr. Asia want?" said Weiss not acknowledging the greeting.

"Trouble with our short position against the Sing dollar, he reckons, and against the unissued bond, David."

"What? He told us to get short."

Portas wasn't a courageous man before his bank superiors, but he liked the truth. "Well, not exactly, David. In fact, he has repeatedly urged caution."

"Fuck him!" roared Weiss. "What line is he on?" Weiss perched at the adjoining desk and picked up the phone.

Oh shit, thought Portas. Just when I might have gotten some useful information. "He is on line 6080, David. Remember, today we are calling Singapore 'Belgium.' "

Weiss grunted angrily and stabbed a button on the phone. "Chambers? Weiss here. What the fuck is going on?"

Holden slammed his fresh drink down on the table in front of him, spilling half of it. Ah King rushed up with a cloth, mopped, and then took the glass away to refill, clucking and muttering in Cantonese. "Good morning, David," he said evenly. Portas and I could have worked this out, he thought. Weiss will never listen to the vague tale I have to tell.

"What the fuck is going on?" repeated Weiss.

"Well, as I was telling Frank, I have reason to think the bad news about Belgium which has been circulated recently may be misleading and that TBI's short position could be very vulnerable."

Weiss covered the mouthpiece with his hand and turned to Portas. "Why is this idiot blathering on about Belgium?"

" 'Belgium' is this week's code name for Singapore, David," Portas repeated, trying very hard to keep his voice even. "Look, it's technical stuff he wants to discuss. Maybe I should just talk to him and summarize the discussion for you later."

Weiss shook his head and spoke into the phone. "Chambers, we have been getting information, from you and from others, that strongly suggests Sin—Belgium could be in deep shit. We also know that the issue was priced yesterday, and that under the terms of the indenture, it must come to market in the next four days, unless the *Belgians* pull it, which the lead underwriter, who is here in *London*, Chambers, says they refuse to do. Capiche?"

"David, I know all that. The point is—"

"The point, sweetheart, is that the market in *London*—the *real* market, bubby—says this bond will go through the floor and probably take the currency with it. Now, what do you, eight thousand miles away from the action, have to add in the way of new *facts* which might suggest the market is wrong?"

"David, stop shouting. I know how you love to beat on me, but there is serious money at stake."

"Facts," said Weiss, his voice somewhat lower.

"David, the reason Belgium was chosen for this issue is that it has been a very stable, growing economy for a very long time." Another statement any listener would easily recognize as false, thought Holden helplessly. "Confidential information, available so far as we know to only a few, has caused some to believe that recent events, not unusual in themselves, foreshadow a severe destabilization of the political and economic situation."

"Information which you in your colorful way have to a certain extent confirmed," said Weiss.

"I told you then that I wasn't sure what that all meant and that it felt staged. I now have reason to believe someone close to the deal wants us to believe the rumors and thus to expose us to a squeeze."

"Jesus Christ, Chambers!" Weiss's voice was rising again.

"What have you been smoking? Who in the hell would benefit from such a deception?"

Holden took a deep breath. "Someone with a nervous underwriting group, David. Someone considering a bear squeeze."

Weiss spoke very softly now. "Well, laddie, the lead underwriter here in London has given no such signal, and the short selling continues. But I will return to that at the end of this conversation, now barely minutes away. What has the lead underwriter's representative been whispering in your little ear?"

Chambers winced and flushed crimson. Weiss had an uncanny knack for being very close to the mark. Could he possibly know about Holden's affair with Barbara? "David, I only know the lead underwriter has a very strong desire to break into this market, and I believe they will support the bond. If nothing happens in the political arena, if the rumors were false from the beginning, the bond will be sold and the shorts burned."

Weiss again covered the mouthpiece and turned to Portas, who had listened to the conversation in silence. "Can you make any sense of this rambling tale?"

Portas shook his head. "It seems farfetched. Besides, Philip Meyer—"

Weiss grinned. "I am saving that for last. But what do you think of Chambers's story?"

"Well, there is no question he thinks he is on to something."

"But we know that this Raza has control of the army, and he doesn't."

"Well, that is rumor, too. Holden has always had a keen sense of the Asia market."

Weiss shook his head. "I think all our darling Holden has ever had that was of any use is a pair of brass balls, and I think he has lost them. He doesn't know how a short squeeze works, and he is losing his nerve. And his little escapade in Singers rattled his tiny mind."

Portas shrugged. "I think he is more solid than that."

"Perhaps," said Weiss. "But we know something else he doesn't." He uncovered the mouthpiece. "Still there, Chambers?"

"Yes, David." Chambers was now certain his hunch—the more he thought about it, he realized it was no more than a hunch, however strongly he felt about it—would be ignored, and he saw no reason to tell the story of Elias's missing lavender scent and be further ridiculed.

"Summarize your conclusions for us, if you would." Weiss's voice dripped sweetness.

Holden sighed. "I think Belgium is safe. I think the rumors

were planted to create a short position and thus a demand for the bonds when issued."

"You think Sea Lion is a fake?"

Chambers winced. Any listener who hadn't figured out the meaning of the conversation would have it now. "A ruse. A red herring."

"And how do you balance this new insight with the colorful tale of your abduction to Malaysia and subsequent arrest and expulsion from Singapore?"

He is doing this on purpose, thought Holden, growing angry. My humiliation is more important to him than anything I have said. "That could have been set up."

"You fucking idiot!" Weiss exploded. "You can't even go back to Singapore for three months! What fucking use are you anyway, Mr. Asia?"

"I want this on record, David. I warn you to get out of that short if you still can. I may not know your wondrous and all-wise London market, but I know a con, an Asian con, when I see one." He said it angrily, but he knew it sounded lame.

There was a pause of several seconds. Holden emptied his drink and leaned back, awaiting the tirade. When Weiss spoke again, his voice was almost caressing. "Let me tell you one thing, one thing only, that you don't know about this affair. Last night Philip Meyer—who, you may remember, is the chairman of Roland, Archer Limited—had dinner with Alex McLean, the editor of *Euromarket Insider*. Do you remember Alex?"

McLean was the editor of the most influential of the Euromarket newsletters. "Yes."

"Good. Philip expressed a certain dissatisfaction with the way the whole bond issue in question has been handled, and he even divulged that his Asian rep may have given the Singaporeans to believe that RAL would support the issue beyond its stated underwriting commitment."

Holden squeezed his eyes shut. My God, poor Barbara.

"Further, after Alex and Philip had gotten well on into the champagne, Philip stated that he had no desire to own the entire issue"—here Weiss's voice rose to a triumphant shout—"and he specifically disavowed any attempt at a bear squeeze! Good night, Mr. Asia!" Weiss slammed down the phone.

Chambers threw the silent receiver at its cradle and missed. He threw his empty glass after it, and it skidded across the floor and shattered against the iron leg of a plant stand across the room. Ah King rushed up and began gathering the pieces in her apron. She turned to him and shouted, "Masta, you clazy! You clazy evah since May-Ling go away!"

Holden looked at the old *amah*, and saw her eyes were streaming tears. Maybe so, he thought. What have I done to my life? Perhaps I *have* taken leave of my senses. "I'm sorry, Ah King," he murmured. "I will clean that up."

She put the rest of the shards she could pick up in her apron and strode heavily toward the kitchen. At the door she turned, still crying. "I get supper now, Masta. Supper *cold!*" She burst through the kitchen door with a thump, shouting in angry Cantonese.

Portas put his phone down gently. David Weiss sat staring straight ahead, his face set in a stiff smile of triumph. Portas motioned to one of his bond traders. "Ned, call over to Stanley Ross and Partners. Check on the Singapore when issued."

"He's fucked," said Weiss with a cackle.

"You don't want to unwind the position?"

"Hell, no. My gut says we will make a lot of money. Think of it: a coup, even a repetition of the rumor, and nobody will want that bond."

Portas leaned forward. "David, I know Chambers didn't say anything specific, but my own gut always gets uneasy when the man on the scene says to go the other way."

Weiss stood up. "I have to fly back to New York this afternoon. Watch it closely, but stay short. Watch the Sing dollar as well."

"David, what will happen if he is right?" asked Portas.

"He's fucked either way. He confirmed Sea Lion, remember?"

"But surely . . ." began Portas. Christ, see reason, man, he thought.

"I will call you from Heathrow before I take off," said Weiss, and he left the trading room.

39
London, 3 August

WEISS CALLED PORTAS FROM Heathrow at six. "How did the bond trade today?"

"Soft," said Portas, looking at his quotron. "Off a bit to 94.25. No news."

Weiss chuckled. "That's good. Whatever Chambers thinks he knows, the issue will fail. Roland's has to put it out by when?"

Portas checked the tip sheet. "Today is Tuesday. Friday at the latest."

"Great. You know, if Chambers hadn't lost his nerve, this could have been a great coup for him. The biggest investment bank in the U.S.A. tries to break into his market and ends up tramping all over its dick in its first deal."

If that is what happens, thought Portas. "Well, I am ready to go home, David. Shall I pass the position back to Asia?"

"Yeah. Tell New York to watch it, then put it back to Hong Kong. Give it to the trader. What's his name?"

"Benny Yu."

"Yeah, give it to Benny. Don't even talk to Chambers."

"David, surely—"

"No. And tell this Benny just to watch the bond, not to trade without calling you. I gotta catch my plane. I will talk to you tomorrow midday."

Hong Kong, 4 August

Typhoon Karen paused for a few hours during the night, seeming to hesitate. An hour before dawn, the storm intensified, with observed winds at its center of over 140 knots, then curved slightly north and accelerated toward Hong Kong. The Royal Observatory on Mount Kellet recorded wind gusts of forty knots at 0515, and directed the Signal Three, Threat of Dangerous Winds and Seas, to be displayed throughout the colony. At seven, the storm once again paused. The colony received heavy rains and the wind abated somewhat.

Holden Chambers arrived late at his office. He felt listless and depressed, afflicted with a hangover from the whiskey he had drunk as well as with the sour taste of defeat and despair from his conversation with Weiss and Portas the night before. He had slept little.

Ah Wong let him out of the car directly in front of the entrance to Gloucester Tower. He sprinted the twenty feet to the doorway as a blast of wind burst through the narrow canyon of Pedder Street, filled with rain as solid as a wave and gritty with blown trash. The wind nearly tore his briefcase from his hand, and the rain left him completely soaked on his right side.

The head foreign-exchange trader, Benny Yu, was having a heated argument with Margaret at her desk outside Chambers's office. Holden brushed past and threw off his dripping jacket. Benny and Margaret spilled in after him, still shouting at each other in Cantonese. "Tea, please, Margaret. And would both of you kindly stop shouting?"

Margaret looked hurt as she nodded and withdrew. She was protecting me and I caused her to lose the battle and therefore face, thought Holden. His head was beginning to pound. Benny stood silently, a truculent look on his sullen, waxy features.

Holden took a deep breath and sat down behind his desk. He did not invite the trader to sit. "What is it, Benny?"

Benny took a single step toward the desk and handed him the long telex that passed the foreign-exchange positions from New York and certain securities positions from New York and London. "Mr. Chambers, all day yesterday you ordered me to buy Sing dollars! All day long you make me lose money! Now look! London went short, and then New York as well!"

Holden studied the telex. New York had indeed passed a major short position in Sing back to Hong Kong. In the securities listing he saw that TBI had a short position against the Singapore bond of nearly twenty million dollars, unchanged from the night before. "I spoke to London last night, Benny. It seems they take a different view of the Sing than we do."

"*We* do? No way, Mr. Chambers! *I* watch the market, see it soft, and want to hold my short position! You went over your authority and told me to buy in at a loss!" He pulled a sheaf of pink foreign-exchange trade-authorization tickets from the side pocket of his baggy jacket and slammed them down on top of the telex. Holden jumped at the sound, and he felt his jaw quiver. Insolent bastard, he thought, looking hard at the Chinese man. He looked at the tickets, then at his hands, which twitched slightly as he held the telex. He struggled to control the rage that flowed with the rhythm of the pounding inside his skull. Benny rambled on in his high-pitched whine about how he had lost face with other traders, as well as with his colleagues in the trading rooms at TBI and at Traders in New York. Holden thought through the act of rising from his seat, reaching across his desk to take Benny by the throat, and slowly squeezing first the sound and then the life from the arrogant little trader. The thought calmed him and he smiled. When Benny saw the smile, he abruptly stopped talking and his contemptuous sneer dissolved.

"So you want me to sign for those trades personally, Benny?" Holden's throat was dry and tight, and his voice had a hissing quality.

"Y-yes. Your responsibility, not mine." Benny's voice was small, and he took a step back from the desk.

"Is there anything else I can do for you, Benny?" Holden imagined his hands on the man's fat neck again, and his smile broadened. He closed his hands into fists to keep them from shaking.

Benny stared at Holden's fists. "No. You sign, please."

"I will. Now, Benny, you can do something for me."

"Yes. Yes, sir."

"Get out of my office at once," Holden whispered.

At ten o'clock Typhoon Karen lurched forward. The winds in the harbor increased to sixty knots and the barometer dropped seven-tenths of an inch in less than an hour. Signal Eight, Typhoon Imminent, was ordered displayed at ten-fifteen. Businesses began to close and heavy shutters were placed over windows and doors.

Holden told his staff to go home as soon as the Signal Eight was announced over the radio. The Hong Kong and Far East Stock Exchanges announced at 1025 that they would close because of the typhoon. The two smaller exchanges swiftly followed suit. Central District emptied of its Chinese workers and most of its Europeans as well, except those who decided to party the storm through in the hotel bars. Chambers considered going down to the Yacht Club, but he felt sure that his boat boys had tied *Golondrina* down as well as could be, and he didn't feel up for a drunken afternoon in the bar.

So Weiss and Portas decided to ignore my advice completely, he thought sourly, his anger smoldering as Ah Wong drove him back to his empty apartment. Ah King had gone to her family in the New Territories immediately after slamming his breakfast down in front of him two hours before.

In Singapore, an announcement was made just before noon that the Trades Union Council had accepted the government's latest offer and that those dockworkers still on strike were already returning to work. At two, Prime Minister Lee appeared on the balcony of Parliament House to announce a reorganization of his cabinet, in order to improve efficiency and to promote better relations among Singapore's diverse ethnic communities. The Minister of Home Affairs, Abdul Raza, was named Deputy Prime Minister and the government's chief spokesman on intercommunity relations. The Minister of Social Affairs, Yusef Ibrahim, resigned, complaining of fatigue and failing health. The head of the Singapore Malay Students' League appeared with the Prime Minister and the Deputy Prime Minister and pledged to work for order and discipline among the secondary-school students in the Malay-language schools.

At 2:15 P.M., Roland, Archer (Singapore) Pte. Ltd. announced the issue of the first-ever fixed-rate Eurobond for an Asian-government entity and said that trading would begin at once in the exchanges in Singapore, Luxembourg, and Hong Kong. Because Hong Kong was closed due to the typhoon, and because London and Luxembourg would not open for four and one-half hours, the Singapore Eurobond began to trade in Singapore and nowhere else.

Barbara phoned Nigel Cross at 3:30 P.M.—7:30 A.M. in London—and got him out of bed. "Nigel, we're issued. The bond's in play."

"Jesus, Barbara, I thought we had agreed to wait until London opened!" He felt a flash of anger and a twinge of dread and was instantly awake and carrying the phone out of the bedroom, away from his sleeping wife.

"We did, Nigel, but much has happened since last night. The government announced a cabinet shake-up this morning and named Abdul Raza Deputy PM."

"Christ! Then this whole Sea Lion rumor—"

"Exactly," she cried, cutting him off. "The dock strike was also declared settled. As soon as these announcements were made, the Sing dollar started to trade sharply higher, as did nearly all shares on the Singapore Stock Exchange. We had to put the bond in play. Buyers were calling up, clamoring for it."

"You had enough buy orders in Hong Kong and Singapore?"

"Better than that, Nigel. We have plenty of buy orders here in Singapore, and Hong Kong's exchanges have closed."

"*Closed!* Barbara—"

"There is a typhoon. The exchanges shut down at ten-thirty this morning." Barbara raced on, her voice animated and happy. "We have buys here from local investors, and we think the MAS and friends are buying as well. Nakamura Securities Singapore have sold their suballotment and want more. I asked them if they would wait for their London to open, but they say their Tokyo wants more now."

"Jesus. You've done it. How is your own book?"

"The Singapore suballotment is sold, Nigel, and I don't think much went to traders. I called you to get authority to start selling off London's book." Nigel could hear her excitement through the wire. His own adrenaline began to rush, and he realized he was pressing the phone into his ear hard enough to hurt. He took a deep breath, forcing himself to think. "Let's go a little slow, Barbara. Are the shorts coming in?"

"It's hard to know for sure. Neither Canadian Bank of Commerce nor BSI are set up to sell here, so we think we are seeing all the non-Japanese interest. Traders Bank in Singapore isn't active in the securities markets, and Pacific Capital hasn't been seen. My guess would be that PCC here wouldn't trade except on specific instructions from Hong Kong."

"But wouldn't the local people have sense enough to call their masters in Hong Kong?"

"Like as not, they can't get through. Long-distance service is being disrupted by the storm, and local service has probably been knocked out as well. I tried phoning my office just before we opened and couldn't get through."

"*Just* before?"

"Five minutes before," she giggled.

"Clever girl. Pray the lines stay down a few more hours."

"It's possible, of course, that the bears could be trading through intermediaries, but there have been no large orders, only a steady stream of small ones. I have unfilled orders for close to another sixteen million, and Nakamura wants another fifteen million."

"All right." Nigel took another deep breath and sat down at the dining-room table. "Give Nakamura his fifteen mil. You take eighteen million from RAL Hong Kong's limit, but feed it in slowly. I want you to start marking the price up."

"But aren't we committed to sell at the issue price?"

"Technically, yes. But I want that position passed to me at a premium, Barbara. When the bears wake up, I want to hit them hard. Use the same intermediaries the bears used to stick it to us all last week."

"All right. What else?"

"I'll get to the office as soon as I can get dressed. Under an hour, I should guess, and then I will call you immediately. In the meantime, you had better thank the god of typhoons, if there is one."

Barbara laughed, a trill of pure delight. "There is, Nigel, and I have." She was as sure as she was happy that Lee But Yang had held his announcement of the unity government until Hong Kong's exchanges had closed, knowing full well that all Singapore issues would soar on the news.

"Congratulations, love, you may have saved us all."

"We did it, Nigel."

"Stay by the phone."

Holden Chambers sat in his darkened flat, watching the lightning and the lashing rain as the windows bulged frighteningly at every gust of wind. Power had failed at one o'clock, and the phone had gone out a half-hour later. His battery-operated radio reported a gust of one hundred twenty-one knots measured at the Star Ferry pier in the past hour. Holden guessed that had been the one which had caused the window in the servants' quarters to shatter explosively. He had heard the glass shards bounce around the kitchen and even strike the kitchen door, a good thirty feet from the broken window.

All the interior doors in the flat were closed and, where possible, locked, as the typhoon instructions stipulated to limit the damage from flying glass. The glass doors to the balcony overlooking the harbor were protected by heavy wooden boards, which he had slid into grooves on the floor and ceiling just outside. The glass doors and all the windows were heavily taped on the inside. Still, the glass doors bulged in the higher gusts, as did the smaller windows, through which the black rushing clouds could still be seen.

When the storm reached its maximum strength at two-thirty, he had taken his radio, a glass, a decanter of whiskey and a soda syphon, and a dining-room chair into the alcove between the two back bedrooms, so as to be as protected as much as possible from flying glass should more windows fail. The darkness suited his mood, so he didn't waste the flashlight he had at hand.

The wind reached a low-pitched roar, like a thousand jet engines, rising in pitch and volume as the demon-jet went to takeoff power and then falling back. Each time the pitch and volume rose, the noise was louder, and the falling-back took longer to return, until at last it didn't return at all. The wind tore at the massive apartment block, and the building began to vibrate, then to shudder, and then to sway. He braced himself against the creaking door jamb and tasted fear, washed down quickly with whiskey. The wrath of God, he thought. The measure taken of our folly of greed. I should pray, he thought, but I am not deserving.

The radio continued to report on the progress of the great storm, with stories of ships breaking free of their moorings and careening through the harbor. One container ship dragged its anchor through the telephone trunk cables between Kowloon and Hong Kong Island, knocking out all international service to the island, before fetching up on the breakwater at Kai Tak Airport and beaching itself halfway up onto the long runway. Air operations at Kai Tak had been suspended when the warning signal was raised to Ten, and the radio reported a DC-10 had been blown off its chains and into the terminal building. Another cargo ship had struck the breakwater at the Causeway Bay Typhoon Shelter and narrowly missed going right in among the massed boats within, among them, Holden thought, his yacht *Golondrina*.

The radio warned all citizens to remain indoors because of the danger of debris flying in the wind. The large metal hanging signs favored by Chinese merchants were said to be flying up and over buildings and crashing through walls. Flooding in the squatter estates on the hillsides caused whole villages to collapse in avalanches of red mud as the dragons beneath Hong Kong's ancient hills bled. Still the storm came on, its awful calm eye passing northward, just east of the eastern approaches to Victoria Harbour and later into the villages in Mirs Bay, home of the Hakka boatpeople and frequent cruising stops of the colony's yachtsmen.

The eye passed, and the wind dropped suddenly to a mere banshee scream as the colony, like a ship at sea, passed from the storm's dangerous to its safe semicircle. The wind decreased abruptly because the speed of the storm's passage, more than twenty knots, began to subtract from the cyclonic winds rather than add to them. The wind shifted abruptly from northeast to southwest, and the rain increased, but the monster had passed. Chambers crawled out of his shelter and cautiously entered the kitchen to examine the damage caused by the burst window.

The lights came back on at five o'clock, dimmed and died half an hour later, and then came back on for good at six-fifteen. The rain let up for spells, and Holden could see the harbor, still whipped to a froth, with surviving ships bouncing nearly out of the water in the monstrous chop. The wind continued to drop, and the sounds of sirens could be heard in the city below. The radio announced the typhoon signal had been dropped to Three, and at six-forty-five the phone jangled to life.

"Holden, are you all right?" asked Frank Portas. The line quality was far worse than usual.

"Yes.. We've had a typhoon, a big one. I suppose you know."

"It was on the Reuters. I don't guess you have heard what happened today in Singapore."

Holden's heart sank. Not the bloody coup! "No. Radio has been all the storm, and the telephone only just came back on."

"While you were battened down and the civilized world slept, Holden, Roland-fucking-Archer opened their bond."

Holden leaned back in the deep chair. His body went as limp as a rag doll's, and for a moment he couldn't breathe. In a flash it came to him who had created Sea Lion and why. Suddenly all the puzzle pieces that had been rattling around in the bottom of the box fell neatly into place, and the picture mocked him. He took a deep breath and began to giggle, and then to laugh. He realized he hadn't really laughed in a week, and the thought so pleased him that he threw back his head and laughed until he was short of breath and his face was running with tears.

"I am afraid it isn't funny, Holden. Not for me, and certainly not for you."

Holden swiped at his tears with the back of his hand. He still shook with stifled laughter. "Christ, but it is, Frank. RAL didn't have enough underwriting authority to stabilize the whole issue but more than enough to hold against any selling pressure in Singapore. And let me guess: There was good political news from Singers, say, shortly before they opened the issue?"

"There was. It seems the government crisis is passed."

"Or never was."

"Or never was. Look, Holden—"

"It's perfect, Frank. Admit that it is dead solid perfect." Holden began laughing again and had to gasp for breath.

Portas chuckled despite himself. It was perfect, and the fact that TBI had followed the ruse all the way to the slaughter didn't make it less so. "All right, Holden, your lady friend Barbara What's-her-name really put it to us. But now we have to think about damage control."

"Barbara Ramsay is her name. I guess you will remember it, Frank, probably forever."

"Quite," said Portas dryly. "Now, if you have had your laugh, can we get on to the subject of saving our skins?"

"Does David know yet?" asked Chambers, letting out one last guffaw.

"No. I called as soon as I got in, but his wife told me he was off on one of his bizarre five-thirty A.M. runs."

"How much have you lost?"

"Well, we don't know. My good old friend, the lovely bastard Nigel Cross, is offering at 102 and getting takers. We tried buying from the other comanagers, but Banque Suisse d'Investissement are scrambling to cover their own positions and have marked it up as well."

"Have RAL released the comanagers' allotments?"

"I think so, else the Swiss and the Japanese wouldn't be trading at all. I am pretty certain Nigel is holding the Canadians' piece. Nakamura have been buying for clients even at the marked-up price."

"What is your position?" asked Holden, pouring himself a drink from the decanter and shaking a cigarette from the red Dunhill's box. He smiled as he lit the cigarette. He knew that his career was over, but he couldn't but admire the mastery of Singapore's coup.

"I have bought a few odd lots, so I have about fifteen and a half million left short, sold at an average price just below 96."

"Christ, Frank. Shouldn't you reduce further?" Chambers blew smoke at the ceiling.

"Of course I should, but this position was not mine but David Weiss's, and I intend it should remain so. Anyway, the price might drop back when Nigel gets tired of holding the lot."

"That's a paper loss of nearly a million dollars."

"Bit over, actually," said Portas. "Not enough to sink Traders or TBI, but certainly an embarrassing loss on what amounts to a single transaction."

Chambers sighed and sipped his drink. The cigarette tasted foul and he put it out. "I suppose it would be churlish of me to bring up the fact that I told you, emphatically told you, and our gracious leader, to get the hell off that position just last night?"

"Well, no, but that is why I called."

"I don't get it, Frank."

"Look, old man, Weiss is going to crucify you no matter what. I know that you told us to get out of the short, and I will tell you, as I told David when last we spoke, that we should have heeded your advice, vague as its grounding may have been. David will not remember it just that way."

"I still don't see—"

"If I stand up like a proper Brit and declare that you were right and David was wrong, it probably wouldn't save you, and I would go down as well."

Holden felt a sudden flush of anger rise to his temples. "But surely—"

"And I wish to tell you that I am prepared to stand by you to any extent you like, if you want to fight David Weiss."

Chambers's anger disappeared as quickly as it had come. "Thanks, Frank, but there is no need to share the noose. What was it the lawyer said in the *Caine Mutiny Court-Martial?* 'Better one lonely hero than a bunch of disgruntled sons of bitches.' Besides, I am out of this. I will never be able to work for Weiss again."

"Well, you think about it, lad. If you want me, I'll be there, never fear."

"I know you will. But just keep it, like a loaded dueling pistol pointed at his skull. I'll make my own way."

"All right, for now. My other line is flashing, and I can only guess who is on. Watch your back, old son."

"No fear, Frank. Confusion to the enemy."

"Just so. Be careful."

Holden put the phone back in its cradle. He shook his head and smiled. Frank is right, of course. It won't matter to David that I was right all along. I am totally fucked, and Barbara, the woman I couldn't help but love, did it to me. Yet I cannot really blame her. She got us all with our own greed, our own self-importance.

He got up, made himself a fresh drink, and carried it into the kitchen. He took two lambchops out of the fridge and placed them on the gas grill above the stove. As he sliced some squash to sauté, the phone began to shrill in the living room: the double ring of an overseas call. Holden ignored it, and it stopped after twenty or so rings. Fuck you, David, he thought, turning the chops. The phone rang again, but he made no move toward it. Time enough for the end of this part of my life tomorrow. The thought of leaving Traders filled him with unexpected pleasure, though he felt a profound regret that he would have to give up Traders Asia and Hong Kong. The phone finally became silent as he dumped the chops onto a plate with the lightly cooked squash and carried it into the dining room, along with a bottle of wine. Outside, the typhoon slowly died.

 **40**

5 August

HOLDEN CHAMBERS CLIMBED INTO the car behind Ah Wong at eight, an hour earlier than usual. The weather had cleared, although heavy clouds continued to stream overhead, occasionally dropping dense showers through twenty-knot winds. The fierce tropical sun began to dry the puddles alongside the road. Uprooted trees had been pulled to the roadside, but leaves and palm fronds were littered everywhere, along with bamboo poles, which had blown off construction sites, and all matter of natural and manmade debris. Police directed traffic around the Garden Road flyover, where a goods lorry lay on its side, wrecked. Traffic was slower than usual, and it took Ah Wong half an hour to reach Central.

Margaret rose to meet Chambers as he walked into the office. She looked apprehensive, so he smiled broadly at her. He felt surprisingly cheerful, almost relieved, and felt he was mentally prepared for the showdown with David Weiss. "There are many telexes on your desk, Mr. Chambers," she said, smiling back at him. "And Mr. David Weiss just called. He wants you to call him at his home in Connecticut the moment you come in."

"I'll just have some tea first, Margaret. And send for Benny Yu, please."

"Yes, sir. Hannah will get the tea. Shall I book the call to Mr. Weiss?"

"Not just yet, Margaret. I'll tell you."

"But he insisted." Her chin began to quiver and she looked close to tears. "H-he shouted at me."

"All the more reason to let him wait, wouldn't you think?" Poor Margaret, he thought. "I'll see Benny first."

She smiled faintly. "Yes, sir." She turned and left the office.

Holden sifted through the telexes quickly. There was a short one from Frank Portas: "Finally cleared off Nigel at between 101–2. Lost over 1.2 mio. Best you batten down for second typhoon two days. All the best, Portas." Holden smiled and set it aside. He felt, rather than heard, Benny Yu standing before his desk. The little trader had entered without a sound.

Holden looked up, still smiling. Benny looked shrunken. Holden knew he was twenty-six, but he looked fifty. His suit was rumpled and his tie askew. On his sweaty face he wore a look of terrible personal tragedy. Chambers had an awful feeling that the trader must have suffered a loss in the typhoon. "Benny, is everything all right? Is your family safe?"

"Everyone is fine, Mr. Chambers," Benny whispered. "Some broken windows, some water came in." He raised his hands in a small additional gesture of despair and fell silent.

"Sit down, Benny," said Chambers softly. Benny took a jerky step forward and dropped into the chair with a loud sigh. "Where is your position?"

"I passed my Sing dollar to Michael Chow in Singapore before I left yesterday morning. He had to buy it out. I lost a lot of money."

"How much?"

"One hundred fifty thousand Hong Kong dollars. All the foreign-exchange trading profits for the year, Mr. Chambers." Benny seemed to shrink further with another little sigh.

"Well, things were far worse elsewhere, as I am sure you know. Nobody gets it right all the time, Benny."

"You were right. I disobeyed your instructions. I shall resign."

"Let's take this one step at a time. Can you give me a report, today, of movements of the Sing against the U.S. over the last ten trading days?"

"Of course," Benny pushed himself painfully up from the chair. "But I was wrong and I shall resign."

"Let's talk about that later, Benny. I'll need that report as soon as possible."

"I shall do it at once." Benny turned at the door and peered back at Chambers. "How did you know?"

"I didn't. But I felt it."

"Everyone here says you have the good *joss*. I should have listened." He turned and slipped soundlessly through the door.

Poor sod, thought Holden. He took up the position sheet. Singapore dollars had finished the day before up twenty U.S. cents, a rise of roughly eight percent. He buzzed Margaret on the intercom. "Call David Weiss, please."

Hannah, the receptionist, set his teacup in front of him. Holden continued to read telexes until Margaret buzzed that his call to Weiss was on. He told her to put it through and to please close his office door. He took a couple of deep breaths, a sip of tea, and picked up the receiver. "Hello, David."

"Hi, sweetheart." Weiss's voice was low and husky, and seemed to seethe through the line. "I suppose you are feeling pretty smug this morning?"

"No, David. I don't like to see the bank lose money."

"I had a particularly unpleasant chat with the chairman this afternoon, Holden. More than money will be lost."

"More's the pity," snapped Holden, making no effort to keep the irritation out of his voice.

"I want you in New York at the latest Monday of next week, asshole!" screamed Weiss. Chambers winced and held the phone away from his ear. "I want you and Portas and that poofter Tony Wren all in a room with me, and then we will discuss what the fuck went wrong, and then I will decide who among you will get to fall on his sword on the chairman's new Shirazi rug."

"David, surely you can't expect to place *all* the blame on your subordinates—"

"I'll get my share. I am already getting my share."

"Especially in view of the fact that the three of us all counseled caution, while you—"

"That isn't the way I see it, bubula."

"While *you*, David," Holden pressed on, knowing he would never get another chance to speak his piece, "insisted on taking a monster short position based on a rumor—"

"Which you confirmed!" bellowed Weiss.

"The hell I did! I reported what I saw, and I always said it looked fishy. And the night before last, I flat-out told you and Frank Portas that it was a con."

"And that's your story." Weiss's voice had dropped to a normal tone and sounded almost amiable. "You actually think you can weasel out of this, O Prince of Asia, and send me to the wall?"

"The least you can do is stand next to us, if the wall is where this ends."

"But Holdy, this is the real world, and that isn't the way it works. Just be here Monday, bright-eyed and bushy-tailed, and you might learn something."

Holden felt suddenly drained of all emotion, all energy. "David, if you are going to fire me, I would prefer to get a few things in order here before coming back."

"Aw, Holdy, don't give up so easily, it isn't like you." Weiss chuckled. "But of one thing you may be absolutely sure, sweetheart: When I fire you, whether this time or at some future date, you may be sure I will do it in person."

"How very kind of you."

"Tut, tut. Sarcasm ill becomes you. Just be here Monday at eight A.M."

"David—"

"*Be* here, asshole!" There was a clang as the phone was slammed down in distant Connecticut.

Holden waited with Ah Wong in Ice House Street, in front of St. George's Building. He had telephoned May-Ling just after talking to Weiss and begged her to see him for lunch. She seemed reluctant, and her voice held an aloofness he had never before heard, but when he told her he would be leaving for New York very soon, she relented, providing she could choose the restaurant.

May-Ling ran down the steps to meet him. She was beautifully dressed in a suit of blue linen and matching bag and shoes. Holden thought she looked achingly pretty despite the taut, chilly expression on her face. She stopped in front of him and extended her hand. He took her hand automatically and shook it, and immediately he felt enormously foolish. She said a few words in rapid-fire Cantonese to Ah Wong, and he nodded and slipped back into the car. "We won't need the car, Holden," she said. "I told you I would choose the restaurant, and I want to show you some things."

She started off up Ice House Street at a rapid pace and he followed. He wanted to touch her, to take her arm, but he wasn't sure how she might respond. On Des Voeux Road, she jumped aboard a tram, and he had to sprint to catch it as it rumbled off east, swaying and ringing its chime. In all his years in Hong Kong he had never ridden one of the ancient trams, nor would it have occurred to him to do so.

She stood in the center of the tram, which was impossibly crowded. The driver pointed to the fare box. "How much?" asked Holden in Cantonese. The driver held up two fingers. Holden found a two-dollar coin in his pocket and dropped it in.

"Aye, yah," said the driver with a laugh. Holden saw the Chinese man behind him drop in two ten-cent coins. Holden forced his way back to May-Ling. The tram was airless and he began to sweat.

"Have you ever ridden the tram before, Holden?" May-Ling asked cheerfully.

"No, and now I know why," he said irritably. "Why couldn't we have used the car?"

"Because I want you to see Hong Kong in a different way from the glass and greed of Central and the shallow parties of the Peak and lunch in the Mandarin Grill or Jimmy's Kitchen."

"Fair enough," he said, grasping the overhead bar and snatching a whiff of air from an open window. Sweaty bodies pressed against him on all sides, and most of the air he breathed had just been exhaled by someone else.

"I know about the bond deal, Holden," she said gently. "Mr. Adams told me. I'm sorry."

He cracked a smile. "It has been a rough week all 'round."

She touched his chest with the tips of her fingers. "Look out the windows, Holden. We have left your Hong Kong and are entering mine."

He stooped and looked out. Hennessy Road, Wan Chai. He'd been here many times, usually entertaining Japanese bankers in the restaurants and night clubs. But he knew May-Ling hadn't brought him here to see nightclubs. Just let it flow, he thought, feeling the sweat running down the channel of his spine and soaking his shirt, front and back. I guess this is punishment, and I guess it is deserved.

The tram rattled on, exchanging new passengers for old every fifty yards or so. When Hennessy Road became Yee Wo Street, May-Ling grabbed his arm and got down. Immediately they plunged into the alleys behind Jardine's Crescent. The alleys, where all manner of cooked food was being prepared and sold, seemed even more oppressive than the tram, even though the stalls were shaded by overhead awnings. Holden felt that without his substantial height advantage over the Chinese mob he would have suffocated. May-Ling pushed on, stopping at various stalls where God-knew-what was being fried in hot oil or grilled over tiny charcoal fires. She collected tiny parcels in a plastic shopping bag she had taken from her purse, paying a few coins to each vendor after much discussion in shouted Cantonese. She looked quite content, not hot in the slightest.

He in turn was disgusted by the squalor and the crowding. The whole place seemed to reek of dirt and disease, and dogs, chickens, and other farm animals darted around beneath his feet. How can May-Ling propose we eat this shit? he wondered, but then he followed her eye as she went from stall to stall and saw that the cooking areas were in fact very clean and the uncooked food carefully protected from the swarming flies. He also watched as she seemed to glide slowly through the crowd. People bounced off him but seemed to flow around her. He tried to emulate her and found the way smoother.

May-Ling's last purchase was from a wizened old man who

carried two large wooden buckets of ice at the ends of a stout bamboo carry-pole. She bought a cola for herself and a San Miguel for him. She glanced at him, shared a joke with the vendor, and then bought another San Miguel. When they emerged into the sunlight at Great George Street, she once again took his arm. "Let's find a shady spot in the park to have our lunch, Holden," she said.

Shady spots proved hard to come by in the vast park, but she found one to suit her in an area filled with mothers chatting on benches surrounded by hundreds of running children, energetic despite the liquid heat. Holden and May-Ling found half a bench in the midst of the melee. As he took off his jacket and placed it beside him, he noticed it was as wet as his shirt and filthy from his passage through the alleys. She opened a beer for him and laid out her purchases. She had skewers of succulent and spicy meat, crisp fried dumplings containing scallions and vegetables with either fish or meat, and little steamed dumplings with shrimp and other shellfish. All were good and delicate, and he thought better not to ask for details as to the origins of the meat. As they ate, the breeze off the harbor gradually cooled his skin, though the humidity was too high for his shirt to dry. They finished the meal, and he started the second ice-cold beer. "May-Ling," he said gently, "thank you for lunch, but why did you bring me here?"

"For lunch," she said, the cool expression returning.

"May-Ling—"

"You want to apologize, to explain," she interrupted. "I don't want to hear you apologize, and there is nothing to explain. I prefer to remember you as strong."

"Strength has little to do with it. I treated you badly and I'm sorry."

She waved the thought away. She looked hurt. "I wanted you to see Hong Kong as I know it, Holden. Look at these people. Look at their vitality. Compare this to the languid life of the European long-noses selling nothing to each other at great profit."

He felt a trace of anger. "You liked the life well enough once."

"I did!" She took his hand in both of hers. "It was new to me, and strange, and it had a rhythm of its own. And the money that flew around! Chinese like money as much as Europeans, perhaps more." She touched his face. "And I loved you, a little. You were so earnest in trying to learn Chinese custom and Chinese sensitivities."

"But I failed with you, and that is why we are here."

"You didn't fail completely. Neither did I." She leaned forward and kissed him lightly, oblivious to the women and children, many of whom were watching. "We are just different, and I had to learn that. You are a good person, Holden, and for a while I thought I could live in your world, but in the end I realized you would always be you, a lovely *gwai-lo*, and I just wanted to be Chinese."

"So my affair with Barbara—"

"Mattered only because you loved her."

He nodded slowly. "I think I understand. As always, you are wise."

"Please don't think badly of me, or of yourself."

"I don't. In fact, I feel much better since we had this talk."

She stood and picked up her purse. "Stay here and finish your beer, my love. There is something I have to do before I return to my office."

He got up, sweeping the remains of lunch into the plastic bag. "I'll get a taxi and take you back."

"No, please. Stay here awhile and watch the people, especially the children. This is my Hong Kong, Holden, and I want you to remember it as part of yours."

She walked away and he sat. He finished the beer and still he sat, watching the children. He wondered idly where he was and then realized: of course, Victoria Park. He had driven past it on the harbor side hundreds of times but never come in. He threw the trash and the second beer can into a litter barrel. I can walk to the Plaza Hotel and get a taxi back to the office. Or I could walk through the streets again and go over to the yacht club, where I am pretty sure to find John Malcolm. Holden Chambers decided to walk, to have another look at May-Ling's Hong Kong.

 **41**

THE SINGAPORE AIRLINES 747 descended south of Hong Kong, flying west of the city of floating junks in Aberdeen harbor and then the high-rises and crowded beaches of Repulse Bay. The captain announced they would be landing to the southeast. Barbara sat on the starboard side of the first-class cabin, and she looked out her window as the big aircraft banked over the harbor. Western District rose below her, its skyscrapers seeming to reach for her, and then they were over the harbor, still choppy from the typhoon, with patterns of white water around the moored ships and ferries and lighters scurrying about in the chop. The air above the harbor was turbulent as well, and the plane shook as it turned over Lai Chi Kok and she saw the orange-and-white checkerboard pattern on the mountain, which marked the final turn for Kai Tak Airport, whose long concrete finger jutted out into the harbor. The plane sank in the wind, and the apartment blocks seemed so close that the landing gear might sweep away the drying laundry that fluttered in the strong breeze. Barbara pressed herself into her seat as the plane made a perfect landing, turned, and taxied in.

She swung along the long corridor of Kai Tak Airport, her heels clicking on the black rubber flooring. She was in high spirits, almost wanting to run to get through immigration and customs and on back to her office but at the same time savoring each yard of the long corridor that led to Hong Kong. For the first time in the many in which she had walked the long passage, she felt Hong Kong was her city, that she belonged. She was a Lion now, for all to see, and she couldn't wait to shout it from the rooftops. A Lion with balls of purest, heaviest brass.

She passed quickly through the Hong Kong residents line at immigration. The officer said "Welcome back" without any trace of expression. Barbara smiled and said thanks, then danced into customs. She was carrying her hanging bag and another leather case with a shoulder strap, as well as her purse and her briefcase. Lions didn't check luggage, she thought joyfully. There was never time. Her driver met her just outside customs, and she gave him the two larger pieces and then sauntered to the curb while he ran to get the blue Mercedes from the multistory carpark. Barbara breathed deeply, savoring the damp heat and the varied smells, all of which had seemed so alien and threatening when she had first arrived just six months before. It seemed a very long time, a different era. She had arrived as no one at all, just some banker's wife. Now she was Barbara Ramsay, Lion. "Roar," she said to herself with a giggle of glee, as the car swept up. She tossed her case and purse into the back seat and climbed in.

"Home, Missy?" said the driver, threading the big car into the traffic.

"No, Timmy, the office."

"Yes, Missy."

Iris met her at the reception and took her things. As she passed through the bullpen of securities salesmen, they clapped and cheered, and some even stood up to applaud. She flushed and smiled. None of these men had ever taken the slightest notice of her before. She slid into her cramped office and shuffled through her telexes for the one from Nigel: "Well done. Position closed out on final distribution. Bears blasted, and we made an obscene first-day trading profit. Please come to London earliest. Congratulations, and I want that dinner. Best regards, Cross."

She thrust the remaining telexes aside, glowing with joy. I wish I could just tell someone! Perhaps I should go over to the American Club for a late lunch. I would have to see someone there.

Iris slipped into her office, carrying a cup of Chinese tea. "There is a Miss Wong to see you, Mrs. Ramsay. She asks for only a minute."

Barbara frowned. "Do I know her?"

"She works at Danger, Close, the law firm."

Traders's law firm, thought Barbara. We have never used them. "All right, Iris. I will go out to her in reception." There was no way she could receive anyone in her tiny office, with prospectuses and other papers stacked on every surface, including piles on the floor. "Ask her to wait a moment."

Barbara sipped her tea and then stood up. Her cream-colored dress of natural silk was wrinkled from the long flight, but she straightened it as best she could. She took a compact from her purse, prodded her hair into place, and made a few adjustments to her light makeup. She slid around the piles of paper and made her way back to reception. "Hello," she smiled. "I am Barbara Ramsay."

"I am Marylin Wong," said the woman. She was tall for a Chinese and darker than most. Her eyes were huge and damp, and she was luminously pretty despite her sad expression. She was faultlessly dressed in an expensive European-style suit of blue linen. She looked faintly familiar, but Barbara couldn't recall where she might have seen her.

Barbara motioned for her to sit in the U-shaped banquette farthest from the receptionist's desk. "How may I help you?"

"You can't," said the woman, her voice cold and with the sharp-edged accent of the educated Hong Kong Chinese. "I only wanted to see you." The woman stood up abruptly and looked down at Barbara. "I wanted to see a woman who could take a man's love and then turn it on him to make his ruin."

Barbara gasped and raised her hands to her face. "You—"

"I was Holden Chambers's friend," the woman said sadly.

The woman who had danced all night with Holden in Manila, thought Barbara. Because she was dark, Barbara had thought at the time she might be Filipina. "But-but, I didn't ruin him," Barbara whispered. "I tried to warn him."

"Holden Chambers was the only European I ever knew who genuinely tried to develop an understanding of Asian sensitivities," hissed Marylin, leaning over the other woman. "The others remained the coarse and greedy pigs they had arrived as, but he changed. *You* brought him back to blind greed, by making love to him and then saving your business at his expense." Marylin curled her lip at the word "business."

Barbara felt frightened by the Chinese woman's fury, and then she felt ill. The room began to spin. She got to her feet unsteadily, swaying. "I can't talk to you," she said helplessly. Her nausea was increasing by the moment.

"There is no need. I wanted to see you, and now I have. There is no more to say."

"Excuse me." Barbara pushed past the woman and bolted for the ladies' room. She fell into a stall and was violently sick, struggling with her arms to keep her head from plunging into the water. When the heaving stopped, her head cleared quickly. She pulled herself upright and flushed the toilet, then bathed her face and rinsed her mouth with cold water from the basin. She was trembling, but the nausea had gone. She looked at her face in the mirror and took deep breaths until her color returned, gradually obscuring the two spots of scarlet on her pale cheeks. She drew herself up, and felt a bruise on her leg. She looked down and saw that she had torn her hose in her dive into the stall. *Damn* that woman, she thought. The rush of anger made her feel better. She marched out of the ladies' room and back into reception. The trim Chinese woman had gone. Barbara realized she had already forgotten her name.

"Are you all right, Mrs. Ramsay?" asked the receptionist.

"I am a little tired, Hilda," said Barbara, sitting carefully on the banquette. "Please call my driver. I think I will go home and lie down."

"Yes, Mrs. Ramsay."

Damn her, thought Barbara, fighting back tears. I didn't use Holden's love, I didn't! I even gave him a warning to clear his short! But I didn't tell him why. I let him fall for the good of the deal. He would have done the same. Any Lion would have, she said to herself, but she knew at once it wasn't true. Lions protected each other. She had betrayed one of the pride. But I didn't use his love! She shook her head as though to confirm the truth of this, but she knew the Chinese woman was right.

"You don't believe the bastard Weiss will actually sack you?" asked John Malcolm, sipping beer from a pint mug at the bar in the Royal Hong Kong Yacht Club.

"No, he couldn't, it would be too obvious." Holden drank from a half-pint glass, for this was the right way to match John Malcolm beer for beer. "But he is sure to take away Traders Asia, and that is the only job I want."

"What will he do?"

"He will put me in some meaningless staff job, reporting to him, doing something silly like a six-month study of the syndication business."

"Reinventing the proverbial wheel," said Malcolm, waving at the barman to refill the mugs. The barman brought fresh ones, icy-chilled. "Traders is already a leader in syndications."

"Quite," said Holden, sipping the light San Miguel beer. "Some say our London could learn a bit about the bond end of the game."

"Aw, squire, surely that Berk can't blame you for his getting buggered by good old Roland, Archer!" John Malcolm scowled, genuinely angry.

"The point is not whether he really blames me—although, John, even in his black heart of hearts, he will never blame himself—but whether he can use this incident as a stick with which to beat me."

"So what will you do?"

"Quit." Holden sipped his beer and smiled. "I can't wait."

"Hm." Malcolm grinned. "Get the boot in then."

"Right in the middle of David's little kangaroo court." It was Chambers's turn to call for the round and he did. "The chairman of Traders is a funny man, John. He believes in the chain of command and will want to back Weiss up, no matter how it looks. But he hates nothing more than a mess, and I intend to give him a mess. I have Margaret making copies of every telex and memo surrounding this affair, most of which are from me expressing opposition to the short position and in general advising caution in the Sea Lion business. I will have copies of similar telexes from Tony Wren; he is sending them up today. My head FX trader is giving me chapter and verse in the Sing dollar-trading over the last two weeks. And I have my own notes on my conversations with Weiss and Frank Portas, TBI's head of trading."

"Why quit, then? Why not just make a fight of it?"

"Because unless I quit, and state why I am quitting, I will never get a hearing from the chairman. If I don't quit, any meeting will be David's meeting, and no one in Traders knows how to control a meeting as well as David."

"Wouldn't they ask you back if you carry the day?"

Chambers hitched himself upright and placed a hand on his friend's broad shoulder. "John, you were with Traders long enough to know that won't happen, and you know Weiss. I couldn't beat him unless I could show his direct involvement controlling the short positions, and I can't without endangering Frank Portas. The best I can achieve is to prevent Weiss from fucking over my people here and a few others who are blameless, first among them Tony Wren and Frank."

"They are blessed to have you as a friend," Malcolm grunted into his mug.

"Besides, John, I wouldn't stay on even if the chairman asked. It would compromise the purity of my quest." Holden laughed and straightened. He clinked his mug with Malcolm's. "I have concluded that this business, and maybe the things we call Hong Kong and Asia, are really like a great party, but one should never stay too long at a party. To do so lacks style."

Malcolm nodded. "No one ever said you lacked style and good timing. You shall truly be missed, squire."

"Take heart, John; this final battle with Weiss will be excellent theater. I have to tell you I am looking forward to it. You know, one of the reasons I hate that bastard so much is because he really has intimidated me over the years."

"And doubtless expects to do so again," said Malcolm, once again waving for the barman. "Jolly little ambush."

Holden looked at his mug. It was half full, and his head was beginning to buzz. "This had better be the last round, old friend. I have to pack the evidence."

Malcolm nodded and frowned. "I hate to think that bastard can just railroad you out. You are worth a hell of a lot more to Traders than he could ever be."

"Thanks, John, but as Weiss told me just this morning, such things don't matter in the real world."

"Well, don't forget you have a lot of friends in Hong Kong who would gladly speak up for you."

"Thanks, John." For the first time Holden felt sad. "But this war will be fought in New York."

"Nevertheless, squire," said John, with a broad wink, "your friends may well take an interest." Holden studied his friend's face for a sign of meaning in the cryptic remark, but Malcolm merely grinned his Long John Silver grin. "When are you going?"

"Tomorrow. The noon flight to San Francisco. I'll spend the weekend with my sister in Menlo Park, losing the jetlag and framing my case, and then fly into New York Sunday evening."

"What will you do when all this is over?"

Holden shrugged and lit a cigarette. "I don't know yet."

"I could get you a spot with Llewellyn's; that is, if you wouldn't mind working for a former subordinate." Malcolm's manner was suddenly stiff and very British.

Holden laughed. "Thank you very much, John. You and I both know you are better at this game than I ever was, and I certainly would be honored to work for you. But this whole affair has put an awfully sour taste in my mouth. I want to get away from banking, and especially from big banks, at least for a while."

Malcolm nodded, raising his bushy blond eyebrows. "Well, squire, I can certainly see that. Anything I can do whilst you are away?"

"Actually, there is one thing. I tried to reach my boatboys this morning but couldn't. They are all too busy cleaning up after the storm. Could you call Ah Lai next week and have *Golondrina* hauled and painted and generally tarted up? I think I might do a cruise to the Phils and maybe even Indonesia when the typhoon season's truly passed."

"I'll do that easily," said Malcolm, signing for the final round. "In fact, why don't I have a word with the lads and see who might be available as crew? I know I could use a month of sea air and exotic debauchery."

"Good. I'd like that."

"Call me from New York before you come back," said Malcolm, clapping his friend on the shoulder. "I'll pick you up at the airport, lest you have the embarrassment of taking a taxi after they cut the buttons off your tunic and break your sword."

"Good lad, John," said Holden, smiling and following Malcolm's broad back from the nearly empty bar.

Holden Chambers worked quickly but distractedly into the late afternoon, arranging his files. He had labeled each of the storage boxes strewn around him: hold in file; send by DHL courier to New York; destroy. Margaret knelt beside the cabinets, sorting. Her eyes were damp, and she moved with uncharacteristic slowness, turning over each file, studying it, although he was quite sure she knew the contents of every one.

"Margaret, this does not have to be a sad time," he said gently. "Life goes on."

"I can't believe you are truly leaving us."

"You will be fine. Traders Asia will be fine."

She bowed her head and swiped at her eyes with a crumpled handkerchief. "But who will come and manage? Who will look after us?"

"Well, I haven't officially been relieved yet. But Traders Asia is important, Margaret. I am sure they will send someone good."

"They should let you stay! You are well regarded, the staff likes you—"

"The staff is loyal, you especially. But you have seen how American banks work. If something goes wrong in your territory, you are blamed."

"But you have said many times that if you stayed strictly within your authority, you could do no business."

Holden smiled, throwing a large bundle of files he had been holding into the "destroy" box. "Maybe New York will make you MD, Margaret. At least you know the business." He got up as Hannah entered his office and give her inevitable slight bow. "Yes, Hannah?"

"Excuse me, Mr. Chambers. Mr. Marston-Evans and Mr. van Courtland have just arrived."

"They don't have an appointment," said Margaret, frowning as she stood by the file cabinet.

Holden shook his head. Did they know he had been called back to New York for a formal beheading? What had happened to them? He realized he had no idea what van Courtland had done with his short position, nor what Marston-Evans and the Bank had lost or won. I don't want to see them, he thought. I hope they got as fucked as I did, but even if they did, I do not wish to share even a defeat with those two. But I can't very well just send them away.

"They should have called for an appointment," repeated Margaret, drawing herself up and clasping her hands in front of her, her face showing stern disapproval that his dignity and position were being disrespected.

Poor Margaret, he thought. In her way, she is as much a loser in this mess as I am in mine, and none of the blame is hers. "It is all right, Margaret," he said. "You are sweet to defend my face even after it has been taken away by events." He rolled down his sleeves and fastened his cufflinks. Margaret's eyes fluttered as she tried to conceal her sense of loss. How I love these people, thought Holden. How sad that I screwed it up for them as well. They won't suffer any penalty that a European would care about, but the loss of face was real. Yet I know that all of them, even Benny Yu, would never have respected me or even cared if I existed if I hadn't taken risks to make Traders great and me a Lion, including even the last risk, which never was mine but which nonetheless has brought me down. Chambers placed his hand gently on Margaret's shoulder. As she smiled crookedly and leaned a bit away from him, he realized he had probably never before touched her. "Ask them to wait for me in the boardroom, Margaret."

She bobbed her head and left his office, her hands still clasped tightly in front of her. He put on his jacket and buttoned it, shot his cuffs, and touched the knot on his tie. Count to one hundred, he thought. Let Margaret, scowling her defense of my face, lead those sods into the boardroom and leave them, on the promise of tea or coffee. Let them wait for me, to remind them that I am the top Lion and that they come as supplicants. Then he grinned broadly. How funny this was, yet how important! Take courage from Margaret: Her face remains, if mine has gone. Yet why should I think my own face gone? Because I lost a game? Because that grinning asshole David Weiss now has me in a position where he thinks he can fire me without risk to himself? But that game is not over, either, he thought, smiling.

He turned toward his vast desk, straightening the few personal objects that remained on the polished surface: Margaret would pack those last and only after he had gone. He counted in his mind another hundred slow seconds. Let them wait a bit longer because they had not telephoned Margaret to ask for an appointment.

He burst into the room at a rapid stride, his shoulders squared. He thrust his chest out and smiled broadly, extending his hand to the two men, who jumped to their feet as though surprised, rooted up from behind cups of yellow Chinese tea set in front of them on the long table. Marston-Evans looked nervous and confused; van Courtland looked flushed and distracted, his tie carelessly askew and his shirt-tails starting out from under his fat belly. "Gentlemen, this is an unexpected pleasure," said Chambers. The words were for Margaret, who closed the door behind him.

Chris extended his hand awkwardly as Holden withdrew his own and dropped into a chair on the opposite side of the table. He pulled his cigarette case and lighter from his jacket and lit a cigarette, pushing the case and lighter just far enough toward the center of the table so that either man would have to reach if he wanted a cigarette. Van Courtland looked stricken as he dropped heavily back into his chair. Marston-Evans tried to turn his face toward a smug expression as he sat down slowly, clasping his spurned right hand with his left and pulling it to the security of his crotch. Chambers smiled behind his cigarette and waited for his "guests" to speak.

"H-holden," Chris began, his forehead suddenly shiny with perspiration. "We only just heard you have been, ah, called back to New York."

"Consultations. Routine, of course." Chambers grinned, not even wanting them to believe him.

"Bloody hell!" roared van Courtland, leaning forward and projecting his fleshy red face. "Singapore's announced a unity cabinet, the Sing dollar is soaring, and the bloody bond issue is way oversubscribed!"

"That all happened yesterday," said Holden, edging his grin toward a smirk.

"True, Chambers," spat van Courtland. "I happened to have gotten the news just after midnight, when the phones at the Foreign Correspondents Club came back on."

So van Courtland had been caught holding his short position. "I thought you told me you had been advised to level your position, Richard." Holden's grin was now genuine.

Van Courtland's face contracted with anger. "Perhaps I was. Perhaps I had other information that certain major positions remained against both the currency and the bond itself."

"Indeed?" Chambers waited for the explosion, which came immediately.

"You bloody pompous bastard!" choked van Courtland. He thumped the heavy oak table with his fist and rose partially to his feet. Saliva wet the corners of his mouth, and his face turned the color of a mottled aubergine.

"Richard," said Marston-Evans, placing a restraining hand on van Courtland's forearm. The fat man shook him off and stood, leaning on his hands on the table, shaking with rage. "Richard, it will do no good to carry on."

"Oh, shut up, you simpering fairy!" spat van Courtland. Chris pulled away as though struck and gasped for breath. "Chambers, did you clear your short positions or didn't you? My trading room says you didn't."

Holden smiled, letting van Courtland wait for his answer. "I did make some trades, back into Sing dollars, before the typhoon sent us home."

"But my trader—"

"I traded off exchange, Richard, and through the kindness of other houses."

"Aha!" Van Courtland seemed to recover immediately from his rage. "There is no way you could have leveled your position trading off exchange. And I know your London took a right royal bath in the bond."

Holden smiled once again, and again he let Richard wait for his reply. He was sure now that First New York and Pacific Capital Corporation had gotten clobbered, having to buy in both currency and bonds after the announcement. "You are right, of course, Richard."

Van Courtland seemed completely recovered, almost buoyant, as he stood up and began to pace. "Well, if the losses were shared, perhaps all is not lost. I am to fly to London to, ah, explain things. If it appears that the apparent sudden turnaround in the fortunes of Singapore were a surprise to all—"

Holden laughed. He leaned back and propped one foot carefully on the other knee. "You still don't see it, do you, Richard? There wasn't any consensus against the Sing dollar or the bond. It was an inside job, remember? How many people had access to the very hush-hush Sea Lion reports?"

Van Courtland stopped pacing, and his cunning look collapsed. "But surely others followed our trades—"

"How short was the Bank, Chris? And how short was Warren's?"

Chris reddened slightly and looked at his hands, flat on the table in front of him. "You know the Bank normally buy foreign exchange only to settle clients' trade accounts."

"Fine, that is for the record," said Chambers evenly. "And Warren's?"

"Well, trading isn't my area, Holden."

"Come on, Chris, out with it!" boomed van Courtland, his voice rising out of control.

Marston-Evans looked for help across the table at Chambers, who merely arched his eyebrows in question. "Well, my understanding is that Warren's was buying Singers for, ah, the last several days."

"You bastard!" hissed van Courtland, his throat constricted. He sat down heavily at the head of the table. "Your London was pushing this Sea Lion fellow off on us as late as the day before yesterday!"

"Richard, I told you on the way over here, I have been locked up in the bank for two days. No outside calls. They made me take my meals there and even sleep in the musty bunkroom downstairs. They only let me go home when the Signal Eight was raised yesterday morning."

"Bloody convenient, I'd say," growled van Courtland. "What did you know they didn't want told?"

"N-nothing." Chris thought of his last conversation with Sea Lion. "If anything, Sea Lion's last information suggested even more strongly that the coup was imminent."

"Then what about your bloody traders?"

"Richard, I don't work with the traders. They apparently didn't credit Sea Lion or had another source."

Van Courtland looked at Chambers, who continued to smile, pushed well back in his chair. "What the hell are you looking so happy about? You got killed too!"

Holden sighed. "Richard, surely there must be some satisfaction in knowing that you have been fucked with delicacy and finesse?"

"*Delicacy* and *finesse?* Are you mad? The Singaporeans patched up their political squabbles, and we got a bad signal."

Holden dropped his foot to the floor and sat up straight, his hands clasped before him. His voice was suddenly cold. "Richard, you perfect ass, the whole thing was a setup. There was *no government crisis!* The Malay threat was no more than the disorganized splinter group it has been for years. Ask yourself who benefited from this turn of events."

Van Courtland whitened. "Surely you don't mean to suggest—"

"The bond issue, Richard, the bond issue. You said yourself last week, gloating happily, that Roland, Archer didn't have enough power in their puny syndicate to stabilize the bond at opening unless they wired out half their capital from New York. They knew that as well as you, as doubtless did the government of Singapore. So they planted a rumor and bet on our greed, Richard, and it worked."

"But Sea Lion was the Bank's source! It came through bloody Chris, here!" Richard's voice was small, almost a whisper.

"Think back, Richard. Sure, the Sea Lion reports came through

Chris. Who better? He would never have had the knowledge to ask the right questions, and the Bank never vetted the source."

Marston-Evans spread his hands in front of him. He looked like a frightened rabbit. "I never knew who it was. I-I just passed it on!"

"And Warrens' was quietly long Sing dollars by yesterday afternoon," said Chambers, pointing a finger at Chris. Marston-Evans shrank from the gesture.

"But why, Chris?" The question from van Courtland was a quavering plea.

"Because the Bank is going to get its banking license in Singapore at last," said Holden, still pointing his finger.

"Is that true, Chris?" croaked Richard.

"Well, I think, ah, the Monetary Authority may now begin processing the final approvals. That will take time, of course." Chris opened his hands in front of him in a supplicating gesture.

Chambers stood up. "Well, gentlemen, I thank you for your visit, but I have much to do before I catch my plane tomorrow. Stay here as long as you like. I will send Hannah with more tea."

"But who in the hell was Sea Lion?" asked Richard, his head bowed, almost touching the table.

Now he sees the magnitude of his defeat, thought Chambers. I almost hate to tell him the even greater magnitude of his embarrassment. "Sea Lion," he said gently, "was almost certainly your wife."

Van Courtland rose slowly from the chair, his head bowed and shaking. He shambled past Chambers, nodding without speaking, seeming not to see him. Marston-Evans followed behind, staring at van Courtland's back in terror. Chambers walked them to the lift lobby and waited until the car came. Van Courtland entered, turned, and gave a lopsided smile and a pathetic little wave of his hand. Marston-Evans entered the car with obvious reluctance and shrank to the corner farthest from the bigger man, seeming afraid to be confined with him and his deadly agony on the short descent to the street.

"Holden?"

Chambers held the telephone tightly. Margaret had buzzed him as soon as he had returned to his office and announced that Mrs. Ramsay was on the line. The vision of her husband, shrunken and speechless, devastated by his wife's victory, burned behind his eyes. He had told Margaret he could not take the call and heard her grunt of joyful approval in the intercom. He pressed his fingers into his eye sockets, trying to push away the images burning from within. Barbara. Margaret buzzed through again to say that Mrs. Ramsay begged him to take the call. She was at Kai Tak and ready to board her flight. He agreed to take it, and Margaret put it through. This time her voice expressed sadness, and Holden felt tears squeeze from under his closed eyelids.

"Holden?"

"Yes, Barbara. I'm here."

"Holden, I am rude to call. I-I know you cannot be pleased to hear from me, the way things . . . turned out."

Can you really know how I feel? he wondered. "It's kind of you to call. Are you off to London?"

"Yes, via Singapore. I am invited to meet the Prime Minister and the press. Then I shall be back here. I'm to be in charge of a new Capital Markets department."

Holden dropped his hand from his eyes and leaned back. Tears splashed on his cheeks, and he smiled. I am human, he thought. I feel. I loved and I lost. "You are to be congratulated on the success of your bond issue, Barbara."

"Thank you." There was a long pause. By the warm color in her voice, Holden sensed she must be smiling her beautiful soft smile. The vision warmed him. "Holden, will you be here when I get back in two weeks?"

Clearing out my flat, most likely. "I am not sure. My New York thinks I may be ready for a new assignment."

"Holden, I hope you understand—"

"I do."

"Holden?"

No matter how far he leaned back in his chair, the tears would not stop. Yet he felt peaceful. How rich the present feels when the future has been erased, he thought. "You made it through, Barbara. You succeeded in doing what you set out to do. Now you will be respected as you deserve, but you will also be envied. People have been waiting for me to slip for years, and now I have. I hope you have as long a run."

She was silent for a moment. He waited, wondering whether his warning would have any effect on her. "Holden, I never meant to hurt you. I never meant to use you. But I . . . had to do it, because—"

"I know, Barbara. It's the game. In the end, it catches us all."

She fought to control a sob. Was his Chinese girlfriend right? Have I made it as a Lion only by seducing and destroying my lover? "Holden, I have no right to ask, but did you ever really love me?"

Now he felt the tears behind her voice, and he felt sad. I loved you enough to let you break my heart, he thought. I loved you enough to grow outside of myself, even to relinquish the shield of my ego. I loved you with the clarity of pure light. And it was my fault that I came to realize all this too late. "Yes, Barbara. From the very first time I saw you, I think, although I didn't know it until . . . later."

He gripped the phone, not knowing what response she might give, suddenly afraid that she might even laugh. The receiver hurt his ear, so desperately did he hold it to him. He heard the background hiss of the telephone line as he listened to her silence.

"Do you? Do you really?"

"Yes. Have a good flight."

"Holden?"

"Good-bye, Barbara."

"Good-bye. Big kiss."

IV
The Summing Up

42

Singapore, 6 August

MINISTER WOO AND ELIZABETH Sun passed through the door of the Prime Minister's office, held open by Doctor Fong. They found Lee But Yang seated at the head of the long table. Deputy Prime Minister Raza, in his police colonel's uniform, sat to the Prime Minister's right, sipping coffee. Lee smiled and waved the finance officials to come to the head end of the table and sit. The old Cabinet Secretary placed teacups before the newcomers and poured, then sat down himself, his notebook ready.

"Mickey. Elizabeth. In the hubbub of the last few days, we haven't had time to congratulate you on the successful launching of the bond issue for the republic," Lee began. "I understand the issue was, ah, oversubscribed, I believe is the expression?"

"Indeed, Prime Minister," puffed the Finance Minister. Elizabeth merely smiled.

"Yes," said the PM. "Oversubscribed, even after there was, I have heard, some short-selling before the issue came out?"

"Well, yes, Prime Minister," said Woo, frowning across at Elizabeth. "Actually the short position helped create some of the demand—"

The PM waved his hand, dismissing the explanation. Elizabeth held her smile and suppressed a laugh. She had spent two full hours explaining the short position in the gray market and its probable effect on the bond to the PM a week before the bond had been issued. Woo looked at her quickly and fell silent.

"What is the price of the bond now?" asked Raza, leaning back.

"It traded yesterday in London in the range of ninety-nine and three-quarters to a hundred and an eighth, which is consistent with movements in interest rates for first-rate bonds," said Elizabeth. "Just above where it first opened."

"But it traded higher the first days, didn't it?" Raza looked at the Finance Minister, then at Elizabeth. She thought the DPM looked faintly amused.

"Well, Abdul," said Woo slowly, as though unsure of his ground, "when the bond was issued, there was an immediate, somewhat artificial demand. The people who had sold short—that is, sold bonds they had borrowed—couldn't find bonds to buy to cover their positions, so the price shot up. . . ." His voice trailed off, and he looked across at Elizabeth for help.

Poor bugger doesn't yet know what happened, thought Elizabeth, although Lee does, and I'll bet Raza does as well. "The short positions were covered at prices as high as 104, Minister," she said. "Once the bond was truly distributed to investors, it fell to a price that reflects yields on other bonds of like quality and similar maturity. It won't likely trade actively in future."

Raza seemed satisfied, and Lee smiled. "Well, in all events, Mickey and Elizabeth, we thank you for a job well done. You proved the nay-sayers who thought Singapore was not ready to enter the prestigious Eurobond market entirely wrong." He looked at Elizabeth, who smiled and bowed slightly, and then at Woo, who fidgeted and looked away. "We thank you," repeated the PM, signaling the meeting over. Woo and his deputy filed quietly out of the office. Dr. Fong picked up his notebook and followed them out, closing the door behind him.

"Are you going to give her the Finance Ministry?" asked Raza.

Lee nodded. "Soon. Mickey has friends—few in number but powerful. When the dust settles, though, she'll have it."

"She took a risk."

"We all did, Abdul, but she played her part well, even when she didn't know what it was."

"Did she know about Sea Lion?" asked Raza, reaching toward his shirt pocket and then pulling his hand away.

"Go ahead and smoke, Abdul," said Lee. "You have earned the right."

"But sir, it offends—"

Lee made his dismissive wave. "It really doesn't. It is to me a mark of self-discipline to eschew tobacco, but you have certainly proved your self-discipline. And your loyalty."

Raza shrugged. He pulled a packet of Player's from his pocket and lit one with a plastic lighter. "I'm a policeman. I do what I am told. But did you tell the Finance Ministry about Sea Lion?"

"No. They heard the rumors, of course. In fact, Elizabeth came to me two weeks ago and demanded that you be told to find and quash Sea Lion or be sacked."

Raza smiled broadly. "So she never guessed it was our operation."

"Yours," said the PM with a slight smile. "Yours."

"Of course, Prime Minister," said Raza, exhaling a jet of smoke toward the ceiling.

"By the way, Abdul, what became of your military camp in Johor?"

Raza coughed and put his cigarette out. "How did you find out about that?"

Lee's eyebrows shot up while the rest of his face feigned innocence. "That doesn't matter. Successful politicians find things out. But you ought to have told me."

Raza looked directly into Lee's black eyes, which were impenetrable as always. "I decided against it. I wanted to maintain deniability for you. The Johor trip for young Chambers was the most risky part of the operation."

Lee nodded. "You are right. I could hardly have approved of such an undertaking, not only the kidnapping of the American but your own unannounced movements in and out of our good neighbor nation. But I am curious as to how you set it up."

Raza decided to have another cigarette. He decided he might like being an insider. "We got a call from Sea Lion that Chambers had a meeting set up with someone called Elias who was to give him proof of Sea Lion's existence. Sea Lion had no idea who this Elias was, but she said that she could divert Chambers and force the meeting with Elias to be delayed to the next day. We found Elias, who turned out to be a telephone-telex supervisor at the Mandarin Hotel, and a former employee of the Cabinet Secretariat. We brought him in and sweated him. He admitted to having the habit of listening to telephone calls of the hotel's guests when he worked at night. It was a near thing. He had no idea who Sea Lion was beyond the name, but of course Chambers would have known, and the game would have been up."

"She should never have used a hotel telephone," said the PM, frowning.

"Quite, Prime Minister, but I don't suppose she felt she had much choice. Her office here would have been a greater risk to her, and we gave her absolutely no support. She never even knew we were supplying her with the information she passed on."

"Did she believe the coup plan was real?" asked the PM.

"Almost certainly not, but after the first couple of tidbits we passed to her proved plausible, she saw the utility of the information to her own need to build demand for the bond. She played the game remarkably well." Raza lit his cigarette.

"Well, it's sure she will never tell," said Lee, noting the facts. "If it ever got out she was involved in a deception of this sort, her career would be put paid. But tell me about the Johor thing.

I assume your cousin, the good General Mohamdir, helped you with it. Were the soldiers Malaysian Army troops?"

Raza frowned. "No. My cousin agreed to fix the border for me, and I asked him for a company of special-forces troops who might have been able to slip into Johor and out again when the show was over, to simulate a light but powerful force ready to march across the causeway to support a Malay rising. He refused; he thought there was too great a risk someone in Johor might see something, or that one of his soldiers might let something slip. He was right, of course. If Singaporeans, or worse, foreigners, believed there really was an army concentration just over the causeway, we would have had a real panic, especially if General Mohamdir could be found to have issued the orders."

"Then how did you get men in uniform together so quickly? I surely hope you didn't invade Malaysia with half the Singapore police force."

Raza smoked, enjoying reliving the operation. "We were lucky. There was a joint summer-training exercise of cadets from the Malaysian Officers' Training Class, along with contingents from Thailand, Indonesia, and the Philippines, in addition to Singaporeans, in the Johor Forest; it's an annual thing. If they hadn't been there, we would have had to limit the operation to the silencing of Elias."

The PM frowned. "With Elias safely on ice, why take Chambers on the ride at all? Why take the extra risk?"

"The risk was manageable," said Raza carefully. "If Elias had simply failed to meet Chambers, we reckoned that he would have been more firmly convinced than ever that Sea Lion was a fraud. We saw an opportunity to introduce a little doubt into his mind, and a little useful fear."

"Tell me exactly what you did," said the PM, his tone commanding and edged with anger.

"We replaced Elias with one of our own motorcycle patrol sergeants, and he took Chambers to Johor. We got the cadets out on military parade, and I made a speech about the honor and importance of national service. I spoke in Bahasa Malay, which the Malaysians and most of the Indonesians understood, but was so much jibberish to Chambers. My cousin sent a couple of police cars into the camp with their roof lights on, and Chambers was whisked away."

"My God, Abdul," said the PM, getting up and beginning to pace. "You took a hell of a risk! If this Chambers had realized what he was being shown, he could have blown the Sea Lion operation, maybe even linked it back to you—to the government."

Raza stood and stared down the PM's anger. "I took *no* risk, Prime Minister. The illusion was quite complete, and Chambers saw someone who could be me surrounded by armed men. Even to a trained eye, a seventeen-year-old cadet with a rifle in his hand looks little different from a seventeen-year-old conscript."

The PM looked at his deputy and saw something new. All trace of deference was gone from his manner. "Abdul, you mean to tell me that our American guest mistook a group of high school cadets toting ancient Lee-Enfield rifles, mostly with the bolts out—"

"All with the bolts out," said Raza.

"—for a serious invasion force?" The PM laughed nervously. His laugh was high-pitched, almost feminine.

Raza sent another plume of smoke toward the ceiling. "We checked. This Chambers has no military training. Besides, 'Elias' kept him quite far away, and Chambers doesn't understand Malay."

The Prime Minister frowned and spread his hands in a gesture of polite disbelief. "But Abdul, even without military knowledge, a group of cadets, from five different nations?"

Raza stubbed the cigarette. "All wogs look the same to Europeans, Prime Minister. And I have to admit we policemen do have ways we occasionally use of clouding the powers of observation." The PM's eyebrows rose into a *V*. "You won't want the details."

"I suppose not." Lee sat down, still shaking his head. "I still think you took an unwarranted risk, Abdul."

"And I insist I did not," said Raza, quite sharply. "The trip to Johor was icing on the cake. We could as easily have simply made Elias disappear, but we saw an opportunity to push a credible debunker of the Sea Lion illusion at least into doubt. If he had somehow been absolutely certain he had seen cadets, which I maintain would have been virtually impossible from the distance he was with only torchlight, what could he have done? Told his London he had seen cadets? *Armed* cadets? *They* wouldn't have been sure, even if he was. And may I remind you that when you authorized the Sea Lion rumors, we agreed that the whole operation was to be entirely riskless and deniable. Absent someone's tracing Sea Lion's information back to this office, there was *no* risk. If Sea Lion was believed, perhaps the bond would succeed. If not, the bond was no worse off than if Sea Lion had never been run."

The Prime Minister's eyes widened with sudden realization. "You are a right clever bastard, Colonel Raza. If anything had gone wrong and the operation had been traced to you, it would have been you leaving the cabinet, not old Yusef Ibrahim with his silly questions, and not Monkey Woo, either."

"Sir," said Raza, lighting another cigarette.

"Instead, you, and *your* Sea Lion, and your bloody cadets have forced me to make you the second most powerful man in Singapore."

"It can't hurt to give a somewhat greater voice to Malay concerns, Prime Minister," said Raza, his tone carefully neutral. "I want nothing more than the security and prosperity of the republic."

"As do we all," said the PM, his tone sarcastic. "And we will be pleased to see your attendance at *all* cabinet meetings from now on."

"Sir," said Raza, and got up and left the room without waiting to be dismissed.

Hong Kong

Captain Sean Kelley sat in his office on the third floor of the U.S. Consulate, studying the Royal Hong Kong Police folder in front of him. Inside was copy number 11 of a Republic of Singapore case file on a man named Jan Willem van Hoorn, Dutch passport 887665e, a.k.a. six other people with six passports, two each from Australia and New Zealand, and one each from Britain and Luxembourg, and two different Hong Kong identity cards. "Why is this of interest to the United States Government, Superintendent?"

"It isn't, Captain," said Superintendent Bruce Maxwell, seated opposite the Defense Intelligence Officer. "It's the man who broke into Holden Chambers's office a month ago and knocked him around."

"Are you sure?"

"Yes, sir. If you look in the enclosed envelope, you will see the photo the Singapore cops took and the Identikit drawing our artist made under Chambers's direction are practically twins. Further, Chambers reported that he had bitten his attacker on the right hand, between the thumb and the first finger. The van Hoorn has a badly infected bite wound in just the right spot."

"How was he identified?"

"Interpol. Fingerprints," said Maxwell. "This lad's been a wrong'un for a long time."

"Will he be brought back here for trial?"

"No, and that is the reason I am here. Read from the first paragraph on page four."

Kelley turned over the first sheets to page four. The man was being questioned, and the report was set out like a script. "VH will be our man; who's R?"

"One Inspector Rashid, according to the preamble, but it could be . . ." Bruce Maxwell raised his eyebrows.

Kelley nodded and began to read:

R: On the night of 7th July, you broke into the offices of Traders Asia Limited in Hong Kong, and subsequently assaulted the Managing Director, one Holden Chambers—

VH: Hang on, Inspector. I've said I was *there*. But I didn't break in, I had a perfect right to be there, and this fellow Chambers assaulted *me* as I tried to leave.

R: Escape, you mean?

VH: No, Inspector, just leave. I was instructed by a senior officer of Traders to enter those premises as his agent and to look for certain documents. He told me that since he was Chambers's boss, the premises in effect were open to him, and therefore to me as his agent.

R: And then Chambers attacked you?

VH: Yes. I tried to leave and he knocked me down. I merely defended myself.

R: What was the name of this official of Traders Bank?

VH: David Weiss. I was known to him as Mr. Dennis. I verified that he is the head of the international capital-markets department, and Chambers does indeed report to him.

R: I don't suppose this Weiss gave you any of these bizarre instructions in writing?

VH: No, he didn't. But I recorded all of our conversations. Some of the tapes are in my kit, and the ones you want are in a safe-deposit box, number 1123, in the main branch of the Wing Lung Bank in Des Voeux Road Central.

Kelley raised his eyes. "We have the tapes, Captain," said Maxwell. "They bear Van Hoorn out. That's why the magistrate doesn't want him back here."

Kelley returned to the report.

R: Was Mr. Weiss aware of the fact that you were recording, and did he consent to it?

VH: No, Inspector.

R: I am sure you know it is illegal to record a conversation without the knowledge and consent of the other party, both here and in Hong Kong—even when the recording could be evidence of a criminal conspiracy?

VH: I know that, Inspector, but I had to protect myself; this Weiss is a right slimy bastard. Besides, I am willing to wager taping a conversation is a whole lot less illegal than breaking and entering and assault, or robbery with violence.

Kelley turned the page. "The rest won't interest you, Captain," said the superintendent.

"Do you know Chambers?"

"Very well, sir. He is my skipper on *Golondrina*. I shall miss him if he is to be recalled to New York, as is rumored."

"I see," said Kelley. The report was numbered 11 on every page, and every page was headed Polis Republik Singapura—For Official Use Only. The paper was grayish and soft, with threads of pink fabric. The report was typed in red, not able to be photocopied. "And what would you have me do with this?"

"It's logged out in my name, and I really should have it back in a few hours," said Maxwell blandly. "I just thought you might want to make some notes."

Kelley nodded. "Could I bring it to you at midday? Perhaps we could have lunch."

"That would be fine, Captain. In fact, some of Chambers's other friends are having a bit of a wake for the skipper at the Yacht Club at one o'clock." Maxwell stood and retrieved his uniform cap. "We'd like it if you'd join us."

Kelley stood and smiled at the young superintendent, and shook his hand. "Until one, then."

"One more thing, Captain," Bruce Maxwell turned toward the door. "Your solemn word that none of this information ever sees the light of day in Hong Kong or Singapore."

"Agreed. See you later."

Maxwell left the office. Kelley immediately scanned the entire report, and decided that all he needed was on page four. He buzzed for his secretary. "Maria, ask Mr. Robbins to come up here, most urgently."

Frank Robbins appeared two minutes later. He was the legal officer on the Consulate staff, and like all legal officers at important embassies and major consulates, he was a Special Agent of the Federal Bureau of Investigation. "Hello, Sean. What's up?"

"Thanks for coming right up, Frank," said the DIO. "I need a copy of this page, and that no one handling this report after me can tell it has been copied."

Robbins picked up the folder. He did not touch page four, which was uppermost. "We certainly can't just Xerox it; special paper. The red letters will bleed right into the paper under the harsh light."

"I figured as much. But you guys are wizards at documents."

Robbins smiled. "Well, I do have a new man, absolute genius at taking low-light photographs. Lenses and filters and all that; I don't understand a word he says. When do you need this?"

Kelley looked at his watch. Nine-thirty. "Eleven o'clock, at the latest."

"Whew!" said Robbins. "All I do know is that it is a slow process, but we will take a crack at it."

"Great, Frank, but tell your man that no traces can be left on the document."

Robbins winked. "I'll let you know as soon as possible."

Kelley fidgeted in his office, glancing at his watch every fifteen minutes or so. He penned a short note as to what could and could not be done with the information, and inserted it in a plain manila envelope of local manufacture. He called the Marine Guard duty sergeant, and arranged to have a marine in plain clothes standing by with a car.

At five minutes to eleven, Robbins returned, followed by a man with thick glasses wearing a stained apron. Robbins laid the Hong Kong Police folder on the desk, and the other man opened a plain manila folder to reveal the copy. The print stood out clear and black against the shiny white of the photographic paper. It was far easier to read than the original. Robbins smiled and put a finger to his lips, and the two men left the office without uttering a word.

Kelley put the photo and his note in the envelope and sealed it, and summoned the marine messenger. "Take this to Kai Tak, Davis, and deliver it to Holden Chambers, on Pan Am flight 8 to San Francisco. Give it to him on the plane; it's all arranged with the police and immigration people."

"God, sir," said the marine. "That flight leaves in fifty minutes. There is a lot of traffic in the tunnel and through Kowloon at this time of day."

"You'll make it, Davis. I have arranged for the aircraft to be held at the gate, if need be. But hurry. We don't want Pan Am to look bad."

"Aye, aye, sir." Davis picked up the envelope. "Anything I should say to Mr. Chambers?"

Kelley smiled. "Just tell him it is a present from his good friends in Hong Kong, but that he cannot open it until he is airborne and has a glass of champagne in his hand."